Jordan's Star

Other Books by Gilbert Morris

Edge of Honor
Jacob's Way

Jordan's Star

GILBERT MORRIS

BOOKSPAN LARGE PRINT EDITION

ZONDERVAN™

GRAND RAPIDS, MICHIGAN 49530 USA

This Large Print Edition, prepared especially for Bookspan, Inc., contains the complete, unabridged text of the original Publisher's Edition.

Jordan's Star
Copyright © 2002 by Gilbert Morris

Requests for information should be addressed to:
Zondervan, *Grand Rapids, Michigan 49530*

Published in association with the literary agency of Alive Communications, Inc., 7680 Goddard Street, Suite 200, Colorado Springs, CO 80920.

ISBN 0-7394-2760-1

Printed in the United States of America

**This Large Print Book carries the
Seal of Approval of N.A.V.H.**

Jordan's Star

This book is dedicated to Doug Patak, my friend.

If everyone had your compassionate heart, this would be a fine world! One of the old Greeks defined friendship as: "Two bodies—one soul." We all meet numbers of people, but how few do we encounter who fit this definition!

Thanks for being my friend, Doug, and for loving my family!

—Gilbert

PART ONE

"Orion the hunter . . . Bootes the herdsman . . . Leo the lion . . . ," Jordan Randolph murmured dreamily. "See, Charlie?"

Sitting beside her on the oak swing, Charlie Maddox obediently searched the night sky with a wrinkled brow. "Ah—*lion*, did you say?"

Jordan ignored him, staring upward, her lips slightly parted. She was not a woman who would appeal to every man's taste, but there were those who found her beautiful—clouds of auburn hair forming a halo around her head, wide-spaced, entrancing gray-green eyes, a trim, shapely figure, a whisper-soft voice.

"Ursa Major, Ursa Minor . . . did you know, Charlie, that *ursa* is the feminine form of *ursine*, or 'bear,' so they should actually be called the Great She-bear and the Little She-bear?" Jordan whispered.

"Bears?" Charlie repeated helplessly, once again sweeping the sky with mystified eyes. He was a rather heavy young man of thirty with brown hair, blue eyes, and a ready smile.

Jordan sighed and turned slightly on the swing to face him. "Ursa Major and Ursa Minor, Charlie. You probably know them as the Big Dipper and Little Dipper."

"Oh, sure I know them. There's the Big Dipper and there's the Little Dipper, right over there," Charlie said, relieved. It was difficult for him to follow when Jordan went off into her fantasies. She would use a dreamy, unconnected voice, soft and almost inaudible, and the things she said rarely made sense to Charlie.

"Big Dipper," she repeated, and sighed. "Such a boring name for such wondrous stars."

Charlie was an earnest, solid kind of man. "Well, speaking of dippers, Jordan, we've got some new well dippers down at the store. Fit right on the swivel of the well bucket, you see, so—"

"Oh, Charlie! How can you even *think* of well buckets on a night like this?"

"A night like this?" Charlie repeated, staring around. "It's dark and cold, just like nights in February always are."

Dark and cold, that's all he sees! Why

can't he see the beauty all around us? To Jordan the night was dramatic, with winter's last cold breath sending shivers over her hot cheeks and bare shoulders, the smell of wood smoke acrid on the air, the stars distant and godlike in their frosty brilliance. The only touch of warmth on the scene was the golden aura of the house they'd left to come outside, and the faint strains of lively music that ran by them like quick-flying birds on the wing. Bemused, she stared at Charlie and pulled her wool shawl closer about her. Suddenly she looked vulnerable, childlike.

Charlie stared at Jordan, suddenly overtaken with awkward tenderness and clumsy longing. "Jordan, you're so pretty!" He turned and threw his arms around her and kissed her roughly.

"Charlie! What do you think you're doing?" Jordan cried, pushing him with all her might.

"Jordan, listen, I—I—," Charlie began, still hoping to somehow show her how he felt. "You know how I feel about you."

"Charlie," Jordan said brusquely, jumping up and disentangling herself, "this is *not* the way to romance me. Assuming, of course, that that's what you are trying to do."

"Of course that's what I'm trying to do!"

Charlie said earnestly. "You know how much I want us to get married."

She stared down at him. "You want us to—you mean, *that's* your marriage proposal? 'I want us to get married.' That's *it?*"

He jumped up, rubbing his hands together nervously. "Well, yes," he gulped. "I mean—what else is there?"

Jordan whirled, her long full skirts making a crisp arc around her stamping feet. "I'm going inside!" she said between clenched teeth.

Closely trailed by Charlie, Jordan practically ran across the flagstone patio, then swept inside the French doors. Charlie stared after her, then went toward the refreshment table that flanked one wall, while Jordan paused at the edge of the polished oak floor crowded with dancers. She tried to compose herself, hoping that the anger she'd felt for Charlie didn't show on her face. Nervously, she fussed with her hair, tucking a few stray tendrils up, unaware that this only mussed it more.

Glancing around the dance floor crowded with couples laughing and enjoying themselves, Jordan felt a sudden sense of alienation. She'd always loved the parties held in this room. Charlie's parents, Phillip and Clara Maddox, had built a beautiful home, and this large ballroom was their greatest pride. The room was large enough for a ball such as this, and over fifty guests now filled it, along with the twelve musicians and the piano sandwiched into a corner. The colorful dresses of the women flashed like a kaleidoscope as they swept around the dance floor. Hundreds of candles from the crystal chandelier overhead cast their light down on the dancers wheeling around the floor.

"My dear, is anything wrong?"

Jordan turned quickly to find Charlie's mother standing beside her. Clara Maddox was wearing an expensive dress of taupe-colored satin. The bodice was tight-fitting with row after row of delicate white lace running the full length to the waist. It was a dress that would have looked very well on a younger woman, but it did not suit a woman of Clara's years. Giving Jordan a close examination, she said rather sharply, "I thought you'd be dancing with Charlie. Don't you feel well, Jordan?"

Jordan knew that Clara had seen her leave the ballroom with Charlie, and that she had also witnessed her flustered appearance as she returned. Clara Maddox was a small, sharp-faced woman who had done everything to persuade Charlie *not* to pursue Jordan Randolph. She had higher ambitions for her son, and now she looked over at Charlie who had come to stand beside Jordan. "You shouldn't take Jordan outside, Charlie. It's too cold. She'll become ill."

"It's all right, Mrs. Maddox," Jordan said quickly. She had no illusions about Clara Maddox's opinion of her—which was that her family did not have enough money for her to be a suitable wife to Charles.

Charlie stepped forward quickly, taking Jordan's arm. "Come on, Jordan. Let's dance."

"If you don't mind, Charlie, I don't care for the polka. I think I'll sit down for a moment," she said quickly. She turned and left the pair, knowing full well that Mrs. Maddox would use her refusal to bolster her arguments to Charlie. Jordan did not care, however.

As she made her way down the long room she heard her name shouted over the vigorous polka music. She turned to see Charlie's sister coming toward her.

Martha Maddox was a small young woman of twenty, not actually pretty but so winsome that people scarcely noticed it.

She had the same reddish brown hair as her father and brother, and the same bright blue eyes. She had been Jordan's best friend for many years, though they were about as alike as buttons and elephants. The traits that Jordan loved in Martha—her solid temperament, her down-to-earth humor, her bulldog loyalty—were much like her older brother Charlie's. It confused Jordan to realize that what she found lovable in Martha she found tiresome in Charlie.

Martha's eyes were laughing now as she demanded, "Well, did Charlie manage to insult you again?"

Jordan had to smile. "He always finds a way, it seems. Can't you give him instructions on how to treat a young woman?"

"I'll try, but it's hard to teach Charlie anything." Martha shrugged. "Let's go sit down. I'm tired of having my feet stomped on by Louis Evert. My toes will be black and blue for a week!"

After the pair seated themselves, Martha consoled Jordan. "I know Charlie's just like a silly little bear, pawing and bumbling around. But he truly does seem to care for you, Jordan. When he's around you, he acts like he's following a princess."

Jordan was only paying scant attention; she had been distracted when Martha had called Charlie "a silly little bear." *I wonder what the masculine form of Ursa Minor is,* she wondered idly, for Jordan didn't actually know any Latin. Her education had hardly been classical; mostly she had taught herself. *Ursus? Would that be correct? So Charlie is—Ursus Minor?* she reflected whimsically, and then made herself pay attention to her chattering companion.

"The problem is, Jordan, that Charlie's a real man. Not a dream of a man."

"I know that," Jordan said, frowning. "But he doesn't even *try* to be romantic."

"You dream of a knight on a white charger?"

"Well, yes."

"Jordan," Martha said practically, "how silly do you think Charlie Maddox would look, swooping around and swooning at your virtue and your charms? How silly do you think any man would look?"

"All the ones we know would look silly," Jordan said imperturbably. "But there has to be a man somewhere with some romance in his soul!"

"Jordan, do us all a favor and marry Charlie," Martha said, her bright eyes serious. "You'd be secure and content, and he'd be happy. My father could have some peace again, because my mother would bow before the inevitable. And"—she looked around, gesturing expansively—"then they would give balls for me and invite lots of young men, instead of giving balls for Charlie and inviting too many girls to try and tempt him away from you."

"Martha, you're incorrigible!" Jordan smiled.

"What's that mean?" she asked with no trace of self-consciousness.

But Jordan had no time to explain, for a tall, gangly man suddenly loomed up in front of them and murmured in a low, cultured voice, "Jordan, I believe this is the waltz you promised me?"

Maylon Simms, a professor at Delmar College in St. Louis, was home for a vacation. He was thirty-five years old, six feet tall, and very thin. His black hair had become gray at the temples, and he had beautifully shaped dark eyes.

"Of course, Maylon. I've been looking forward to it."

Jordan rose, and as they began the simple but grand steps of the waltz, Maylon smiled down at her. "I believe it's appropriate for a gentleman to tell a lady how lovely she looks. So I will now avail myself of that opportunity."

She liked Maylon a great deal. He had courted her in a rather halfhearted fashion at one time, but nothing had come of it. "Very well," she teased. "Proceed."

"Oh. Yes, of course." He cleared his throat. "Miss Randolph, you remind me of Byron's poem, 'She walks in beauty like the night of cloudless climes and starry skies.'" He eyed her, then grinned. "How was that? Romantic enough for you?"

Jordan laughed. "Say some more poetry for me."

"I think I said all the poetry I knew when I was trying to court you."

"I think not," she said calmly. "You know everything anyone's ever written in English."

"Hardly," he sighed as he expertly whirled her around the floor. Though Maylon was gangly, and sometimes looked awkward because of his long legs, he somehow managed to be a fine dancer. "But, knowing of your literary preferences, perhaps I should have quoted this: 'Long live the Lady

Rowena, the chosen and lawful Queen of Love and Beauty! Long live the Saxon Princess! Long live the—'"

"Shh—Maylon, not so loud," Jordan protested.

"But I'm the herald," Maylon teased her.

"Well, be a quiet one then," Jordan admonished him, her eyes twinkling. "I am flattered, though, that you compare me with the lovely Rowena."

Simms enjoyed teasing Jordan about her favorite novel. "How many times have you read *Ivanhoe*? Three times? Six?"

She averted her eyes. "Mmm—perhaps."

"Or perhaps ten or twelve times?" he prodded. "It's a wonder you don't speak in Middle English. Jordan, my dear, don't you see that books like *Ivanhoe* are just a let's-pretend game? You love it because it portrays a perfect world. You love the beautiful dresses of the women and the pageantry of the court. Knightly chivalry, courtly love, men in chain mail, women on ivory pedestals, Robin Hood in the forest—"

"Boar's head on the table, dogs underneath, rushes on the floor," Jordan added mischievously. "Oh, how I long for it!"

Then without warning Maylon asked

abruptly, "So you're going to marry Charlie Maddox?"

"What? Oh, I don't know, Maylon," she answered, flustered.

"You'll make him miserable."

"Well, of all things to say! *I'll* make *him* miserable? I'll have you know, Professor Simms, that he's very much in love with me!" Jordan bristled.

"I know that, Jordan, a blind man could see the way he looks at you," Maylon went on carelessly. "But it's the truth, Jordan. Charlie Maddox has two hardware stores, and his fondest dream in life is to have three. When he gets three his next dream will be to have four. That's what your life will be, Jordan, measuring out nails and bolts and selling shovels. Some day—probably sooner rather than later—you'd hate him for it. And, as I said, you'd make him miserable."

Simms' words troubled Jordan, for he had touched on the core of her unhappiness. She had long understood that there was not a romantic bone in Charlie Maddox's body. But somehow, with what seemed the inevitability of their match, she had managed to convince herself that she should settle down, act like an adult, be practical, and take Charlie Maddox as a husband because he did love her as much as a man like him could. She had always liked Charlie, and his clumsy devotion had endeared him further to her. It hadn't occurred to Jordan that she might not be able to settle down and make do, that she might, indeed, come to hate Charlie and her life with him. But now, with an unpleasant shock, she saw the truth in her old friend's words. "I shouldn't be discussing Charlie with you," she said lamely.

"I'm sorry, Jordan, but there it is, and you should know it. Perhaps it's because I'm as romantic as you are," he said, shrugging. "I think life ought to be like one of Byron's poems. You think love ought to be like Rowena and Ivanhoe."

"There's nothing wrong with that, is there?" she entreated him.

"Nothing wrong with it," Simms answered. "It's just that I haven't seen many knights in silver mail riding glorious white stallions around Independence, Missouri."

"Then," Jordan said with regained equanimity, "maybe I'll go looking for one. Even beyond the far reaches of St. Louis."

"You mean, like, all the way to Dodge City?" Maylon asked, winking.

"Maybe so, Professor. Maybe so."

Twelvetrees, the home of Daniel Randolph and his family, barely merited the name, for there were only seven large oak trees in front of the house. The others had died of disease, but no one thought of changing the name. It had once been a very large estate located some five miles north of Independence, but Jeremiah Randolph, Daniel's father, had been an imprudent man. He had invested in the New York stock market, and in the financial depression of 1837 he had lost heavily and mortgaged Twelvetrees to the hilt. The estate had never really recovered, and from time to time Randolph had been forced to sell off parts of the holdings to keep the rest. Now it was a relatively small property, and all that remained of the grandeur was the stubborn pride of Daniel Randolph and his wife, Josephine—that and the big house.

It was indeed a beautiful house. Not as large as the Maddox place, of course, but it was still a fine example of antebellum architecture. The house was a two-story of red brick featuring a white portico with great Corinthian columns. Two colonnades connected the main house to its two wings, one the kitchen, the other the carriage house. High windows accented the front of the house on each level, with a set of French doors in the middle of the house on the second story that led to a balcony. The oak double doors on the lower level were set off by tall windows along either side.

Despite the loss of much of the land, and therefore many of the sharecroppers, Twelvetrees still had an overseer, a middle-aged man named Claud Ventner. His wife, Lily, was the housekeeper. The rest of the workers were all black, but none of them were slaves. The Randolphs were rigidly opposed to slavery and would never have contemplated having a slave on the place.

The Maddox's ball had lasted past midnight, and though Jordan hadn't gotten home until the wee hours, she had risen early. Shivering in the raw morning, she washed her face at the rosewood washstand and dressed quickly, donning woolen drawers and undershirt over which she put on a chemise with a bandeau and with shoulders of elastic knitted webbing that crossed in the back. Her dress was plain for an at-home day: a blue gingham dress with a ruffled hem. She fumbled a little with the buttons of her high-top shoes—her fingers were cold—but managed to pin her hair up fairly presentably to go downstairs.

The kitchen was hot and steamy and fragrant, for Lily Ventner's new cast-iron cooker had been fired up since before dawn.

"What can I do to help, Lily?" Jordan asked, sniffing the aroma of fresh-baked biscuits.

Lily Ventner, a tall rawboned woman with a homely but always cheerful face, frowned a little. "Miss Jordan, you always were a good child to help, but I've just about got everything ready, you see."

"No, I'm glad to help, Lily. What are you doing—oh, I can beat the eggs. Here, let me." Jordan took the big earthenware mixing bowl and grabbed the whisk and the wire basket of fresh brown eggs Lily had gathered just that morning.

"Yes, miss," Lily said, defeated. Sometimes Jordan's help did not exactly make Lily's lot any easier.

Jordan started humming and cracking the

eggs into the bowl, conscientiously beating them after adding each one, as Lily had taught her. Busily Jordan hummed an old English ballad, "Barbara Allen," as she started counting the eggs she'd cracked . . . but then she began to wonder who exactly had written the song. Was it Henry the Eighth? He'd written "Greensleeves"—at least, that was the traditional belief. But was "Barbara Allen" from an earlier period? Henry the Eighth was fifteenth century—

Jordan had lost count of her eggs. With a quick guilty glance behind her at Lily, whose back was to her, she tried to count the broken shells, but she'd cracked them too hard, and there were so many pieces . . . in her confusion she dropped the egg she was holding into the bowl—into the raw eggs—tried to grab it—grabbed it too hard, and the thin shell dissolved into five little pieces, suspended at all levels in the eggs. "Oh, dear," she murmured.

Lily peeked over her shoulder and said, deadpan, "Easiest way is to dip them out with a bit of eggshell, Miss Jordan."

"It is? Oh, thank you, Lily. By the way—could you, perhaps, guess how many eggs are in there already? I've sort of lost count."

"Yes, miss. I'd say that was eight there. Do four more and that'll get it."

In spite of Jordan's "help" Lily soon had breakfast ready, and by the time the food was on the table, Daniel Randolph and his wife, Josephine, had come down to breakfast. Josephine was herding Jordan's brothers—ten-year-old Albert and Frank, who was twelve—while Daniel was scolding Beth, who was eight, and could never get dressed and her hair combed in time for breakfast.

"Look at your hair!" Daniel scolded. "It looks like a rat's nest."

"I couldn't help it, Papa. I didn't have time to comb it."

"You had as much time as anybody else," Albert snorted. "I got my hair combed, didn't I?"

Beth stuck her tongue out, and Albert reached over to swat her.

"Albert, you stop that!" Josephine snapped. She was of medium height and as a young woman had possessed some beauty, but that had faded. Now at the age of fifty she wore a disgruntled look. She had thought she was marrying into a great family, and the discovery that the Randolph name and house were about all that was left had not made her a happy woman.

Finally all sat down, and after a perfunctory blessing they began to eat. During the meal Jordan had little to say. Her parents talked about the farm; her brothers and sister argued and made faces at each other and generally made loud nuisances of themselves. Sometimes Jordan felt as if she were a foreign interloper who had been born into this family by some cosmic accident. Her mother was a severe and pragmatic woman, her father a hardheaded businessman, her brothers and sister unimaginative children. Jordan sometimes thought that none of them had ever had any dreams, either waking or sleeping.

When the meal was over Jordan said with all the brightness she could muster, "Time for school!"

"Aw, I don't want to study today," Frank protested. "I'd rather go with Claud."

"None of that," Daniel said instantly. "You listen to your sister. You don't want to grow up to be a thick-headed fellow, do you?"

"I don't care if I do." Frank shrugged.

"Well, you're not going to! You mind what your sister says. One word from her, and you'll have a caning!"

Jordan paid little attention to this argument, for it went on with a monotonous regularity. She tutored her brothers and sister, a task which she took seriously. She went into the study room which had once been a bedroom but had been converted to a schoolroom with tables and chairs and bookcases. It was a cheerful enough room, with bright green-and-white striped wallpaper and a large window reaching almost from the floor to the top of the tall ceiling. She pulled the dark green velvet curtains back, and the room was flooded with golden sunlight.

Both Albert and Beth liked their schoolwork, but Jordan supposed they were obliged, being normal children, to protest every day. Frank never let on that he enjoyed a minute of it, but he did have an aptitude for arithmetic, and sometimes he begrudgingly showed some eagerness. Unfortunately, math was not Jordan's best subject; in fact, she was and had always been hopeless at it. But she did try her best for Frank's sake, and courageously she had decided to try some simple geometry to see if it would interest him.

"Arithmetic first," she announced, and all three of the children gave an obligatory groan. "Today we are going to start with a review of our geometry." Rising, with a last hesitant look at her math textbook, she pointed to her chalkboard. "Equilateral triangle—isosceles triangle . . . um . . . calene triangle—"

"Jordan," Frank said triumphantly, "that there you're pointing at is an isosceles triangle. Not a scalene triangle."

"It is?" Jordan asked. "Then what's this?"

"It's a right-angled triangle, silly," Frank declared. "Which is also an isosceles triangle."

"It is?" Jordan asked again, bemused. "Oh, of course. It is. Um—well, then. What in the world is—oh, never mind!" Her eyes brightened. "I have an idea, then, Mr. Frank Mathematician of the World. Why don't you teach us the math hour today?"

"Really?" Frank looked rebellious, but then his eyes brightened. "You mean it, Jordan?"

"I certainly do."

"Can I hit Albert's knuckles with the ruler?"

"No, you certainly cannot!"

"Aw, shucks! But I know it better than you do, huh?" He swaggered as he rose to stand by the chalkboard and grinned up at her.

"Yes, as a matter of fact you do." Jordan

smiled back at him. He was a precocious child, but Jordan thought that, of all of them, in some strange way, she was more like Frank than anyone. At least his boyish tricks and troubles showed a little bit of imagination, such as the time he'd shot the heads off all of his mother's prized tulips, imported from Holland, with his slingshot. He had hardly objected to his caning, and had grinned when he'd told Jordan that he'd gotten every single one of them with one shot apiece.

Jordan resisted an impulse to ruffle his hair—he hated baby stuff like that—and said, "But that's all right, Mr. Frank. You just wait until we get to geography. I'm going to stuff your hard head full of information about Pango Pango."

"Okay, but for now you gotta sit down, Jordan, and learn about these here triangles." He shook his head and made a very adult face of disdain. "Girls can't figure an inch with a ruler. Now, this here is called an equilateral triangle . . ."

As conscientious as she was, Jordan was always relieved when lessons were over, perhaps more so than even the children. Her

parents required the children to have lessons in the morning, and then her father
took the boys to work the farm. Beth still
had an obligatory nap, but then was allowed
to play all afternoon.

But afternoons were Jordan's best times,
for then she was on her own, without household obligations, for the Randolphs still had
three servants besides Lily to do all of the
unending chores of running a large household.

And so, every afternoon Jordan read until
she was called down to supper, and even
then went reluctantly.

She was reading *The Pioneers* by James
Fenimore Cooper for the third time. Now she
lay down on her bed, bundled up in a warm
woolen shawl, for this February had no por-
tent of warm spring weather in it. Soon she
was lost in the adventures of the pioneers
who were headed west for romance and adventure.

She had read all of the Cooper novels and
all the novels she could get by Sir Walter
Scott. The bookcase in her room was filled
with books by these two writers, along with
every book she could get about the Far
West. America was becoming more con-

scious of the vast lands lying westward, and Jordan devoured every scrap of information in the newspapers about California and the Oregon Territory.

Perhaps it was where Jordan lived that drew her attention and her imagination to the westward migration. Independence, Missouri, was a departure point for the long trains of big canvas-topped wagons that rolled out across the prairie headed for the exotic lands of California and Oregon. For the past five years Jordan had loved going to town and watching the wagon trains as they formed into rolling towns. She talked often with those who were headed for the distant lands, for she found their pilgrimage fascinating.

Her wholehearted absorption in *The Pioneers* was interrupted by a businesslike knock on her door. "Come in, Mother."

Her mother stepped inside. "Are you busy, Jordan?"

"No, Mother. Just reading." Jordan put aside her book. Her mother's face was troubled, and she took some time seating herself on Jordan's bed and smoothing her skirt.

"Did you have a good time at the ball last

night, dear?" she asked, the lines around her mouth and a flinty look in her eyes signifying displeasure, or perhaps merely disillusionment.

"Well . . . ," Jordan answered awkwardly, "I—I was glad to see Mr. Simms again, after so long. And Martha, of course."

"And Charlie?" her mother asked sharply.

"Yes, I was glad to see him," Jordan said cautiously.

Josephine Randolph shook her head sadly. "I'm worried about you, Jordan. Here you are nineteen years old. It's true, you have the kind of beauty that will last—at least, you will always have that fragile air, and you do have such good skin and hair. But even you will age, Jordan. You're already older than many girls in Independence who are married. In two or three more years you'll already be an old maid, and what man who can marry a seventeen-year-old will marry a twenty-one-year-old spinster?"

"I don't know, Mother, it's just that I don't believe that Charlie Maddox is the man for me," Jordan ventured timidly. "We're not—suited."

Josephine stared at her daughter with narrowed eyes. "Suited? He's a man; you're a woman. He comes from a fine family, and his prospects are good."

"Yes, three hardware stores, maybe four," Jordan sighed. "What more can a woman ask for?"

Josephine looked pained, but then she softened and took Jordan's hand. Josephine, in spite of the fact that Twelvetrees was not as prosperous and grand as she wished, still had never had to do any actual household labor, such as cooking or washing clothes or cleaning. Her hands were soft and warm, tiny, with the blue veins of age just starting to show. With uncharacteristic gentleness, Josephine stroked her daughter's hand for a moment, studying it. Jordan stayed very still, for such expressions of tenderness from her mother were rare. Finally Josephine sighed and looked back up, her cool blue eyes squarely meeting Jordan's otherworldly gaze.

"What more could a woman want?" Josephine repeated in a hard voice. "Nothing. Nothing at all, Jordan. Charles Maddox is an honorable and respectable young man, and it's obvious that he cares for you very much. Just because his name isn't Sir Boodle of Waddle or Lord Fancy of Frenchy, and just because he speaks American instead of King James English, and just because he wears breeches instead of satin pantaloons, doesn't mean that he's not suited to you. It just means that you've made up your mind that you're not suited to mortal, living men."

"But, Mother, he's so—so *normal*," Jordan said, her voice dropping in shame. That wasn't what she'd meant to say at all, but she was incapable, it seemed, of expressing her innermost longings and desires to her mother.

"Normal?" Josephine's eyebrows shot up.

"Umm—yes, he's just so perfectly—normal," Jordan said miserably.

"So you prefer a man with an abnormality," Josephine said icily. "I see. Would this odd preference of yours be for a man with a physical aberration, or a mental deficiency? Or perhaps both, just to make life interesting?"

Though Josephine was stern, Jordan could detect just the tiniest bit of exasperated amusement in her voice. Timidly Jordan peeked up at her mother's tight face and said, "Perhaps a—a sword swallower? With one leg, maybe? And a tendency toward melancholy?"

"You're just as likely to meet and marry one of them as you are to meet a knight in shining armor!" Josephine snapped. "Listen to me, Jordan. Will you at least *try* to brush the clouds away from your face and blink the stars out of your eyes long enough to think about your future? And at least take some time, a few days, anyway, and consider Charlie Maddox as a suitor. Think about his good qualities, Jordan, for he does have many. Will you do this for me and for your father?"

"Yes, Mother, I will," Jordan said meekly. "I promise I will try to be sensible."

"That will be a day of great note," Josephine sighed, rising. "Speaking of young girls with no sense, your cousin Jolie Doucett is coming for a visit. You recall Jolie, don't you?"

Irene Doucett was Josephine's only sister. She had married a man named Lonnie Doucett who lived just outside Baton Rouge, Louisiana , and the two sisters had visited infrequently in the last ten years.

"Oh yes—I remember Jolie, though the last time I saw her I was nine or ten. And she's a year younger than I, isn't she?"

"Yes, and just like you. Irene writes that

Jolie lives in a make-believe world too, thinks she's going to be a great actress or some nonsense," Josephine scoffed. "If Irene's sending her here to be cured of her fancy notions, I'd better warn her that you're no fit companion for Jolie. Likely there won't be a sensible conversation in the house while she's here."

"I hope not," Jordan said slyly. "This sensible conversation has been enough to last me for a while. I'm quite exhausted."

Her skirt making crisp crackles as she swept to the door, Josephine turned and said, "I'm not surprised, considering it's an effort that you rarely make. Don't be late coming down for supper, your father gets so upset. And Jordan?"

"Yes, ma'am?"

"Remember your promise."

"Yes, ma'am," Jordan said obediently. "I will brush the clouds from my face, blink the stars from my eyes, and think on all the manly virtues of Charles Maddox."

Josephine nodded wearily and Jordan heard her mutter as she went out the door, "Oh, Charlie—you and your blasted hardware!"

TWO

The ancient steamboat with the rather grandiose name of *Glorianna* had docked at the wharf in Independence, and a steady stream of passengers flowed down the gangplank. Jordan anxiously studied the faces of the passengers as they hurried by, uncertain that she would recognize her cousin whom she had seen once ten years ago.

She heard her name shouted enthusiastically by a youthful, high-pitched voice. "Jordan, Jordan! Here I am!"

Jolie Doucett fairly bounced down the gangplank and hurried to Jordan's side. She was a most attractive young woman, with glossy black ringlets, dancing brown eyes, and a rich olive complexion inherited from her father's forebears, the Creoles. She was tiny, fully six inches shorter than Jordan, who indeed was taller than most women at five feet eight inches tall. Jolie's hourglass shape was enhanced by a traveling costume of maroon velveteen with black corded trim;

the jacket hugged her small waist most be-
comingly.

The girls exchanged quick kisses, and
each exclaimed over how pretty the other
was, and how much they'd grown. Jordan
said, "This is Jackson, our stableman and
driver. Where can we get your baggage?
What do you have?"

"One enormous trunk and two smaller
ones," Jolie said. "But I'm sure Jackson can
fetch them for me. They're tagged—oh, can
he read?"

"Of course," Jordan said a little stiffly.
Jackson was one of their Negro servants,
but then she realized that Jolie's experience
with Negroes was probably very different
from her own. Baton Rouge, in the deep
South, had many slaves. Abruptly Jordan
wondered if her aunt and uncle Doucett actually owned slaves, for Jordan didn't know.
Jolie looked prosperous enough; her dress
was much, much finer than anything Jordan
had ever owned.

"I'll take care of yo' trunks, Miss Jolie,"
Jackson was saying quietly. "What you want
to do, Miss Jordan? Go right on home, or is
you gonna take Miss Jolie around the
town?"

"Oh, I want to see the town; I'm not tired at all," Jolie said quickly. "Can't we, Jordan?"

"Of course, let's walk," Jordan said enthusiastically. "I haven't been to town in ages. They don't let me out in public much, you know."

Jolie giggled and threaded her arm through her cousin's. "I know exactly how that is. My mother tries to keep me locked up, too. And I can't believe they let you come to fetch me unchaperoned."

Jordan said airily, "Oh, I'm a respectable old spinster. Much too old for chaperonage."

"Nineteen? Oh, yes, you're creaking with age! A perfectly proper chaperone for me."

They talked avidly about their families, catching up on the long years and remembering the fun they'd had on the one visit they'd had together as children. "Remember the time we stole Mama's gloves, the red satin ones with the pearl buttons?" Jolie said.

"*You* stole them," Jordan retorted. "I was an unwilling accomplice."

"You were nothing of the sort! You said they were magic gloves and if we slept with them under our pillows we'd wake up and be princesses with golden hair and satin dresses!" Jolie said indignantly.

"I remember. Too bad we got caught before we could make the magical transformation."

"We didn't get caught—you told on us!"

The girls looked at each other with sparkling eyes, then burst into laughter. "Yes, that's how it was." Jordan nodded. She paused and waved dramatically at the street before them. "Well, there it is, Cousin Jolie, the main street of Independence, Missouri. I'm sure you're very impressed."

The main thoroughfare of the town differed little from most small towns in the South. In essence, Independence had grown up around its dignified steepled brick courthouse. The main street surrounded the fenced courthouse square on three sides. Independence had all the businesses vital to a growing population, housed for the most part in two-story wooden buildings with steep roofs: a general store, a hardware store, a bank, a hotel, a livery stable, a laundry, a blacksmith shop, a post office, a sheriff's office and city hall, two saloons, a church, a dentist's office, and a doctor's office.

The two young women walked energetically, and Jolie, surprised at the crowded streets, remarked, "Goodness, there are certainly a lot of people here for a town that doesn't seem that big."

"Most of them don't live here, Jolie. They've gathered here from all over the country to start for Oregon."

"But where do they stay? The hotel is so small."

"Most of them are living in their wagons outside of town—just as they'll be doing for the next several months."

"Good heavens, what a horrible thought!" Jolie said with an affected shiver. "Living in a wagon!"

Jordan glanced at her in surprise. "Oh, no, Jolie, I think they're very courageous and noble and—and—"

"Dirty?" Jolie grinned.

"No!"

"But how are they bathing? In the horse trough?"

"I don't know, but it doesn't matter, Jolie," Jordan said with exasperation. "That's not the point. Anyway, would you like to walk over to the west end of town? That's where they camp, getting together to form up the trains."

"Yes, it sounds like fun."

They walked along the boardwalk, and at

the edge of town, as Jordan had promised, a host of wagons were swung together in groups. Many of them were drawn up in circles to form an encampment. Large herds of oxen, horses, mules, and milk cows were kept in a corral set aside for each group. Groups of roughly dressed men stood around talking as the women cooked over open fires. Children of all ages were running and playing, their voices high in the air.

"Why are they all stopped here?" Jolie asked with interest. "Why don't they start?"

"They have to wait until late April—or even May. The trip's got to be timed just right. If they leave too early, the grass won't be ready for their animals. If they go too late, the grass will have been trampled down, and the water holes polluted. And if they go very late," Jordan went on somberly, "they could get caught in a blizzard—which is awful from what I hear."

"Getting caught in *any* weather in one of those wagons sounds awful to me," Jolie said. "What do they do when it rains?"

"Try to get in out of it, if they have good sense," a voice broke in behind them. "I got four young patients here with catarrh after playing out in the rain last week."

Jordan turned and held out both her hands with evident pleasure. "Why, Dr. Leverett! I haven't seen you in so long!"

"That's because you're so disgustingly healthy." Leverett was in his mid thirties, but touches of gray appeared in his crisp brown hair. His eyes were a sharp gray, and his gaze went at once to Jordan's companion.

"This is my cousin from Baton Rouge, Jolie Doucett. Jolie, I want you to meet my favorite physician, Dr. Paul Leverett."

"My pleasure, Dr. Leverett." Jolie smiled. She could no more help flirting than she could help breathing. "I'll try very hard to get sick while I'm here on my visit," she said, giving him her most brilliant smile.

Leverett nodded, a glint of amusement in his eyes. "I'll look forward to it. So, you ladies are out on the town?"

"Yes, I'm showing Jolie all the sights," Jordan answered. "I mean, the sight. This is it."

Dr. Leverett nodded, turning to consider the mass of wagons and livestock and busy people. "Trains are getting organized, and it's just the middle of February. Wonder how many more will come in before April."

"There are more and more all the time."

Jordan added wistfully, "Sometimes I think I'd like to go to Oregon."

Leverett gave Jordan a quick glance. "I'm considering that myself."

"Oh, dear," Jordan said. She glanced at the doctor at her side, who was staring intently at the groups of wagons. "You—you're not thinking of going west, are you, Dr. Leverett?"

"I've thought about it." Leverett gave them a short bow, then said, "Happy to meet you, Miss Doucett. Give my best to your family, Jordan."

Both young women watched as the doctor wheeled and walked rapidly away. "He's not bad-looking," Jolie mused. "Married, I suppose?"

"No, he's not. Everyone speculates on why that is. I think it's because of his brother, Les."

"Why would he keep Dr. Leverett from getting married?"

"Les is pretty wild, Jolie. Always into some sort of trouble. As a matter of fact, Dr. Leverett had to leave St. Louis to get him out of trouble."

"What kind of trouble?" Jolie demanded.

"He shot a man over a woman, and Dr.

Leverett had to get him away or see him go
to jail." Jordan's eyes clouded as she added,
"Les is a sad case, Jolie. He's nice-looking
and smart, but he can't stay away from the
wrong kind of women and he drinks all the
time. I get the feeling that Dr. Leverett's had
to spend his life taking care of him."

Jolie, subdued, murmured, "What a
waste!"

The two young women wandered around
taking in the activity. The prospective travelers across the plains were far more interesting to the two than any city group.

"Well, hello, ladies." A tall young man
wearing buckskins and carrying a rifle suddenly joined them. He had a lean face, a pair
of bright hazel eyes, and white teeth that
made his skin look very dark indeed. "My
name's Seth Hawkins. Don't reckon as how
we've met."

"I don't think we have." Jordan smiled.
Some of the young men from the trains were
very forward, as she had discovered. "I'm
Marie Antoinette. This is Lady Sonya from
Russia."

Jolie giggled, and the young man's eyes
came to her at once. He winked at her.
"Now, Miss Sonya, you ort not to be laughin'

at me like that. Come along, I'll show you ladies around."

Jolie apparently would have gone, but Jordan was wiser. "No thank you, Mr. Hawkins."

"When will you be leaving? Aren't you afraid to travel all that way to the ocean?" Jolie asked, her large brown eyes wide.

"Why, Miss Sonya, I done been there twice already."

"Aren't you afraid of the Indians?" Jolie asked.

"Why, ma'am, all them pesky redskins can do is kill me. And they couldn't kill me but once, could they now?"

Seth Hawkins was an engaging young man, and despite herself Jordan stood there listening as he spoke of making the journey west. Finally she said, "I wish I could go. It must be wonderful."

Hawkins turned his bright eyes on her. "Wal, now, I don't rightly know about *wonderful*. It's downright exciting all right, but it ain't exactly for fine ladies like you."

"Oh, I'd love to go!" Jordan said fervently. "I read all about it in James Cooper's book *The Pioneer.*"

"Don't reckon I've read that," Hawkins admitted. "But it's pretty tough goin'. You ladies would be better off going to New York City."

"That's what I'd like," Jolie said instantly. "New York City."

The two girls talked with Hawkins for a while. When they finally parted, Jolie smiled. "He's handsome."

"Yes, he is."

The two made their way back to Main Street, then stopped to have something to eat at a restaurant. The menu was not particularly exciting, but they settled finally on soup and a pork chop for each. Jolie said, "Look at that sign over the door."

Jordan looked and laughed, for it said, "If you don't like our grub—don't eat here!"

"Not a very elegant café, I'm afraid," Jordan apologized. "I've heard about New Orleans cooking. It's famous all over the world. I remember when I was visiting you we ate crawfish and shrimp."

"Oh, yes. The cooking is good in New Orleans—Baton Rouge, too—but I get tired of it."

"I think so often of our visit there, Jolie— and I remember your beautiful house."

"Oh, it's all right," Jolie shrugged, sipping her tea. "But I get bored to death."

"So do I. I wonder if young women every-where get bored like we do."

"Do you have any beaux?"

"Well, I have one. Charlie Maddox is his name. His family is rather well-to-do, and he's already gone into business for himself." She determined to be a little bit more positive. "He has two hardware stores," she said with as much excitement as she could muster.

"Who cares about them! What about *him?* Is he an exciting lover?"

"No, not at all!" Jordan said with more emotion than she should have. She already felt very close to Jolie, for both of them, ap-parently, were dissatisfied with life. "He's dull as dishwater—but don't tell Mother I said so."

"Maybe I should tell *him.*" Jolie grinned.

"I've already told him."

"Well, he didn't run away, so he must love you very much."

"I think next to his hardware stores, he loves me better than anything."

Jolie giggled, and Jordan asked, "Would you like to go see his hardware store?"

"Oh, I can't wait, Jordan! If there's any-thing I love, it's visiting a hardware store!"

Jordan led Jolie to the main part of town,

then stopped in front of a store with a large sign: Maddox Hardware. "This is Charlie's store. Would you like to go in and meet him?"

"Of course! Don't *you* want to see him?" Jolie asked curiously. "I thought that you were going to marry him!"

"My mother hopes so," Jordan answered, "but I hope not." Her own words, uttered without forethought, struck her forcibly. She had obediently been trying to talk herself into accepting Charlie's proposal, and had been singing his high praises to herself often, as she had promised her mother. But now, even as the words had come out of her mouth, Jordan realized the grim truth of them.

"I'm anxious to meet your Romeo."

"He's hardly my Romeo." Jordan shrugged. "He's got no more romance in him than one of his coffee mills."

"Jordan! How shocking!" Jolie said, giggling.

"You'll see," Jordan sighed. "All right, come along."

The two young women entered the hardware store, holding their skirts carefully because it was cluttered from floor to ceiling with various, mostly metal, objects. Wide full skirts proved awkward to maneuver when bins of nails and stands of picks and rows of plowblades seemed to deliberately reach out to snatch at them.

Charlie Maddox, in a three-piece suit, was working as usual. He spotted Jordan and came at once, beaming. "Why, hello, Jordan," he said. "What are you doing in town?"

"I'm meeting my cousin. Jolie, may I introduce Mr. Charles Maddox. Charles, this is Jolie Doucett."

"Come for a visit, have you, Miss Doucett?" Charlie asked, taking in the lovely, bright-eyed girl with some appreciation, which merely amused Jordan. Jolie was pretty, and very vivacious, but Jordan wasn't the type of woman to feel any sort of jealousy.

"Yes, I have, and it's so wonderful to see my cousin." Jolie looked around, her dark eyes shining with apparent fascination. "What a perfectly *marvelous* hardware store!" she exclaimed, winking slyly at Jordan.

"Do you really like it?" Charlie grinned happily. "I'm pretty proud of it. I've got another one over in Westport. It's not as big or fine as this one, though. Do you know we've got the largest selections of hinges in this part of the world?"

"Really? I'd just *love* to see them."

"Why, I'd be proud to show them to you, Miss Doucett! Here, come right this way."

Jolie shook her head admiringly at the display Maddox led her to. "Why, Mr. Maddox, I've never *seen* such hinges in my whole life! Why, the stores in New Orleans don't have anything to match this! Amazing, isn't it, Jordan?"

"Breathtaking," Jordan said, rolling her eyes behind Charlie's back.

Staring at the display, Jolie waxed eloquent. "I declare, I have *never* seen such hinges in all my life! My, look at this one! Have you seen it, Jordan?"

"I don't believe I have, but it is magnificent. You never told me you had such wonderful hinges, Charlie."

"Why, I thought you knew. Everybody knows that if they want a hinge, Maddox Hardware is the place to come," Charlie said grandly.

"You must have hundreds of—of—things here!" Jolie cried. "I declare I am overwhelmed!"

"Thousands, actually," Charlie answered

her with a superior air. "It takes us a week to do a complete inventory."

Charlie Maddox, a guileless young man, never caught onto the fact that the two girls were leading him on. Jordan threw herself into the joke, and she and Jolie went all over the store exclaiming over nails, bolts, anvils, ax handles, and Charlie's wonderful new well dippers that had gotten him into so much trouble the night of the Maddox's ball.

Finally Jolie sighed, "I declare, I am just exhausted. So many wonderful tools and things to see."

Charlie was beaming with excitement. "You bring her back tomorrow, Jordan, and I'll show you the new cream separators that are coming in."

"I'll do my best, but we mustn't overwhelm her so early on her visit. Good-bye, Charlie," Jordan said lightly. Charlie gave her a light peck on the cheek, and because she felt guilty she allowed it.

As the two girls went back out on Main Street Jordan exclaimed, "You are just *awful*, Jolie! Making fun of poor Charlie."

"You're just as bad, cousin. He is quite a catch, though. Just think of all the hinges you'd have!"

THREE

Jolie Doucett was energetic, exhilarating, never boring, and it seemed, never bored, despite what she'd said about herself. She even insisted on helping Jordan teach the younger children, and to Jordan's surprise, she was an excellent teacher—of drama, that is. Beth idolized her; Albert thought she was "a good 'un, for a girl." Jordan suspected that Frank had a crush on Jolie, but of course, he would never admit such a thing. Jordan noted that Frank blushed a lot and, once or twice, awkwardly held Jolie's chair when she sat down. To Jordan's surprise, Jolie didn't tease him or make fun; she treated him with kindness while at the same time teaching him properly of their respective places in the world—that of a grown woman and a boy who was not yet a man.

As Jordan noted this, she recalled with a pang her first crush. At the age of thirteen she had fallen madly in love with the sheriff, Cameron Taylor. To her he had seemed dashing, daring, impossibly romantic. She had been especially impressed by his sweeping, thick mustache. Now she re-membered that he had treated her very much as Jolie treated Frank, with a grave courtesy because she was a well-brought-up girl; but also he had shown her a good amount of kind condescension because she was, after all, just a child, and it had made her conscious of the fact. She thought sadly that like her cousin Jolie, Cam Taylor had a certain wisdom that she herself did not have. After all, she had treated poor Charlie Maddox with much less respect than the sheriff had shown her.

Over the course of the week, Jolie took over the classroom. She wrote a play for the youngsters, giving them each a small part, while she was the Queen of May. Beth was an elf, Albert was a shepherd boy, and Frank was a woodcutter. Jordan was impressed as director, and it was great fun. Once Josephine came into the schoolroom and said in a voice like doom, "I have never heard such screeching and giggling and car-ryings-on. What are you two girls teaching them?"

"Oh, dear Aunt Jo," Jolie said breath-lessly, "we're teaching them a play, and they are exceptionally good actors. It's based on *A Midsummer Night's Dream.* By Shakespeare? William Shakespeare?"

"I *know* his first name, Jolie," Josephine said dryly. She gazed around the schoolroom suspiciously, and all of the children—including Jordan—felt guilty for some reason and dropped their heads. "Very well," she said finally. "Your father and I will see the performance on Friday night." She closed the door solidly behind her.

Jordan's eyes grew round as she looked at her cousin. "What?" Jolie asked innocently. "I think it's a wonderful idea!"

"But—but, Jolie! This play is wonderful for the children, but—based on *A Midsummer Night's Dream*?" Jordan worried. "It's more like playing Ring Around the Rosy!"

"Who cares? I promise that your mother and father will be so happy to see what excellent actors they have in the family"—Jolie beamed at Beth, Albert, and Frank—"that they won't notice that it's a very broad interpretation of Shakespeare."

To Jordan's great surprise, her parents did seem very pleased by the little theatrical production; her father even asked Jolie to write, produce, and star in another play featuring his children. He winked at Jordan and pronounced, "And why don't you put a part in it for Jordan? All you'd have to do is have her walking around with a cloud around her head, humming. She plays that part very well."

"Until she trips over something," Frank scoffed. "She never does look down to see the earth she's really walking on."

After school Jordan and Jolie rode every day, even when the wind blew sharp and cold, heralding a blustery March. The Randolphs had several good saddle horses, and Jordan and Jolie were always laughing about riding their "palfreys" and "knightly steeds."

One freezing cold Monday afternoon, the two young women cut their ride short because a wind out of the east was blowing savagely enough to numb their faces. Jolie and Jordan came into the kitchen, which was steamy and fragrant, and demanded hot apple cider from Lily.

Claud Ventner, the overseer of the plantation, came in, stamping mud from his boots. "I'll just bet you two young ladies would be interested to know that there's one of them what-you-call-it—theater groups in town."

"A theatrical troupe?" Jolie asked excitedly. "When? Are they there now? What are they performing?"

Claud, a cautious and deliberate man, shook his head slowly. "Ain't rightly sure about all that, Miss Jolie. I seen a poster at the barber shop was all, but I'm thinking it was something by that Shakespeare fellow."

"*Hamlet*? *King Lear*? *The Merchant of Venice*?" Jordan demanded.

"Yep. Something with a funny name like that." Claud nodded.

"Oh, it doesn't matter anyway," Jolie said, her eyes bright. "We must go, Jordan, we must!"

"Yes, we must!" Jordan agreed. This was the first time she could recall a professional theatrical troupe coming to Independence. She had seen some street performances, mostly very short comedic sketches by ragged, hungry actors, but she had never seen a real play.

The play, *Romeo and Juliet,* would not have been well received in New York. There were not enough actors and actresses to go around, so some of them had to play double or even triple roles. And the town hall wasn't exactly a distinguished theatrical site. However, the stars, Brian Defoe and Helen Foster, were very fine—or so it seemed to Jordan. Defoe was a tall, well-built man of thirty-six with dark hair and rather haunting black eyes. His costume was tasteful, and the tights showed off his muscular figure well.

"Well," Martha Maddox whispered, "now there's a fellow that could break your heart. He probably has sweethearts all over the country."

Helen Foster, who played Juliet, was small, blonde, and rather pretty. It was hard to judge her age, but she was not in the first flush of youth. Approaching thirty was Jordan's best guess.

Both girls enjoyed the play tremendously. Jordan started crying steadily in the first scene of the first act, when Benvolio and Montague talk about seeing Romeo on his lonely walks. Jolie leaned over and hissed, "What are you crying about already? No one's even dead yet!"

Jordan replied weakly, "But it's so—so *beautiful!*"

As the play unfolded, Jordan was completely caught up in it. She knew the play well, having read it three times, once only a month earlier. But how different when the words were spoken! She watched the tragedy unfold as the star-crossed lovers found each other, and then felt a sense of grief as their lives began to fall apart.

She was lost in the play, oblivious to the audience around her, and finally when Romeo died and the actors left the stage, she found herself rising with the audience to give a standing ovation to the cast. She applauded until her palms hurt, then turned to see that there were tears in Jolie's eyes. "It was moving, wasn't it? They are very good."

Martha said, "I think I'll come back tomorrow night and bring Charlie with me. Maybe you could come again."

"I don't think so, Martha," Jordan said quickly.

The crowd began to file out, and Jordan turned to go after saying good-bye to Martha, who left to join other friends. Jolie said, "Come on. Let's go meet the actors."

Jordan would not have thought of such a thing. It was beyond her, and she stared at Jolie in consternation. "Why, we can't do that!"

"Yes, we can. Come along."

Filled with apprehension and some embarrassment, Jordan followed Jolie. They passed through the doors leading to the rear section of the hall and found a beehive of activity. Jolie stopped one of the minor actors, saying, "We'd like to see Mr. Defoe and Miss Foster."

"They're over there. Mr. Defoe's in that room. He's got his name on the door. Miss Foster's is the one beside it."

Jolie led the way and without hesitation knocked on the door with a sign "Brian Defoe" pasted to it. It opened almost at once, and the actor stood before them, still dressed in his costume. Jordan fully expected him to be displeased, but he smiled cordially. "Good evening, ladies. How can I help you?"

"We just wanted to come by and tell you what a wonderful performance you gave, Mr. Defoe." Jolie spoke quickly, her eyes alight with pleasure.

Defoe smiled. "What a generous thought! Are you ladies from Independence?"

"I'm Jolie Doucett from Baton Rouge." Jolie smiled.

"Ah, yes. I have been there many times. And this lady?"

"My name's Jordan Randolph. I live five miles north of Independence."

"Acting is hungry work. Miss Foster and I are going to go out and get a bite to eat. Would you two ladies like to join us?"

"Oh, that would be wonderful!" Jolie said, her eyes sparkling. "Are you sure it wouldn't be an imposition?"

"Not at all."

"On the condition that you let us pay for the dinners," Jordan said quickly.

"Why, I couldn't permit that."

"Please. You gave us so much pleasure. Let us do this little thing for you."

"Well, actors never refuse a free meal. Suppose you let me change, and then I'll introduce you to Miss Foster."

The rest of the evening was a joy to both young women, but especially to Jolie. Helen Foster looked somewhat older in street clothes with the heavy makeup removed. She looked rather tired, and as they ate in the restaurant, she mentioned, "Acting is a hard life."

Jolie said, "Oh, but it must be worth it! I'd give anything if I could be on the stage."

Helen Foster smiled at the young woman. "You remind me of myself when I was your age. How old are you, my dear?"

"Eighteen."

"I started much younger than you. My parents were in show business, and it was a natural move for me. But I often wished I had married and led a more stable life."

Brian Defoe smiled and laughed softly. "You'd be bored to death, Helen." He studied Jolie. "Have you done any acting, Miss Doucett?"

"Oh, nothing like you do. Just small things in local productions, but I did Lady Macbeth once."

Brian was sitting across from the young woman. "I can't believe it! You played that wicked woman! An innocent child like you?"

"I'm not a child. I'm eighteen." Then she relented, "But I was only sixteen when I played that role. She was a wicked thing, wasn't she?"

"Well, if you ever decide you want to go on stage, look us up. Both Helen and I will be glad to have you in our troupe."

"Don't be foolish, Brian," Helen chided. "This young woman will marry a rich husband and not have to be traipsing all over the world."

Jordan, for the most part, simply listened. She was fascinated by the actors, who spent the evening relating stories. She did not recognize some of the names they mentioned of fellow actors that they had worked with, but Jolie knew them all. The young woman had apparently memorized everything about the theater. Jordan saw also that Brian Defoe was a ladies' man, probably having vast experience with stagestruck young women. Once Jordan glanced at Miss Foster, and as their eyes met, something passed between them. Miss Foster shook her head slightly as if to say, *Don't let this beautiful young woman fall into the clutches of Brian Defoe.*

As they left, Brian Defoe did all he could to persuade them to stay over and attend the next day's performance. Jolie was eager to do this, but Jordan saw some danger. "I don't think that would be possible, sir," she said. "But it's been a wonderful evening."

Jolie tried hard to persuade Jordan to stay for the following evening's performance, but Jordan was adamant. "We can't do it. Jackson will be here in the afternoon to take us home." The two girls were staying in a hotel that evening.

"Well, at least we can have breakfast together," Brian said. "Suppose we meet here at this restaurant at nine o'clock."

"Oh, that would be wonderful."

"Then you might want to attend the rehearsal," Brian said quickly.

"Yes," Jolie agreed at once.

Something about all this disturbed Jordan, but there was nothing to do back home. *After all*, she argued with herself, *what harm can come of it? I'll be right there.*

Jordan and Jolie were right on time for breakfast and for the rehearsal. Miss Foster was not involved in most of the rehearsal, and it was Brian Defoe who said, "Why don't you help me a little with the balcony scene, Miss Doucett? I can never do that quite right."

Instantly Jolie was alive with excitement. "Will that be all right, Jordan?"

"I suppose so," Jordan said, hiding her doubt.

She sat in one of the seats and watched as Jolie did the balcony scene. She had a book in her hand that she had to refer to often, but Jordan was amazed at how much passion she put into the part. The talent simply flashed out of her.

Brian Defoe went through the love scene, and when it was over he said, "I can't believe it! You play that role better than actresses that have been doing it all their lives."

"Oh, that can't be true," Jolie denied, but her face was flushed with pleasure.

"I'm not above flattery, but this isn't flattery," the actor replied. "I've been around the theater a long time, and it's a pretty grim business at times. Helen was right when she said it's a hard life, but out of that darkness, once in a while, something glitters. And I think that's you, Miss Doucett. I don't know what your plans are, but with your talent, you might consider the theater as a profession."

At that point Jordan came quickly and said, "We've got to go, Jolie. Jackson will be waiting."

Defoe extended his hand. "Let me give you my card. It has my address on it. I'm there between tours. I'll be in New Orleans later on in the year. Perhaps your family could bring you to the performance, and I'd get to meet them."

Jolie took the card eagerly. "Thank you very much. I'd love to do that."

The young women made their way back to the carriage, and most of the way home Jolie talked and talked and talked. Jordan had never seen her so excited. Finally she said cautiously, "You'd better not get too involved with the theater. It's not a good life."

"Oh, I think it would be. I'm going to go see Brian when he's in New Orleans if I have to run away from home."

"I think you'd need to be careful around Mr. Defoe," Jordan said carefully. "He's probably quite a ladies' man."

"Oh, I suppose so, but that wouldn't have anything to do with me."

She continued to talk about the theater, especially about Brian Defoe, all the way home, and it troubled Jordan. She thought of writing to her aunt Irene and warning her, but knew that she would never do that.

"Jolie, dear, he fell in love with you, as all men do after they've talked to you for two minutes," Jordan teased. "Of course he's going to tell you what you want to hear."

"I don't care what you say, I'm going to

New Orleans in the spring and audition for a troupe," Jolie replied. "I think I'll be a perfectly wonderful actress."

"Actually, I think you would," Jordan said thoughtfully. "And just because the man was drooling over you doesn't mean he wasn't being truthful about your talent."

"Drooling or not, he is a very accomplished actor, well-respected in the South, anyway," Jolie told her with satisfaction. "He was highly acclaimed in Atlanta and Charleston and New Orleans for his Romeo."

"Mm," Jordan said noncommittally.

Jolie gave her a sharp glance. "What's that mean? Didn't you see what a fine actor he was?"

"Well . . ."

"What's that mean?"

"You've already asked me that," Jordan said.

"But you didn't answer me," Jolie parried.

"I know. Um—yes. I suppose Mr. DeFoe is an accomplished actor. But he's so—I mean, when you see him—that stage makeup is—backstage he was—so—" Jordan gestured helplessly. "I don't know. I enjoyed the play very much. But when we went backstage and saw Miss Foster and all of the actors up close, I felt sort of—deflated."

Jolie's dark eyes narrowed as she considered her cousin. They reached the buggy, with Jackson waiting faithfully for them. They climbed in and he tucked wool robes around them securely for the long cold ride home. As they left Independence Jolie said quietly, "I know what's wrong, Jordan. We may have only been together a week, but I can see exactly what's wrong with you."

"What's *wrong* with me?" Jordan blustered. "Nothing's wrong with me! It's just that it was all so shabby, when you looked closely. It just sort of startled me, that's all."

Jolie shook her head, smiling. "Dear Cousin, even your little brother Frank understands that your world of knights and ladies and chivalry and romance is more real to you than this buggy you're riding in. Now you've decided you didn't like the play because you found out that Brian DeFoe isn't really Romeo Montague, and Helen Foster isn't really Juliet Capulet."

"That's silly, and untrue," Jordan denied indignantly. "Of course they aren't! I'm not so fanciful as to believe that Romeo and Juliet are real people."

"No, you just wish they were. I declare, Jordan, you can look at a good solid coal oil lantern and get upset because it's not a star."

Jordan stared at her cousin, then made a face. "A plague on both your houses," she muttered.

Jolie laughed, then quoted melodramatically, pointing at the lopsided almost-full moon, "'Lady, by yonder blessed moon I swear—'"

Jordan said eagerly, with great anguish, "'Oh, swear not by the moon, th' inconstant moon—'"

"You didn't let me finish," Jolie said peevishly. "Where was I? Oh, yes. 'By yonder blessed moon I swear/that tips with silver all these fruit tree-tops . . .'"

She and Jordan spouted Shakespeare with, perhaps, more eagerness than skill all the way to Twelvetrees. They arrived around seven, cold and suddenly conscious of exhaustion. As they wearily climbed out of the buggy and told Jackson good night with thanks, Jordan stole one last look up at the moon, distant and cold, and whispered, "'Alas, that love, so gentle in his view/Should be so tyrannous and rough in proof!'"

FOUR

Jordan, with great resolve, squeezed her eyes shut and willed sleep to come. But all such exercises were merely frustrating. She became more wide awake than ever as her mind fought her own body.

"Typical," she muttered. Jordan was subject to insomnia, as her mind busily, sometimes frantically, chattered along late at night, when quiet settled over the house. Jordan Randolph had no more control over her active mind than she did over her high emotions.

Resignedly she sat up, then groped down at the foot of her bed, underneath two wool blankets and a heavy quilt, to grasp the handle of the warming pan. Pulling it up to the head of the bed, she warmed her hands over it. Her feet were toasty, but her hands were freezing. For some reason Jordan had never been able to sleep with her hands under the covers; it made her feel as if she were smothering. Once she'd tried sleeping with wool gloves on, but she'd awakened, clawing frantically at the air, from a nightmare. She'd dreamed that her hands were paralyzed, with no feeling at all, and the deadly paralysis had begun creeping up her arms. Mercifully Jordan had awakened then. She'd never tried sleeping with gloves again.

Restlessly she leaned over and opened the drapes; her small bed was right by the window. Outside, the full moon was brilliant and the landscape stark, simple bare branches and naked earth. An icy easterly wind keened around the house, high and lonely. The heavy winter drapes shivered. Jordan's eyes brightened. The melodramatic night fired her imagination.

Impulsively she jumped up and began to dress, quickly but quietly. Thick woolen underclothes, a simple workday gray woolen skirt, a white blouse. With a small smile she took her new cloak, a present from her mother and father on her nineteenth birthday, from its muslin drape. It was the loveliest thing she'd ever owned. Made of fine white alpaca wool, it was a simple cape that reached to her toes. The hood was framed with white rabbit's fur. Instead of a clasp the hood tied under her neck with braid that was dusted with real gold, and the hood had a tassel in the back of the same fine thread.

Her father had grumbled that it was much too expensive and was also impractical, while her mother had remarked coldly that it was not even fashionable; short pelerines and pelisses were more stylish. Still, Jordan had seen it in *Godey's Lady's Book* and had asked for it, and Daniel had ordered the wool from Brazil and bought the rabbit skins from a trapper, and Josephine had had a seamstress in Kansas City make it. Jordan treasured the cloak. She hadn't worn it much—once to church, on Christmas Eve, and once to a New Year's Eve dance at the Maddox's—but she had often taken it out and swirled around her room in it, admiring it in her full-length cheval mirror.

"I say, how ghostly I look, wot?" she whispered, stifling a giggle. She was speaking in her newly acquired British accent. At *Romeo and Juliet* she had been fascinated to hear the way the actors pronounced the words, and Jolie had been aghast to hear that Jordan had never heard a British accent. Jordan had demanded that Jolie teach her, and in the last four days since the play, they had been speaking "British" constantly. Daniel

Randolph had muttered that they sounded as if they had marbles in their mouths, and Josephine had sniffed and reminded Jordan that she had predicted that there would be no sensible conversation in the Randolph household with two such silly girls there. But Jordan didn't care; she thought that Queen's English was a thousand times more beautiful than Missouri twang. She had made Jolie read aloud—in British—from *Ivanhoe* for so long that Jolie had gotten hoarse.

Pulling on her white kid gloves, Jordan crept down the stairs, through the entrance hall, and out the door, with hardly a creak from the wooden floors. When she stepped outside, she stopped and gasped—the cruel wind seemed to snatch her breath from her—but raised her head to gaze at the moon, exhilarated. Slipping silently down the long drive between the seven oak trees, she took a well-worn path to the left, down a gentle slope to the pond. It was a manmade pond, designed and built by Daniel Randolph's father. A small creek trickled beside the road that ran south to Independence. Jeremiah Randolph had dredged a small pool, built a spillway of native stone, and surrounded the hidden pond with weeping

willows, clumps of Dutch iris, and tall cat-
tails. Jordan was the only member of the
family who ever came here; the boys fished
and swam in a small swatch of the Blue
River that was the northern boundary of
Twelvetrees, and her mother and father, for
all Jordan knew, had forgotten all about the
place.

She stood still beside the little pond, rev-
eling in its quiet beauty. Though the wind
still rushed around her, the pond was down
in a low hollow and the tall pines shielded
her, their voices like whispering women in
the strong wind. Jordan sighed, entranced
by the beauty of the cold clear night and the
feeling of complete solitude. Though she
had enjoyed her cousin Jolie's visit very
much, she had missed her long afternoons
of reading in her room. Jolie wasn't the type
to be content with reading for very long.

The full moon, a perfect round disk, was
reflected cleanly in the pool; no breath of
wind stirred the black water. "'Swear not by
the moon, th' inconstant moon . . . ,'" Jordan whispered. *I suppose Jolie would say
that I'm looking at that perfect reflection of
the moon, and like it better than the real
moon . . . am I that fanciful? That—foolish?*

Perhaps I am . . . I find that reflection, a moon made of water, fascinating. What's wrong with that? Nothing! Except—except—what if it's true, that in other things, important things, I can't tell the real thing from the—the—vision? Like with Charlie . . . now I only think of him as Bottom, that poor, foolish man with the ass's ears, worshipping Queen Mab from afar. But that's not Charlie at all. He's a good man, hardworking, loyal, honorable, and honest. How can one know the Truth?

Her thoughts made her feel desolate, vulnerable. She walked along the edge of the pool, staring at the Water-Moon. It wavered, very slightly, and Jordan stopped, trying to see what had disturbed the water. The wind still blew, but it was high above her, moaning through the thick pine trees. She focused and searched around, suddenly conscious of a strange feeling that she was not alone. She wasn't frightened—it was not that odd, shivery feeling she got when she knew someone was watching her—but she felt a little wary. *Who could be out here at this time of night? Perhaps it's a raccoon, or maybe a fox?*

It was neither.

A horse, a great silvery-gray stallion, came picking his way delicately down the slope from the road. He eyed her, and Jordan stared back at him, enchanted. He had a long wavy mane, and he was enormous, but in the moonlight he seemed ghostly, just a lovely vision from her dreams. After watching her for a moment, he lowered his head to drink from the Pool of the Water-Moon.

Colin Bryce simply could not understand how the stallion had managed to throw him. One minute he'd been slouching along, dozing a little, minding his own business, and the next minute he'd been rudely awakened by the pain in his backside as it solidly thumped onto the dirt road.

Colin looked up in shock at the traitorous animal, and the horse had sidled a little, snorting with disdain, Colin thought, and then had trotted complacently off straight down the road, empty stirrups jingling merrily.

Abruptly Colin jumped up, wincing with pain, and shouted, "Hey, you villain! Caesar, come back here!" He stooped, picked up a rock, and threw it toward the stallion, his face twisted with rage. His cry was useless, of course. Shouting at a runaway horse to come back was about as effective as shouting at a thief who was running away with your purse. Throwing the rock was the action of a man who had a temper, but sometimes lost it.

Colin Bryce was no fool, however, and he was generally a good-natured man. As he brushed his trousers and pulled his canvas overcoat closer around him, a wry grin played on his lips. "Blasted animal needs a rudder and an anchor!"

Colin knew much more about those items than he did horses, for he'd been a sailor most of his life. Sweeping up his wide-brimmed felt hat, he settled it firmly on his head and started walking down the road. He was thankful it was a bright night, for the moon clearly outlined the road ahead of him and glowed down into the mysterious darkness of the thick woods on either side. He walked steadily, all sleepiness forgotten, though he was tired. He had gotten off the steamboat at St. Joe several days earlier and after checking around had decided that Independence was his best bet. Now he berated himself for trying to ride instead of taking the mail coach. He had seen Caesar in a corral, a magnificent pale dapple gray, with a silvery mane and long tail, finely groomed. That was all he knew about the horse—how he looked—and that was why he'd bought him and his tack for one hundred and ten dollars that he could ill afford. The gimlet-eyed, grinning little man named Peters that had sold Caesar to Colin could have told him that the stallion had a tendency to take a quick jolting sidestep every once in a while, when he could feel the least indecision in the reins. This would, quite effectively and quickly, dump an unsteady rider onto the ground. But Peters didn't think it was necessary to relate these things to Colin Bryce, who was green enough to pay twice as much for Caesar and the tack than he'd been prepared to take. That pretty much told Peters what kind of horseman Bryce was! Colin himself was finding out the hard way.

As he moved along, Colin Bryce's gait clearly revealed that he was a seaman, not a horseman. Years spent on board ships had given him a sailor's rolling gait instead of the straightforward heel-and-toe march of the landsman. Now he regretted that his experience at sea had hardly prepared him for the complexities of landlocked life. *How am I going to catch that horse? And—wait—how am I going to* find *that horse? Blast him! I could try the old sugar cube thing, but you have to actually be in the horse's presence to try to lure him!*

He stopped and looked around helplessly. He might as well be in the jungles of darkest Africa for all he knew. Even if there was a house nearby, would a person—a dumb tenderfoot sailor—go to ask for help in catching a runaway horse? Did one go to the sheriff? Send out a posse?

Colin shrugged, then walked on. One thing was certain, he couldn't expect Caesar to just humbly walk up to him while he stood in the middle of this road. He was conscious of the hard-packed earth beneath his feet, grimacing a little at the way each step seemed to jolt through his body. He hadn't really gotten his land legs yet, and the fixed earth seemed cruel to him. He'd been at sea for a long, long time.

His decision to leave the sea had not been sudden. He'd thought of it for several years, conscious that somehow, though he did enjoy his life, he wasn't made of the same stuff that many of his shipmates were. He simply wasn't in love with the sea. He didn't dream of being at sea when he was in port; he didn't long for it. It was just his chosen career, and he hadn't done badly. At twenty he'd finally made first mate of a tea clipper, then at twenty-five he'd finally gotten commissioned as a captain. True, he'd been captain of an ancient scow of a two-masted brig barely waddling along from Boston to France with tobacco and rice. But it had given him the much-coveted title *Captain* Colin Bryce. *Not that anyone around here's much impressed,* he reflected dryly. *Still, I did it. Now I'm glad I'm moving on . . . at least I* was *moving on until that horse tossed me . . .*

Colin stopped dead and strained his ears to the utmost, trying to decide if the sound he'd heard was real, or just a banshee trick of the wind. No, he decided, it was just the soft moans of the thick pines high overhead, a sort of dry sigh that he found very poignant, even as his sailor's mind registered that the wind was coming round now from the northeast, and the raw coldness in it had gotten even icier. But whatever he'd heard wasn't a horse sound. Still, he headed over to the left side of the road, for he'd seen something, some glimmer that had barely registered on his eyes. Yes, it was water, the slight dark gleam of water. Perhaps—if his luck was changing with the wind—Caesar might have come here to drink?

He looked down, but from the road the ground dropped about six feet, a rocky undercut that looked treacherous. Hastily he backtracked to where the shoulder was less precipitous, and he jumped down about four feet, landing solidly on a soft bed of pine needles that must have been two feet deep. He started for where he'd seen the water, breathing appreciatively of the dusty but still sharp scent of pine.

Ahead he saw something bright, incandescent. The reflection of the moon on the pond seemed to dart playfully in and out of his vision as he passed the tall thin trunks of the trees. He was almost to the clearing when he stopped dead still, his breath indrawn sharply.

What is that? What—

Colin was not a man who frightened easily, and neither was he a man given to flights of wild fancy. But something he couldn't quite see wove in and out of his vision, a white shimmer floating along the edge of the pond, not fog, not light, not animal—

Instinctively he grabbed the butt of his Navy Colt .45, secure in its holster at his side, but it gave Colin no comfort. He remembered the time he'd seen a siren . . . after eighteen days of the heat and blinding light and thirst of the doldrums, and they'd finally made landfall at Kiribati, and he'd seen the half-fish, half-woman, her long green hair soft and silvery looking, singing to him . . .

With a small start he almost smiled. He'd been eleven years old, a captain's steward on his second voyage, and it had been no siren but merely a curious growth of coral.

But this was no will-o'-the-wisp. It was a woman, he saw, and stopped dead still. She was lovely enough to be a dryad, however, with her long hair, thick and curly, escaping from the snow-white fur of the hood she wore closely around her face. She was tall and seemed to glide along, as if she walked not on the hard, unforgiving earth, but on air cushions under her feet.

Colin stood absolutely still, watching, until she drew near, her head lifted, and his startled gaze met her faraway, dreamy one.

She stiffened abruptly, and at once whirled, her long white cape floating about her. Then with a most human and earthy grunt, she fell to the earth, the impact of her body in the pine needles making Colin wince.

"Miss—pardon me," he said inanely. "Are you hurt?" He took a step closer and saw her flinch.

She rolled over into a sitting position and shot a look over her shoulder. "You—you scared me!"

"I know, I'm sorry," Colin said contritely. "I just couldn't think of the—er—proper—" He took another step closer.

"Don't come any nearer!"

To Colin's dismay, he heard a loud wet snort, and then he spotted Caesar, on the other side of the pond. The horse turned, struggled up the slope, and once again made his escape.

"Caesar! Come back—oh, forget it," Colin grunted, turning his attention back to the young woman.

She was still staring at him suspiciously, but she asked in a less hostile voice, "Was that your horse?"

"I'm afraid so," Colin answered. "His name is Caesar. My name is Colin Bryce."

"How do you do. I'm Jordan Randolph."
The mindless niceties came out of Jordan's
mouth before she realized it, and then she
and Colin stared at each other and both
laughed. Jordan now became very self-conscious and tried to struggle to her feet. A
sharp pain knifed at her right ankle, and with
a gasp she sat back down.

"Miss Randolph, may I take the liberty of
assisting you?" Colin asked formally. It did
seem to make the odd situation a little less
tense.

"I—I've done something to my ankle,"
she said in a small voice, her head down,
the hood completely hiding her face. Slowly
she looked up, and reached up with long
white fingers to pull back her hood. The
moon made her face very white and stark
and her eyes were dark pools, but to Colin
she still had an almost supernatural beauty.

"Are you real?" he half-whispered.

"I—I think so . . ." Jordan found herself
looking into the eyes of the stranger, and
she knew then that she would never forget
this moment as long as she lived.

FIVE

Colin Bryce carried Jordan as easily if she were a child. From the pond to the house was a distance of almost an eighth of a mile, but he never wavered, never even seemed to be breathing heavily. Jordan was very conscious of his arms, as steady as pillars, encircling her, and the muscular strength of his shoulder against her cheek. Secretly she inhaled deeply of his scent, a combination of carbolic soap and the clean wind-whipped tang of his new canvas overcoat.

They didn't speak; Colin was staring hard at the house, trying to decide how best to announce their rather unorthodox appearance. Jordan was silent because she was speechless; she was so entranced. But the dogs solved Colin's dilemma, for as soon as they entered the grounds the low baying began. Before Colin had reached the steps a light appeared on the upper story, and soon Daniel Randolph threw open the door, holding a flickering candle in one hand and a shotgun in the other.

"Father! It's me!" Jordan said as Colin came to a quick halt on the porch.

"Jordan? What in blue blazes?" Daniel blustered. "And who are you, sir?"

"Father, please, I've had a small accident," Jordan said quickly. "This gentleman is helping me."

"What were you doing out this time of night!" Daniel said again. "Well, bring her on in, Mr.—who the blue blazes are you?"

Colin carried Jordan into the house. She pointed him left, toward the parlor, and he set her gently down on the sofa. Behind him Daniel Randolph followed, muttering to himself. Jordan stammered, "F—Father, may I introduce Mr. Colin Bryce. Mr. Bryce, this is my father, Mr. Daniel Randolph."

Colin stuck out his hand; bemused, Daniel shifted the shotgun to an awkward position under his arm, fidgeted with it a moment, and finally managed to shake Colin's hand. "Who are you?" Daniel repeated.

They heard quick footsteps on the stairs and loud whispering. Josephine entered the room and instantly demanded, "Who are you?" Jolie's gamine face popped around her shoulder, her eyes wide.

"Ma'am, I—," Colin began, but was interrupted by Daniel Randolph, who turned and began berating Josephine for letting Jordan run wild, and a loud argument ensued. Colin stepped closer to try to explain, but Josephine shrieked again, and Colin hastily stepped back, his hands up in an I'm-harmless-I-surrender gesture.

Jolie, lovely in a red velvet dressing gown, slipped to Jordan's side and whispered, "How in the world did you find *him?*"

"I fell and hurt my ankle," Jordan murmured incoherently. Her eyes were wide as she stared at Colin Bryce.

"No kidding," Jolie muttered, staring at her face.

"He's handsome, isn't he?" Jordan whispered.

"Yes, indeed," Jolie readily agreed. "I want one!"

Eventually Colin managed to calm Daniel Randolph down by speaking very slowly and distinctly. "Sir, I was riding to Independence, but my horse threw me, and so I was walking. I saw your pond and thought Caesar might have stopped there to drink—and as a matter of fact, he had. But when I got there I interrupted your daughter on her—

walk. I startled her, I'm afraid, and that's why she fell and that's why she twisted her ankle. Please accept my apologies."

Daniel's confused face and Josephine's disbelieving one turned slowly to Jordan, reclining on the sofa. "I—I stepped in a hole," she said guiltily.

"What hole?" Daniel asked blankly.

"Never mind, Daniel, she's been out wandering on her midnight haunts again," Josephine said in a businesslike manner. Bustling to Jordan's side, she pulled her skirt up and gently touched her right ankle. It was badly swollen, and Jordan winced when she touched it. "I don't think it's broken . . . ," Josephine muttered.

"No, I don't either," Colin agreed. Josephine gave him a look that would have burned water and he hastily added, "Ma'am, I felt it necessary to check her ankle before I tried to move her. I'm—I've dealt with injuries before, and I knew I'd have to splint it if it was broken, and—"

"Mother, it's quite all right, Mr. Bryce has been very proper and very gallant. After all, he did have to carry me to the house," Jordan said with a smile.

"*Carry* you?" Josephine said despairingly.

"Mr. Bryce, I can assure you that our family is much more respectable than you would ever know from meeting my daughter."

Behind them, still standing with his nightcap askew, his candle firm, his shotgun tucked under his arm, Daniel Randolph said helplessly, "That's right, Mr. Bryce. We're normal."

Colin shrugged but managed to direct a surreptitious wink at Jordan. He said, "I'm a pretty normal man myself, but I must say that tonight's been really—unusual. Now I'd better head on out and try to find that blooming horse. He's probably all the way to Kansas City by now."

Jordan cried, "Oh, no!" Then she quickly said, "Father, of course Mr. Bryce must stay the night, mustn't he? I mean"—she groped for words—"I'm the reason he didn't catch Caesar, after all!"

"Who's Caesar?" Daniel asked, bewildered.

"His horse," Jordan said reasonably. "Caesar was drinking at the pond, but he ran off when I—when I—"

"Bewitched him," Colin added with a small smile. "Will-o'-the-wisp, bewitched my horse."

Jolie, still kneeling by Jordan, looked up and gave Colin her most brilliant smile. "Mr. Bryce, I think you may be right about my cousin. Perhaps she is a will-o'-the-wisp. I'm Jolie Doucett."

"Happy to know you, Miss Doucett."

With a sigh of exasperation Josephine rose and said, "Daniel, call Lily to come get the blue room ready for a guest. Jolie, take Mr. Bryce's coat and hat, and go warm some milk. I'm going to make some cold compresses for Jordan's ankle. I hope you won't be afraid to accept our hospitality, Mr. Bryce, even though we must seem to have a lunatic asylum here instead of a home."

Colin laughed and his teeth were very white against his deeply tanned skin. "Ma'am, I can assure you that I'm not at all afraid. Thank you very much. I would be honored if you could see fit to put me up for the night."

The next morning Jordan woke with a start when her door creaked open. Jolie slipped in, closing the door softly behind her, and ran to leap onto Jordan's bed. Jordan winced as her swollen ankle bounced up and down, but Jolie ignored Jordan's grimace of pain. "He's up already!" Jolie whispered, her eyes dancing. "I can hear him moving around!"

Jordan's eyes, sleep heavy, widened suddenly. "Oh, dear. It's not even dawn yet!" Helplessly she touched her hair, which was in wild tangles since she hadn't brushed it out—much less put it up in curling papers—the night before. Jolie was already dressed with her dark glossy hair arranged in a bouffant with ringlets bouncing over her left shoulder. Jordan stared at her cousin, then said pitifully, "Help me!"

"Of course I will," Jolie said, smiling. "Why do you think I'm here? Now, what will you wear?" She rose and rummaged through Jordan's oak armoire. "Here, Jordan," she said, taking out a morning ensemble, an underdress of white cambric with a corsage of white eyelet embroidery over muslin, and an overdress of white muslin trimmed with pale yellow grosgrain ribbon on the sleeves and hem.

"I'll freeze!" Jordan objected.

"What are you going to wear?" Jolie retorted. "Your schoolmarm's plain white blouse and gray flannel skirt and apron? Just like it's any other day?"

"No," Jordan said decisively. "I'll just freeze. Here, Jolie, help me get to the wash-stand. I must wash and—whatever shall I do with my hair? And horrors, just look at me! I'm all pale and have shadows under my eyes and my lips are blue already!"

"That's fine, you look all frail and con-sumptive, like the heroine of a French novel," Jolie said by way of reassurance. "Hurry up, Jordan, for if you don't, then your father will likely go fetch Claud to carry you downstairs."

"Oh, I see," Jordan said breathlessly. "If we can time it just right, then Mr. Bryce will be obliged to carry me downstairs, won't he?"

Jolie rolled her eyes. "Jordan, you may have bewitched his horse, but you certainly have a lot to learn about entrapping men. I declare, I've already considered three or four ways I could fall down and break my leg so he'd have to carry me around. If I was the damsel in distress I'd have already had Mr. Colin Bryce carrying me all over Twelve-trees."

"But you're not. I'm the lucky one who

twisted my ankle," Jordan said with a sly smile. "So you're just going to have to stand in line, Jolie. Now here, hand me my cologne from my dressing table. I'm going to pour some of it in the water . . ."

Hastily Jordan washed, then hopped over to her dressing table, ignoring the dull throbbing in her ankle. Jolie expertly pinned up her hair, using at least thirty hairpins, but she did manage to tame it enough to tie it up with a wide yellow ribbon that matched the trim on Jordan's morning dress. Then, with much fumbling and giggling and one-footed hopping on Jordan's part, they managed to get her dressed. Jolie was still buttoning her up when they heard a quiet knock on Jordan's door.

"Yes?" she called.

"I'm sure I'm not being very proper," Colin Bryce said quietly into the closed door, "but either you're trying to jump around on one foot, or you've got a kangaroo in there, Miss Randolph. I just wondered—"

The door jerked open, and Jordan hung precariously on it. She smiled brilliantly, and now her cheeks were pink from the icy wash water and the sleep dullness was gone from her eyes. Jolie slipped up to hurriedly finish the last button, for Jordan had leapt—one-footed—to the door when she heard Colin's voice. Now she breathed, "Oh, Mr. Bryce, I'm so ashamed to be so helpless, but once again I must beg your assistance."

"Of course, it will be my pleasure once again." He smiled. "Good morning, Miss Doucett."

"Good morning, Mr. Bryce," she said, giving him her most brilliant smile. "Poor Jordan. She's quite unable to walk."

"No trouble, I feel responsible for her injuries anyway," Colin said. "Are you ready for your palanquin, my lady?"

"Why—how do you know what a palanquin is?" Jordan asked, her eyes shining. Jolie surreptitiously pinched her, and Jordan said, "Oh, yes, I'm ready, sir."

Colin swept her up easily and walked down the hall to the stairway. "I was in Java once," he explained. "Saw a lot of them there, some in India, some in Canton."

"You've been in all those places?" Jordan exclaimed breathlessly.

"Yes, Miss Jordan. I'm a sailor—well, I *was* a sailor. Just a landlubber now, though," Colin said as he slowly descended the stairs, watching his steps carefully. He shifted his right arm a little, hugging Jordan more closely.

"Oh, I'm so sorry to be so much trouble," she said, clinging to him tightly.

"No trouble. You're not as heavy as First Officer Gibbons," Colin said lightly.

"First Officer Gibbons?" Jolie, from behind them, repeated curiously.

"He was our navigator, big man, weighed about two hundred pounds. He broke his leg, and we were lost on the Tropic of Capricorn. Had to carry him topside for his watch. He was a lot heavier than you, Miss Randolph. And he didn't smell nearly as nice," he added, smiling.

Jordan's heart seemed to leap in her chest. "Thank you very much," she managed.

They entered the dining room, and Jordan was surprised to see that her father and mother were there alone, and Lily was setting five places. "I've already fed the children and banished them to the schoolroom," Josephine explained. "They would just pester you to death, Mr. Bryce. Here, you certainly don't have to hold Jordan all through the meal."

Colin got Jordan settled into a chair, and

he and Jolie sat down. After an absent-
minded blessing by Daniel Randolph, Lily
served them, which was unusual in the
Randolph home. Generally breakfast was
placed on the sideboard and they helped
themselves. Jordan decided that her
mother was treating Colin Bryce as an honored guest, which was good; perhaps Josephine's ire for Jordan's unorthodox
midnight adventure was assuaged by Colin
Bryce's gentlemanly appearance and com-
portment.

Jolie said mischievously, "I'm sure the
children wouldn't pester you with questions
nearly as much as we're going to, Mr. Bryce.
Why don't you just surrender, start at the beginning of your life, and end when you rescued our damsel in distress last night?"

Josephine sighed deeply. "Mr. Bryce, I
must apologize for both my daughter and
my niece. My daughter can hardly keep her
head out of the clouds long enough to carry
on a lucid conversation. My niece Jolie has
been so indulged that she talks all the time,
usually impertinently."

"Not at all, ma'am," Colin said with a
smile. "Both your niece and your daughter
are charming young ladies. And it doesn't

seem to me to be at all impertinent, to inquire what kind of stranger you've so graciously invited into your home."

"You've certainly proved your gallantry to me, Mr. Bryce," Jordan said. "I would have had a terrible time last night if you hadn't been there to help me."

"If I hadn't been there you wouldn't have fallen down," he insisted.

"Oh, you just don't know our Jordan," Jolie teased. "For such an elegant young woman she certainly does trip over things and drop things and entangle her skirts a lot."

"Jolie!" Jordan said, blushing painfully. "You make me sound like such a great clumsy mump!"

Jolie waved a dismissal. "You're not clumsy, Cousin, you're just—easily distracted."

"Speaking of clumsiness," Colin interposed, "my horse certainly showed me up last night. As you've probably guessed, I'm no horseman. Can anyone here tell me how I might go about finding that devil? And catching him?"

Daniel said, "I've already sent my foremen and a couple of men out to look for him. My guess is that he found my north hay field, probably been there munching all night."

"Thank you, sir," Colin said with evident relief. "I thought ships were mysterious, willful creatures. I just didn't know that a horse could put one over on me so fast. Caesar didn't really throw me, you know. I was just sort of bumbling along, dozing, and somehow he just figured a way to walk out from under me."

Daniel laughed heartily. "Oh, they can be sly, all right. Especially for an inexperienced rider. So, Mr. Bryce, you say you know ships? Sailor, are you?"

"I was, up until about a few months ago," Colin replied, settling in to tell his history. "My father was a carpenter, worked for Clancy Shipbuilding in Boston. He and my mother were from Wales, but they came here two years before I was born. My mother died when I was nine years old, of typhus, and then the next year my father was killed when a boom gave way and crushed him."

"How very sad," Josephine said quietly. "So you were orphaned?"

"Yes, ma'am, but I don't really think of myself as an orphan. After all, I had two good parents for ten years, and that's enough to feel that you have a family," Colin said, shrugging. "Anyway, another family from the shipyard offered to take me in, but they had eight children, and times were hard. So I went to sea."

"At ten years old?" Jordan said in astonishment. "You were just a child!"

"Not really. Our lives were—different from yours, Miss Randolph," Colin said quietly. "Actually, when I got taken on as a captain's steward at ten, I was older than all the other boys, cook's helpers and powder monkeys. Some of them went to sea when they were six years old. Anyway, I started off as a captain's steward on an East Indiaman. I just showed up at their wharf and announced I was an able seaman," he said, grinning. "They laughed, but the captain said I sounded like an educated little monkey, so he took me on as his steward. He had another boy, too, a black boy, and we were sort of like the captain's showpieces. We wore white gloves and fine blue coats and satin breeches and powdered wigs. We were a pretty showy pair."

Daniel shook his head. "British gentry, no doubt. I've heard they're odd sorts of birds."

"You do seem very educated, Mr. Bryce," Josephine remarked coolly. Her blue eyes bored into him.

"Yes, ma'am, thanks to my mother," Colin explained. "She was a very educated woman. She told me once that she'd been a governess to a viscount's children before she and my father married." He dropped his eyes, slowly and methodically spreading raspberry jam over a fat biscuit. "My parents were sort of an odd couple; I can see that now. But as a child . . ." He gave a slight shrug. "You don't think about those things. One grave regret I've always had is that I never found out their story, their history. Anyway, she educated me at home, a fairly rigorous schooling. And then Captain Blackburn—my first captain—allowed me to attend school with his midshipmen. He was a retired naval officer, you see, and he had that Royal Navy mindset that he was responsible for his young men's education."

"That's very fortunate for you," Josephine said approvingly. "It's a general conception that sailors are an ill-educated, boorish lot."

"Mother!" Jordan blustered. "That's insulting to Mr. Bryce!"

"Not at all, Miss Randolph," Colin said good-naturedly. "It is true, you know. Men who've made the sea their lives are usually raw brutes in port. And it's also true that most of them have no education at all, except their knowledge of ships. The sea is a harsh school and doesn't give a fellow fine manners."

Josephine then asked with rigid politeness, "And so you are a sailor, Mr. Bryce. How is it, then, that you are here, so very far from the sea?"

"Great day in the morning, Josephine, give the man a chance to eat! He's hardly been able to take two bites," Daniel grumbled. He had long finished his hearty breakfast of eggs, chops, oatmeal, and biscuits.

"It's really all right, sir," Colin said politely. "I can understand Mrs. Randolph's concern. Ma'am, I worked my way up, you might say, through the ranks, until three years ago I finally got commissioned as a captain. I had an old brig—in fact, she was an old Baltimore schooner—on regular runs from Boston to France. But she finally gave out about a year ago, and when she did I decided to try something different. I guess I never was what you'd call a born seaman, even though I did like it well enough to do it for fifteen years. But then I decided I'd try a new career. I had some money saved, and I thought I might open a small import-export business. But somehow"—he smiled engagingly at Josephine—"it never worked out. I've been—traveling, you might say, for the past year. I was in Charleston for a while, then New York, then I wandered down to New Orleans. Then I started reading about all the lands to the west, and I decided on a new profession."

"And—and what is it?" Jordan asked breathlessly.

"I'm going west." He smiled at her. "To Oregon Territory."

"Are you really?" Jordan exclaimed. "How exciting!"

"Exciting, yes," Josephine said stolidly. "But do you know anything about farming, Captain Bryce?"

"Not a blessed thing, Mrs. Randolph," Colin answered easily. "But I'm young, and the sea has toughened me up. I'll learn as I go along. For instance, I've already learned that I don't know how to choose, buy, or ride a horse," he said, grinning unself-consciously. "But I'm learning. So I was on my

way to Independence to try to make con-
nections with a wagon train."

"They won't be leaving for another six
weeks or so," Jordan said quickly.

"They won't?" Colin was surprised. "But I
thought there was a steady stream of wagons heading west."

Daniel settled back in his chair, noisily
sipping a third cup of coffee. "They can't
leave this early, Captain Bryce. There
wouldn't be any grass for the animals along
the trail. Most of them start out in the latter
part of April."

"Well, there's another lesson learned the
hard way," Colin gamely said. "I guess I
could go on to Independence and get outfitted. Think I'll try and talk to some people,
get some expert advice before then, though.
Wouldn't like to think I was putting out to
sea in a sieve."

"I can help you, Captain Bryce," Jordan
offered, her eyes alight.

"I can, too," Jolie said eagerly.

"Nonsense," Josephine said dryly. "Why,
you two girls barely know how to button
your shoes! What makes you think, Jordan,
that you could advise a man on how to get
equipped for a wagon train west?"

"How hard can it be?" Jordan said stubbornly. "You just—think of what you'll need, and get it."

Colin laughed. "Miss Randolph, that's exactly what I thought when I bought Caesar. Look how that turned out."

Jordan's cheeks turned a delicate pink, but she asserted, "But, Captain Bryce, I could have helped you buy a horse. I know a lot about horses, don't I, Father?"

"She does," Daniel agreed. "How a woman can be such a good rider and can't walk across the room without breaking something is a mystery to me."

"I'm a good rider, too," Jolie said coquettishly. "Perhaps, Uncle, you would allow me and Captain Bryce to ride this morning? Of course, Jordan is a better horsewoman than I—but unfortunately, dear, your poor ankle will keep you from riding for a few days, won't it?"

Jordan was downcast. "I'd forgotten about that."

"Forgotten about it?" Josephine repeated with disbelief, then cast a sharp, knowing glance toward Colin Bryce. "Nonsense. As soon as Claud returns I'm going to have him go to town and fetch Dr. Leverett. I don't think it's broken, Jordan, but he really should advise us about the best way to care for it."

"Why don't Captain Bryce and I go to town?" Jolie suggested brightly. "He could ride Sally; she's very gentle. That way he could get a riding lesson and also see Independence."

Jordan opened her mouth with dismay, but quickly her mother cut in. "I think that's a marvelous idea, Jolie. If Captain Bryce doesn't mind, of course."

"My pleasure, ma'am. It's the least I can do," he said, turning to Jordan and making an elegant small bow, "for this damsel in distress."

Jolie and Colin returned from town with quite a party. They had found Dr. Leverett at Maddox Hardware, and when Charlie heard the news about Jordan's mishap he insisted on riding out to Twelvetrees too. The doctor examined her ankle and pronounced it a minor injury. Because it was so late Josephine insisted on everyone staying for dinner, and so they had a merry company of seven that night.

"Good news on Jordan's ankle," Dr. Leverett reassured everyone as soon as grace was said. "It's not broken. Just a sprain, but it's a bad one. Keep cold compresses on it in the morning, since it will swell some at night. During the day, stay off it, Miss Jordan, and keep it elevated."

"Oh, no," Jordan cried, with a swift glance at Colin Bryce seated beside her. "I wanted to—that is, I don't want to stay in bed for two days!"

Across from her, Charlie Maddox noted Jordan's expression and frowned. "I brought you a walking stick, Jordan. Not very pretty, I guess, but it is hand-carved from fine ash."

"I don't want a walking stick! I'll look like an elderly matriarch hobbling around!" Jordan said petulantly.

Very deliberately Josephine laid her fork to the right of her plate, and laid her knife precisely on the left. "Jordan Randolph, how thoughtless and rude of you. I'm ashamed."

Jordan's face reddened suddenly, and she bowed her head. "You're right, Mother. Please forgive me. And, Charlie—thank you so very much. I'm sure it's a lovely walking stick. It's very kind of you."

"It's okay, Jordan," he said gruffly, embarrassed for her. "It's really not that pretty. Maybe you can tie some ribbons on it or something."

"We'll paint it, Jordan, with black and silver and gold gilt," Jolie suggested enthusiastically.

"Excuse me, ladies," Dr. Leverett said dryly. "Am I speaking in a foreign language? I said nothing about *walking*, as in *walking* sticks. You're supposed to stay *off* the ankle for two days, Miss Jordan."

"Oh, pshaw," Jordan said, fully recovered now. "Surely I'll be able to get around. Maybe—ride? Maybe tomorrow?"

"Absolutely not!" Dr. Leverett objected.

"Riding wouldn't put any strain on my ankle," Jordan reflected. "It's my right ankle, and I mount with my left. Dismount—well, perhaps I could—"

"I give up," Dr. Leverett grumbled, apparently to himself.

"Perhaps Mr. Bryce could simply sweep you up?" Jolie suggested. "He's so very good at it."

"Heard you've been hauling Jordan around like a pack mule, Mr. Bryce," Charlie said suspiciously. "How'd that come about?"

"She bewitched my horse, and then fell from the sky," Colin said, winking at Jordan.

"Enough nonsense," Josephine said sternly. "Captain Bryce, I'm surprised at you. You seem a sensible man, but then again, you have been in the company of my daughter and my niece for a day and a night, and that's enough to make a reasonable person slightly lunatic. Anyway, Jordan, you will not be riding, you will be doing exactly as Dr. Leverett advises. For the next two days you will be here, in your room or on the parlor sofa. You will not be walking, you will not be hopping like a rabbit, and you will certainly not be riding. After two days we shall see. Now, Dr. Leverett, I'm so glad you're joining us for supper, it's been so long since we've seen you."

"Mrs. Randolph, it's my pleasure. It's been a very long time since I've had some home cooking. Sophie's in town is close, but there are so many people in Independence now that her home-cooked meals are starting to get something of the flavor of a camp cook's." Dr. Leverett looked appreciatively at his chuck roast, baked and basted all day with Lily's special butter-and-red-pepper marinade.

"You should get yourself a housekeeper and cook, Dr. Leverett," Josephine said, smiling. "Men are quite incapable of keeping a house."

Dr. Leverett gave her an amused glance. "Are you trying to get me married off again?"

"Perhaps," Josephine replied. "I've noticed that Mrs. Williams at church has been bringing bread and cakes to you."

"Nice lady, Mrs. Williams. Widowed two years, she is," Dr. Leverett told Colin across the table. "Has four young children. I'd probably kill the whole lot of 'em off in a month, just from aggravation."

"Hard way to start a family, sir," Colin said, suppressing a grin.

"No ready-made families, not for me," Dr. Leverett said succinctly. "I'm just not the marrying kind, never was. Besides, I decided yesterday that I'm going to start a whole new life—and four kids with measles and runny noses don't come into it at all."

"Why, what do you mean?" Josephine asked. "What new life?"

"I'm heading west, for Oregon Territory," he announced with satisfaction.

"What!" Josephine said, shocked. "But—but, Dr. Leverett, Independence is your home! How could you possibly just fly off the handle on a wild goose chase like that?"

"Mother, you're mixing your metaphors," Jordan said, amused. "Dr. Leverett, I think that's perfectly wonderful! Oh, how I wish I were a man, and I could just—just—clap my hat on my head and ride off to Oregon!"

Charlie Maddox said stolidly, "Jordan, that's a wild notion. You've got no idea, the planning those people have to do, the supplies they have to have, the hardships they face."

"But they're explorers, Charlie, courageous pioneers," Jordan argued. "I'm sure it's hard and dangerous, but glorious too."

"Not so glorious once you start buying a wagon and animals and supplies and equipment," Dr. Leverett stated. "I really didn't have any idea what a big project it is to get yourself all the way across America and stay alive. I'm finding out quick, though. I talked to Horace Farr, one of the wagon masters, and joined up with his train. Found out I'd talked myself right into being on the council. We have to figure out who can come with us, who can't, exactly what route we're going to take, estimate water requirements, set minimum standards for equipment and food and supplies for every member of the train. It's sort of like a military expedition."

"Really?" Colin asked with interest. "I'm going west, too, Doctor, and I'd sure appreciate it if I could talk to some people, get some advice, find out what I need. Think this Mr. Farr would give me a hand?"

"Doubt it, he's got his hands full just managing the eighteen wagons he's got now, sitting still," Dr. Leverett said succinctly. "But maybe I could help you out some. I've found out about the wagons and the animals. If you can get outfitted up right, Captain Bryce, you could join up with our train. But I must tell you, we're trying to set some requirements for the wagons that some of the other wagon bosses sneer at. Looks to me like some of the other trains are kind of just clappin' their hats on their heads and riding off into the sunset, as Miss Jordan here said. Mr. Farr, and our council, are rather strict about what our wagons need."

"Sounds expensive," Colin said, frowning.

"Guess maybe it is," Dr. Leverett said. "But I've been with those people down there, talking with them a lot, because I'm the only doctor that'll care for the people on the trains. I've gotten to know most of the wagon bosses, and I think Horace Farr is the best man. He's smart, he's tough, and he doesn't cut corners. You want to come down and talk to some of the wagon bosses, get a feel for it, Captain Bryce, I'll be glad to introduce you around."

"That would be very kind of you, sir," Colin said gratefully. "Would you let me go back into town with you tonight? I'll get a room, and maybe tomorrow we could go over and meet some people."

"Not tonight!" Jordan objected. "Aren't you staying with us tonight?"

"Well, I—," Colin began.

"Clean forgot to tell you, we found that horse of yours, right where I said he'd be," Daniel said. "Up in my north field, chomping on my cattle's hay. Claud brought him back, and he's all cleaned up and bedded down in the stables. You might as well stay here tonight, Captain Bryce, and get a start in the morning."

Josephine cast a cautious glance to Charlie Maddox, who was frowning severely. But then resignedly she agreed, "Of course, Captain Bryce. You're welcome to stay tonight; it would just be silly for you to go back into town."

"Thank you, Mrs. Randolph," Colin said happily. "To tell you the truth, I'm already sore from all the riding today. I'm wondering if I'm going to be able to walk tomorrow. I might be in just as bad a shape as Miss Randolph."

Jordan brightened at that, but once again, Josephine brought her back down to earth. "The more you ride, Captain Bryce, the easier it becomes," she said knowingly.

"Sure hope so," he said wryly. "Because from my experience so far, I'd rather be riding a jolly boat in a gale than trying to ride a horse."

"I thought you did very well today, Captain Bryce," Jolie said. "After all, you didn't fall off once."

"No, I didn't, not even once." Colin shrugged. "But Caesar's not much like that sweet little mare. He's out to get me, that horse is."

"He's a fine animal," Daniel put in, "but he's sneaky smart. Claud told me that he almost had his stable gate unlatched. Would've made a clean getaway if Claud hadn't gone back just to check on him. He was trying to lift the latch with his teeth."

"Just what I need, a horse that's smarter than I am." Colin grinned.

"He's sturdy and healthy though," Daniel said. "He'd be a good mount to take west."

"That's fine," Colin said dryly, "if I ever get to ride him. Do you know that I don't even know how to saddle up a horse? When I bought Caesar, the man I bought him from saddled him up for me, and"—he glanced at Jordan and smiled—"then I just clapped my hat on my head and rode off into the sunset."

Jordan laughed, while Charlie Maddox glowered. But he did manage to say with awkward good grace, "Well, Captain Bryce, when you get ready to get outfitted you just come to Maddox Hardware. I'll be glad to help you out, make sure you don't get loaded up with a lot of things you don't need."

"That's very nice of you, Mr. Maddox," Colin said warmly. "Guess you can see I'm a real tenderfoot. I'm going to take all the help I can get."

"Perhaps tomorrow I'll ride back into town with you, Captain Bryce, and we can visit Charlie," Jolie said with a glance at Jordan. "He's got some new cream separators that you really *must* see."

Jordan felt a twinge of envy, but she couldn't possibly stay angry with her cousin. Jolie Doucett was never one to let a good-looking man escape her attention, but it was always just mild flirtation, and Jordan was not really the jealous type.

Besides, she had much more serious plans for Captain Colin Bryce, and no little things like flirtatious cousins or sprained ankles or even would-be fiancés were going to change that.

Jordan thought serenely, *Colin and I are just meant to be!*

"What do you mean?" Jolie asked, her clear brow wrinkling.

"Colin and I—we were just meant to be," Jordan said in a soft voice.

Jolie reached up and pulled a long, dangerous-looking pearl hat pin out of her veiled top hat. Her riding costume was of midnight-blue velvet, with a matching hat, and was one of Jolie's favorite ensembles. She and Colin had been out riding. Colin had been staying with the Randolphs for the last three days; the hotel in Independence had been full. He and Jolie had been riding each day while Jordan was nursing her sprained ankle.

Jolie sat on Jordan's bed, fiddling with her hat and hat pin. "Jordan, dear," she said with unusual deliberation, "it's hard for me to understand exactly what you mean. I assume you're saying that you're in love with Colin Bryce?"

"It's much more than that," Jordan said with some surprise. She had thought her cousin would instantly comprehend the revelation Jordan had had. "I just know that Colin and I are meant to be together. We are soul mates, kindred spirits. Sometimes two people are just destined to be together forever. Like Romeo and Juliet."

"Don't forget they were star-crossed lovers, together only in death, dearest," Jolie said dryly. "Which brings me back to my first question—lovers? I mean, Jordan, Captain Bryce is a charming man, and there's no doubt that he has a—certain—regard—for you, but—"

"Oh, he doesn't know it yet," Jordan said confidently. "But he will. He'll have to."

"But it just doesn't work that way, Jordan," Jolie argued. "I mean—how do you know that this is—real? That this is"—she groped a bit—"that this is the real thing?"

Jordan's eyes focused a thousand miles away. "I know, because my heart tells me . . . and my dreams tell me."

Jolie sighed. Such a premise could hardly be refuted with logic. "Well, Jordan, this may be all very clear to you, but oddly enough I've spent more time with Captain Bryce than you have, and I'm afraid I've seen no indication that he's aware of his— destiny."

"He doesn't have a positive dislike of me, does he?" Jordan asked, wide-eyed.

"No, of course not," Jolie answered hastily. "And—no, dear, I can already hear your next question. He's not enamored of me, either. We enjoy each other's company, and of course you know I flirt with him outrageously, and he likes that. Most men do. But he just rarely speaks of you, except in passing, you understand. I say, 'Jordan and I were riding here once and we saw a fox,' and he says, 'Miss Randolph is so fortunate to have these fine horses to ride every day, blah, blah . . .' You know, we speak of you as a mutual acquaintance. He likes you, I know; you make him smile. But, Jordan, it would be tragic for you to think that something is inevitable when it's not."

"But it is," Jordan insisted. "I just know it, Jolie!"

"All right," Jolie said, surrendering. "For

your sake, I hope so. But what about poor Charlie Maddox?"

Jordan frowned. "What about him? I never made him any promises."

As if she were speaking to a wayward child, Jolie explained, "But, Jordan, you've been keeping company with him for almost a year now. He feels that you two have a commitment, and rightly so, whether or not you've said the exact words, 'Yes, I will marry you.' He told Captain Bryce that you were engaged."

"What?" Jordan exclaimed, wide-eyed. "Well, there you are, Jolie! If Colin thinks I'm engaged, then of course that's why he hasn't been spending much time with me!"

"But, Jordan—," Jolie began, then gave up. This conversation was just a little too one-sided for her, and besides, she certainly was no oracle. Maybe Jordan was right. Maybe she and Colin Bryce were thrown to-gether by Fate or Kismet or Destiny; their meeting was certainly unique. But Jolie Doucett, at heart a pragmatic woman, won-dered if perhaps Jordan's dreams had not blinded her at last.

SIX

Colin Bryce finally got a room at the Independence Hotel, and he left Twelvetrees with
promises to come back and visit often. When
Colin did come to see Jordan, he was gallant
and attentive, but not overly so. In spite of all
of Jordan's maneuverings, she had been unable to get a single moment alone with him.
But she was not at all discouraged.

On Friday it was time for Jolie to return to
Baton Rouge, and Jordan insisted on ac-
companying her to town. "Mother, I've been
stuck in this house for an entire week, and
I'm walking just fine now; I don't even need
the walking stick," she told Josephine firmly.
"I need an outing, and besides, I can pick up
the things you need from Drury's General
Store."

Her mother had relented, and it was a fine
cheerful March afternoon for a drive. It was
windy, but the sun was bright and warm.
Jordan felt as if she'd been released from
prison. They went straight to the wharf, for
Jolie had had some last-minute flurries in

packing, and they were almost late to catch
the steamboat, the same *Gloriana* that made
her eternal loops from Baton Rouge to Independence.

"Oh, dear, I have to fly," Jolie said, hastily
kissing her cousin as they heard the stew-
ards making final boarding calls. "Jordan, I
can't tell you how much fun I've had this last
month. Please, please promise me to come
to visit soon!"

Jordan smiled serenely. "Maybe I will,
Jolie. I certainly will miss you."

Jolie gave her one last fervent hug, whispering, "If he's what you want, dear Cousin,
I hope you get your heart's desire."

Jordan stood on the wharf and waved
good-bye to Jolie until the steamboat
rounded the south bend. Then she turned
and instructed Jackson, "Please take the
buggy to Courthouse Square, Jackson, and
just wait. I've got several errands to run, but I
want to walk for a while. Here's a quarter; get
yourself a sarsaparilla while you're waiting."

Leisurely Jordan strolled into town, somewhat depressed over the loss of Jolie. Early
spring was her favorite season, when the
days were warm and the nights still cool.
Town was crowded, as usual; it seemed

even more so since people joining the wagon trains were still pouring in. *About two months is all I've got before Colin leaves,* she thought, and the realization of it was like a cold shadow flitting over the sun. Jordan walked more quickly.

She made her way to Maddox Hardware, walked in, and went straight to Charlie, who was in his shirtsleeves, earnestly talking to a man in rough clothing and a worn wide-brimmed gray felt hat. "Now this is a Collins ax, sir, the finest ax ever made! You can't find a better ax—"

"Charlie?" Jordan said politely, laying her hand on his arm.

He looked around with surprise and frowned momentarily. "Hello, Jordan. I'll be with you in just one minute." He turned back to the man who was listening with narrowed eyes and went on, "As I was saying, sir, you can't find a better ax for the money. Now, it's true, this is more expensive than some, but you see, the guarantee is made, essentially, for a lifetime . . ."

Frowning, Jordan wandered off to look around. Now that she wasn't distracted by Jolie's—and her own—little making-fun-of-Charlie games, she was impressed, in a sort of mechanical way, with Charlie's store. It was meticulously clean, which was unusual for a hardware store, and organized in a methodical, practical manner. *Just like Charlie,* Jordan reflected with amusement. *Everything in its little bin, everything precise, nothing whimsical or fanciful . . .*

"Jordan? I'm sorry, but I was in the middle of explaining axes to that gentleman," Charlie said with a hint of reproach.

"I heard," she said absently. "Do you have some time now? I'd like to speak to you if I may."

He glanced at her curiously, but answered politely, "Of course. Would you like to come into my office?"

"Please." She followed him into a small cubbyhole that was just as well-ordered as his store. He indicated a straight chair in front of his desk, which had papers on it in a very neat pile just to the left of his blotter, with edges squared and a large, glistening quartz crystal as a paperweight. Jordan stared at it curiously; it seemed foreign to Charlie's nature. She would have expected him to have a paperweight made of a solid, unadorned wooden block.

He seated himself behind the desk and

steepled his fingers as he leaned over. "Well, ma'am, what can I do for my favorite customer today?"

Jordan, contemplating the paperweight, quickly gathered her thoughts. "Oh, yes. Well, Charlie, I felt that I ought to tell you as quickly as possible. You see, I've just decided that we're not at all suited for each other, and though I'm honored by your proposal, I'm afraid that it wouldn't be wise for us to marry."

Charlie was unmoving, as still as if he were made of stone. His freckled face turned white, however, and his boyish lips tightened. Jordan was a little disconcerted. She'd spoken matter-of-factly, even lightly, and she'd thought that Charlie would shrug and smile. He was doing neither. Especially not smiling. In fact, he looked—stricken.

"Oh, dear," Jordan stammered, blushing. "Charlie, I didn't mean to be—brusque. I really thought you felt the same way I do."

Tightly, his fingers still steepled, he muttered, "Why should you think that, Jordan?"

"I—I don't know," she said, bewildered. "I—I just thought so."

"You thought," he growled. "No, Jordan, you did *not* think. You never think! You just flitter around like some kind of dandelion fluff, not knowing and not caring."

Jordan's eyes grew wide. "But that's not true! I—I do care, Charlie. I care for you; I've known you all my life! But we shouldn't be married, Charlie. I wouldn't make you happy at all."

His indrawn breath was sharp; he squinted and his eyes closed with pain. Jordan waited, not knowing what to say. After a long, heavy silence he dropped his hands, leaned back as if he were very tired, and looked up at her. "I'm not going to argue with you; that would be stupid. Just tell me one thing. It's Bryce, isn't it?"

Jordan was shocked, first of all because she couldn't believe that she was that transparent, and secondly, because somehow she felt it was rude of Charlie to mention it. "Why—why—that's absurd, Charlie," she retorted. "I refuse to discuss it."

Slowly Charlie nodded. "It *is* absurd. That's why I know it's the truth." He stood, his shoulders rounded as if he were thirty years older. "If you'll excuse me, Jordan, I'm busy today."

Flustered, Jordan rose and hurried to the door. Charlie was standing still behind his desk, watching her. She turned with an angry retort, and saw the hurt in his eyes and the defeat in his stocky, solid body. "Charlie, I—I—"

"Never mind, Jordan," he said quietly. "Just—leave. Please."

She left, closing the door quietly behind her. In great confusion she hurried out of the store. This hadn't gone at all as she'd pictured it, and she was confused, and upset that she'd hurt Charlie so badly. It had shaken her. She turned and began to walk blindly on the sidewalk, making her way with some difficulty, as it was thronged with people. Only after she'd walked past three stores did she notice that she'd turned the wrong way, and she whirled around, bumping into an elderly lady and knocking her bonnet askew. Jordan apologized profusely, and the lady warily straightened her bonnet and hurried off muttering about rude young women. But at least now Jordan was heading in the direction of Drury's General Store.

It was all the way at the other end of the square. Jordan, absorbed in her thoughts about Charlie Maddox, absently decided that she'd cut across the street, and stepped off the plank walk, barely noticing when two carts rumbled past her. *I can't be-lieve Charlie was so upset . . . I thought he was just sort of . . . going along, as I was, for lack of something better to do . . .*

Jordan was brought up short as a buck-board passed by within inches of her toes. "Well, now, Jordan, do I need to rescue you again?" an amused voice called.

She whirled. There in the muddy street, Colin Bryce was towering over her, mounted on Caesar, who was prancing nervously. The sun hit Colin's hair, deepening it to blue-black, and he was very broad-shouldered and erect in the saddle. Jordan was speech-less for a moment, but she quickly recov-ered. "I haven't fallen in a hole again, Captain, but I would like to be rescued, if you're inclined," she answered.

He dismounted, not smoothly but ade-quately, and took her arm. "I'm at your ser-vice. I'm thinking of starting my own business: Maiden's Rescues, Limited. Any Day, Any Hour, Any Danger."

Jordan held his arm closely and smiled. "I'm your first client, sir."

"If you keep falling down and walking in front of moving horses I won't need any other clients," Colin teased.

"That would be fine with me," Jordan said.

But Colin seemed to take no notice of her gravity. "Here we are; I've delivered you safely to this side of the street. Are you going to Drury's?"

She hesitated. "I have some purchases to make, but—" She waited, eyeing him, hoping he would suggest something for the two of them to do together.

He waited politely, then said helpfully, "But you've forgotten what they are?"

"No, silly!" she said, laughing mostly at herself. "The truth is that I had intended to spend some time in town, make it a sort of an outing, since I've been stuck in the house for a week. It just occurred to me that if I'm going to walk around I really don't want to be carrying parcels."

He grinned engagingly. "Why, Miss Randolph, I do believe I've been misled about your state of mind. That makes perfectly logical sense."

"Thank you," she said dryly.

"I'm going to buy some horses," he said expansively. "I believe you offered to help me once? And now that it appears you have horse sense, I can't think of anyone better to advise me."

"I'd love to," she said delightedly, taking his arm again. "Where are you going?"

"Man named Fred Bates has brought some stock into town," Colin answered as they picked their way down the street, leading Caesar. "They've set up a corral over behind the livery stables, close to where the wagon trains are camped. A lot of the farmers and stockmen around have started bringing their stock into town to sell. People going west have been snatching them up."

He and Jordan talked animatedly about the people he'd met and the things he'd found out about traveling west. Jordan was interested in everything, from the route they took down to the kind of water barrels they used. It never occurred to her that she'd been bored to death when Charlie spoke of such things. In fact, she'd forgotten all about Charlie Maddox and their painful scene.

They reached the west end of town, and found that now there were not one but three temporary corrals put up to display animals for the wagon trains. "Business must be real good," Colin said. "All three of these corrals are full—and look over there, must be thirty oxen lined up. They're big scary brutes, aren't they?"

Before Jordan had time to answer a man, short and swarthy, with a huge swooping mustache, came to greet them, rubbing his hands together in an oily kind of way. "Hello, folks, glad to see ya. Name's Bates, Frederick R. Bates. Looking for some stock to take you all the way to Oregon Territory?"

"Sure am," Colin answered. "All of these animals yours?" In the first corral were twelve horses and eight mules.

"Yes, sir, my own stock. Used all of 'em on my farm, Red Hand River, east of town. Got eight hundred acres, but I'm over-stocked with my animals," the man said grandly. "Decided to sell some of 'em, even though I'm not really hard up. Figured you pioneer folk can put 'em to good use."

"Red Hand River?" Jordan repeated, her brow furrowed. "I've never heard of that farm. I'm sorry, sir, what did you say your name—"

But Frederick R. Bates was quick, and he shot Colin a shrewd glance and saw that he wasn't really paying attention to Jordan. "Now, sir, I can see you know good horse-flesh when you see it, 'cause that's a fine saddle horse you got here." He slapped Caesar's rump as he rounded the horse, talking, so that Colin turned away from Jordan to hear. "Yes, sir, fine animal. So, you looking for a pair to pull a wagon?"

"Yes, sir," Colin answered as Bates stepped some feet away from Jordan, and Colin stepped close to him. Jordan followed, thinking to herself that Colin hadn't tightened Caesar's girth strap properly. Horses, especially smart horses like Caesar, blew out their sides when they were being saddled so that the girth strap seemed tight enough. Some greenhorn riders—like Colin—had a rude awakening when they were riding along and the saddle slid out from under them. Idly she wondered if Mr. Bates had noticed it, but Jordan was so bemused by Colin Bryce that she could hardly do anything but watch him, drinking in his dramatic good looks, his masculine ease, the set of his shoulders, his muscular hands.

". . . that pair right there, had 'em pulling hay carts," Bates was saying, rubbing his hands together briskly. "They pulled 'em like they was lady's little coaches, good strong horses. Pretty too, ain't they?"

"They sure are," Colin said admiringly. The two horses that had drawn his eyes were a matched pair of bay geldings, one with a blaze and one with a star. They were high-stepping, lively, even in the dusty, crowded corral. Even as he watched, the one with the blaze reared a little, then danced sideways, snorting.

Bates's black eyes were shrewd. "Had a feller wanted to buy that one with the blaze this mornin', but I kinda wanted to sell 'em together. They been paired all their lives, you see, and that makes a fine team. I told that feller I'd let him have the blaze this evenin' if I couldn't sell the two of them. Tell you what. I was gonna charge him a hunnerd dollars for the blaze, but if you'll buy the pair, I'll let you have both of 'em for a hunnerd sixty, mister. They're kinda like my kids, you know? Hate to separate 'em."

"They are fine-looking horses," Colin said, considering. "Jordan? What do you think about that pair? The bay geldings, with the star and the blaze?"

Jordan was considering the horses un-certainly. Truth to tell, she knew how to sad-dle a horse, how to groom one, how to feed one, even how to deliver a foal. But she knew absolutely nothing about buying one. She knew she could tell an ancient old nag from a young horse, and of course she could tell if they were spavined or sway-backed. But how much money to pay for one was quite beyond her experience.

Suddenly Colin brushed past her and hurried to a man walking by, calling out to him. The man stopped, listened to Colin, then nodded. The two returned and Colin said eagerly, "Jordan, may I introduce you to Tyler Sublette? Ty, this is Miss Jordan Randolph. Her father, Mr. Daniel Randolph, owns Twelvetrees," Colin said.

Jordan shaded her eyes from the bright sun as she looked up at the man. He was very tall, over six feet. Built sturdily, with broad shoulders and a thick chest, he had the lightest, coolest blue eyes Jordan had ever seen. His face was deeply tanned, with crow's-feet at the corners of his eyes and hair that had been sun-bleached. His nose was thin, but Jordan saw a small crook in it as if it had been broken sometime in the past. She guessed his age at somewhere in the mid thirties. He had a tough, well-used appearance, in worn buckskins, but he gave her a ready smile.

"I've met your father, Miss Randolph, and—Miss Doucett? Isn't she a relation?" Ty

Sublette asked, extending his grin to Colin Bryce.

"So you've met my cousin," Jordan said, smiling back at him. "I'm so sorry to say that she's returned to Baton Rouge, leaving a string of broken hearts behind."

"She's a right charming young lady," Sublette said cheerfully.

Colin explained to Jordan, "Ty is a mountain man, and he's been over the trail all the way to Oregon and back. Dr. Leverett introduced us. He's been trying to talk Ty into going with Mr. Farr's wagon train as a scout and guide."

"Is that right?" Jordan said, her eyes shining. "Mr. Sublette, you've been all the way across to Oregon? I'd love to hear your story."

"Long story, ma'am," he replied easily. "And probably not that interesting to a town lady like you."

"I'm not a town lady—," Jordan said, but Colin was eager to make his purchases, and interrupted her.

"Listen, Ty, I'm getting outfitted for the trail, and I'm green as grass. Maybe you might help me out a little here," Colin said, leading the man toward the corral, and a scowling Mr. Bates.

"Hello, Fred," Ty said evenly.

Bates just grunted, "Hello, Sublette." He brightened up amazingly, however, as he took Colin's arm and tried to lead him away. "Now, sir, see them two horses is over here, I can cut 'em out for you—"

But Colin turned back to Ty. "See that pair? I really like the looks of those horses."

Ty stuck his hands in his pockets and studied them, his stance relaxed, but his gaze coolly assessing. "Fine-looking pair."

"Well—what do you think?" Colin asked. Jordan hovered close, watching Ty Sublette curiously.

"They're nice-looking horses," Sublette said slowly.

"I think so, too," Jordan said eagerly.

Colin, forgetting that Bates hovered right behind him, said, "Price is dirt cheap, too. Man's only asking one hundred and sixty dollars for the pair."

The corner of Sublette's mouth twitched. "You've bought dirt that cheap, have you, Colin?"

Bates stepped up, his eyes black with anger. "If you ain't buyin', Sublette, then maybe you'd better keep out of it."

Sublette shrugged. "Man just asked me a

fair question, Fred. I'm going to give him a fair answer."

Colin frowned and looked at Jordan, mystified. But she was no help; she didn't know what Sublette's taciturn comments meant, either. Colin tried again. "You think the price is too high?"

"It's a little high, Colin, but they are a nice pair of horses. It just kinda depends on what you're looking for," Sublette said quietly. He saw that Colin was utterly confused now, and added, "Those two horses are going to look real pretty to Indians. They'd love to have a couple of good-looking, spirited horses like that."

"Oh, you mean they'd be more likely to steal them? But they wouldn't be loose in the herd animals, you know. I wanted them to pull my wagon."

Bates stepped up and said loudly, "That's right, Mr. Bryce, and I've done told you they'd be a real good choice, they've pulled heavy hay wagons all over my farm, and—"

Ignoring him, Sublette asked in a quietly amused voice, "Where you going to pull your wagon to, Mr. Bryce? Across town?"

Colin also ignored Bates, frowning.

"You're saying—two horses won't do it? Well, how many do you have to have?"

Bates almost shouted, "Now, I done told you, them two horses—"

Quietly, calmly, Sublette said, "Now, Fred, I didn't say a word about you overcharging this man, because I figure every man has to learn some lessons the hard way, and it's really none of my business about a man's finances. But I can't stand here and let you sell that pair to pull a wagon to Oregon."

Bates bristled, then wrinkled his face up with disgust. "Them is good hosses, Sublette!"

"I've said they are," Ty agreed easily. "But they'd never get a wagon over the mountains. I know it and you know it, too."

Bates glared at Sublette, then said loudly, "Well, I got them mules, too! Sublette, don't you go a-telling them that mules won't do!"

Carelessly Sublette said, "No, I'm not going to tell them that."

Jordan and Colin had been listening, both of them wide-eyed. Now Jordan spluttered, "Well, of all the nerve! Do you mean you were going to charge double what those horses are worth? And they're not even the right breed?"

Colin's inevitable good nature triumphed, and he laughed. "Jordan, I think that things like this happen all the time. Mr. Bates here is just a good horse trader, as they say."

"But it's dishonest," Jordan said indignantly.

Colin laughed again, but Ty Sublette studied Jordan gravely. "You're both right, you know. Fred here is a good horse trader, but it was dishonest. You ashamed of yourself, Fred?"

"Keep your nose out of my business, Sublette!" Fred muttered grumpily as he walked away.

"Well, I think someone ought to tell the sheriff about that man," Jordan said angrily. "It's a disgrace!"

"I guess all's fair in love, war—and horse trading, Miss Randolph. Just don't tell anyone what a dupe I am," Colin said, still grinning. "You either, Ty. I'd never be able to raise my head again if the whole train knew I was so dim-witted."

"Guess I'd be pretty dim-witted about buying a boat," Ty Sublette said. The three slowly began to walk toward the second corral. Ty glanced back at Caesar, his eyes appraising.

With dread Colin asked, "Now what? Is he

forty years old, or dying of consumption, or
something? I mean, he is a horse, isn't he?"

Ty grinned, and Jordan thought that he
was not the kind of man who smiled very
much, but when he did, it was a slow, wide
smile, filled with warmth. "That's a fine horse,
Colin. Good legs, good breadth of chest, fine
straight line from withers to rump."

"And you're wondering how I managed to
pick out a good one, I bet," Colin grumbled.
"And don't even ask me how much I paid for
him. I'm not telling."

"Fine with me. But, Colin—," Ty said reluctantly.

"Yes?" Colin asked warily.

"You saddle Caesar by yourself, do you?"
Ty asked.

"Yes, I do, I didn't want the stable hands
to do it because I wanted to learn myself,"
Colin said. "Why?"

"Well, that girth strap, you're going to
have to tighten it more," Ty said evenly.
"With it hanging loose like that, well, these
horse traders are going to spot it first thing,
and . . ." He shrugged expressively.

Colin blinked. "Okay. What's the girth
strap?"

Jordan couldn't help it; a giggle escaped.

Ty Sublette kept his face admirably composed. "It's that strap under his belly. Here, let me show you." Ty went to Caesar, expertly pulled the strap loose from the cinch, kicked his leg up, and pushed against Caesar's side with one booted foot. "See here? He puffs out his sides so it'll be loose. You just be a little more stubborn with your foot than he is with his puffin', and you'll get it good and tight."

Colin watched carefully. "Blamed horse is too smart." He glanced at Ty's face and asked, "Thing like that would tell a horse trader I'm a greenhorn, huh?"

"Probably," Ty agreed reluctantly. "But mostly I'm figuring they're waiting to watch you ride that horse upside down."

Colin shook his head ruefully. "Can't tell you the times I've laughed and poked fun at some poor landlubber trying to take in a sail or man a buntline. I'm paying for those sins now."

Jordan bristled. "Well, I think it's just downright mean to laugh at people's honest mistakes, or to make fun of them."

"Reckon you'd never do that to anyone," Sublette said idly. But his blue eyes were intent, as if he were looking inside her, measuring her in some odd way. Suddenly Jordan was ashamed, remembering how she had often made fun of Charlie Maddox.

Jordan felt her cheeks burn, but tossed her head a little and grabbed Colin's arm again. "Don't take it so hard, Captain. I know horses, but obviously I don't know about *buying* horses. I had no idea that people would lie to you bald-faced like Bates did. And another thing I don't understand at all, Mr. Sublette. You say that horses can't pull the wagons to Oregon? But I see wagons here all the time with horses pulling them."

Ty nodded. "Some of them can, if they're good, big workhorses. That pair you admired, Colin, they were a nice team, no joshing. They'd make a good matched pair to pull a light buggy, or they'd make good saddle horses for fun riding. But they weren't workhorses. Their legs were too long and they were too antsy. You gotta have at least six big horses, like plowhorses, with short thick legs and wide chests and hopefully some fat on them, both to keep them from starving in the thin times and to insulate them against cold. Those high-flyin', prancing kind just aren't sturdy enough to pull a heavy wagon over a thousand miles. Personally, I think a six-mule team or a coupla good teams of oxen are much better."

"Really?" Jordan asked. "Which is best? Mules or oxen?"

Ty considered this. "If I were choosing, I'd get me two good pair of oxen, not young ones. Oxen can live a long time, and they can work—well, they can work pretty much until they die. You can't beat them for stamina, or for strength. And if you're lucky enough to get a pair that have been matched, then you get—I guess you'd call it—sweet-natured beasts. Not like mules. Mules are hardy enough to pull a ton for a day and a night, and they can eat rocks and go without water for a long time. But nobody would ever call them easy to handle."

Jordan was astonished. Daniel Randolph had never used mules or oxen at Twelve-trees. "But you said oxen are sweet-natured? They look so fearsome!"

"Oxen are some of the most loyal animals I've ever seen. To their teammate, and to their owner, if you treat them right. When they're teamed up, you know, they form a bond for life. If one of them dies, it's real hard to team up the other ever again. Sometimes they just kinda get sick, and give up, and die."

"How sad," Jordan said quietly. "I had no idea."

Colin was listening closely and staring at the teams strung out under the trees by the corral. "Sounds like oxen are really the best bet," he said.

Ty shrugged. "Just my opinion, you know. You could walk around here and five other men would probably tell different."

Colin glanced at him. "Maybe. You know, Ty, I may not be able to tell when a horse trader's cheating me, but I can tell when a man knows what he's talking about. I don't want to impose on you, but I would like to ask you a question. How much do good teams of oxen—like you were talking about—cost?"

"They're expensive," Ty said bluntly. "Not as much as mules, but more than horses. And you have to have good oxbows. If you don't, and they break, you're just plain out of luck."

"What are oxbows?" Colin said in bewilderment.

"They're those great big yokes around their necks," Ty explained patiently. "They weigh around two hundred pounds, so you can't carry a spare on the trail. I've seen men make 'em out of thin reeds, then cover 'em with one turn of leather. Likely some of these teams here are outfitted like that. First time oxen turn their heads separate ways they'll snap in two just like that." Ty snapped his fingers, a loud crack like a gunshot. "Anyway, to answer your questions, I'd expect to pay, probably around one-twenty to one-fifty for a good team, and another fifty or so for the yoke."

Colin whistled softly. Ty nodded sagely.

Jordan said, "Well, Captain Bryce? See any you like?"

"I'm going to have to think this over, and maybe do some figuring on my finances." Colin grinned. "See if I can make it come out to more than I've really got."

Both Ty and Jordan chuckled at that. "Always knew I should've learned more about arithmetic in school," Ty said. "Just sounds like something that makes you more money."

Colin, Ty, and Jordan all turned back toward town, and Colin said, "Would the two of you join me for supper? It's the least I can do for picking your brain all afternoon, Ty."

"Glad to help out," Ty said, "but I can't make supper. I was heading over to Doc Leverett's for a meeting with the train council to look at some maps they've got. But it was a pleasure to meet you, ma'am. I'll see you later, Colin." He sauntered off, taller than the crowd, his gait slow but sinuous, like a panther's.

Colin watched him leave. "Dr. Leverett and Horace Farr sure are trying to get him to join the train. He must be a good guide."

"He seems like a competent man," Jordan agreed. "Anyway, I believe you asked me to have supper with you? I'm starved."

Colin looked a little surprised. "Won't it be awkward for you?"

"What do you mean?" Jordan asked, mystified.

"Well, I was thinking that Charlie Maddox might object to his fiancée having supper with me alone," Colin said awkwardly.

Jordan exclaimed, "No! I mean—Charlie won't mind. That is, I'm not his fiancée. We were never formally engaged."

Colin stared at her, his dark eyes slowly taking her in, his expression changing from wariness to smooth appraisal. Jordan felt a little self-conscious at the sudden heat in his gaze, but her heart beat faster with excitement. "Well, now," Colin said softly, "that changes things."

"It does?" Jordan whispered.

"Why, of course it does." Colin took her hand again, moved close to her, pressing against her side, and pulled it close. For a moment he kept his hand covering hers. His hand was brown, with long fingers, and it was very warm and sea-roughened. Then he took Caesar's reins again and they started walking back around the corrals.

Jordan gazed up at him, hardly breathing. "So you are glad I'm not engaged?"

"I am," Colin said, smiling down at her. He had a heartbreaking smile, with strong white teeth, and his eyes crinkled at the corners. "Ever since I first saw you, the beautiful will-o'-the-wisp by the enchanted pool, I've had a hard time keeping my distance, you might say. But I never move in on another man's property. As Ty Sublette said, it just ain't right."

"No, it's not," Jordan breathed. "So— would you like to see me? A lot, I mean?"

Colin laughed. "You're sure straightforward when you want to be, aren't you?"

"I don't know," Jordan replied, bemused. She could hardly think, she was so excited. "I suppose I just don't know how to flirt and tease."

"That's refreshing, actually. And nice to know that you would like to flirt with me," Colin said warmly.

"I would if I knew how," Jordan said, a little shyly. "But since I don't, I suppose I'll just have to say what I want."

"Sounds like a good place to start. So, Miss Randolph, what do you want?" Colin asked, his eyes sparkling.

She searched his face, trying to speak, but she could hardly breathe. Finally she said in a hushed voice, "I—want—I—"

But Jordan was incapable of telling him her true feelings at that moment. She was still stunned by the ardent response she'd drawn from him, and her head was spinning as if she'd been suddenly struck a blow. He was watching her intently, clutching her closer against him, but Jordan pulled back a little and managed a small smile. "I want you to take me to supper."

"Is that all?" Colin smiled.

"No," Jordan said calmly. "But it is a good start."

SEVEN

Due to Dr. Leverett's recommendation, Colin Bryce had been accepted into the wagon train led by Horace Farr. Now he was attending his first council meeting, run by his new wagon master. The small group of men gathered beside Farr's wagon, standing or squatting before a small fire and drinking hot coffee.

Farr was a tall, rough-hewn farmer from Tennessee. He had light brown hair, dark brown eyes, and there was an air of easy competence about him. He was a slow-talking man but a thinker, and he had been elected wagon master unanimously. His wife, Ellen, three years younger at thirty-seven, came over to stand beside Colin, greeting him with a smile. "Dr. Leverett tells us you're going to join our train."

"Yes, ma'am. I hear your husband is the best wagon master around."

"He didn't seek it, but I have to say he'll do his best."

Farr began at once by saying, "I think the

biggest problem we've got right now is settling on a guide."

"I've been talking to Tyler Sublette," Dr.
Leverett spoke up. "I think he'd be willing, if
we made a formal offer."

Ira Barnhill, the richest man on the drive,
spoke up. "I don't see why we need one. We
know the way. You head west until you hit
the coast." Barnhill was forty-one years old
with thin gray hair. His eyes kept going over
toward his wife, Avis. They made a rather
strange couple. Avis was not yet twenty with
dark hair and eyes, a most attractive
woman. She was Barnhill's second wife and
close in age to his three sons, Ace,
Theodore, and Cornwall. Barnhill was in-
tensely jealous of his young wife, but as far
as anyone knew there was no cause for it.

Farr listened as Barnhill made his argument but then shook his head. "It's not like a
trip from the farm to the county seat, Ira.
We're going to hit some rough territory.
Everyone admits that."

Dave Minton, a short man with black eyes
and hair, spoke up at once. "I agree with the
doctor. We should hire Ty Sublette. He's
been over the trail, and everybody says he's
a good man."

"We don't need him! It's a waste of money, and even if we did hire someone, I don't want Sublette on the drive." The speaker was Pete Gratton, a strong fifty-three-year-old Texan. His wife, Carrie, rarely spoke. Her hair was going gray at fifty, and her faded blue eyes and bent form showed a hard life on a Texas cattle ranch.

"What have you got against him?" Farr questioned.

"He's a bit too brash," Gratton said. "We can find another man."

The argument went on for some time, and finally Farr said, "I've heard enough argument. We're hiring Sublette, if he'll have us, and I don't want to hear any more about it. Now, we have other matters we need to take care of. We need to decide final qualifications for a family to make the trip in our train."

"What do you mean by that?" Gratton asked. Like Colin, he'd joined the council only recently, and hadn't heard the many discussions the weeks before on how to outfit the train and who to take on. "A man's free to go if he chooses, ain't he?"

"It can't be like that, Pete," Farr said slowly. He searched for the words, and finally they came. "It's going to take all we've got to get there. Someone leaves without enough food or without the right kind of animals, we can't abandon them, and they'll become a burden."

"I'll agree with that," Ira Barnhill spoke up quickly. "There are some already here who don't have any business making this trip. We'll wind up feeding them and taking care of them." His eyes went over to the wagon of Orville Crane and his wife, Fanny. They had arrived at the camp only three days earlier in a wagon that was tied together with wire and the wobbliest wheels that anyone had ever seen. The wagon was packed with six small children ages one to eight, and it was obvious that they had nothing.

"What are you thinking in the way of qualifications, Horace?" Colin spoke up.

"Every family ought to have spare stock. We're going to lose some on the way," Horace said quietly, although his voice carried over the open space. "Every wagon should have enough provisions, and there really ought to be cash because we'll have to buy supplies at Fort Laramie and Fort Boise."

Most of the men agreed to this, and with

further talk came up with some basic standards.

Finally Farr said, "I think I can help the Cranes a little. Maybe some of the rest of you would like to pitch in." At once Colin spoke up, volunteering to help, then several others joined in. Gratton and Barnhill made no offers to help, but enough help was raised to admit the Cranes.

"I'm glad you offered to help," Ellen whispered to Colin.

"Well, they're down and out," Colin observed. "Won't hurt us to do for others."

Colin appeared at Twelvetrees that afternoon, and Jordan met him at the door. "The bad penny turns up again." He smiled.

"Come in, Captain Bryce," Jordan said at once. "My family is out visiting neighbors, but I can entertain you."

She led him into the parlor. They sat on a horsehide sofa in front of the fire, and she listened with pleasure as he gave her an account of the wagon council. He told her of the personalities, and of the decisions that they'd made. And he poked fun at his own inexperience. "Don't know why they're willing to take me on," he said. "I'm the greenest of the green."

"But you'll learn. Oh, how I envy you!"

"Let's wait and see if I make it." He stretched his feet toward the fire and asked, "Jordan's such an unusual name. Were you named after a river in Palestine?"

"Oh, no. It's my mother's maiden name, Captain."

Colin shook his head. "You don't have to bother with the 'captain,' Miss Randolph. I was only captain for one voyage. That was on an old scow that I thought would sink before we could come to land. Colin will do fine."

"All right. So it will be Colin and Jordan. Now—tell me about the places you've been."

For over an hour Jordan listened enthralled as Bryce spoke of India and the islands of the Caribbean. She made an attractive audience, and he finally laughed. "I'm becoming a bore." The wood in the fireplace snapped and crackled, sending fiery sparks up the chimney. Colin rose and poked at the log with a poker, watched it settle down, and the blaze grew even higher. "Always loved a fire," he said, replacing the poker. He came back to sit down beside Jordan, stretching his long legs out for comfort. "No fires like this on a ship—just in the galley."

"I never thought about that."

"Ships are the most uncomfortable things in the world, I suppose. The only fire allowed is in the galley, no matter how cold it gets—even if you're among icebergs. You just put on all the clothes you have and shiver and shake."

"Tell me some more about the whaling voyage."

Colin turned to her and smiled. His teeth were very white against his sunburned skin, and he had shaved so closely that his cheeks were smooth. The line of his jaw and the short, English nose gave him a most masculine appearance. He had a wide mouth with two deep lines on each side of his lips, and there was a pale scar over his left eyebrow that she had never noticed before. The last two days, the two had been together most of the time. They had ridden during the day with Colin helping her on, almost lifting her up and putting her in the saddle. At nights they had gathered, and Jordan had played the pianoforte and sung.

The two had learned to sing well together, and the family had enjoyed the fine voice of Colin as he sang the old Welsh melodies he had learned from his parents.

Now, however, a sense of depression settled on Jordan, and Colin, who had been watching her face, caught the expression at once. As he sat beside her, he appreciated the supple lines of her body. She was in that first maturity after girlhood. She had, he had discovered, a tremendous capacity for emotion and could swing from the extremes of laughter and softness to anger. Most of all she was a girl of great vitality and imagination. He saw it now, this hint of the will in her, for there was pride in the corners of her eyes and lips.

"What's wrong, Jordan?"

"Oh, nothing really."

"Yes, there is. I know you well enough to know that. What is it?"

"I guess I'm jealous of you."

"Of *me!* What in the world for?"

"Oh, you've gone all over the world and seen all those wonderful places—and now you're going to Oregon."

Colin studied her for a moment, then shook his head. "I've sensed you weren't satisfied, but why? You seem to have such a good life here." He reached out and took Jordan's hand. "Maybe you're not a woman who likes to be confined. You're like a bird. You need to be free."

Jordan was very conscious of his warm hand holding hers, and she did not attempt to withdraw it. "That's exactly how I feel—like I'm in a cage." She hesitated, then said, "You're the first one who ever understood what I feel, Colin."

Squeezing her hand, he said, "I never thought of it, but women are pretty much tied down."

"Tied hand and foot! Oh, how I envy you! You're going to have a great adventure, and I'll be stuck on this grubby farm!" She blinked suddenly, then whispered, "I'm sorry you're leaving, Colin. I'll miss you."

"I'll miss you too, Jordan." Colin had known women in his life, for he was an attractive man and had traveled much. But he was a lonely man as well, and sometimes the hungers of a lone man will move like a needle of a compass to the thought of a woman. Now as Colin sat holding Jordan's hand, she caught his glance and held it, and it was as direct as his own. But there was also a woman's mystery that drew him and caused him to reach out and pull her close.

He half expected her to resist, but she did not. As he kissed her, he was utterly and totally conscious of the softness of her lips that responded to his. He felt her hand come up on his neck, and something old and timeless came to them, and he knew she felt it as well. She had the power to deepen his hungers, and when he finally lifted his head, he whispered huskily, "You're so sweet, Jordan!"

As for Jordan, she was shaken by something that had taken place as he had held her and kissed her. She had been kissed before, of course, but something in this man reached out to her. It was as if she had suddenly come into a harbor, and she knew that she would not forget his embrace for days or even weeks.

"You must think I'm awful," she whispered.

"I think you're a beautiful woman, and you're very unhappy. But we've got two months—let's make the most of it!"

Jordan sat on a flat boulder, munching an apple and contemplating the perfect pink blossom floating near the bank. After the children's lessons she had grabbed a light lunch, snatched up her well-worn *Ivanhoe*, jammed an old bonnet on her head, and hurried down to the pond. She was studiously avoiding her mother, indeed had been avoiding her since she'd broken off her "engagement" to Charlie Maddox. Her mother had persisted in calling it an engagement, despite Jordan's protests.

Colin Bryce had called at Twelvetrees every day since their time alone together. Daniel Randolph, oblivious to the obvious reason for Colin's visits, always asked him to stay for supper, and he always did so. Daniel liked Colin, found him interesting, and Colin, with his curious and active mind, seemed to find everything about Twelvetrees and farming of great interest.

Josephine Randolph, however, was not at all blind to the signals between her daughter and the captain. She had been polite to Colin, but she watched him and Jordan carefully. Jordan, in spite of intensive efforts, hadn't been able to wrangle a single moment alone with Colin.

Now, as her attention strayed from the adventures of Wilfred of Ivanhoe, she considered what she might do, both with her mother, and with Colin. Time was growing short.

But the perfect blossom drew her attention, for she loved water lilies. They looked so perfect and so fragile that it seemed they would wilt at the least human touch. But Jordan knew they were actually very hardy, tough plants. She knew this because ever since she'd been able to use a hoe, she'd been the one who kept the water lilies down to one manageable corner of the pond. If they weren't rigorously cut back twice every spring and summer, they would choke the pond.

After she finished her apple she carefully put the core back into her canvas bag. All garbage was valuable, for the pigs would eat anything and everything, and the Randolphs, though they weren't poor, were frugal.

As she bent to wash the stickiness from her hands, she considered the perfection of the flower. "Herald of spring," she murmured. The bloom was almost six inches across, white with delicate rose shading in the center. The three round emerald flat leaves surrounding it were perfect, unblemished. Jordan thought how lovely it would look, floating in her mother's old Baccarat crystal bowl.

She leaned out, but the lily was just beyond the reach of her fingertips. "Drat it all!" she said. Water lilies were notoriously hard to gather. They had fat, tangled roots dug deep into the mud. Once they were picked, they had to be immediately placed in water or they would instantly begin to turn brown. Jordan sat back on her heels, considering if she could risk going back to the house to get something to pull in the elusive flower, and a bucket of water to put it in. *My walking stick would be perfect*, she reasoned. But she knew her mother and father were having dinner. Could she risk sneaking into the kitchen without her mother demanding an intimate talk?

Jordan was still trying to make up her mind when she heard the distinctive snap of a dry pine twig breaking, and the soft shuffle of footsteps through the carpet of pine needles. She stood up, surprised, for no one ever came down here. *Except Colin, to meet his destiny*, she thought with a small smile.

It wasn't Colin but her mother. "Hello, Jordan," Josephine said. "I decided that if I was ever going to have an opportunity to speak alone with you, I'd either have to come down here or have Frank tie you to a chair in the schoolroom."

"Hello, Mother," Jordan said. "It's true, I have been busy lately."

"Yes, you certainly have," Josephine replied emphatically. She looked around at the stand of flat boulders that formed part of the landscaping for the pool. "Come and sit with me. We need to talk."

"Of course." Jordan and her mother settled down, and Jordan took off her bonnet and lifted her face to the gentle sun, closing her eyes.

"You're going to freckle," Josephine said at once. But she said nothing else for such a long time that finally Jordan turned to her in surprise. Jordan could discern a small hint of—was it perplexity?—in her mother's gaze. Finally Josephine said quietly, "You know, Jordan, I've always regretted that I don't understand you better. Sometimes it seems that you're like a foundling put on our doorstep."

Josephine stared at her for awhile longer, searching her daughter's face as if she were a stranger. "I—Jordan, I do love you."

"Why, I love you too, Mother," Jordan said

quickly, touched by the scene. Tears were starting in her eyes. Her mother was not given to revealing her emotions, but she was obviously moved.

Josephine ducked her head and plucked at her skirt. But her discomfort didn't last long, and she settled in her usual ladylike posture, her back erect, her shoulders straight, her feet tucked neatly to the side. By contrast, Jordan was perched on the rock, her feet up, hugging her knees.

"Jordan, I want to talk to you—no, I want you to talk to me. I know you've broken off your engagement to Charlie Maddox, but how do I know this? Because Martha Maddox was in Drury's the other day, and she told me. How do you think that made me feel, Jordan?"

"But, Mother, we weren't really engaged," Jordan protested. "I never did tell Charlie that I would marry him."

"But you never told him that you wouldn't, either, did you? Not until last week when Colin Bryce started calling on you every day."

Jordan dropped her eyes. "Yes, Mother, that's true."

Josephine asked sharply, "It is really over between you and Charlie, then?"

"Yes, ma'am."

"And are you absolutely *positive* that this is what you want?"

"Oh, yes, ma'am! I—I love Colin!" Jordan burst out.

Josephine's mouth tightened into a thin line. "But it's been only a month! Jordan, how could you?"

"How could I?" Jordan repeated dramatically. "How could I not? I can't help it!"

"That is absurd," Josephine asserted. "Of course you can 'help it.' You're a grown woman with a free will."

"But, Mother, don't you know that sometimes people fall deeply, helplessly in love at the moment they meet? Sometimes two people are just *meant* to be together."

Josephine made an effort to speak calmly. "Jordan, you are too young, and too naive, and too fanciful. Won't you please just trust me for once? I don't want to see you make a terrible mistake."

"But I don't have time, Mother," Jordan said softly. "Colin's leaving next month. I want to go with him, as his wife."

Josephine sighed deeply. "I realize that. But does Captain Bryce feel the same way you do? Is he helplessly floundering in love, too?"

Josephine's sharp tone stung Jordan, and

she jumped off the rock and went to the edge of the pond, staring down at the lovely water lily. "I'm sure he does," she said quietly. "But we haven't had hardly a moment alone together. It's not as if we've had much opportunity to—talk."

"Doesn't that tell you something, Jordan? If he's as helplessly in love as you think you are, it seems that he would be shouting—" She broke off abruptly, for Jordan had bowed her head and her shoulders were trembling. Josephine rose and said gently, "I'm sorry, Jordan. I know that I'm always too sharp with you. I had hoped—well, I'll speak to your father. We'll give you and Captain Bryce some time alone tonight after supper."

It took a moment for the words to sink into Jordan's abject misery, "Oh, thank you, thank you, Mother!" She turned and threw herself into her mother's arms. "I do love him so!" she whispered, her face pressed against her mother's breast.

While waiting for Colin, Jordan had changed clothes three times, put up and taken her hair down four times, had considered and discarded three fichus, and had changed her shoes twice. She finally settled on her second-best church dress, a pretty muslin with a tight corsage and fashionable long pointed bodice that, along with the wide skirts, made her waist look impossibly small. The muslin was sprigged with lavender flowers, and she had a lavender woolen shawl to match.

When Colin arrived, Jordan hurried downstairs and she and her parents sat in the parlor. Daniel Randolph seemed slightly bewildered, his mystified gaze roaming back and forth between Jordan and Colin. Amused, Jordan wondered exactly what her mother had told her father, but she could see no sign of discomfort or strain on her mother's face. She was polite, as always, and she seemed resigned.

Finally Lily called them to dinner, having fed the children an early supper and sent them to play in their rooms. The four settled down at the polished oak table, and Daniel said his usual short grace. Jordan was so nervous she could hardly eat; indeed, she was barely able to follow the conversation. However, she did come to strict attention when Colin started telling them about his latest preparations for going west.

"I've been shopping around and calculating, and by the time I buy everything I'll be just about broke. But I have to get the essentials— a wagon, oxen, tools, food, supplies. I know what you're thinking—I don't know anything except the sea. But that's a pretty tough sort of outdoor life, always exposed to rough weather. Sailors don't get to retire to a comfortable cabin every time it rains or snows."

"But won't it be hard, riding all day?" Josephine asked pointedly.

"Well, Mrs. Randolph, riding all day and night for months on end *is* a lot scarier to me than the weather," Colin told her. "Caesar and I have come to a sort of understanding, but I'm not sure he'd be so patient with me after I've been bouncing and jerking in the saddle for hours. But of course I'll be on the wagon seat, not in the saddle."

"The council took you on, did they?" Daniel asked.

"They've approved me, yes, sir," Colin said. "In fact, Dr. Leverett got approval and approached *me* about it, not the other way around. It seems that they'd have some use for me, maybe, because I can navigate by the stars. So far they haven't been able to get a guide they're happy with. They're just about to settle on a man named Dutch Bremer, but none of them are too happy about his abilities, it seems."

Daniel nodded. "Yes, I know all about him. This is his second trip west. Now, you gotta understand, back here we hardly get word about how the wagon trains make out, unless it just happens that some local goes west, and they write home and tell about the trip. These guides that take them over, then come back to pick up another train, they're not going to tell you if anything went wrong, are they? No sir, they're not!"

"So I understand. Horace Farr's brother and his family were on Dutch Bremer's first train. Dutch took over sixty wagons in that train, and only forty-one of them made it to Oregon Territory. Bremer swears that they were people who weren't well-equipped enough—broken wagon wheels, not enough supplies, people got sick and died. But Horace's brother wrote back and said Bremer got them lost in the Rocky Mountains, searching for the southern pass. And the train, when it moved on, left some people behind that weren't buried yet, if you take my meaning. Larry Farr took two sick people in his wagon that died along the trail, but finally they got to where they had to move on, and left one couple and two families behind. They haven't been heard from in Oregon, that's for sure."

"But how can that be?" Jordan asked in a startled tone. "Surely no caring human being would just leave people behind!"

Colin answered quietly, "People do strange things when their lives are in danger. I've seen men in a boat after abandoning a sinking ship, pushing men in the water away with oars, men who were their shipmates, their friends. Once I even saw a man cut off another sailor's fingers as he grasped the boat's sides. They were messmates, too."

Jordan gasped. "I can't believe it! I would never, never do something like that! And Colin, I don't believe you would either!"

"It won't come to that. There are some very responsible men on our train."

Supper lasted a long time, for the Randolphs did enjoy Colin Bryce's company and conversation, but afterwards Jordan wasted no time. As soon as she decently could, she said, "Colin and I are going to take a walk. Come along," she said, tugging at his sleeve. Colin barely managed to bow to Josephine as Jordan dragged him outside.

Jordan closed the door behind them, leaned back against it, and took a deep breath. "Oh, what a heavenly night! Thank heaven we've escaped!"

Colin smiled. "You are such a strange girl, Jordan."

"So I've been told at least twice a day all my life," she replied.

"Strange and beautiful," he said gallantly.

She flashed him a quick smile, then threading her arm through his, said, "Let's walk down to the pond."

They walked out of the circle of the warm lights beaming through the windows of the house. Both of them, in a single moment, turned their eyes up to the stars. It was a clear night. No clouds shadowed the star canopy. "You navigate by the stars," Jordan whispered. "Teach me their names."

Colin glanced at her and felt the same bewitchment that always seemed to settle on him when he was with her. "There is Arcturus and down below is Spica . . . Virgo the virgin . . . Hydra . . . and there are the twins, Castor and Pollux . . ."

"Which one? There are so many!"

Colin smiled at her. "They're part of a constellation called the 'Twins.' Look, right up there—can't you see the figure of two people?"

Jordan stared but was dazzled by the multitude of the stars. "I can't see them."

Colin said, "Here—I'll show you how to spot them. It's the way I was taught." He pulled an envelope from one pocket and took a pencil from another. "It's bright enough for me to do this," he said as he made some marks on the envelope. Turning it to her he asked, "There—can't you see the twins?"

Jordan stared at the dots he'd made, then shook her head. "All I can see is a lot of dots. I can't see any twins."

Colin took the paper and quickly made some marks on it, then handed it back. "How about now?"

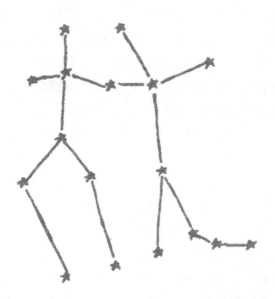

Jordan took one look at the drawing and cried, "Why, I can see them! They're holding hands."

"Yes, I've always thought they were lovers, Castor and Pollux."

"Where are they?" Jordan asked.

"Over there—the two bright ones, one over the other. The highest one is Castor. It's really six stars, though to us it looks like only one bright one."

"I've read about them in my mythology book—Castor and Pollux, twin sons of Zeus, reunited in the sky after Castor's untimely death."

"Did you know that they are regarded as the patrons of soldiers, athletes, and sailors? Sailors always wish for good sailing on them, in the night watches."

Jordan looked up at the glittering stars and whispered, "I'd like to have one for my very own! Oh, not mine like I *owned* it, just one very special to me—to remind me of this time with—with you."

Colin studied her face, then took her shoulders and stepped behind her. He put his arm over her shoulder, pointing high into the sky. "You see those three real bright stars right where I'm pointing?"

"Yes." Jordan was very conscious of his hand on her left shoulder and his right arm resting on her right. "They're Orion's belt, aren't they?"

"Yes. Now, follow down from the three stars—down, down, to the right there. See that bright star, the brightest in the sky?"

"Yes, I see it."

"That's Sirius. It's the brightest star in the sky. It's called the Dog Star because it's the brightest star in the Canis Major constellation, which is called the Big Dog. Pretty, isn't it?"

"Oh, yes! It glows like a diamond!" Jordan stared at the star, then turned to face him. "That's going to be *my* star, Colin. I'll never have a real diamond, but Sirius will be my own diamond."

"All right, it'll be yours."

She glanced up at his face. In the dim light his profile was stark, his eyes black, the hollows of his cheeks deep, his high pronounced cheekbones a sharp plane. He stared down at her as if he were trying to memorize her face. With deliberation she put her arms around his shoulders and caressed his neck, stepped close to press against him, and raised her face to his.

He bent to her, kissing her at first gently and tentatively. But she returned his kiss with such warmth that his arms, his hands, his lips, grew urgent. Gasping, she finally drew back, but didn't step out of the tight circle of his arms. "Colin," she whispered urgently, "I love you. Please, please don't leave me. I couldn't bear it."

His eyes narrowed, and he grew very still. "Jordan, I was never lonely in my entire life—until I met you. Now every moment I'm away from you I'm thinking of you. And when I'm with you, I can't think of anything else. I must love you, too."

"Yes, you must," Jordan said, though whether in agreement or insistence she hardly knew.

He kissed her again, but tentatively this time, running his finger down her cheek and neck. She shivered involuntarily, clinging to him. He asked hesitantly, "Jordan, could you consider marrying me?"

Jordan could hardly speak, and for a long moment she looked into his face, her eyes great silvery pools, caught in starlight. "Yes, Colin. I will marry you, and I will love you until the day I die."

Martha Maddox stared at Jordan, an expression of shock marring her face. She had arrived five minutes ago, and as soon as Jordan had seated her in the parlor and revealed her decision to marry Colin, she exclaimed, "I can't believe it! You're not really going to marry that sailor, are you?"

"Yes, I am."

"But, Jordan—that's the craziest thing I ever heard! You can't be serious!"

A smile lifted the corners of Jordan's mouth. "Why do you think it's so crazy? Don't you like him, Martha?"

"Oh, of course I like him. He's one of the handsomest men I've ever seen, and charming as well—but he's going to be a farmer out in Oregon. I think you're making a huge mistake."

Jordan looked down at her hands for a moment, then broke the silence by saying, "So does everyone else, Martha. But I love Colin, and he loves me."

With an impatient gesture, Martha shook her head, and her lips drew tightly together. The two had been best friends for years, but now she felt certain that Jordan was about to make one of the worst mistakes possible. "But it'll be so hard," she said. "You've never had to work—not like they do in Oregon."

"I'm not worried about that. I've never minded work."

"But there's not even any land there to farm. The trees all have to be chopped down."

Jordan rose and went over to Martha. She sat down on the sofa beside her and put her arm around her. "It's sweet of you to be worried about me, but this is what I want."

Still terribly disturbed, Martha shook her head. "You always were romantic. You see this as a big adventure, but I don't think there's any adventure to working yourself to death. I've heard that those pioneer women get old before they're thirty years old. Just one baby after another, and grinding labor from dawn until bedtime." Turning to Jordan, she got control of herself. "You'll do it, I suppose. You always did have a stubborn streak."

Reverend Thomas Grooms was a tall, heavy-set man with a thatch of iron-gray hair and a pair of steady hazel eyes. He was a good pastor, thinking always of the needs of his flock, and as he considered the young woman who sat across from him, his thought was, *I've failed with Jordan. She's not ready for a marriage like this—or for any marriage.* He'd had a long talk with Jordan's parents, and they had agreed that she was far too delicate for a frontier life. Grooms had been in favor of their asking Jordan to put off the marriage, but had learned that Jordan would never agree with this.

"Jordan, I've known you since you were a

child," Grooms said quietly, "and you know I have your best interest at heart. I think you should think seriously about this step."

"But I love him, and he loves me!" Jordan said earnestly.

Always the same—young people think the marriage ceremony is some sort of magic that will ward off all trouble. For some time Grooms tried gently to get Jordan to see some of the problems that lay ahead if she made this marriage. He pointed out the terrible hardships of living on the frontier, but she had settled it in her own mind that this would be no handicap for her.

Finally Grooms said, "I didn't want to mention this, Jordan, but you don't have a firm enough faith to go into this sort of marriage."

"Why, Reverend, you don't think I'm a Christian?" Jordan exclaimed.

"I didn't say that. I think you do know the Lord, otherwise I would never have baptized you. But you've led an easy, comfortable life. Your faith has never been tested, has it? But you're marrying a man you don't really know, and you'll be facing problems you've never even considered."

For a considerable time, Grooms tried to

show Jordan that she was plunging into a life that would require more than just a token faith, but he could see that she was hurt.

"I don't think you're being fair, Reverend," Jordan said, her chin high in the air. "I know I'm young, but I love the Lord. What else is there?"

At that moment Grooms knew that Jordan was beyond his reach. He'd seen it before, many times. Young people in love seemed to develop some strange impediment in their ears, which kept them from hearing any wisdom from their elders. Leaning forward, he said gently, "I'll be praying for you, Jordan, that God will be with you every step on the way to Oregon, and afterwards, too."

Jordan took his hand, relieved that the pastor said no more about the difficulties. "Thank you, Reverend Grooms. It will be fine—you'll see!"

For a long time after Jordan left, Grooms sat in his chair regarding the wall across the room, but not really seeing it. He was praying that Jordan Randolph would survive the ordeal that lay ahead. Aloud, he said, "Lord, I don't know which is harder, to make a new marriage work or to survive the trip to Oregon—so I ask that you get this young woman through both those dangers."

Jordan wore her mother's wedding dress, which had been her grandmother's, too. It was of satin, faded to a cream color by the long years, but still lovely. She carried a bouquet of white lilies, and her father had managed, somehow, to find some apple blossoms in a nearby county and had arranged for them to be brought fresh that morning, for Jordan's hair. The church was full to overflowing, but afterwards, and all her life, Jordan never could remember where anyone was. She saw everything through a mist of tears. She remembered how heartbreakingly handsome Colin was in a new gray suit, and she remembered that her mother cried softly. But that was all.

The wedding march sounded, and Jordan stepped out and made her way down the aisle. She felt her heart beat faster as she saw Colin standing there waiting for her. When she arrived at the front, Colin smiled at her, and the ceremony began. Reverend Grooms began reading the old words, and Jordan listened carefully. As she made her vows promising to love, honor, and obey, she saw the pride in Colin's eyes, and it seemed that all the faces and everything faded out except his face as he smiled at her. He put the ring on her finger, and then finally the words came. "I now pronounce you man and wife."

She turned to take his kiss, and even under such public circumstances, she could not help but respond as his lips came to hers.

And then they made their way out, and as soon as they had cleared the sanctuary Colin grabbed her and lifted her off the floor. "You'll never get away from me now! You're all mine, Jordan."

Jordan's breath was almost cut off by his strong arms, but she loved it. When he put her down, she touched his cheek and whispered, "Yes. I'm yours forever."

Mr. and Mrs. Colin Bryce had a two-day honeymoon. It was not very impressive, but two days in St. Joe was all they had time for. The two days—and nights—passed much too quickly for Jordan. She learned on her wedding night that she was a woman capable of a deep passion. Both she and Colin were surprised, and considerably happy, that their coming together seemed as natural and joyful as their courtship had been.

On their first morning together Jordan had awakened to find Colin resting his chin on one arm in bed beside her, regarding her closely. She flushed, but he smiled, reached out, and tucked one of her locks back off her forehead. "I didn't know I was marrying such a tiger," he said quietly.

"How long have you been awake, groom?" she said, blushing.

"I've been watching you sleep, bride," he answered. "You don't even look like a real person when you're asleep. You look unreal, soft-focused, like a man's best dreams."

"Do I?" she said, stretching luxuriously. "I'm so glad I wasn't snoring, or drooling, or something like that."

"You? I can't imagine it," Colin scoffed. "You always look like some illustration in a child's fairy-tale book. But, bride, I hate to tell you that you married a mere mortal, and we get hungry. How about some breakfast?"

She put her arms around his neck and kissed him long and warmly. "Groom," she whispered throatily, "how about later?"

EIGHT

When Jordan and Colin returned from their honeymoon they got a considerable and delightful surprise. Both Daniel and Josephine Randolph seemed reconciled, even pleased, with her marriage to Colin. As they came out to meet the new bride and groom, Daniel was excited, his stern face alight, his blue eyes shining. Even Josephine seemed expectant. They took the pair inside. As Colin and Jordan were enjoying ice-cold apple juice, Daniel grinned broadly at the two. "We have some gifts for you."

"Oh, Father, you've been so generous already," Jordan protested. Her parents had given the couple the sturdy little mare Princess, and had completed Jordan's scanty marriage chest with a vast array of fine linens.

"Come outside," Daniel said. "We've got a surprise wedding present for you."

As soon as she stepped outside, Jordan gasped with surprise. In front of the house, Jackson stood proudly by a team of oxen yoked to a brand-new covered wagon. Jordan's eyes grew big and round, and then stung with tears. She threw her arms around her father, hugging him tightly, and then ran to her mother. For once Josephine allowed Jordan to embrace her. "Oh, Mother, how very generous of you! It's marvelous, just perfect! Thank you, thank you a thousand times!"

Josephine stiffened slightly, disentangling herself from Jordan's arms, but she did give her a cool kiss on the cheek. "You're welcome, dear. And your father and I have decided to give you enough cash to hire someone to do the driving and help with the cooking and chores. After all, we haven't exactly raised you to be an expert at driving oxen or cooking venison."

Colin was shaking Daniel's hand. "Sir, I can't thank you enough for your generosity! I've promised to take good care of her, and I'm grateful to you for helping me do that."

Frank and Albert came running out of the house, whooping like wild Indians, with Beth following at a more sedate pace, holding a doll. Before any of the adults could say a word Frank and Albert scrambled up onto the broad backs of the oxen, two great solemn brutes with large gentle eyes.

"Is—is that safe?" Jordan asked, coming down the steps slowly, holding out her hand tentatively to the team, as if trying to tame a tiger.

"'Course," Frank scoffed. "They're just big ol' babies. Me and Albert been riding 'em ever since we got 'em. They don't even know we're here."

"That's the truth, Miss Jordan," Jackson said, stroking one great wet nose. "Oxen, they're more like pets than work animals, if you're of a mind to pay them attention."

"Oh, yes, I am," Jordan said happily, petting one just as if he were a dog, stroking his hard head. His coat felt like short rough wool. "What are their names?" she asked her father, who was standing beside her.

"Their names?" he said blankly. "Why, I don't know."

Colin sidled up to pet one, frowning with concentration. The ox rolled a great gentle brown eye up as Colin scratched his ear. "You name them, Jordan. Anything you want."

With a warm, intimate glance at her husband, Jordan said softly, "Then I should like to name them after the stars. This is Castor, and that is Pollux."

Frank sniffed disdainfully. "Sounds like Bible names to me."

Colin gave Jordan a secret smile of remembrance of the last time they had picked those stars out of the night sky. Then he turned to study the wagon, and he and Daniel Randolph engaged in a cheerful and fairly technical conversation.

Jordan and her mother withdrew to the parlor, leaving the men and boys to their new toy. "They're lovely oxen, Mother," Jordan said enthusiastically. "I love them already."

With her long-suffering sigh, Josephine said, "Jordan, the oxen are not pets, and you are not embarking on a carriage ride in the park. Do you have any notion of what your life is going to be like for the next four or five months? Do you have any picture in your mind at all of the difficulty, the hardships, the privations, perhaps even the tragedies, you are facing?"

But Jordan was not to be disenchanted. "Oh, Mother, I'm married to a man I've dreamed of all my life. He loves me, and we're going on a great adventure together! How can I possibly have a long face and be filled with dread? My life is going to be wonderful, just wonderful!"

Josephine, who was already starting to feel the desolation that she knew would fill her heart when her daughter left her, perhaps forever, relented. She nodded and made herself smile. "Dearest, you're right, and once again, I'm sorry that I'm being such a glum old thing. I'm happy for you, Jordan. I wish you and Colin all the joy in the world!"

Jordan climbed into the wagon and knelt before a small stack of books, her brow knit with the struggle of choice. The wagon was pulled around behind the house, and she'd been making decisions about what she would take on the journey. She and her mother had spent hours deciding what household goods she could best use, while Colin and her father had given much thought to tools and farming items.

Jordan had spent two hours making painful decisions about which books to take. She had many books, and loved them all, but Colin had limited her to only three, because of their weight. She had narrowed her choices down to ten, but now the thought of leaving the books she loved so dearly pulled at her. She picked up a worn copy of *Pride and Prejudice* and stared at it, then said, "Oh, fuzz! I can't leave this one!" She looked around guiltily, then shoved the novel into a sack of seed corn. *I can't let Colin find it—he'll think I'm crazy.*

"Hello? Anybody here?"

Jordan scrambled out of the wagon to find a man waiting expectantly. "Yes, what is it?"

"Mrs. Bryce?"

"Yes, I am."

"Feller told me you need to hire an extra hand for the trip to Oregon." The speaker was a homely man of some forty years. He was a gangling individual, rawboned and roughly dressed. "My name's Gus Dabney, ma'am. Shore would admire to go along with you."

"Did you walk all the way out from town?" Jordan asked, astonished at Dabney's determination.

"Oh, no, ma'am, I got a ride with your neighbor, Mr. Fellows. Right nice feller."

"You'll have to talk to my husband, Mr. Dabney."

"'Course, Mrs. Bryce—and I'm just Gus."

At that moment Colin appeared, striding around the house with a box in his arms. When Colin arrived, Jordan said, "This is

Gus Dabney, Colin. He's looking to go to Oregon."

"Heard you needed a man, Mr. Bryce." Dabney nodded.

Colin nodded and studied the man carefully without appearing to do so. He was a good judge of men. "Ever been to Oregon?"

"Nope, not me. Been around quite a bit, but never seen the big water." Dabney grinned suddenly, saying, "I don't look like much, but I'm tougher than I look. I can drive a team, cook a little bit, and I'm a fixer. Can mend whatever needs it."

"It's a hard trip, Gus. You got a family?"

"Me? No, I ain't got anybody. Spent too much time tryin' to see whut's over the next hill to get tied down." He went on, "Understand you have just one wagon. I can sleep outside, or underneath. Don't matter to me."

"All right, Gus, you're on. Come along and I'll show you our stock. I hope you know more about oxen than I do."

"Stay for dinner, Gus," Jordan said. "And we've got a room over the barn if you'd like to stay there until we leave."

"Right nice of you, Miz Bryce. Be pleased to."

Jordan smiled. "Can you do anything else that's handy, Gus?"

"I was with a circus for a time." Dabney smiled at the thought. "I was a knife thrower."

"Why'd you quit?" Jordan asked.

"It was one of them acts where somebody would stand in front of a board and I'd outline them with knives." He shook his head regretfully. "I kept hittin' my partner, so she took off with an acrobat. Never could figure that out. I just nicked her a little—and in a place that didn't count much."

Jordan laughed, liking the man a great deal. "Maybe you can teach me to throw a knife."

They had fourteen scant days until April 15, when the train was scheduled to pull out. Colin rose every day before dawn to go into Independence and finish the arrangements, taking Gus with him. Jordan, her mother, and Lily worked on packing and outfitting the wagon. Lily had the inspiration to sew pockets onto the inside of the canvas covering, for more storage, and though Jordan tried to do it herself, her sewing skills were even more lamentable than her cooking abilities. Along those same lines, Josephine decided to sew Jordan's money—all in small bills—into a quilt that her mother had made, but Josephine had to do all the sewing.

On Tuesday Colin returned from town, jumped off Caesar, and caught Jordan up in a whirling bear hug. "I got you a present, bride," he said. "Look, just look what I found!"

He took a small parcel out of the saddlebag, wrapped in black velvet. "It's gold," he told her proudly.

Jordan was expecting a ring—Colin had not had the money to buy her a wedding band, much less an engagement ring with a precious stone—and the excitement mounted in her when he slowly unrolled the parcel.

She stared, bemused, at the object. Colin grinned, his eyes crinkling with sun wrinkles at the corners. "Isn't it just the most clever little thing you've ever seen?"

"Why, yes, my love, it's very—clever," Jordan replied, giving him a delighted smile. "A necklace! It's lovely!"

"You don't know what it is, do you?" he asked with amusement. "Come with me."

To Jordan's confusion, he led her around the house, back to the kitchen, and demanded a piece of bar soap from Lily. With his sharp penknife he shredded some small bits into a cup of boiling water, then stirred it vigorously. As Jordan and Lily watched with devouring curiosity, Colin took the small object on the chain and held it up with the air of a snake-oil salesman. It looked like a tiny stein, with a curved handle and a rounded finial top. Delicately Colin pulled off the top, and they saw that it was a cork with a small wand on it that had a loop at the end. Carefully Colin poured some of the soapy water into the little stein, and pushed the wand back in. "This, ladies, is a golden bubbler." He pulled out the wand, and blew through it. Four tiny bubbles floated out.

"Oh . . . ," Jordan whispered, her green eyes as huge as a child's. "Oh, Colin, it's magical!"

"For my lady of enchantment," he said, with a sweeping bow. "Only magical gifts, and myrrh and incense and rainbows and shooting stars for you." Colin loved to tease Jordan about her romantic tendencies, and now smiled at her delight.

Jordan—along with the other children, Josephine commented acidly—played with the bubbler for six solid hours. Blunt as usual, Daniel commented that it wasn't a very practical gift, to which Jordan replied that she was particularly grateful for that.

The next day Colin brought her a package back from town, and whispered in her ear that she probably wouldn't want her mother to see this one. That was very true, as Jordan blushed when she saw the elaborate nightgown he'd bought from the back room of Yeager's Dry Goods Store. Tartly she told Colin that she didn't think that she'd be wearing it much on the wagon train, and he replied that they had several days—and nights—before they left.

On Thursday he brought a piece of amber with a tiny leaf preserved in it; then on Friday a James Fenimore Cooper book, *The Red Rover,* which Jordan didn't have, and which delighted her, though the book was much-used and slightly mildewed. "You can't get me a present every time you go to town," Jordan told him playfully.

"Why not?" he replied, clasping her in a strong embrace, and kissing her long and lovingly, in full view of Lily, who pretended to be utterly deaf and stone blind. "I miss you so much, bride, even when we're just away from each other for a few hours."

"I miss you, too, Colin," she whispered. "We are meant to be. We were always meant to be."

NINE

A week before the wagon train left, Colin and Jordan still had not purchased all the necessary food and supplies; Jordan's stout gingham dresses and plain cotton aprons were unfinished; she had no suitable shoes or boots for the trail. On this day, when Josephine had been trying—to no avail—to make Jordan pay strict mind to Lily's instructions for baking biscuits, Colin brought Jordan another gift, and Josephine finally lost what vestiges of patience were left in her worried mind.

"A cat!" she snapped. "Are you out of your mind, Colin?"

"Why, no, ma'am," Colin answered sheepishly. "I like cats. They're lucky."

"Oh, Colin, she's perfectly beautiful." Jordan smiled, taking the ball of white fuzz in her arms. "I've never seen such an extraordinary kitten, such luxurious fur, and such an exotic face! Look, Mother!"

"I see her, Jordan," Josephine said with ominous calm.

"She's a Persian cat, an ancient, noble breed," Colin told Jordan proudly. "They're very rare in this country. Especially pure white ones."

"Oh, Colin, Colin, I'm so very pleased!" Jordan said, hugging him with one free arm as she cradled the kitten, who looked very bored and sleepy.

"I thought you would be," he said with satisfaction. "As soon as I saw the mother cat with her litter, I knew you needed one."

"Jordan, listen to me," Josephine said sternly, stepping off the porch and into Jordan's line of sight. When Colin was around it was extremely difficult to keep Jordan's attention. "Cats don't travel well. What do you think she will do, ride in the wagon?"

"Why not?" Jordan asked, her eyes wide. "See, Colin has bought her a little wicker carrier."

"You can't keep a cat in a carrier all day and all night long for five months," Josephine said with as much calmness as she could muster. "And as soon as you let her out, she'll wander. Do you think that the entire train will hold up while you search for your cat?"

"Oh, Mother, you do worry so," Jordan

said, bending to kiss the kitten's flat nose. "She'll be fine . . . I'm going to name her—"

"Rowena," Colin said, smiling.

"Oh! You knew!" Jordan said, staring up at him.

"Of course I did," he murmured, taking her arm and petting the kitten, whose round green eyes were growing heavier by the moment. "I know you, my love. Now, you see, cats are considered very lucky. We always have them on ships. And this lovely little creature reminds me of you, with her wide green eyes . . ."

Josephine sighed, turned, and made her way heavily back into the house. Daniel had come in for dinner, and with a silent signal she motioned him into the parlor and closed the door. "He brought her a kitten," Josephine said, sitting down rather heavily on the sofa. "A kitten!"

Daniel nodded, collapsing into his favorite armchair and propping his stockinged feet up on a faded embroidered stool. He'd left his muddy boots in the kitchen. "Yup. Saw him when he came in the yard, proud as punch. He seems like a sensible man most of the time, Josephine, but I swear at times he's as bad as Jordan!"

"I think she's bewitched him," Josephine sighed.

"He did do a good job, though, waterproofing the wagon," Daniel said thoughtfully. "Taught me a trick, he did. It was pretty watertight, but since he caulked the seams with tar and double strands of rope, I say not a single drop's going to get in that wagon, even if they have to float down the Columbia River on it." He stirred restlessly, then said in a low voice, "Jordan asked why you had to waterproof a wagon that's going across the prairies. Girl's got no idea in her head what this trip is going to be like."

"Don't I know that?" Josephine said wearily. "So far all she's worried about is taking enough hair rinse and cologne. Can you believe that silly bubble machine Colin bought her? And now a kitten! What can that man be thinking of!"

Daniel, who recalled very vividly exactly what he thought of when he was first married, managed to grin devilishly at his wife. "Can't imagine. Just think how sensible, how down-to-earth we were when we were first married, Jo."

Josephine had to laugh, but then shook her head with disapproval. "We weren't going on a journey through the wilderness, with wild Indians and storms and mountains and starvation and bears and—and who knows what else."

He nodded. "Still, I think Colin is a good man for that. He's lived through dangers we couldn't imagine, being at sea for most of his life. I think he'll take good care of Jordan, Jo."

She dropped her head, and with uncharacteristic nervousness, picked at her skirt. "I hope so, Daniel. I truly hope so."

On Thursday morning there was to be a final meeting of everyone who had joined the train with Horace Farr, the wagon master, and the council. Colin wanted to ride into town—he was getting more proficient by the day at his horsemanship. But the reality of the fact that they were leaving on a two-thousand-mile journey was starting to penetrate Jordan's mind, and she decided to take the buckboard into town and get their final supplies.

Masterfully Colin jumped up on the seat and took the reins from Jordan. Amused, she asked, "Have you ever driven a team before, Colin?"

"No, but it looks pretty easy," he replied carelessly, flicking the whip over the two horse's backs and making the clicking noise he'd heard teamsters make.

The horses were supremely unimpressed. One did flick a fly off his rump with a disdainful swish of his tail.

"Hm," Colin said, frowning. "Didn't I make the right kind of noise?"

Giggling, Jordan took the reins, snapped them smartly, and growled, "Giddup there, hup!" Obediently the horses moved.

"Don't tell anyone about this," Colin pleaded, then took the lines himself.

In about a quarter of a mile he'd almost driven them into the ditch, and both he and Jordan were laughing so hard that they almost let the cart overturn. "Ho, hup, git over there, Jinks!" He yanked on the right rein, and the horses veered over to the middle of the road again—for the time being.

"You're sawing on the reins, Colin," she told him, poking him hard in the side. He jumped, for he was ticklish, and Jordan knew it, and the horses, thoroughly confused by this time, came to a sullen standstill.

"This is a scurvy tub, this is," Colin gasped, still weak from laughing.

"Are you going to let me drive, so we'll get there sometime this week?" Jordan teased.

"No," Colin grumbled. "I can learn this. I mean, what's so hard about it? There's the road, right in front of them. Why can't they just go down it like good little horses? Hup, there, horses, git on there, let's go to town." Shuffling, the two horses made another start.

"Well, I suppose you'll have to learn," Jordan said, settling down close to him. "Gus will drive the wagon most of the time, but you'll have to take your turn."

"You too," Colin said. "You take the mornings, and I'll take the nights."

"All right," Jordan agreed, her gaze turned up to his tanned, strong face. His teeth flashed white, and after a moment she jerked upright and pinched his arm. "Oh, you! You'll take the nights—Colin, we don't travel at night!"

"We don't?" Colin replied with great surprise. "Oh. Well, I'm glad to know that; I've got other things I'd rather do at night . . ." He grabbed Jordan, pulled her close, and kissed her. Promptly the horses wandered over to the right and almost took them into a stand of young oak trees.

This nonsense continued all the way into

Independence. They left the buckboard at the livery stable and arm-in-arm made their way to their camp. At this time there were three distinct groups that had formed themselves into trains, and were already drawn up into the defensive circles that would form their night camps for the next several months. Horace Farr's train was in the premium spot, just at the end of the road past the livery stable. All of the people in the train were gathered around the nearest wagon, for Farr had climbed up into the seat to speak to them.

Because they'd been so busy getting ready for the journey, this was Jordan's first visit to the wagon train that would be her home for the next five months. In a low voice, Colin pointed out various people and named them.

Then Horace Farr began to speak. "Good morning, everyone," he began, lifting his voice to carry to the edge of the crowd. "I'm your wagon master, Horace Farr. Right now we've got twenty-eight wagons in the train, and eighty-four souls. I hope in just a few days I'll know you all by name, and I want to tell you right now that me and my wife will be glad to talk to you anytime. Over there"—

he pointed—"is our wagon, with the blue stripe painted on it. That's our current address. Drop by for a visit anytime."

There were some satisfied chuckles at this, and Farr leaned down to consult with someone for a moment. Jordan, standing on tiptoes, clearly saw Ty Sublette's wide, buckskin-clad shoulders above the heads of the crowd. "Look, there's Ty," she said to Colin with interest. "Has the council persuaded him to join the train as a guide?"

"Don't think so. Not as of yesterday, anyway," Colin answered. "He says he just got back from wandering all over the west for a year and a half, and he's not ready to leave the big city yet. But he's been working with us on the maps we've got. They're not very good maps, but he's been real good to go over them with us—especially me. I'm not too sure about land navigation—I can't tell one tree from another—but he seems to think that I might at least be able to keep us on the right latitude through the Rockies."

"Of course you can," Jordan said stoutly, nestling close to him.

Horace Farr continued, "Right now we're in pretty good shape. Everyone here has some good stock, fine wagons, and as far as I can tell, have taken in a goodly amount of provisions. The council has come up with a few more items that they feel are necessary, so please check with Mr. Barnhill for the list." Some groans accompanied this, but no one actually called out an objection.

"Uh-oh," Colin said in a low voice. "More money."

"We have plenty of money," Jordan whispered. "You just don't worry about that, Colin."

"Make sure you get everything before we leave," Farr said sternly. "It's important for all of us to be well-stocked. Now, I know you're all concerned because we haven't settled on a guide. But Sublette here has been helping the council with making some good maps, big improvements on anything I've seen yet. I'm sure we're going to be all right."

Farr was almost finished when the sound of a wagon approaching caught everyone's attention. Jordan turned with the others to see a wagon with a canvas cover over the top supported by hoops. A woman was driving and a young boy sat at her side. The woman pulled the wagon to a stop and then sat there for a moment.

Farr glanced at the council, then said quietly, "We'd better check on this." He approached and took off his hat. Everyone was quiet and could hear the words that he spoke. "Good afternoon, ma'am. May I help you?"

"Yes, sir. We want to join your train."

Farr was taken aback, clearly not knowing how to reply.

Jordan and Colin were standing very close, and she got a clear view of the newcomers. The woman was quietly attractive, with tendrils of ash-blonde hair escaping from her faded bonnet. Her features were regular and even, rather than pretty. It was her calm, serene expression that made her attractive, even if her features, taken one at a time, were not. The boy was towheaded, with round innocent blue eyes; his features were akin to the woman's, and he watched her and Horace Farr with a darting, pleading expression.

"Ma'am, it's too late. I'm sorry, but the train's all made up."

"My name is Leah Ellencourt. My husband, Mark, is ill, but we must go on the train."

"Why, you can't take a sick man on a journey like this!" Farr exclaimed. "It just ain't possible, ma'am."

Ira Barnhill had approached to stand beside Farr. "We've got some mighty strict rules, Mrs. Ellencourt. You'd have to have at least four animals, and we've got a rule listing what sort of supplies every wagon has to have. I don't want to pry, but can you meet all of this?"

"We don't have much money, but God has called us to start a church in Oregon."

Pete Gratton snorted audibly. "A preacher! Just what we don't need!"

Farr shook his head sadly. "It's a hard trip, Mrs. Ellencourt. I'm sorry, but we just can't allow it."

The young boy sat up straight and kept his eyes fixed on Farr.

Dave Minton, always good-hearted, stepped forward and said, "I hope you understand, Mrs. Ellencourt. It's just that this is a very hard trip we're looking at. And with your husband already sick and maybe you don't have enough animals to make it, you really don't need to join this train."

Leah Ellencourt's face did not change. She sat there holding the lines loosely, and there was a quiet dignity about her that Jordan admired. She felt a wave of sympathy for the woman, but as she listened to the murmuring, she knew that there was little chance of her joining the train.

"We have a council, ma'am," Farr said. "And they're all right here. I'll let them go have a meeting."

"We don't need a meeting," Barnhill said, glancing around at the other members, including Dave Minton. "It's impossible. Sorry, ma'am, you just can't go."

Ty Sublette had suddenly moved out from the shadow of one of the wagons where he was standing. He walked over to the woman and looked up at her. "Your husband, ma'am, is he any kin to Josiah Ellencourt?"

The woman took in the tall figure of Sublette and nodded. "Yes, he was my husband's father."

"You reckon I could speak to your husband?"

Something about the tall man's demeanor seemed to satisfy Leah Ellencourt. "If you'd like," she said. "He's lying down in the wagon."

Sublette followed the woman to the rear of the wagon. The canvas was pulled up, and a man was sitting with his back braced against the side of the wagon. He was slight of frame and had the pale countenance of a sick man, but his brown eyes were clear as he regarded his visitor.

Sublette introduced himself. "I'm Ty Sublette. Your father and I were partners once."

Ellencourt nodded, and his voice was clear, though not strong. "He's spoken to me of you many times, Mr. Sublette. He thought the world of you."

"I reckon I always used him as a measuring stick for other men." Sublette hesitated, then said, "This is going to be a rough trip, Reverend. Not so good for a sick man."

"We feel that God has called us to go to Oregon. I know that may sound foolish, but my wife and I feel we must go."

Sublette turned suddenly to look at the woman. She was watching him intently, a steadiness in her gaze that impressed him. He dropped his eyes to the boy, who was regarding him open-eyed, then turned back to the man. "I owe your father a debt. If you're sure you want to do this, I'll do all I can to see you through."

Ellencourt's eyes brightened, and he put his hand out. "God bless you, Mr. Sublette!"

"Just Ty will do—and I'm not sure I'm doing you a favor." He hesitated, then said, "I'm surprised at your calling. Your father—well, he wasn't much for religion."

"I know he led a hard life," Ellencourt said. "But he was converted after he left the mountains. He was the finest Christian I ever knew. I think it was his example that turned me toward the ministry."

Leah Ellencourt said, "The others don't want us to come. Can you convince them?"

"I think I might—if you're both sure this is what you want."

"It's the hand of God, Ty," Mark Ellencourt said quietly.

Sublette walked from behind the wagon and came to stand before Farr. "You still want a guide?"

"Why sure. You mean you'll go?"

"I'll go if you take this family."

Pete Gratton whipped his hat off angrily. "No! I'm against it!"

The question of a pilot, however, was a pressing matter. They had found no one with any qualifications at all, only one man who had been no further than Fort Laramie, which was no help whatsoever. Farr was staring at Sublette. "You really mean that, Ty?"

"I mean it."

"We can't break the rules," Ira Barnhill snapped. "They don't have enough stock."

"Give me half of the pay for getting you to Oregon," Sublette said instantly. "I'll see that they have stock and supplies."

Gratton glared at the tall man. "We ain't takin' no strays."

Sublette's face was bland, and he did not raise his voice. He made a strong figure as he stood there, and his voice was light as the summer breeze as he said, "I said I'd stand for them. That ought to be good enough for you, Gratton."

"The council will have to meet," Farr said. "Come along."

Colin whispered, "I wonder what's got into Sublette. He's changed his mind mighty sudden."

"I'm glad he did," Jordan said.

The meeting did not last long. Ira Barnhill looked unhappy, but Farr spoke up firmly. "All right, Sublette. It'll be as you say. You agree to lead us all the way to Oregon if we take these people?"

"Yes."

Sublette turned and walked back to the Ellencourt's wagon. He stood looking up at the woman and the boy. A smile touched his broad lips. "What's your name?" he asked the boy.

"Josiah."

"Named after your grandpa?"

"Yes, sir."

"Well, Josiah, it looks like you're going to Oregon."

"I have to thank you, Ty," Mrs. Ellencourt said. "I hate to take charity, but my pride will have to step aside. I think God sent you to help us."

Sublette did not answer for a moment. "Well, ma'am, I don't know much about God, but I'll do my best to get you to Oregon."

He turned and walked away. Colin intercepted him with Jordan by his side. "By George, Tyler, I'm glad you're going! I feel a lot better."

"So do I," Jordan said quickly. She could not help but ask, "I have a woman's curiosity, Ty. Everyone wants to know why you changed your mind."

Sublette studied the two, then said almost idly, "Josiah Ellencourt was my partner in the mountains. We spent two years on the lower Missouri trapping beaver—this was when I was only eighteen. I was caught by a band of Sioux and they were going to boil me over a fire. Josiah sneaked up and potted two of them. I was tied up, and there was still two left, and Josiah didn't have any more bullets. They came at him with tomahawks, and he pulled his Green River knife and killed both of them." A strange smile touched his broad lips then, and his voice was so soft that the two had to lean forward to catch it. "I never saw such a pretty sight as Josiah Ellencourt comin' out of the woods to take on those Sioux."

Jordan said impulsively, "I admire you very much for giving up your own interest to help the son of an old friend."

"Don't deserve much credit for that. I'm just like a leaf in the wind. It might as well blow me to Oregon as anywhere else." He turned then and walked away with his peculiar, soft-footed gait.

"He's a sad man." Jordan shook her head. "I wonder why."

"He'll probably never mention it, but he's a good one to have on the trail." Colin nodded. "I'm glad he's coming." He poked her. "Come on. Time to go shopping."

"Oh, dearest me," Jordan muttered to herself. She was standing outside the door of Drury's General Store, fumbling with her reticule and the list of provisions she and Colin would need for the trip. Colin was buying a few tools at the hardware store and had left her to deal with the food.

"This is—this is—" She turned the list sideways, for her mother had made imperious little appendices, with many exclamation points, alongside the list, trailing down the page and even onto the back of the paper.

"Mrs. Bryce . . . ," a voice sounded in her ear.

She started, then smiled. "Why, Mr. Sublette! I'm surprised to see you here. It seemed to me that you stirred up the beehive so that you'd never be able to get loose!"

"Call me Ty," he said. "People can buzz about me all they want," he said easily, stepping to push open the door for her. "I've got better things to do."

"Like shopping?" Jordan teased.

"Sure enough, ma'am. I see you've got you quite a list there. That is a list, I take it? Not a letter?"

"Mm, both, really. My mother doesn't think I can decipher a simple grocery list; she has very detailed instructions to go with it . . . but I'm ashamed to say that she must be right, I'm at a loss . . . what could—does this say—eggs in cornmeal? 'Place the eggs in the—,'" Confused, she turned the grubby, creased paper sideways, then upside down.

"Maybe I might help, ma'am?" he said, disguising a chuckle with a slight cough.

Jordan looked up to search his face. The store was dim because of the goods that covered the few windows. It was cool and quiet, for Jordan and Ty were the only customers at the moment. It had the permanent scent of a general store: a sawdusty aroma, mixed with vinegary pickle barrels and the heavy fruit drift of black licorice. "You?" Jordan stammered. "But you're a man!"

"Guess I am," Ty said gravely. "I don't mean to be pushy, ma'am, it's just that I figure you're getting supplied for the trip, from the looks of that list. I could help you with that."

"I guess I need help. My mother offered to send a servant along to help me, but I wanted to do it myself." She smiled nervously, adding, "You'll find out soon enough that I'm not the most practical person in the world."

Ty's firm mouth was twitching. "Well, I couldn't help you with a recipe for a sponge cake, or anything like that. Doubt if any man could."

"Exactly!" Jordan nodded eagerly.

"But I just figured," Ty went on calmly, "that your mother was trying to tell you that on the trail, we usually stow the eggs, and sometimes bacon, in the cornmeal. Layer them in the barrel, you see. Then you use up the eggs along with the cornmeal for cornbread, and can cook up your bacon."

"Eggs in cornbread?" Jordan said blankly.

"I'm pretty sure that's the way," Ty said cautiously.

"Oh. Well! That is clever! Well, if you're offering, would you please help me decipher this list of provisions." Jordan smiled up at him. "And I understand that you are the first person to ask about anything to do with going on the Oregon Trail. Could you, please, tell me what this is—this word, here, underlined? Is that 'hard take'? Whatever can she mean—"

"Hardtack, ma'am," Ty said resignedly. "It's over here. But listen, I'm just about to give my list to Mr. Drury, and his boys can draw it all up. Why don't you do the same, ma'am? They'll understand your mother's list very well, I'm sure."

"Really?" Jordan asked, amazed. "I had no idea." Catching a glimpse of his expression before he managed to get his poker face aligned, she wrinkled her nose up at him. "That astounds you, I'm sure. No, really, it's quite all right. I'm ignorant, but I'm learning quickly. By the way, you say you have a list? I'm a little surprised—I thought that you would just sort of exist in a permanent state of self-sufficiency."

"Not exactly, ma'am," he said lightly. "But this list is for the Ellencourt's supplies. I've got a couple of things I want to get for myself, though. Could I interest you in the peaches, ma'am? Which do you like best, honeyed peaches or sugared peaches?"

"Honeyed," Jordan said, her mouth watering. "Tinned peaches are delicious. Which do you like?"

"Honeyed. Wonder which would be best

for Reverend Ellencourt?" Ty said, considering the cans stacked neatly into two little
pyramids.

"I heard Mrs. Ellencourt say that he's not
well," Jordan said quietly. "Is he very ill?"

Ty shrugged, a short dismissive gesture.
"Don't really know. But he'll like honeyed
peaches, I reckon. Guaranteed to make you
healthy, wealthy, and wise."

"Then I shall have many, many tins of
peaches." Jordan smiled. "I may not know
much, but I can see that anything that does
all that is going to be a must for this journey."

"If you learn that, ma'am," Ty said quietly,
"then you've learned a good lesson."

She studied him, noting the confidence in
his stance, the strength in his well-muscled
shoulders, arms, hands, and the aura of natural authority and decisiveness that surrounded him. "You know, Ty, Colin and I are
very happy you'll be going with us."

He nodded, modestly but not overly so, a
mere acknowledgment that she was right to
feel reassured. "Thank you, Mrs. Bryce." He
gave her a sharp, bright sidelong glance. "I
don't feel awkward about asking you for a
small favor."

"Why, of course, Ty—and please call me Jordan."

He frowned, a small grimace of worry. "It's pretty hard for a woman on the trail, especially with a family, and one of them sick. Mrs. Ellencourt needs friends, loyal friends. Now, I'm going to make sure that the Ellencourts are taken care of as far as keeping them safe and provisioning them and all, but if you could just—"

"I understand," Jordan interrupted quickly. "I'll try to be a good friend to her. After all, I need close friends myself." She added, "I'm so glad we'll have a minister along. Are you a Christian man, Ty?"

A shadow crossed Sublette's face. "No, I'm not," he said simply, then turned and walked away. Jordan was somewhat shocked at his response. *I must have offended him—I'll have to be more careful.*

It was still dark, the small hours just before dawn, on April the fifteenth. After tearful good-byes from her family, Jordan and Colin had spent their first night in their wagon, while Gus slept outside.

In the gray stillness the jarring crack of a

rifle shot sounded. Jordan jumped, still half-asleep. "Colin! That was a shot!"

"Sure was," he moaned. "Time to get up and fix my vittles, woman. This here train's gonna be movin' outta here, headin' west, at first light!"

They dressed, not quickly, and with many giggles and playful shoves and pinches, in the cluttered confines of their wagon. Finally Colin jumped out and took Jordan by the waist and swung her around, much as her father had done when she was five years old. "Put me down, you brute, or I'll be too dizzy to cook!" she cried.

"Can't have that," he said, setting her down.

Still clasped tightly together, they turned to look at the encircled wagons, their first hometown. Everyone was already stirring, calling out. Ty Sublette had the Ellencourt's fire going; their wagon was just in front of the Bryce's. Several other fires made cheerful yellow glows in the cold damp predawn. Children already were playing, calling out and running, and two dogs barked loudly.

Colin pulled Jordan closer, then put his fingers under her chin and tilted her face up to his. "We're leaving today, in just an hour or so. It's going to be a long journey, and a hard one. How do you feel, Jordan? Are you happy?"

She kissed him, long and warmly, then pulled away and rested her face against the rough, clean-smelling muslin shirt. "Happy? I don't think I ever, in my life, knew what happiness was, until now." She pulled back to stare up at him, into his beloved face. "Leaving? No, we're not leaving anything, and we're on no journey, and there is no long and difficult road in front of us, Colin. That's not where we are."

"Then where are we, bride?" he asked gently.

"Home, my love. We two are home—no matter where we are!"

PART
TWO

The sharp crack of a rifle brought Jordan from a sound sleep with a jolt. She hadn't yet been able to adjust to the sounds of gunshots beginning her day, particularly as they came at four o'clock in the morning. For the tenth day in a row she jerked, then fell back in the pallet in the wagon with a groan. Colin, however, jumped up, bright-eyed and fresh as always. "New day on the trail, my love! Good morning!"

Jordan pulled the quilt over her head, saying thickly, "It's not really morning. It's still dark."

"Mm, lady's grumpy today," Colin said, prodding her gently with one already-booted foot. "Any breakfast on the schedule? Or do I need to go a-begging?"

"No," Jordan said, choking down a prodigious yawn and sitting up to gaze blearily around. "I'll cook breakfast."

"Be much obliged to you, ma'am." Colin pulled up the flap and jumped out of the wagon.

Shivering in the bleak predawn chill, Jordan longed to pull the blanket over her face and sleep. She closed her eyes, but at that moment, something soft touched her face. She opened her eyes to see Rowena perched on her chest, touching her with one paw. "You gorgeous thing!" Jordan exclaimed, and picked up the ball of fur. She had become very attached to the kitten, and for a few moments played with her. Then she sighed and put her down. "Got no time for playing, Rowena."

Outside the wagon, Jordan washed her face and hands in a bucket of water, wishing, dreaming, lusting after a hot head-to-toe bath. *How long will it be until I get a hot bath?* she wondered, disheartened. The discontented murmur reminded her of her long-ago conversation with Jolie, when Jordan had so blithely dismissed such minor setbacks on such a noble journey. Now she grumbled to herself, "It sure doesn't seem like such a minor thing now, noble quest or not!"

Splashes in cold water were presenting much more of a problem to Jordan than she would have thought possible. She never, ever, felt clean. As for hot water, she didn't have time to heat up a bucketful in the mornings, and at night she was usually too tired. *Maybe after I get settled down, get used to the routine, I'll be able to organize better.*

But the most meticulous organization wouldn't help Jordan's most pressing problem after ten days on the trail, and that was that her body was stiff and sore from the long hours in the saddle and on the wagon seat. *What would I do if we didn't have Gus?* Indeed, the lanky hired hand made life much easier for Jordan. He had taught her how to cook some simple foods, and done most of the driving while she and Colin rode their horses.

Fifteen miles a day they had to cover—for months. Somehow that had not seemed so difficult in Independence, but now the distance stretched out beyond her comprehension.

Jordan had not said a word of complaint about her sore body or even given a hint of it by such tactics as heavy sighs or pained expressions. She was, on the whole, a good-natured woman, and now that natural effervescence bubbled up as dawn slowly lit the sky behind them.

As she dried off her face with a rough towel, the daily routine began. People, young and old, poured out of their tents and wagons. Slow spirals of smoke began to drift up into the lightening sky from the many campfires. At the Ellencourt's wagon Leah was already buttering high, fluffy biscuits, and the delicious smell wafted to Jordan's nostrils. Gus had started her fire and set up her tripod, but Jordan was not very hopeful about the bread she'd mixed and allowed to rise all night; upon opening her Dutch oven, she saw with dismay that the dough looked more like log-chinking than light bread. Still, she gamely hung it on the tripod and set up her rock-grill for her frying pan, to make bacon and eggs.

The men, including Colin, who looked after the large herd of beef cattle and milk cows and saddle horses generally tended to them until about six o'clock. Then they returned to eat breakfast. Jordan's bread was indeed still a lump of heavy gray dough by breakfast time, but Colin only teased her a little, and ate all the bacon and eggs. Gus ate a huge breakfast and complimented her, "You're getting to be a fine cook, Miss Jordan! Ain't that right, Jos?"

Jos Ellencourt, who was a great admirer of Jordan, had filched one of his mother's biscuits for her, which Jordan ate with immense enjoyment. *I've got to get Leah to teach me how to make biscuits!* The men began to water the fires, strike the tents, load the wagons, and yoke and hitch the teams. Colin accomplished all this much more quickly than many of the men, and as usual, he told Jordan, "I think I'll go on with the hunters, Jordan. Do you mind?"

"No, of course not," Jordan said, smiling and kissing him lightly. "Shoot me a big buffalo."

The hunters were probably five or six miles ahead at seven o'clock when the wagon master, Horace Farr, blew the trumpet, a shrill clarion call that set the train into motion. His wagon drew out of the circle first, and slowly the caravan formed into a line behind him. Jordan was already mounted, enjoying the rough warmth of Princess's coat as she stroked the mare's neck. Behind her Gus drove their wagon, and right ahead of her Leah Ellencourt, driving her team of oxen, waved, and Jordan waved and smiled back.

The April sun overhead was a pure azure, and large fluffy clouds as white as cotton balls drifted lazily along. As far as the eye could see in any direction, the bright gold of black-eyed Susans and the cheerful yellow of dandelions, blobs of deep green wild henbane, and the muted khaki tints of sagebrush and prairie grass stretched ahead. Far off to the south a smudge of storm clouds brooded, and Jordan thought they might have a shower later. They'd already had two spring storms, and Jordan had thought them both delightful, standing out in the warm deluge with her face lifted to the sky and her arms spread wide, laughing.

For now, however, the day was bright and warm and benevolent, and Jordan, despite her aching body, enjoyed the vista, the sounds of creaking leather and jingles of harness, the scent of wild sage.

The morning passed, measured by the slow, sure tread of oxen and the sun creeping up on them from behind. By the time the train halted for lunch, Jordan could barely dismount. She called ahead to Leah Ellencourt, "Are we stopping by a stream, Leah? Do you know?"

Leah shook her head, but motioned Jos to her, and the boy took off running, presumably to find out. Meanwhile the train was laboriously coming to a stop, wagon by wagon.

Jordan went to the back of the wagon, lowered the back gate, and climbed up to sit down for a few minutes. They only stopped for about an hour for dinner, so no fires were lit and no cooking was done.

Finally Jos came running back to her wagon. "Miss Jordan, we're not at a stream or anything right now, but this afternoon we're going to cross the Big Blue."

Jordan smiled at the thin, earnest boy. "Thank you, Jos. Guess I'll just have to wait until then to soak my feet."

"Yes, ma'am," he said with blank politeness, then hurried back to his friends.

Jordan sat quietly, daydreaming a little as she watched the boys play. Finally Colin came riding down the line with Ty Sublette, and the two men spoke a word or two to every one of the wagons. Jordan watched and noticed how very different they were. Colin was smiling, joking, his eyes sparkling, his boyishly rowdy laugh ringing out. Ty smiled, touching the brim of his hat to all the ladies, his demeanor calm and solid in contrast to Colin's tearing high spirits. Jordan smiled affectionately, admiring her husband's handsome profile and winning smile.

"Bride!" he called.

"Groom!" she answered.

"What's for dinner, woman?"

"Turtle soup? Lobster? Or maybe you prefer fresh-fried trout?" Jordan asked gaily as Colin dismounted—now with extravagant grace—at her feet.

Colin came to plant a quick but sound kiss right on her mouth. "I was hoping for some hardtack and jerky and tinned peaches."

"Well, if you insist," Jordan said, clambering up to rummage around in the wagon. Immediately a loud metallic crash sounded, followed by two hollow wooden thumps, and Jordan mumbled, "Ouch! Gosh, that really hurt!"

As Sublette rode by he grinned at Colin. "The bride's cooking dinner, is she?"

"Dunno for sure," Colin admitted, his eyes sparkling. "Mrs. Bryce? You all right in there, or do I need to get Doc Leverett?"

"I'm fine," Jordan said in a muffled voice. It sounded as if she had her head stuck down in a barrel.

Colin added conversationally, "This is the only wagon on the train that has to have a doctor in attendance when meals are being prepared." Ty chuckled.

From inside the wagon Jordan called,

now clearly, "Mr. Colin Bryce, just you keep your sass to yourself, please. And that goes for you too, Ty!"

Ty grinned, winked at Colin, then kicked his horse into a walk. Colin came to peer into the wagon. "You all right?" he asked.

"Yes! Now here, have your old dinner!"

They ate lunch quickly, then Colin rode off on Caesar, dashing up to ride with the scouts. Wearily Jordan threw the slight dinner litter back in the wagon, closed it up, and took her place on Princess again. "Girl, what do you think?" she murmured to the mare. "Do you think we'll make it?"

Afternoons were always much harder than mornings. The sun glared straight into their westward-seeking eyes. The dust rose, fine and gritty, to choke them in the dry part of the long day. Even a very small dinner made them sleepy . . .

Jordan had learned to take little naps even while riding, but she awoke with a start. She jerked with a sudden cry of sharp pain, and then realized that she must have been sleeping for hours, for the sun was late-afternoon orange hovering low. She looked around wildly, and spotted Jos Ellencourt coming her way, waving.

"Looky, Miz Bryce—it's the Big Blue River!"

"River looks real shallow," Pete Gratton argued heavily, his big face hot red. "I say we camp here and cross in the morning. The people are tired, right here's a nice cool stream, and it's late."

Horace Farr looked wearily at the big man, with his shadow, Ira Barnhill, hovering behind him. "Ty said we need to cross tonight," he finally replied as patiently as he could. Every single time the train stopped— for dinner, for water, for the night—Gratton and Barnhill, along with their half-dozen or so followers, came up to Farr's wagon to complain about something.

"And why'd he say that, I wonder?" Gratton shot back belligerently. "It wouldn't be because I been tellin' him all day long that Catlow told us this little spot's the sweetest one for a long pull? And Sublette's just being contrary because he doesn't like Catlow?"

Behind him, like a big smelly oxen himself, Al Catlow guffawed. He was a big barrel-shaped man, with pugnacious jaws and long matted brown hair.

Horace Farr said quietly, "Gratton, Ty Sublette's got a good reason for crossing this evening. I didn't question him very closely about it because he's the pilot of this train, and we all agreed that what he says about the trail is the final word. Now, he'll be riding back up here just as soon as he finishes getting everyone ready to cross, and if you've a mind to, you can take it up with him. But I'm the train captain, and it's my responsibility to move this train along, and I'm not going to let anyone hold us up to stand around and argue about something that's been settled long ago."

"It ain't been settled long ago, and it ain't settled now," Gratton grated.

"Fine, Pete. You can stay on this side of the river if you'd like," Farr said politely.

"Now, wait just a minute, that ain't—," Gratton blustered.

"Trouble, Horace?" Ty Sublette, riding up, asked mildly.

Farr shrugged. "Pete here, and some of the other men, want to stay on this side of the river tonight. I tried to talk them into staying with the train, but it seems like they don't want to cross."

Ty nodded thoughtfully, then said, "Gratton, I knew of a train that decided to wait and cross the Big Blue in the morning. That night there came a storm, and the river rose up past where we're standing right now, and it was thirteen days before they could make their crossing. This is a nice spot, I'll admit, but I don't think anyone wants to camp here for the next two weeks. Do you? Especially with those clouds rolling up on the horizon." He nodded to the west.

"No, but—," Gratton frowned, couldn't seem to work out why he was still angry, and finally muttered, "Well, that's all I wanted to know, Sublette—why all the hurry to cross tonight."

"Now you know," Sublette said evenly.

"'Bout time too," Gratton grunted, turning on his heel. "C'mon, boys, I guess we better get ready to swim."

Horace Farr watched them go with cool blue eyes, sucking his teeth thoughtfully. "That man would argue with a rock. We ready to cross?"

"Ready when you are, Horace."

"Then let's head 'em up and move 'em out."

* * *

It was full dark before all twenty-nine wagons forded the Big Blue and got themselves arranged into their customary circle. It was a prime campsite, with cool grass and the bubbling, cheerful river right at hand. Jordan did get a chance to soak her feet for a little while, just before she had to start the arduous evening chores.

The hunters had ranged ahead in the afternoon and had found a herd of antelope. Everyone on the train had a feast of fresh, tender meat that night. Colin had killed one, and some of the other men had to show him how to skin it out and butcher it. Everyone pitched in and built a big fire pit, the men made a crude grill, and everyone had a chance to smoke their choice cuts. Ty had brought the Ellencourts an antelope, and Leah invited him and Colin and Jordan to supper.

This was the first time Jordan had been around Mark Ellencourt. He generally came out for breakfast, and Jordan had privately observed that he tried to help his wife and son with all the chores. But usually Leah would smile, take his arm, and lead him back to the wagon, where he would disappear. He was evidently very ill.

Now Jordan surreptitiously studied him as he, like the rest of them, sat cross-legged on a blanket around the Ellencourt's campfire. He had a good face, not classically handsome but attractive, with fine tawny brown hair and gentle brown eyes. His face was thin and pale, but his countenance was kind. He spoke of his and Leah's struggles to join a wagon train moving west.

"I came down with the fever just before we reached Independence," he was saying between healthy bites. "This is really the first day I've had any appetite at all. I must thank you again, Ty, for providing us with this excellent meat. I feel stronger already."

Ty said casually, "No trouble. But you'll have to thank the cooks for the meat. Leah, I reckon this is the best steak I've ever had. You're a mighty fine cook."

Leah Ellencourt's green eyes twinkled. "Yes, it was only due to my secret recipe for throwing a steak on the fire that makes it so delicious, Mr. Sublette. But thank you anyway."

"Jordan has some pretty mysterious recipes, too, Leah," Colin said, grinning. "By my count, it took her eighteen minutes, four separate tools, and a set of instructions for her to open a tin of peaches for my dinner."

"Well, from here on out you may open your own tinned peaches," Jordan said good-naturedly. "I cut my finger twice, and I don't think I've gotten nearly enough sympathy for it. But anyway, Leah, I obviously don't have any recipes to trade with you, but I would love for you to tell me how you make your delicious biscuits."

"So would I," Colin agreed enthusiastically.

Leah smiled. "I could write it down for you, but it would be so much easier to show you. Why don't we join forces in the morning?"

"Why, that would be fine—and I'm sure my husband would greatly appreciate it," Jordan responded, giving Colin a little jab in the side with her elbow.

Colin smiled at Jordan. "Maybe I tease my bride too much. She's very smart, but her smarts run more along the lines of books and poetry than cooking."

At the mention of these intellectual pursuits, Jos Ellencourt made a hideous face, but Jordan assured him, "Don't worry, Jos, I'm not going to collar you and make you do lessons."

"She's been after me to make her a book rack to mount on Princess's back," Colin said. "Sort of a book saddle for a horse."

Ty Sublette's white teeth showed in a wide, delighted grin. "I knew an old, old mountain man named Samuels that had just that kind of rig for his mule. It was a little wooden stand, like, that held the Bible—that was all he ever read, the Bible—upright, with a little lip along the bottom that held the book open, the whole contraption strapped down with harness leather."

"Do you hear that, Colin?" Jordan teased. "I expect delivery in a day or two."

"That must have been old Ned Samuels," Mark Ellencourt said. "My father spoke of him quite often, wondering what had happened to him."

Ty shrugged. "He was a real mountain man, stayed up there for months and months at a time, in the High Rockies. He's either still up there reading his Bible, or he might be dead by now. Come to think of it, I haven't seen or heard tell of him in a long while."

Mark Ellencourt smiled. "Doesn't sound like such a bad way to die. Alone, communing with God, in the mountains."

"Might sound good to you, Reverend," Ty

replied lightly, "but most people don't exactly want to die all alone up in the mountains. Takes a special kind of person, I think."

"Mark is that special—and that strong," Leah said quietly. "I'm certainly not. I'd be terrified. That's why I'm so glad that you're our guide, Ty. By all accounts you are the man to keep anyone from getting lost anywhere on the trail. I've certainly heard Mark's father speak highly of you very often."

"Yes, ma'am, I'll never forget roaming the mountains for a couple of years with Josiah Ellencourt," Ty answered. "He sure was a strong, tough man."

"Not like me," Mark said unself-consciously. "It grieved him that I wasn't like him. But he treated me right, and was proud of me, just the same. I miss him still."

"How long has he been gone?" Colin asked.

Ellencourt's gentle gaze was focused far away in remembrance. Finally he stirred. "It's been three years now since he's gone to be with the Lord."

Ty gave Ellencourt a strange look. "How did he come to be saved?"

Mark smiled. "Just facing his own mortality. He told me that everything—including

the Lord Jesus and his words—looks different when you start getting older. He said he
thought a lot about the things that were
ahead when he died. He said, and I quote,
'Any critter with any sense is going to want
to go to heaven to be with the Lord Jesus
'stead of hell with that ol' Satan tormentin''
'im. So I'm going to figger out how to get to
heaven.' And so he did."

"But it's not really that simple, is it?" Ty
asked quietly.

Mark Ellencourt looked mildly surprised.
"Why, of course it is! It's the simplest decision we ever make. Whether to live with the
Lord or whether to live with the devil. That's
for eternity, that's for tonight, that's for the
next five minutes. It's all the same decision."

Ty nodded, but it was clear that he didn't
fully agree. However, Mark Ellencourt was
not a pushy, preachy type of man, and he
went on smoothly, "Now, my esteemed
guests, I believe we all face a very crucial
decision to make right now. Will you have
vinegar pie or apple tart?"

ELEVEN

Jordan walked alongside the yoke of oxen, her hand resting from time to time on the rough coat of Castor. The week on the trail since crossing the Big Blue River had given her complexion a light golden tan and brought out a few scattered freckles across the bridge of her nose. From time to time she glanced across the five wagons that spanned out on each side of her and then back at the rest of the train. Somehow it had been in her mind that the wagons in a train would go single file, but here on the prairie Sublette had suggested they spread out in this manner so that there would be less dust on those that brought up the rear.

Now as she strolled along, a smile came to Jordan, and she thought, *I'm really starting to enjoy this trip.* It had taken two weeks to get the wagon train shaken down, for most had never been on such a venture before. Since the train moved rather slowly, geared to the pace of the oxen, it was a pretty sight to Jordan to see the youngsters spanning out from the wagons plucking wildflowers, shouting and playing, and their mothers trying to keep track of them.

At noon the teams were not unyoked but turned loose from the wagons. They would graze leisurely while the women prepared a cold meal.

The evenings had been particularly fine to Jordan. At first she had been too tired to do anything but fall into bed with Colin. He was an ardent lover, and in effect this was their honeymoon, so she grew accustomed to his reaching for her and pulling her close. But now that she had grown stronger, she stayed up later fixing the evening meal for Colin and Gus. There was plenty of fresh game, and Gus turned out to be a surprisingly good campfire cook.

Sometimes they would set up camp near a river, and a violin would strike up, joined by a flute that sent an eerie sound over the open prairie. Finally all would grow hushed, and only the guards would stay awake. It was during those times that Jordan would lie in Colin's arms, and the two of them would laugh and talk until they fell asleep.

Jordan's thoughts were interrupted when Sublette appeared from a distance. She had learned to recognize his tall form, and now she knew he was coming to lead the train to the campsite for the night. Ellen and Horace Farr were in the wagon to her left. Ellen called out, "I guess it's time to set up camp. There comes Sublette."

The two women watched as Sublette came closer and called out, "Single file!" The Farrs moved into first place, and Jordan fell behind them. She looked back to see Colin smile and wave his hand.

Ty Sublette moved his horse beside her and said, "You're doing fine, Jordan."

"Why, thanks, Ty."

"Were you named after a river?"

Jordan smiled, for she had been asked this question before. "That's what Colin asked me. No. It's my mother's family name."

"Mighty pretty. Often thought about the Jordan River."

Sublette flashed her a smile, his teeth very white against his bronzed skin, and then he wheeled his horse around. He rode to the head of the train and expertly guided the Farr's wagon in a sweeping circle. Somehow he was always able to space the wagons so that the last exactly filled in the gap. When the circle was made, he moved along speaking to several, and then when he came to the wagon of the Ellencourts he stepped off and was greeted at once by Jos. "Hey, Ty."

"Hey yourself, Jos. You have a good day?"

"Sure have. Did you shoot that deer?"

"Yep, but it's an antelope. You want to help me clean it?"

"Yes!"

Sublette pulled an antelope off from behind his saddle where it had been lashed with rawhide thong and carried it outside the camp, stopping first to say, "I'll get this critter skinned, and then we'll have us a good supper."

"All right, Ty," Leah said. She watched him, tall and straight, her green eyes following the pair as they left.

Turning, she went to the back of the wagon and unloaded fragments of wood she'd picked up during the day's ride. Quickly she built up a fire and then turned to Mark, who had gotten out of the wagon. His face was pale, but she said cheerfully, "Ty brought us an antelope. We'll have good steaks tonight."

"Fine." Mark smiled at her. His thin face was leaner than it had been at the beginning. He had gotten over the fever that had plagued him, but there was a lack of strength in him that concerned Leah. "I'll help you build the fire."

"Already done. Why don't you just read until supper's ready?"

"All right, Leah. I do feel helpless, though."

"Plenty of time for you to help when you get your strength back."

As usual, Mark Ellencourt began reading a book. He had the habit of putting himself out of the world around him, and now he was soon lost in the printed page.

Sublette came back soon, his hands bloody, and gave a quarter of the small antelope to Leah. "I'll take the rest of this and divide it up."

"Be sure you give some to the Cranes," Leah said quickly. "They don't have much."

The Cranes, Orville and Fanny, were not particularly strong. They were both thin almost to emaciation—so thin and worn that it was hard to believe that their six small children running along from an infant of one year to a boy of eight could have sprung from such an unlikely pair.

Sublette left Leah and walked around the circle until he came to the Cranes. "Hello,

Fanny," he said. "I brought you some fresh meat."

"Why, thank you, Ty." Fanny Crane was a small woman with thin hair and blue eyes. There was a nervousness in her that never seemed to leave. "Did you see any Indians?"

"Not likely to, not around here. Don't you worry."

Orville, hardly larger than his wife, walked up. He was wearing a pair of faded, patched overalls and had the baby in his arms. "We appreciate the meat, Ty."

"It's a stringy little thing, but it'll do to eat."

Sublette talked for a moment with the Cranes, studying them thoughtfully with his clear blue eyes. He had been apprehensive about the family joining the train. They would be more at home on a farm back in Arkansas than on this particular venture.

As he made his way back to his camp, Pete Gratton suddenly made an appearance, staring at Sublette belligerently. He still resented the fact that they'd hired Sublette.

"We didn't make very good time today, Sublette."

"Reckon we did fairly well."

"I think we could have gone another hour on the trail."

"Maybe so."

They were joined by the Barnhills, who moved closer to hear the conversation.

Ira Barnhill said, "I think Pete's right, Sublette. We could have made a few more miles."

Avis Barnhill suddenly turned to her husband. "I think Ty knows more about things like that than any of the rest of us."

Quickly Barnhill's eyes narrowed, and he reached out and took his wife by the upper arm. "Sure, Avis. I'm just anxious to make good time. Come on. I'll help you fix supper."

Ten feet away the three sons of Ira Barnhill lounged around. They were stair-stepped up. Cornwall at seventeen was a tall lanky boy and a better man than his father and his brothers. Theodore, twenty-three, was a carbon copy of his father. Ace, twenty-five, was a handsome man with black hair and eyes. He dressed better than the rest of the men on the train and made a romantic appearance. Now as the three waited, watching the little scene, Ace murmured to his brothers, "Pa's afraid to let Avis even talk to a man."

"Shut up, Ace!" Theodore grunted. "I won't hear that kind of talk."

Cornwall glanced at his father and noted the possessiveness of the man and knew that Ace was right, but he hated for it to be spoken.

Ira came back without releasing Avis's arm. "Why don't you fix us some of that stew you make so good, Avis."

"All right," she said. Avis rarely argued with her husband, but now she winked at Ace. "You boys can watch me to be sure that some man doesn't run off with me."

"That's not funny, Avis!" Barnhill's pride was hurt, and he glared at his three sons, waiting for a reply, but they had learned to keep quiet at such times.

The Farrs were a close-knit family. As they sat around the campfire, Horace grinned at Ellen, his wife, and said, "You know, Ellen, it's good to have a red-haired woman around."

"Stop your foolishness, Horace."

Their three children were sitting around the small campfire. Jack at seventeen longed to be a man. He and Cornwall Barnhill had become good friends. Rita, sitting across from Jack, was sixteen. She had her mother's red hair and blue eyes and was on the verge of womanhood. She was a lively girl, with a strong interest in young men that troubled her parents. Payton, her younger brother, also inherited Ellen's red hair and blue eyes and was as full of life as any ten-year-old.

Horace Farr's mother, Dorcas Farr, at the age of seventy-one, was thin and wiry and active, but at times she would fall into a quiet period when she said almost nothing. She was an herb woman and believed deeply in signs. When a bird flew into the house, she would always say, "There's going to be a death soon." She was not, however, a dour woman, for she looked life straight in the face, and now she moved over and sat down on the blanket beside Rita. "I saw you lookin' at that Corny Barnhill."

"Oh, I didn't either, Gran!" Rita protested.

"You're gonna have to show him a little more interest if you want him to chase after you."

"Ma, stop that," Horace said mildly. "She spends too much time thinkin' about young men as it is. You'll teach that girl bad habits."

Dorcas sniffed. "I don't reckon I taught you any bad habits, Horace."

"I might argue that," Ellen said with a

smile. "But you have to filter out everything your grandmother tells you, Rita."

Rita smiled and put her arm around her grandmother, whom she loved dearly. She leaned over and whispered, "You tell me how to do it, Gran."

Sublette suddenly appeared at the fire, and Jack at once straightened up. He came to his feet and said, "Hello, Ty."

"Hello, Jack. How's it going?"

"Good. We got some meat left."

"Already ate. Might take a little of that coffee though."

Sublette, as always, brought a sense of confidence with him. The tall pilot said little, but there was something about him that people looked up to.

As he drank his coffee, he suddenly winked at Gran. "Well, Sister Farr, you're going to have to speak to that granddaughter of yours. I saw her making eyes at Corny Barnhill."

"Oh, I did not! Everybody's making fun of me!"

"I was just teasing. It was him lookin' at you. Don't blame him either."

Rita was pleased at Sublette's gentle teasing and went to fill his coffee mug.

Suddenly there were shouts, and Sublette's head turned quickly. Everyone followed his gaze, and they saw two men struggling and scuffling in a fight.

"That's Ace Barnhill," Horace said, a worried expression on his face. "Looks like he's whippin' the doctor's brother. They've both been after one of the young women on the train. I figured there'd be trouble."

"I guess I'd better see about it," Sublette said quickly. He handed the cup to Rita, then turned and walked swiftly away.

Sublette stepped at once between the two men. "You'd better save this. You'll need it down the line," he said.

Ace Barnhill had dark hair and eyes, and at six feet was well-proportioned. "This is none of your put in, Sublette!"

"You don't have to take care of me." Les Leverett was five years older than Ace Barnhill. He had fair hair and rather soulful blue eyes. He was also a heavy drinker, as the entire train had learned, but no one was called upon to reform him.

Suddenly a husky man with hazel eyes and stiff black hair stepped forward. His eyes were laughing, but there was something arrogant about him. "Why don't you stay out of it, Ty? Let 'em have it out. I never saw you break a fight up back in the mountains."

"This is different, Al." Sublette studied Catlow. The two of them had known each other while trapping beaver in the mountains. Al Catlow was a dangerous man, and Sublette somehow understood that the burly trapper would never be satisfied until he tried his strength out on Sublette himself. He waited to see if this was the moment, but Catlow simply laughed and said, "Appears to me you ain't got time to baby-sit drunks."

Sublette did not answer. He grabbed Leverett's arm and said, "Come along, Les."

Jerking his arm away, Leverett snapped, "I don't need your help!"

Ace Barnhill called out, "This ain't over, Leverett."

Leverett's face was bleeding, but he merely laughed. Sublette pulled Leverett away.

"Come on, Les. I'll clean you up."

The two walked away down the line until they came to the Leverett wagon. Paul was squatted before a fire frying meat, and he stood up at once. "What's going on?" he asked quickly.

"Nothing," Les said.

"You've been in a fight. Sit down and let me clean you up."

"Just a scratch."

Sublette stood by idly watching as Leverett cleaned the cuts. There was a certainty in the man's movements, and he studied the two men who were so different. Doc Leverett was a man people would trust, but Les was a womanizer and a drunk. Sublette had learned in confidence from Paul that it was on his brother's account that he was making this trip. He had told him confidentially, "He killed a man in a duel over a woman back east, and he drinks too much. But I've got to help him, Ty."

Now Sublette nodded and said, "Good night," and left the two.

When Ty was out of earshot, Paul looked his brother in the eye. "Now, what happened, Les?"

"I was just talking to one of the girls, and Ace took exception to it."

"You were lucky you didn't get beat to a pulp. You've got to quit drinking, and you've got to leave these women alone."

Les laughed and rose. He went to the wagon, came back with a bottle, and drank from it. "Now, tell me I drink too much."

"I can't run your life, Les, but you're headed for trouble. These people will kill over a woman."

Les simply grinned and took another sip from the bottle. Putting the cap on it, he said mildly, "All right. I'll try to behave."

Paul stood for a moment watching his brother with a sense of hopelessness. It seemed he spent half of his life getting him out of trouble. It had seemed like a good idea to get him away from civilization, but now he wondered if he had made a big mistake. They were away from all law now, and this would be just the kind of setting that Les would like. He said quietly, "You'd better stay away from the women," then turned and went back to cooking the meal.

TWELVE

Weaving through the wagons, Jordan guided Princess past the head of the train. She waved at Ellen Farr and received her smile. Glancing back, she saw the loose horses far back behind the wagons and the cattle with the riders back of them and to the sides. Out to the windward side of the train women and children were walking and seemed to be having a fine time. Some of them were looking for wildflowers, but there were fewer flowers now as they were coming into the country of the Platte. Cactus was more common and thistle and low sage, which glowed with a dull, silvery color in the sun. Some wildflowers, hardier than others, waved briefly—small yellow-hearted daisies that apparently could grow out of gravel if necessary. Now and then a clump of wild roses would appear.

Overhead the sun beat down upon the white of the wagon covers and on the red and white and black of the oxen. The dresses of the women, at times, added a splash of blue or red or green.

The hunters rode out ahead as usual, but Sublette, for some reason, lingered behind. He glanced up, turning alertly to find Jordan coming, and when she fell in beside him, he spoke softly as he always did. "Good morning for a ride. Fine mare you've got."

"Her name is Princess. She is nice, isn't she?"

Jordan fell in beside him in a natural enough way. Her cheeks glowed with the exercise of riding, and there was a liveliness about her that pleased Sublette. There was nothing flirtatious about her whatsoever, but she had a way of laughing that was very attractive—her chin tilting up, and her lips curving attractively. He admired the picture she made and felt the strange things a man feels when he looks on beauty in a woman and knows that it will never be for him.

"Are there some rough spots on the trail coming up, Ty?" she asked.

He shook his head, his eyes guarded. "Never can tell for sure."

"When do you think we might run into Indians?"

"Not likely we'll see any soon."

"I thought there'd be Indians all the way along."

"Nothing but a few Kansans around here, and they're not dangerous."

Indeed, the few scattered Indians had come in mostly to trade. Jordan had looked forward eagerly to catching her first sight of the noble red man, but the Indians she had seen were a dejected, beaten people. Now she laughed at herself almost ruefully. "I am so foolish."

"I doubt that."

"Oh, I am, though. I've read all the books about Indians, mostly by Cooper, and I was expecting a noble savage."

Sublette was amused by this. He glanced at her, appreciating the rich auburn hair that she allowed to fall down her back this morning. She was wearing a gray dress that deepened the gray green of her eyes. "We'll see some savages. I don't guess I could say about how noble they are."

"What are they really like? The Indians, I mean. You've known a lot of them, Ty."

"They're like us."

His answer took her off guard. "Like us?" she said. "Why do you say that?"

Sublette smiled. His eyes were sleepy although they never stopped moving from point to point across the horizon. "When an

Indian mother plays with her baby, she pokes his cheeks just like you'd do, so he'd make bubbles."

For a time Jordan did not speak. This interested her. "But they're cruel, aren't they? I've heard that they torture their captives."

"Yes. They'll do that all right."

"But you like them, don't you?"

"Some of them."

"You're a hard man to talk to, Ty Sublette." The light of Jordan's eyes held back some sort of laughter, and she watched him with a wide-eyed attention. "Did you wear a beard when you were in the mountains?"

"Most of the time. Came clear down to here." He tapped himself on the chest. "It was curly, too."

She looked at his hair. "Couldn't have been."

"It was though."

She studied him more carefully. "I hope you don't grow another one. I wouldn't like it."

Sublette found this woman highly entertaining. "Don't guess I will. Makes my face itch."

Jordan rode back alone to the train at noon and found Colin short-tempered. "These blasted oxen won't pay a bit of attention to me!" he complained. "A whip doesn't mean a thing to them." Colin had been driving the wagon while Gus took his turn riding herd.

Jordan patted his arm. "You just have to let them take their own time. You know that. That's what all those people say who really know oxen."

Colin had not shaved in three days, and now the bristles of his beard were glinting in the sunlight. His hair needed cutting, and she made a note to trim him up after supper. She reached up and ran her hand across his beard. "You'll have to shave."

"Nobody to see me."

"Somebody to feel you though. It's rough on my skin. Maybe you'd rather sleep alone."

Bryce's eyes sparkled. "Not much chance of that." He put his arm around her, squeezed her, and leaned over and kissed her. "I'll shave tonight though."

As they sat there, he said, "I saw you out there with Ty. What does he talk about?"

"Oh, mountains and Indians, trapping beaver. I asked him about the trail ahead. He won't tell me, but I know he thinks we're in for a hard time."

"It's boring, isn't it?" Colin said and moved restlessly. He was wearing a light gray shirt and a black hat with a low crown. He looked ahead into the distance at nothing but flat country. "I thought it'd be more exciting than this."

"I think it may get exciting enough," Jordan said. "Ty says that the Indians may be more of a danger farther on down the trail."

"I wouldn't mind a little adventure and shoot me an Indian."

"I hope you don't have to."

Surprised by her words, Colin looked at her. "Why, of course we'll have to! Everyone knows we'll have trouble with them."

"Ty says they're just like we are."

"Like him maybe. He lived with them so he's taken up with their ways, but I'd never trust a redskin."

Something about this disturbed Jordan, but she did not remark on it. "I think I'll go ride out in front again." She reached out and grabbed his hair and pulled his face close. "Does it make you jealous for me to talk with another man?"

"Not a homely fellow like Ty. Besides, I think he's woman proof."

"No man is woman proof!"

"I expect you're right about that." He kissed her again, then laughed as she shoved him away, grimacing at his prickly face. "I'll shave tonight," he promised.

Jordan went back to Princess, swung into the saddle, and rode back to join Sublette. The two rode together, more or less, all afternoon, and Sublette became more talkative. He told her a great many stories about his trapping days, and finally he laughed saying, "I've become talkative as an old woman."

"I like it. Oh, Ty, I'm having the best time of my life! I was so bored back home."

"Reckon you'll get bored again. Life's pretty much the same."

"This isn't."

"No," Sublette admitted. "The trail to Oregon is pretty exciting. A little bit chancy. This is the easy part."

By late afternoon Sublette was growing more alert. The sun had swung over and some of the heat had gone out of the day. Jordan was growing drowsy in the saddle but did not want to return to the train. Finally she straightened up and narrowed her eyes. "This country's different."

"You've got sharp eyes, Jordan. The Platte's right over there. What date is it?"

"Second of May."

"We've made good time."

Eager to see this river that somehow seemed to be an important point in their journey, Jordan sat straight in the saddle. They rode through a long set of hills with piles of sand, some of them up to sixty feet high, held together by cactus and thistles.

"What's that white stuff on the ground?"

"Somethin' like salt."

Thirty minutes later, Sublette pulled his horse up and nodded. "Well, there it is."

Jordan had heard a great deal about the Platte and had a picture in her mind about what it would look like. Now, however, she sat on her horse, stunned by what lay before her. "I can't believe that anything could be that flat."

"She's flat all right and goes on for quite a ways."

Jordan stared at the horizon. It seemed that she was looking at an empty world, for before her the land was as flat as her kitchen table had been at home. There were no trees, no mountains, not a break, it seemed. She shook her head in wonder. "I've never seen so much of nothing in all my life."

"Most of us live shut off by trees and hills,

but when you get to a place like this you begin to find out how big the world really is." His voice sounded loud in the silence, for nature seemed to be struck dumb, and there was very little sound.

Jordan sat on her horse, smelling the saltiness and the freshness of the breeze. Overhead the sun's witless stare beat down upon her, and the blue day flickered above the nothingness that rimmed her. She had some vague idea of the unguessed and un-known distances that lay before her, and fi-nally she said, "It's so big, Ty. I never realized the world was so big."

"It makes a man or a woman know how small they are," Sublette agreed.

"I never knew it would be like this," she murmured.

The two sat on their horses quietly listen-ing to the sounds of the wagons approach-ing, and then they moved forward. When they reached the Platte, she said, "It's so wide!"

Sublette grinned at her. "An inch deep and a mile across. That's what they say about the Platte. Well, we'd better get the wagons around in a circle."

* * *

Mark Ellencourt carefully nibbled the tender meat from the bone and then took a sip of the strong black coffee that Leah had brewed. "These are good birds. What do you call 'em, Ty?"

"Prairie chickens. Don't guess that's the right name, but that's what everybody calls them." Sublette had brought in half a dozen of the birds, and Leah had spitted and dressed them. She had cooked them over a fire, adding some sort of seasoning that had made the small birds taste very good indeed. Leah had eaten one, and the men two apiece.

"You keep on eating like that, you'll get well in a hurry, Mark."

Ellencourt laughed softly. "Dr. Sublette prescribes prairie chickens."

"How are you feeling?" Leah asked.

"Fine."

"I asked Leverett to come by and see you."

"You shouldn't have done that. He's got plenty to do."

"He does for a fact." Sublette nodded. "We've got a small town here, and it seems like somebody gets cut or bruised or a bone broken almost every day."

"As long as we don't get cholera, we're all

right," Leah said. "I've heard about it. It's awful, isn't it?"

The question seemed to depress Sublette. He did not answer, but picked up a stick and began to poke at the fire. His silence was noted by both Leah and Mark. They had talked about the big man often enough, but now they saw a sadness in him that they had not noticed before. Ellencourt said quickly, "Think I'll have any trouble startlng a church when we get to Oregon, Ty?"

Sublette considered the question. "Well, it gets lonesome out on the homesteads. Nothing much to do, so people go to church to see their neighbors. Not," he said quickly, "that they're not religious. I didn't mean to say that."

"I don't mean to preach at you, Ty, but I do like for everybody to know the Lord. What about you?"

Sublette smiled faintly. He looked up at the stars that were beginning to glitter overhead. "Well, Mark, somebody made all those. Somebody made us, too. They didn't make themselves any more than we did."

The remark interested Ellencourt. "What about your people?"

"They were Methodists. Took me to church every Sunday of my life until I was fifteen."

"What happened then?"

"My mother died, and then my father and I just made out the best we could. I guess she had the most religion. Father and I didn't. Didn't feel the same with her gone."

"Do you believe the Bible?"

"I guess I do." He looked down at the ground, stirred his shoulders restlessly, then lifted his head to meet Ellencourt's gaze. "Know the Bible, but don't do it. Guess that's my story."

"You will someday."

"Maybe."

"I think you will." Ellencourt's voice was insistent, and an eager look lighted his eyes. "I think you're a seeker—for God, that is. Lots of men don't seem to care about the Lord, but I think you do."

"I've heard some good preaching in my time, Mark. It didn't seem to take."

"God has to call us. When he does, Ty, I think you'll answer."

Leah sat quietly listening as her husband spoke with Sublette about Scripture. She discovered that the tall man knew a great

deal of the Bible, and that he was not antag-
onistic as some of the rough men on the
train were.

Finally Leah said, "How is it you never
married, Ty?"

"I was married."

"I didn't know that," Leah said quickly.

"Well, some people might not call it that."

The sounds of the camp overlaid the
night. A fiddle played, and the sound of a
zither came faintly to them. Someone was
singing a song, but the words could not be
made out. Leah put her gaze on Sublette.
"When was this, Ty?"

Sublette said quietly, "Her name was
Lanonta. She was a Crow. We had a son
and we named him Ty, like me." He sat there
quietly watching the fire, a big man with long
and broad bones, and a face whipped by
the wind. He was usually optimistic but now
sadness was on him, as the couple saw.
They waited for him to speak, and finally he
said abruptly, "They both died of cholera a
day apart." He got up and left silently, not
making a sound.

Leah whispered, "How tragic!"

"I wondered why he was so quiet. Must
be hard." Mark shook his head.

Reaching over, Leah took Mark's hand. "We'll have to pray for him," she whispered.

It was exactly the middle of May when the train reached Big Springs. They were worn thin by the travel now, and Horace Farr asked Sublette, "What about up ahead?"

"The easy part's behind us, Horace. It gets tougher from here on."

Ellen Farr was trying to cook with buffalo chips and finding it difficult. These chips could only be brought to blaze in a well-drafted fire pit, so successful cooking called for a new improvised skill. Horace had been amused at his wife on one occasion. Having kneaded her dough, she watched and nursed the fire, holding an umbrella over it and the skillet for nearly two hours. "You're a stubborn woman, Ellen Farr," he remarked.

"I'm going to have bread or know the reason why!"

Trouble with the Indians had not come as they had expected. The Platte valley lay in kind of a no-man's-land between the warlike Pawnee to the north and the Cheyenne to the south. Nevertheless, precautions were always taken according to Sublette's directions. The wagons were drawn up into a corral in every campsite, and Sublette saw to it that the guards were posted around the corral perimeter. Late one afternoon after camp had just been made, Jordan looked up to see a group of Indians that had appeared from nowhere.

"Look, Colin!" Ellen said with alarm. "Indians!"

Colin took one glance and snatched up his rifle. He stepped outside the wagon train followed by Jordan, and others who had come forward, all of them armed.

The Indians were not impressive. They wore odds and ends of white man's clothes along with their breechcloths and made a rather sorry sight.

"What do you want?" Colin said loudly.

"Want food."

"There's nothing for you," Colin said. He was aware that others had gathered beside him.

"Take it easy, hoss." Colin turned to see that Sublette had come.

Right beside him was Al Catlow. "Good time to take some Indian scalp."

"No trouble, Al." Sublette stepped forward and said softly, "These are Caw. No trouble." He lifted his hand in a peace sign, and the leader who wore a blanket around him gave him the like signal.

Horace Farr came to stand beside Sublette. "What about it, Ty?"

"We'll just give them a little grub."

"We'll give them nothing," Al Catlow snapped. "I'm surprised you're so tender-hearted about Indians. I mind once when the Sioux nearly lifted your scalp. You weren't thinkin' about givin' them food then, Ty."

"That was different. These fellows aren't dangerous."

Catlow made an ominous shape as he stood facing Sublette. There was a wildness in him that lay only a little beneath the surface. He had a tough face, and there was an arrogance in his hazel eyes as he stared at Sublette.

As for Sublette, he had turned to face Catlow, waiting to see which way the man would jump. He knew Catlow was unpredictable as dynamite. Anything could set him off, so he just simply stood there waiting to see what the big man would do.

Catlow seemed to be toying with the idea of having it out, but then he laughed roughly and said, "You nurse 'em if you want to,

Sublette. They'll be back and steal us blind, Farr. You'll see it."

"I think Catlow's right," Colin said quickly. His eyes had not left the Indians. "We'll give them nothing."

Sublette studied Colin for a moment, then said, "I killed an antelope this afternoon. That'll make 'em happy. It won't take anything away from the train." He turned and spoke to the Caw using mostly sign language and a few guttural sounds. The Indians nodded, and Sublette disappeared. He came back with the carcass of the antelope which had not been dressed, gave it to the Indian, and said a few words. The Indians watched him for a moment, nodded, said something, then turned their horses away.

Ace Barnhill stared at Sublette. "I didn't know you cared so much about Indians."

"They're no harm. Later on we may run into some tougher fellows. No point sharpening your horns on people like that."

The crowd broke up, and Jordan said quietly, "I'm glad Ty didn't let the men hurt those poor people."

Colin gave her a dissatisfied look. "He's too soft. I wouldn't have thought it of him." He was edgy and said no more, but for some reason Jordan was unhappy with him. She knew he had a gentle side, but for the first time she'd seen a hardness in him—and it troubled her. She wished he'd shown more compassion for the Indians. The hardness in his eyes as he'd spoken of them gave her a glimpse into a side of his character she hadn't seen.

Now she thought, *I'm being silly—we're all just tired and a little too sensitive.* But the incident had sobered her, and she found she could not forget Colin's callous hatred of the ragged Indians.

THIRTEEN

Jordan stirred briefly, opening her eyes enough to note that the blackness of night had begun giving way to the pale gray in the east. She lay beside Colin, not moving lest she disturb him. Lying there on the bed that they had made in the wagon, Jordan felt a sense of satisfaction with herself and with life in general. She had, as all young women, thought about marriage, the physical side of it, and had been apprehensive about what her response would be. She had had no experience, aside from a few brief embraces and torrid kisses, but this was different.

Now she stretched her toes out, arched her body slightly, and smiled in the growing light. She was alive in the fullest sense of the word and had been able to meet Colin's hungers with an equal passion. Although such things were not talked about among young women of her class, she had sensed that some women did not experience the same receptiveness that had been hers. Turning over on her side, she studied

Colin's profile, and even in the darkness with his hair tousled and mussed there was a handsomeness about him that pleased her. She liked to think that she would have loved him even if he were not so good-looking, but his good looks were a part of what he was. Once the thought had come to her, *What if he were in an accident that marred his face? Would I still love him?* She knew now after their brief interlude of marriage that she would, and it was not his good looks that had made her come to him night after night and to think of him during the day.

From outside the wagon, she heard the stirring of early risers and knew that soon the rifle would sound from the guard signaling to the train to stir and to begin moving. But now for this moment, Jordan lay there simply soaking up the quietness and thinking of the days that had passed and of those to come.

Rowena mewed loudly and came to lie on her chest. She had started doing this at the first of the drive, and seemed to enjoy batting at Jordan's closed eyes as if to waken her. Jordan smoothed the soft fur and felt the tiny rumble as the kitten began to purr.

This was one of Colin's gifts to her, and she knew she'd love Rowena as long as she lived for this reason.

Colin stirred, shifted his body, and reached for her even in sleep. A smile curled up the corners of Jordan's lips. She reached out and brushed a lock of his black hair from his forehead, and even as she did the sudden explosion of a gun on the outside of the camp somewhere broke the silence.

"Time to wake up, husband."

Colin groaned and shut his eyes more tightly. He would have pulled up the coverlet and gone immediately back into a deep sleep, but Jordan put her hands on his face and shook it gently. "Wake up. You can't sleep all day."

Colin's eyes opened as he struggled to come into the world of wakefulness. He shook his head as if to clear it of cobwebs, then his eyes opened to slits. "I don't want to get up." Usually he came awake filled with energy, but he had stayed awake until the small hours of the morning, engaged in a poker game with the Grattons and some other men.

"You have to. We've got to cook breakfast and get ready to leave." She stroked his face and ran her hand over his thick curls in a loving gesture.

Colin turned to face her and drew her close. "I don't want to get up. Hire Corny to ride herd for me today."

"Oh, Colin, that would look bad."

"Man wants to sleep, what's bad about— ow." Colin slapped at Rowena, who had swiped at Colin, catching his nose with her tiny claws.

"You crazy cat!" He slapped at the kitten, knocking her roughly against the canvas top.

"Colin! You hurt her!" Jordan cried. She put her hands out and took the kitten, holding her to her breast.

"That cat has never liked me!"

"You didn't have to hit her. She's so little!" Hurt was in Jordan's eyes as she stared at Colin. She had loved the kitten from the first, not least of all because she was Colin's gift to her. Now she glared at him, angered by the cruelty of his blow.

Colin had lost more than he could afford in the poker game, and was in a bad humor. He liked the kitten well enough, but his nose was bleeding and he snapped, "I wish I'd never gotten that blasted cat!"

His words hurt Jordan, and she turned

away from him, holding Rowena close. She could never abide cruelty to animals, and it shocked her to find that Colin had a brutal streak in him. Tears rose to her eyes, and she put Rowena in her cage and began to dress, saying nothing.

Colin stared at her, and said stiffly, "I didn't hurt the cat." When she didn't answer, a stubborn line straightened his lips. "All right, if you want to be that way!"

The two dressed in silence, and then Jordan gave Colin one reproachful look. Picking up the kitten's cage, she left the wagon without a word. Colin dressed, leaped out of the wagon, and moved over to where Jordan was beginning to put together a meal. He saw the stiff set of her back and felt her resentment. "No breakfast for me," he said gruffly, and walked away to saddle Caesar.

Jordan looked up to watch him leave, then went to take Rowena out of the cage. The kitten mewed and began to lick her nose as Jordan held her up. "He didn't mean to hurt you, Rowena," she whispered. She stroked the silky fur for a moment, struggling with the grief that blotted out her happiness. "It was just a little thing—he didn't mean it!" she whispered, but she knew she had seen a side of her husband that she wished were not there.

Gus slapped the huge oxen on the shoulder. "Be still, Castor. Be good for a change." He laid the yoke on Castor's shoulders, pinned the bow, and then spoke to the teammate. "Come on, Pollux. Your turn." Pollux moved forward obediently, and Gus laughed. "Odd to me how that the female is more stubborn than the male." It was a satisfaction to him to handle stock, and now as he finished yoking the pair, he pulled his watch from his pocket and glanced at it. "Six-forty."

As he moved about gathering chips and starting the fire, he was aware of the camp coming alive around him. There was always a sound and a bustle as men were striking tents and loading wagons. There was the sound of the oxen as they gave their soft calls from time to time. The women were cooking, and the smoke of small fires was rising all around the circle of wagons.

Gus had always liked morning best of all, and now as he moved to get breakfast started he had a sense of purpose. He was a man who had traveled aimlessly over a great deal of country. Now, however, this trip seemed to be more purposeful. He did not know what was coming, but somehow he felt that he had found the right place to be.

Returning to the wagon, he found Jordan holding her kitten, her face pressed against the white fur. "Morning, Miss Jordan."

"Good morning, Gus."

Gus, noting that her voice was muted, saw that she was unhappy. "How about I fix breakfast this morning?"

"I'm not hungry, Gus." She hesitated and added, "Colin's already gone, so don't fix anything for us." She kept her face averted as she put the kitten back in the cage. "Would you mind driving the wagon again today? I'd like to take Princess and go on out ahead of the train."

"Be proud to."

As Jordan left to saddle her mare, Gus moved about setting things in order. He was a handy man in all ways, which was a good thing, for Colin paid little attention to such things. When the breakfast was ready, which this morning was fried ham and eggs and some leftover biscuits that Gus warmed in a Dutch oven, Gus saw Colin coming, leading his stallion. "Breakfast is ready," Gus called out. He saw Colin hesitate, then come and look down at the food. He had a strained look on his face, but sat down and took the plate Gus handed him. Gus noticed that although Colin ate well enough there was something that seemed to be troubling him. He waited and finally said, "It's going to be a good day."

"It'll be like all the rest of them." There was a discontent in Colin's voice that caught Gus's attention. "Every day's just alike. I didn't think it'd be like this."

"Why, I'm enjoying the trip myself."

"Maybe you are, but I guess I was at sea too long. Wasn't made to eat dust every day."

Gus sensed that there was a discontentment in Colin Bryce that he had seen before in other men. He was a rather astute student of human nature and had learned to know men very well—women not so well. He observed Colin bolt his food then walk away without a word, his face stiff.

The train swung into motion, and the voices of children mingled with those of their elders. The clatter of the wagons began as the oxen and mules surged forward, the oxen bawling out steadily. Underneath this sound Jordan was aware of the steady hum of mosquitoes and slapped at her neck as one of them bit her. "It's going to be a nice day," she said to herself. She put the mare at a trot and soon had passed several hundred yards ahead of the rest. She slowed down then, enjoying the view. There were a few wildflowers yet to be seen, the air was crisp, and she felt good.

A sudden sign of a horse approaching drew her attention. She turned around and saw Ace Barnhill pull his big stallion up beside her. There was a rough handsomeness about him, and he said, "Good day for riding."

"Good morning, Ace. Yes, it is."

She had gotten to know the Barnhills well, for their wagon was only three behind hers. She had become good friends with Avis Barnhill and Cornwall, her blonde stepson.

He brought his horse to hers, so close that his knee touched hers. When she pulled Princess away, he laughed. "I wouldn't think a woman on her honeymoon would be so scary about a man."

It was an innocent enough remark, but something about the way Ace said it and the rashness of his smile warned Jordan. She did not answer but said, "I wonder when we'll see buffalo."

"Any day now. How's married life? You enjoy being a wife?"

Jordan knew at that instant that Barnhill was making a move toward her. She suspected he had known many women and been successful, but now she turned to him and put her cool eyes upon him. "I don't discuss my private life with anyone." She kicked the mare's sides, and Princess leaped forward. She heard Ace laugh and say, "I'll see you later, Jordan. We'll talk about it."

The encounter disturbed Jordan. She found herself disliking Barnhill and determined to stay as far away from him as possible.

Jordan pulled her mare up next to Sublette and he nodded. "Going to have a rain," he said. He pulled his pipe from his pocket, packed it, and lit it, shielding the bowl of it with his hand from the light breeze. He said no more, for there were times, Jordan had discovered, when a silence lay over him that he would not break. It was not awkward, and she suspected it had come from his days in the mountains trapping.

Finally she asked him, "What was it like being a mountain man?"

"Too much to eat or nothing at all. But mostly it was being ready for trouble. That was it. The trouble was always there. It got so the hair on the back of my neck stood up and wouldn't lay down." He turned to smile at her briefly. "But no more trapping for me."

"I can't see you as a farmer. Is that what you'll do?"

"I guess I will. I'm old enough."

"How old are you, Ty?"

"Thirty-six."

The two rode along. She had learned that he had an insight into people that was rare so she asked, "What about the Ellencourts?"

"What about them?"

"Have you been sorry that you threw in? I know you came just to help Mark out."

"I owed his father a debt. I always like to pay my debts."

"They're a strange couple to me," Jordan said.

"What do you mean 'strange'?"

"Well, she seems somehow stronger than her husband."

"Physically she is. He's a sick man. Had no business coming on this trip, but he said God told him to."

"Do you believe God tells people things?"

"Can't say. He never told me anything. Of course I haven't put myself in a position to listen."

He suddenly turned to her and said, "What about you? Do you think God talks to people?"

"Yes, I do. Not with the voice so much, although I guess that's possible, too. But sometimes I know when the Lord wants me to do something."

"Must be comforting."

She shifted her glance toward him quickly, wondering if he was making fun, but there was a sober light on his face. She tried to think of an answer but none came.

They rode together for over an hour, and she was amazed at how the time went by. She watched his eyes go from point to point, never stopping, and finally he lifted his arm and said, "Look over there."

She saw something break the horizon— small bumps, almost dots. "What is it? Is it mountains?"

"Buffer."

"You mean—buffalo?"

"Yes. We'll eat well tonight."

"Can I watch you kill one?"

"Sure, but we'll wait until late this afternoon just before camping time. That way I can drive one into camp and shoot it so we don't have to haul it."

Jordan rode back to camp at noon. As soon as she rode up and dismounted, Colin came to her. Taking her hand he said, "I was wrong this morning, Jordan."

At once Jordan felt a lifting of the heaviness that had been with her all day. "It's all right, Colin."

"No, it wasn't. I had no call to be mean to Rowena. I'm sorry. It won't happen again." He gave her a shamed look, muttering, "You should have shot me."

"Oh, Colin, it wasn't that bad!" She put her arms around him, and when he held her tightly, she whispered, "It's all right, sweetheart!"

Colin kissed her, relief sweeping across his face. "I hope we never have another fight. I've felt like a varmint all day!"

"We won't!"

"Next time I act up, just hit me with something!"

Jordan laughed, her eyes misty. "All right, I will. Now, let's eat and make up."

"I thought it was 'kiss and make up.'"

"We'll do that, too!"

Gus joined them for lunch, and they all ate hungrily. Jordan told the men about the buffalo. "Ty says he'll wait until just before we camp, drive one in, and shoot it."

"Are they that tame?" Colin stared at her.

"Ty says they are. He says they'll even mix with the herd and some of the herd will follow them off if the drovers aren't careful."

"I'd like to shoot a buffalo."

"Why don't you go out and ask Ty. I'll bet he'd show you how."

"I don't need anybody to show me how to shoot. You couldn't miss a beast that big."

"Oh, I'm sure you could do it. It's just that Ty said you could put a dozen bullets in the big things sometimes. If you don't hit them right, they just walk off." She knew that Colin hated to be bested by any man, so she smiled and said, "You go shoot me a big buffalo. I'll drive the wagon."

"This is the best thing I've ever eaten," Colin said. Some of the others had joined them and cooked the buffalo that he had shot earlier in the day. The Ellencourts were there along with Sublette, Paul Leverett, and his brother, Les. Bryce had dropped the buffalo with one shot, and Ty had told him, "Not many do that the first time. You're a good shot, hoss." The phrase had pleased Colin, and now he took another bite. "Never thought I'd like to eat a buffalo tongue."

"Best part," Sublette said. He was sitting cross-legged eating slowly and held up a bite that he had speared with the point of his knife. "I like the liver best myself."

Paul Leverett turned to Les. "Not bad having somebody else shooting the game and cooking it for us."

Les Leverett winked at him. "Maybe we could do it every night. How about it, Sublette?"

"Ask Bryce there. It's his buffalo."

Paul leaned back and stared at Sublette. "It's rougher up ahead, you say, Ty?"

"Pretty tough—but we'll make it." He lit his pipe, then added, "There's one section that I'm already worried about. It's called Sublette's Cutoff."

"Named after you?" Leverett demanded.

"No, after a distant relative. It's as tough

as anything on the trail. Very little water and lots of cattle have died—people, too."

Later when Sublette walked away to check the stock, Paul said, "I'm glad that fellow is along." He took another bite of the meat, then added, "I'm surprised that we haven't had more trouble than we have."

"It'll come, Doc," Colin said, and a moody light touched his eyes. "Trouble always comes."

FOURTEEN

Sublette slanted his body sideways in the saddle as his eyes went over Fort Laramie. From where he sat he noted the slope to the southeast, and his eyes picked up the forts themselves, which had an almost pristine whiteness in the afternoon sun. Long shadows from the trees were beginning to fall, and he shifted his gaze to take in the camp where the Sioux had pitched their tepees. His eyes narrowed as memories came drifting back to him from the past. He had respect for this tribe as being, perhaps, the fiercest fighters on the plains. They did not bother him, however, for he knew that they would be good Indians this close to the fort. He watched as the copper-skinned children ran between the lodges shouting, playing their games as all children do. The men and the women moved more slowly in the shadow of the tepees, and the skeleton-thin Indian dogs moved about searching for scraps.

"I'm glad to see the fort, Ty." Paul Leverett sat on his horse rather awkwardly, like a man who did not feel completely at home. Indeed he did not, for he was a man of the city, of carriages and buggies, and the trip across the plains had not been easy on him. Even now his face seemed thin from the strain of the trip. He lifted his hat and ran his hands through his crisp brown hair, and his gray eyes fastened on the Indian camp. "Are they dangerous?"

"No, they'll be good Indians as long as they're this close to the soldiers."

Leverett turned to face Sublette and envy came to him. He admired the tall, rangy hunter and wished that he had some of the toughness that Sublette bore so lightly. Ty Sublette was not a man, Leverett had learned, easily touched by small problems. He was, however, a man greatly troubled by deeper things than those on the surface.

Now, though, there was a lightness about Sublette, and his mood was easy. "I'm glad to see Laramie, Doc," he said. "Some folks are running low on supplies."

"I hope they've got medicines of some kind here. I didn't bring near enough." Leverett ran his eyes over the fort and glanced at the wagons that were rolling forward. "Not much of a town, is it?"

"Not to you, I guess." As he sat his horse, who stood grazing on the thin grass, Sublette was flooded suddenly with memories. He remembered how he had seen this country for the first time, wild and young himself. There hadn't been a post on it then or any tame Indians—only buffalo, beaver, and the long grass waving in the bottoms. The wind had had a lonesome sound to it, and the emptiness of space had filled a man up with something he had never been able to find.

"What are those hills over there, Ty?"

"The Black Hills. Pretty country. Over there's the Red Butte. You can't see them from here, and then the Sweetwater and farther than that the Southern Pass. I spent a lot of time there once trapping beaver."

"What's over that way?"

"The Popo Agie. Prettiest river I ever saw."

"Well, I'm going on into the fort. You coming with me?"

Sublette did not have time to answer, for the sound of a horse approaching at a fast pace turned him around. He relaxed as he saw Ira Barnhill riding up on his large stallion. "Leverett, I'd like for you to stop by and see my wife."

"What's wrong with her, Ira?"

"I don't know. She's feelin' poorly."

"All right. I will."

Barnhill studied the doctor with a trace of intolerance in his glance. It was a way he had toward men of education. He had none himself but had accumulated a great deal of money as some uneducated men will. He was what some called "country smart." He had an excellent memory and a quick eye for the main chance. Impatient, prideful, quick to take offense, he was a hard man to get along with, and now he hesitated as if he wanted to say something else. Then something came to his eyes, and he turned his horse and rode toward the fort without another word.

"Strange fellow," Leverett said.

"He's tough enough. He'll make out all right."

"Well, I'll go see how Mrs. Barnhill's doing, then I guess I'll go into the fort."

Sawing on the reins, Leverett managed to get his horse turned around. He kicked the animal in the sides, and the sorrel turned his head and looked at him curiously. A flush came to the doctor's face, and he turned quickly to see if Sublette was laughing at him. "I wish I could ride a horse better." He saw no sign of humor in the eyes of the tall man, but then Sublette was not a man who showed things easily. "I feel like a fool."

"You can do other things," Sublette murmured. "And you'll learn how to ride. I'm glad you're on this trip, Doc."

The phrase pleased Leverett. He nodded and laughed shortly. "Well, if I can just learn to stay on top of a horse, I'll be all right, I suppose." The sorrel moved forward at a leisurely pace headed generally in the direction of the camp, and Leverett rode with his back tense, expecting the animal to pitch at any minute.

Guiding the sorrel through the camp, he saw Theodore Barnhill unhooking a yoke of oxen and pulled up the horse. "Your father asked me to stop by. He said Mrs. Barnhill's not feeling well."

"She ain't right pert," Theodore said. He looked so much like his father that the resemblance was startling. He looked exactly as the fifty-one-year-old Barnhill must have looked at twenty. "Go on in," he said. "Maybe she needs a tonic." He watched as the doctor swung out of the saddle. "I'll tie up your animal."

"Thanks," Leverett said shortly. He went to the back of the wagon and saw that it was covered with a cloth of some kind. "Mrs. Barnhill?"

"Who is it?"

"It's me, Dr. Leverett."

The cloth moved back, and Avis Barnhill's face appeared, framed by the darkness of the interior of the wagon.

"Your husband said you weren't feeling well."

"I'm all right." Avis's face was a mirror which changed as her feelings changed, and now Leverett saw discontent in her large dark eyes. She drew the curtain back fully and examined him with a strange expression. "Come in," she said.

Leverett hoisted himself up on the back of the wagon, pushing the covering aside. He took in the crowded space containing all sorts of household equipment piled as high as the canvas would permit. The bed was between all of this, a feather mattress covered with a turkey red quilt. Avis moved back and sat cross-legged, the cotton dress outlining the half fullness of her breast. The dim light was kind to her, showing the full, soft lines of her figure, and she studied him in a way that, for some reason, made him nervous.

"Your husband thought I ought to drop in."

"No reason for it. I'm just feeling poorly."

Stretching his hand forth, Leverett pressed two fingers against the side of her neck and caught the beat of her heart. "Do you sleep well?" he asked.

"As well as anyone."

"The trip's been hard on you."

"Hard on all of us. Hard on you, too."

The flesh of her neck was soft and at the same time firm. Something about the intimacy of the touch disturbed Leverett, and he withdrew his hand quickly. The action brought a small smile to the lips of Avis Barnhill. She said nothing, however, and then asked abruptly, "You're not married, are you?"

"No."

"Ever been married?"

"No, not that either. Why do you ask?"

"Women are always curious about things like that. Did Ira think there was something particularly wrong with me?"

"I don't think so. What's your complaint?"

"Nausea. I was sick this morning."

Leverett's eyes narrowed. "You know what that might mean."

"A baby. But I hope not."

"Most women want babies."

"I don't. Not now anyway." She started to say something else but paused and turned her face away from him.

He said, "I can examine you, but it's probably too soon to tell."

Turning back to him, Avis made a thin, white line with her lips. "I never should have married."

The statement caught Leverett off guard. He knew there was a wide discrepancy of age between the two. They also somehow seemed mismatched, although he had thought it was just age. "You're just discouraged," he said finally.

Avis shook her head. "No, I made a mistake." She suddenly laughed, and the sound was pleasant in the closeness of the wagon. "I've never said that to anyone, but I guess doctors are different. People tell you everything, don't they?"

"Sometimes."

"I guess women have tried you too, haven't they?"

A warm flush rose to Leverett's cheeks. He did not answer. His response seemed to amuse Avis.

"You seem almost afraid of women. Are you?"

"No," Leverett said shortly. "Why would you think that?"

"Just a notion that came to me."

Leverett studied her face for a moment, noting the turn of her lips. She had a pleasantly expressioned mouth, though at the moment it was not so. "I suppose most women aren't completely happy in their marriages."

"That's a dark point of view. I might as well tell you the rest. I married him because I had to get away from the life that I had. My name was Satterfield. My folks were sharecroppers, poor as dirt. I never knew what it was to have a dress that wasn't handed down to me. I didn't have shoes to wear to school. There was never enough to eat, and I spent all my time taking care of the babies that came to my ma every year. Everyone felt sorry for us. I couldn't stand to go to town because I didn't want to be seen."

Leverett listened as the words suddenly poured out of Avis's lips. It was not unusual for a patient to confide in a doctor, especially, it seemed, in this circumstance. She was right also in that some women had tempted him, but he had always managed to avoid becoming involved with any of them. Now, however, he knew there was some danger, for something in the attractiveness of the woman drew him.

"Anyway, Ira asked me to marry him. He had money and a fine house, so I did."

"Not uncommon, I guess."

"It was a mistake." Her words were flat, and she shook her head. "There's nothing wrong with me. You may as well go."

He felt a sudden flash of pity for the woman, and without thinking he reached out and took her hand. It was warm and firm, and she returned his pressure. "You'll be all right," he said, and the words sounded inane. He did not speak, nor did she. Her hand was an extension of herself, and he noted the richness of her lips again and how she studied him with a half-lidded attention. A sudden desire came to him, sweeping over him in a way that he had never known. Instantly he dropped her hand. "Well," he said, "I'll be getting along."

Avis studied him as he edged backward. "The women on the train don't like it that you're single."

"Why do they care?"

"They want to see every available man married. They'd love to catch you mixed up with some woman."

"They won't." The words seemed to hang

in the air, and Leverett felt uncomfortable. "Maybe you need a tonic. I'll fix you up something."

"Never mind. I'll be all right."

As Leverett crawled out of the wagon, he found Theodore Barnhill watching him carefully, a bland expression in his eyes. Cornwall, the youngest of the boys, had come to stand beside his brother.

"Doesn't seem to be much wrong with her," Leverett said.

"Maybe she's going to have a baby," Corny murmured.

"Maybe. I can't tell yet." Leverett sensed a tenseness in the situation. Nodding, he said, "I'll bring some tonic back. It might help settle her stomach."

He turned and led his horse away, and wild thoughts ran through his mind. It was a long way to Oregon, and he knew, somehow, that this meeting with Avis Barnhill would be with him in his thoughts and in his memory.

As the doctor walked away, Corny's eyes followed him, then he glanced at the wagon. "You reckon she is going to have a baby, Theodore?"

"I hope not. We don't need a squalling youngun around here."

Corny did not answer but finally turned away, a thoughtful young man unsure of himself, intimidated by his rougher brothers and especially by his father. He murmured, when he was out of the hearing of Theodore, "It wouldn't be bad to have a baby. I think it'd be nice."

"How long do you think we'll stay in Laramie?" Jordan's eyes were bright, and she turned to Colin as the two reached the outer edge of the fort. The idea of being in town was exciting to her. "I hope we stay a few days."

"I doubt if we'll stay more than a couple of days."

"But Laramie's about halfway, isn't it, to Oregon?"

"I don't think it's that far. We've only come about six hundred miles."

"How far to go?"

"Ty says maybe thirteen hundred—and they're the worst miles. I'll be glad when we get there, Jordan. This trip's getting on my nerves."

Quickly Jordan glanced at Colin's face. There was an impatience about him that she had noted, and now she said, "Are you sorry we came?"

"No, not sorry." He turned and smiled at her, his dark blue eyes fond, and he reached out and put his arm around her. Squeezing her, he said, "It's just a nice, long honeymoon."

She leaned against him as they walked along, and then they entered the fort. "I never thought I'd be so glad to see a town. You know what I miss on the trail?"

"What?"

"Chairs. It's either lie down on a bed or sit on the ground or ride a horse. I'm anxious to sit down on a real chair."

Colin laughed at her. "I miss a lot more than a chair. What do you want to do now?"

"Oh, just look at the store and do a little shopping."

"I'm not much for that." He reached into his pocket, took out some coins. "Get what you need, but nothing very heavy."

"What are you going to do?"

"I guess I'll find Ty, and we'll look the fort over."

"All right. You have a good time."

* * *

Sublette caught a glimpse of Jordan as she sat on a chair on the porch in front of the general store. He saw no sign of her husband and after a brief hesitation, turned and walked over to her. "Hello. You look mighty comfortable."

Jordan smiled at him. "I told Colin the one thing I missed was a chair to sit in." She laughed suddenly. "Isn't that a foolish thing?"

"Not so foolish." Sublette leaned against the post that supported the awning that shaded the front of the store. "Been buying things, I see."

"Yes, I have. Not like being at home when you can run down to the store if you need something. Where's the next town?"

"Fort Hall. Not that you'd call it a town. At least there'll be some kind of a store, but not much of one."

"Is the way hard, Ty?"

"Pretty rough."

Sublette smiled suddenly, and his teeth struck a white flash against his dark tan. "What are you thinking right now, Jordan?"

"Oh, about what it will be like when we get to Oregon. What's it like, Ty?"

"Heaviest stand of timber in America, I do think. It's going to take a lot of sweat to cut those trees down and make a farm." He studied her for a moment, then suddenly squatted down on his heels. He wrapped his heavy arms around his knees to keep his balance thrown forward and tilted his head back to look up at her. "It's a long way and a hard way. When we get there it will still be hard. Are you ready for that?"

"Yes."

"You seem mighty sure. You were a town woman, weren't you?"

"Yes, I was, but I can be a farmer's wife."

She faced him fully then, and the determination showed in her eyes. He smiled slowly. "I think you'll make it, but it won't be like you think. Things never are."

"What does that mean?"

"Well, a man gets an idea in his head—or a woman, too, I suppose—and he starts out to find the reality. And when he gets there and finds it, it's not like he thought it would be."

"You think things turn out badly."

"Most things do, I guess."

"I don't think so. Some do, of course," Jordan said thoughtfully. "But I want to believe that things can end happily." She laughed, a good laugh, rich and full, that seemed to bubble up. "I know you think I've been reading too many novels."

"I'm glad you're optimistic," Sublette said. "I hope you always are, but it's going to be a tough trip."

"I'm glad you're with us, Ty. Everybody is."

He did not answer but turned to watch the passersby. It was a mixture of Indians, mountain men, members of several wagon trains that were camped outside the fort, and once again he thought how empty this land had been when he had first seen it as a young man. He had an impulse to tell his feelings to the young woman before him but let it pass. "Where's Colin?"

"I expect he's in a poker game somewhere."

Something in her tone drew Sublette's attention. He stood to his feet and said, "I'll run him down. It's gettin' pretty late. You want me to help you carry that plunder back to the wagon?"

"No, I'll wait here for Colin. He'll come along soon enough. If you see him, tell him I'm ready to go."

"All right."

Sublette had already spotted the most likely place for a poker game. The sun was almost down now, but the yellow lights inside the Diamondback Saloon were glowing through the glass. He entered and saw Colin at once. He was seated at a table with four other men and did not look up until Ty had approached to stand beside him.

"Hello, Ty. Sit down and take a hand."

"Guess not." Sublette hesitated, then said, "Whenever you're through here, Jordan's ready to go back."

"I won't be long. I about got all the easy money."

A thin man with muddy brown eyes was sitting across the table from Colin. He wore a vest that would have attracted attention anywhere, multicolored and tight-fitting. His eyes glittered as he said, "You ain't leavin' here until you give me a chance to win my money back."

"This is Mitch Farrod, Ty. He was the best poker player in Laramie until I came along."

"Shut up and play, Bryce!"

Something in the thin man's demeanor alerted Sublette. He said nothing but kept his eyes fixed on the thin man. He stood there while two hands were played, Farrod losing heavily on both of them. "You win a little bit too easy, Bryce."

Colin was raking in the money that he had just won, but at the words he stopped suddenly, and his face grew cold. "What does that mean, Farrod?"

"You're a cheat!"

The room fell silent, and everyone's eyes went to Colin Bryce. It was an insult that no man could endure in this world. "You're a sore loser," Bryce said. His face was suddenly tight and somewhat flushed from drinking, and he rose to his feet. "I'm pulling out."

Farrod suddenly rose so swiftly that his chair fell over backward. "You're a cheat, I said!" He reached for the gun at his side, and he moved so swiftly that Bryce had no time to move. Sublette did, however. His arm shot out, and he knocked the gun upward. It exploded as the arm was at the top of the arch. Sublette grabbed the pistol, wrenched it from the thin man, and held it, saying, "Settle down, hoss." His words were quiet, but Farrod stared at him with pure venom in his muddy brown eyes.

"That's enough of that!" the owner of the saloon said. "If you got a fight, take it outside." He was a big man with a large stomach, and he had picked a shotgun from behind the bar.

Colin said, "We'll settle this outside, Farrod. I'll go get my gun."

"Come along, Colin," Ty said quickly. He pulled Colin outside, and when they were clear of the door, Ty said, "Let it go."

Anger had ruffled Colin Bryce's demeanor. Now he turned and said, "I ought to go back and take a shot at him."

"Better not."

Colin suddenly shook his head and turned to face the tall man. "Glad you were there, Ty. I wasn't even carrying a gun. Didn't expect trouble."

"Let it slide."

Colin glanced once more at the saloon, then said, "I guess I'd better go find Jordan."

"She was at the general store a few minutes ago. I'll see you later."

Colin said quickly, "Thanks, Ty. I think he would have gotten me if you hadn't been there."

Ty Sublette shook his head. "I'm glad it turned out like it did."

Colin would have said more in the way of thanks, but Sublette turned and walked quickly away. Colin hurried then to the store where Jordan rose to greet him. She saw his flushed face and his agitation. "What's wrong?" She listened as he told her, then he said, "If it weren't for Ty, I'd probably be dead."

Jordan felt a sudden fear. "Come on. Let's get out of this place."

As they made their way back down the street of the fort, Colin said, "That Ty, he's a good one and as tough as they come."

Jordan did not answer for a moment, then finally she said, "Yes, he is. Come on, Colin. I want to go have a meal at the restaurant. We can sit down in real chairs and eat."

Fort Laramie wasn't much, but it had made a pleasant break for the train. As Jordan bent over the bacon sizzling in the skillet, she felt a sudden reluctance to head out into the wilderness again. A nudging against her leg brought her attention, and she smiled down at Rowena. "You're nothing but a worthless beggar," she said, but at once put down her fork and picked the kitten up. Rubbing her face against the silky fur, she whispered, "You've got to be better to your papa—you hear me?" For some reason, Rowena had taken a dislike to Colin, and though he made light of it, she knew it bothered him.

"Breakfast ready?"

Turning quickly, Jordan saw Colin watching her, a smile on his lips—and a cane-bottomed chair in his hands. He held it up, saying, "Happy birthday."

"Colin!" Jordan cried and ran to him, ignoring the claws that Rowena dug into her shoulder. "Is it for me?"

"You can sit down as much as you want to now. Here, try it out."

Colin walked over to the fire, set the chair down, and grinned at her. "There, you lazy hussy. Now sit down and hush." He smiled as Jordan sat down, her face alight with pleasure. "I know it's not your birthday, but I wanted you to have it."

Jordan jumped up and plucked Rowena from her shoulder. Dropping the kitten to the ground, she threw herself into Colin's arms. "You're the best husband in the world!"

"No, I'm not, but I'm glad you think so."

Jordan kissed him, then said, "You sit down in that chair. I'm going to cook you the best breakfast you ever had!"

"What's that in the skillet? A burnt offering?"

"Oh, fuzz! I've burned that blasted bacon."

"Feed it to the cat. But then she's too snooty to eat it—" Colin broke off, for a wagon was approaching, coming from the direction of the fort. "Who's that, I wonder?" They both waited until the wagon drew to a halt. Colin stepped forward to say, "Morning. Can I help you?"

"Lookin' for the wagon master." The speaker was a fair-haired man so fat that he overflowed the seat. A heavy woman sat beside him, obviously his wife. Both appeared to be in their mid thirties. A younger woman walked beside the wagon, the sun highlighting golden glints in her hair. "My name's Jesse Lee, and this here's my wife, Mary, and her sister, Jennie."

"I'm Colin Bryce, and this is my wife, Jordan. You need to see Horace Farr." Colin nodded. "His wagon's right in front of us. He's at the fort right now, but he'll be back soon."

Jordan stepped forward. "Get down and have some coffee."

"That'd be right nice." Lee got down ponderously, then helped his wife down. She was a short, round woman with light brown hair and a pair of bright blue eyes. "Don't want to be a bother." She smiled shyly.

"No trouble at all. If you haven't eaten, I can fix you something."

"We done et, but that coffee smells good."

Jordan found extra cups, listening as the man spoke with Colin. "We left with another train a month ago, but Mary here took sick, and we had to stay over at Laramie. We figgered to join up with you folks if it would be all right."

"Don't think it will be a problem," Colin said at once. "One more wagon won't make much difference."

Jordan handed two cups to the older couple, but then saw that the younger woman had picked up Rowena and was stroking her fur. She poured another cup, then advanced to where she stood by the wagon. "Here's some hot coffee." She extended the cup, but the woman paid her no heed. Awkwardly, Jordan extended the cup again. "Her name is Rowena." Still there was no response, at least for a moment. Then the woman turned to face her, and Jordan saw a startled look in her eyes.

"Oh, thank you," she said and reached out for the cup. Her voice was somehow strange, rather flat and toneless. "What's the kitten's name?" she asked, keeping her eyes on Jordan's face.

"Rowena is her name."

"Rowena—what a pretty name." She was a shapely woman, no longer a young girl. Jordan estimated she must be in her late twenties. Her eyes were blue-gray and her complexion was flawless. As she sipped the coffee, she kept her eyes fixed on Jordan's face, and suddenly it came to Jordan: *Why, she's deaf!*

"Do you like cats, Jennie?" Jordan spoke slowly, forming each word carefully, and saw that the young woman had no trouble understanding her.

"Oh, yes! And this one is beautiful." Jennie put her cheek against the smooth fur of the kitten, and her eyes glowed with pleasure. "I can feel her purring. What a nice sound that must be!"

Jordan had never known a deaf person well, and a sharp pang came to her. *I've always taken my hearing for granted—how awful not to hear voices!*

Mary Lee had watched the two women, and said, "She had scarlet fever when she was only fourteen. It took her hearing, but if she can see a person's lips, why it's a sight how she knows what's said."

"She's your sister, is she?" Colin asked.

"Yes. Her name's Jennie Town. She ain't never married. Guess she never will."

As the Lees waited for Farr to return, Jordan found it easy enough to speak with Jennie. The woman was very bright, and except for the flat tone of her voice and the fact that she kept her eyes fixed on a speaker's lips, she was normal.

Horace Farr returned, and was glad enough to have the Lees join the train. "Have to call a meeting of the council, but that's just a formality." He smiled. "You're qualified. Glad to have you with us."

"Me and Mary, we're musical," Jesse said. "I ain't too fat to play a fiddle."

"That'll go right well." Farr nodded. "Train needs a music maker." He turned then, hurrying to get the train under way.

Jordan said, "Why don't you get in line right behind us? You can keep Rowena with you if you like, Jennie."

Jennie Town smiled sweetly and stroked the kitten. "That would be nice. You'll like the music my sister and brother-in-law can make. Everybody does."

Later as Jordan put the chair into the wagon, she was thinking about the deaf girl. "It makes me sad, Colin—Jennie, I mean. She's so pretty, and she misses so much."

Colin nodded. "Too bad. Guess she'll never marry."

"Why not?"

"Man likes to talk to his wife. Be hard with a deaf woman." He saw that she was grieved, and put his arm around her. "She'll be fine. Now, you can think all day about sitting in your chair tonight."

FIFTEEN

Mornings had become hard on Colin. He had always been an early riser, but the trip had dulled him somehow. He was hard to arouse, and only after he had been up an hour did he feel human again. He forced himself out of bed and ate breakfast, saying hardly a word while Gus and Jordan chattered back and forth over the fire.

Without even a comment on how good the breakfast was, he rose and went at once to yoke the oxen. Picking up the heavy yoke, he pinned the bow and laid it across the neck of the oxen. After yoking the oxen, he glanced at his watch, noting that he was in good time. He glanced around, seeing that some were still striking their tents while others were ready to go. Leaning against Castor's side, he watched idly as the women did the little things necessary before leaving, scraping and scouring the breakfast things, then packing them into the wagons.

As the sun cast pale gleams over the camp, Colin thought, *I used to like getting up early—always my best time.* Somehow early rising was particularly hard on a wagon train, and many sharp things were spoken trying to get the train under way. The young ones sometimes cried or yelled, and over the usual noises was the steady hum of mosquitoes that made a canopy around every head.

Finally Colin shook himself and walked back to where Gus was yoking the other oxen to the second wagon. Colin was pleased with Dabney, for he was a cheerful fellow. The nondescript, rather homely fellow could do anything, it seemed. "Where did Jordan go, Gus?"

"She just went wandering around."

"She'd better not wander too far. We're going to want to get an early start."

"She's gonna ride that horse of hers today."

"All right," Colin said shortly.

As Jordan walked briskly toward the horse herd, she saw a woman standing watching, and her attention fastened on her. The woman was black, and there was some expression in her eyes that caught at Jordan. She slowed her pace, then with a decisive movement she went over to speak. "Hello. How are you this morning?"

The woman was coffee colored, attractive. She was strongly built and wore a calico dress but no bonnet. "Hello," she said rather breathlessly. Something showed through her eyes, and she swallowed for a moment. "You going with this wagon train, you and your man?"

"Yes, I am. Do you live here at the fort?"

"No, ma'am, I don't. My name's Rosie Smith. My husband—he named Cato. We don't live here."

The words puzzled Jordan. She could see that something was troubling the woman, and she realized how little she knew about what went on in the minds of black men and women. Her family had been opposed to slavery, and all those who worked on their place were free. Now the woman was staring at her with a wistful expression, as though she wished to speak but was nervous. Jordan said, "My name's Jordan Bryce."

"I'm right pleased to know you, Miss Bryce." The woman started to speak but then dropped her head and said, "We done have a hard time."

"What's wrong, Rosie?"

Looking up, Rosie Smith said with pain making a note in her voice, "We done been freed by Mr. Jefferson back in Tennessee. My husband, he says we got to get away. There's gonna be bad trouble."

"I expect he's right. Where are you headed?"

"Cato, he said we'd go to Oregon. He says there's land there to be had. He's a hard worker, Miss Bryce. All we want is a chance."

"Did you start out by yourself, Rosie?"

"Oh, no. We got on with a wagon train, but—" Rosie's voice faltered, and then a painful expression crossed her face. "They threw us off the train—the last one that went through."

"Why'd they do that?"

"Some of the men didn't like black people."

Jordan was an impulsive young woman. She said, "Where's your husband?"

"He's right over there. That's our wagon."

"Those are good-looking animals, and you have spares, too."

"Yes. Mr. Jefferson give us some money, and we worked a long time. So now we want to go, but we can't get there alone, Cato says."

"Come on. Let me meet your husband."

Rosie shot a quick look at Jordan. There was hope in it for the first time, and she said quickly, "Yes, ma'am."

The two women passed to the outside of the train where a single wagon stood. A very large black man stood there, well over six-three, Jordan guessed, and weighing nearly two hundred pounds. He had powerful arms and shoulders, and there was an alertness about him as the two came up. He did not speak but waited until his wife said, "This is Miss Bryce, Cato. I been tellin' her about our troubles."

Cato bowed his head. "Mighty pleased to know you, Miz Bryce."

"I'm glad to know you, Cato. What are you going to do? Go back?"

"No, ma'am. We ain't gwine back to Tennessee," Cato Smith said firmly. "Dey's gonna be a war there some day over slavery. I knows that much, an' I don't want no part of it. I just wants to work and raise some chilluns. Me and Rosie will make out fine if we can just get to Oregon."

The plight of the couple touched Jordan, and she said, "Let me talk to my husband. I'd like to see you join our train."

Hope sprang into the eyes of the huge black man. "That would be mighty fine, Miz Bryce. I'd be mighty thankful, me and Rosie."

"You wait here, and I'll go find him." Turning, Jordan ran lightly back to the wagon and found Colin already on the seat. "Colin!" she said. "I've got to talk to you." She scrambled up in the seat and began talking very rapidly. She did not notice how disgruntled Colin looked, for she was accustomed to his bad moods in the morning.

Finally she said, "We ought to make room for them on the train. They seem to be good people."

"They're black people," Colin said shortly.

"Why, yes, they're black, but they're in trouble, and we ought to help them."

If the timing had been better, Colin's reaction might have been different. Actually he had very little feelings about black people, but he had served on a slave ship on a voyage and had decided that blacks were totally unable to rise above what they were. Of course, he had seen them at their worst, crammed into a hold and dying by the dozens, frightened, not knowing where they were going. At the time he had thought that they would never be any more than animals.

"No! They can't go!"

Shocked at the harshness of his tone, the harshest that he had ever shown to her, Jordan was taken aback. She stared at him for a moment, and finally put her hand on his arm. "I know it's early, and you usually don't feel good. But I feel very strongly about this."

"They're like children. They can't take care of themselves."

"You don't know that, Colin. This man is very able. He's big, strong, and the woman, too. Their wagon is as good as any in the train, and they have extra animals."

"I don't care anything about that. It would cause nothing but trouble. You know there are Southerners on this train that hate black people."

"I don't hate them. Do you?"

Colin felt that he was being pushed into a position that he did not like. "I don't hate them," he said shortly. "But they're not going and that's that!"

Jordan stared at him as a sudden surge of anger swept over her. She was an easygoing young woman as a rule, but at the core of her being was a firm determination to do the right thing. Strange feelings stirred painfully through her, for she was suddenly aware that her marriage was being tested for the first time. Speaking in a low tone, she said, "We disagree about this. I think you're wrong, Colin."

"They're not going and that's that!" he repeated.

Jordan stared at him, and for that instant he seemed to be a stranger. She loved him with all of her strength, and pain rose in her as she knew that they had reached a crisis in their relationship. "I'm going to talk to the council," she said bluntly.

She got down and walked away without looking back. Colin almost spoke out, but he shook his head. *They'll never let Negroes go on this train. She'll just make a fool out of herself.*

The council had been having an informal meeting composed of Horace Farr, Pete Gratton, Dave Minton, and Ira Barnhill. Now she simply walked up to them saying, "I have something for the council to decide."

"Why, surely, Miss Bryce." Horace Farr smiled at her. "What is it?" He listened along with the others as Jordan explained the problem of the Smiths and ended by saying,

"I think we ought to let them go on the train."

Ira Barnhill said pugnaciously, "That won't do at all, Miss Bryce. If you knew Negroes like I do, you'd know better than to even ask."

"I've been around black people all my life, and I know good people when I see them."

"You don't know much if that's what you think! They'd steal us blind, and we'd have to take care of them," Barnhill said bluntly. "I'm sorry, but the answer is no."

"I'll have to appeal to the whole council then."

An argument began among the council members, and Jordan stood watching them. Farr and Dave Minton were in favor of taking the Smiths while Ira Barnhill and Pete Gratton were opposed. All were outspoken. Finally Barnhill said curtly, "That's all we'll have to hear about this!"

"No, it's not." Horace Farr was a strong opponent of slavery. "I think we're going to have to take a vote among the rest of the folks," he said quietly.

"Take a vote!" Pete Gratton stared at Farr with angry hazel eyes. Physically he was the more powerful man, but he knew people would not follow him as they did Farr, and it angered him. "We're not taking Negroes, and that's all there is to it!"

Farr stood there patiently listening but finally he said, "The council's split, and there's no other way but to take a vote."

"You could decide against it," Gratton said. "You're the captain of the train."

"Wouldn't care to do that. It won't take long." He turned and walked away leaving Gratton and Barnhill with angry expressions.

Jordan had been waiting, standing off while the men argued, and when Farr came up she said, "What did you decide, Mr. Farr?"

"We'll take a vote of the whole train."

Hope surged through Jordan, and she smiled. "I know this is your doing. They're really good people. Come along and meet them."

The two went to where the black couple stood waiting, and Farr stuck his hand out when Jordan introduced him. Cato Smith looked startled, but he put his massive hand out. It swallowed the hand of Horace Farr, but the pressure that the black man exerted was gentle. "We appreciate anything you can do for us, suh."

"Can't make any promises. It'll be up to the people of the train—and I have to warn you that there are some who don't want black people."

Cato Smith was silent for a moment, then he smiled, and the sadness of ages was in that smile. "I know, suh. It's always that way."

The word had spread rapidly among the families of the train, and within thirty minutes everyone who could get free from any duty had gathered to listen as Horace Farr set the matter before them. Farr cast his glance over the crowd and was doubtful of the outcome. During the trek thus far he had made it a point to meet everyone, and now he thought, *It's like every other crowd. There are some angels and some demons. I reckon we're about to find out whether our train has got more of one than the other.*

He lifted his hand and raised his voice. "All right, folks! Settle down now!" He waited until silence fell over the group and then cast his eyes at Cato and Rosie Smith. The couple were not with the group but stood far off to one side. They were, Farr saw, the object of glances—some curious, some malevolent. Knowing that talk would mean little, he said, "Folks, we have a tie in the council about a decision that's got to be made." Quickly he outlined the problem and ended by saying, "I don't propose to let this run on to a long-winded debate. The problem is simple. Do we let Smith and his wife go with the train or not?"

"I say not!" The speaker was Ace Barnhill. He stood beside his father and his brother Theodore. "One of the reasons we're going to Oregon is to get away from the argument about slavery, and I don't propose to take part of the problem with us."

Mark Ellencourt stepped forward. He looked small when contrasted with the rest of the men on the train, and there was a pallor on his face—the mark of sickness. He had never really recovered, and though he was able to travel now without lying in the bed of the wagon, his continued frailty was obvious. "I disagree with you, Barnhill. We can't solve problems by running away from them. I think we need to take these people along with us. They're in trouble, and all of us need help when we're in trouble."

"We don't need any sermons." Al Catlow was leaning against a wagon wheel, his hazel eyes burning with excess energy. "We don't need any more problems on this train, and I ain't sittin' down with no niggers."

The debate went on for some fifteen minutes, and finally Jordan could stand it no longer. She stood up and faced those who had, more or less, drawn together to oppose taking the Smiths. They were led by the Grattons and the Barnhills. "I've lived among black people all my life, and my people were always against slavery. I'm against it myself."

Her voice rang out loud and clear, and everyone in the train studied her. A quick flare of anger touched her eyes as she spoke, and a summer darkness lay over her skin. Her auburn hair flashed with red tints as she stood without a bonnet, and suddenly the thought came to Horace Farr, *Why, she's the kind of woman that could draw a pistol and shoot a man down if she had to. And then after it was over she could just go about her work and not go to pieces.* He admired her courage deeply, but as his eyes swept the group he saw that not everyone was so inclined. Ace Barnhill didn't attempt to conceal the anger that was building up in him. He jerked his hat off and slapped it against his side and muttered something to his father as Jordan spoke.

After Jordan had finished making a plea, Ace moved over and stood before her. He glanced over her shoulder at Colin, who was standing some distance behind Jordan. Colin had kept silent and hated it when Jordan spoke up, but he had determined simply to cast his vote against taking the pair.

"What do you think about this, Bryce? Your wife's doing all the talking."

Colin shifted his shoulders, and when he spoke his voice was cool like the strokes of a bell without a flaw. "I'm against it just like my wife's for it."

Jordan turned and looked at him. There was something in her eyes that he could not interpret, but a sadness came to him at that moment. He had been as happy with this woman as he had ever been in his life. Her touch and her voice had become necessary to him—as necessary as food or air. He had been a lonely man all of his life, but now he had found a harbor. And the matter of Cato Smith suddenly had dismembered that which he had valued above other things.

"You ought to take your wife in hand," Ace said, his eyes flaring as he stared at Bryce, a challenge in them. "Take a switch to her if she won't mind you."

Colin straightened suddenly and left his position. As he moved there was, as always, the slightly rocking gait learned from years at sea. He came up at once to stand before Barnhill, confronting him, and said in a mild voice, "You keep your remarks to yourself about my personal life, Ace."

Ace laughed, and a rash smile made his teeth look very white against his tan skin. He was totally confident, a larger man than Bryce. He had judged the ex-sailor by the things that were important in his world, and Bryce was a mediocre horseman and knew little about the West. This gave Barnhill a contempt for the man. "Man can't control his wife might as well put on skirts. I guess she's tellin' you how to vote."

Colin Bryce narrowed his eyes and stood there, a half smile pulling his lips into a long, tough line. He said so quietly that those at the outer edge of the group could not make out his words, "You say one more thing, Barnhill, and I'll break your neck."

Ace shoved his hat back and laughed. "You're all talk! Get over with the rest of the women."

Colin moved then with a speed that as- tonished the onlookers. One moment he was standing indolently, it seemed, and the next his arm shot out, and a blow, with all of his one hundred and eighty-five pounds behind it, struck Ace Barnhill squarely in the mouth. It drove Ace backwards, his arms cartwheeling, and he sprawled out on the ground, dazed for a moment. He shook his head and struggled to get to his feet, and as he did Bryce said, "Keep your mouth shut, or I'll break your neck!"

Barnhill had been stunned and shaken by the blow, but he was a fighter down to the bone. He got to his feet, cursed, and advanced toward Colin, who stood, his fists lifted slightly. Barnhill began to reach out with large searching lefts. Colin simply kept his arms up, taking the brunt of the blows on them and on his shoulders.

As always at a fight shouts went up, and Theodore Barnhill called, "Bust him up, Ace! Break his face!"

Bryce had been forced to become a fighter and had faced tough men while at sea. He dodged and ducked, and finally tiring of being unable to take the blows, he threw himself forward. His blows rained upon Barnhill, who was driven backward by the fury of them, and Barnhill gave ground and caught a vicious right in the chest which numbed him. He was tough enough, however, to ignore it, and as a return he caught Colin over the eye with a sharp, vicious right hand that opened up a cut. Instantly the blood began to flow, and Colin was blinded in that eye for a moment. He brushed the blood aside as the two threw blow after blow.

The dust rose in the air as the two men scuffled, and soon the skill of Barnhill began to tell. He landed blows that rocked Bryce backward.

The fight continued until both men were reaching for air. How it might have ended was never settled, for suddenly Theodore Barnhill stepped forward and struck Bryce a sharp blow in the neck that drove him to the ground.

Dave Minton, no fighter himself, ran forward at once. He was a peaceful man, short and cheerful under all conditions, but now his face was angry. "Stay out of this, Theodore! It's between these two."

Theodore Barnhill, a huge, powerful man, simply laughed and swept Minton out of the way, not even watching the smaller man as he fell sprawling. He turned and headed for Colin, who had gotten up, and his intentions were clear. The two brothers were very close, and everyone in the train understood that they were joining together to give Colin Bryce a beating.

At that moment, seemingly from nowhere, a form appeared before Theodore. Ty Sublette had watched the fight in silence. It was his policy not to interfere in other men's quarrels, but when Theodore had moved in he had stepped forward at once, putting himself between the huge form of Barnhill and Colin.

Theodore had never liked Sublette. He had been against hiring him and had been yearning for a chance to challenge him. Now Sublette simply stood there, and a strange half smile touched his lips as he said, "I reckon you'd better stay out of it, Theodore."

"Get out of the way, Sublette, or I'll tear your head off."

Sublette did not answer, but there was something almost indolent in his posture. He stood hip-shot, his hands hanging loosely down at his sides, and his light blue eyes had a mild expression in them. It was as though he were half amused by something that he had often seen, and he simply said, "Don't interfere or I'll have to put you down."

"Put me down! You couldn't put a baby down, Sublette!"

Colin had recovered now, and came to stand beside Sublette. His face was red and bleeding, and he said, "I was all set to vote against taking the black man and his wife." His breathing came fast, and anger smoldered in his dark blue eyes. "But now if scum like you are against it, I'm for it! I vote to bring Smith." He turned and said, "Everybody that will, take a stand against fellows lIke this."

Theodore Barnhill suddenly leaped forward, looping a long, powerful right hand toward Sublette. Sublette's response was as quick as light. He blocked it with his left hand and then drove a powerful right with all of his weight behind it into the pit of Theodore's stomach. The big man was stopped as if he had run into a pile driver. The breath whooshed out of his lips, and as he stood there gasping for breath, his eyes disbelieving, Ty Sublette leaped forward, grabbed the bigger man's head in a headlock, swung him around, and threw him with a lift of his hip. Theodore Barnhill practically turned a flip and lit on his belly. At once Sublette straddled him, reached forward, and grabbing his head pulled it back. "I'll break

your neck, Theodore, if you make a move."
Sublette's voice now was as cold as polar
ice. He turned around and said, "You two
fellows go ahead and have your fight."

"All right with me," Bryce said. He moved
forward, but Ace did not like the situation.

"Stay away, Bryce." He turned toward
Sublette, who was grinning toward him as
he held the big man's head so that he was
unable to move. "Let him go, Sublette."

"Why, I reckon I want to see the end of
your fight. You go right ahead, Ace."

"Yes," Bryce said. And now, although his
face was smeared with blood, he moved forward. "You made a few remarks. I'll hold you
to them."

Ace suddenly pulled his gun and said,
"Stay back!"

A murmur went around the crowd, and at
once Horace Farr stepped forward. He was
the least impressive of any of the men in this
little drama. Tall, rawboned, and his clothes
practically hanging on him, nevertheless he
had some quality that caused other men to
listen. Sternly he said, "That's enough, Barnhill. Put that gun away."

Ace whirled to face Farr, and for a moment the two men stood locked in some

sort of struggle. And then Ace shrugged and said, "All right. It's all over. Let's have the vote."

Sublette released Theodore, stood back, and watched him carefully as the big man got to his feet. Theodore's face was scarlet, and a burning hatred lay in his eyes. But the moment had passed, and he simply said, "I'll see you later, Sublette."

"Anytime."

"All right. Let's have the vote." Horace Farr lifted his voice so that it carried clearly. "Everyone in favor of taking Smith and his wife raise your hand." He glanced over, and Horace Farr was surprised. He had expected an even vote, for he knew that there were many Southerners on the train, most of them holding a poor opinion of black people. However, the result was foregone. "All opposed." He looked at the hands and said, "Anyone want to count them?"

"No. I don't think we have to," Dr. Leverett pronounced. "I'm glad it went this way. I think we're better people than to leave a family stranded here."

Jordan went up to Colin and pulled a handkerchief out of the pocket of her dress. She mopped the blood from his face and smiled. Pride was in her eyes, and she whispered, "Thank you, Colin."

"Well, it's not that I'm so good. It's just that I can't stand those Barnhills."

"Come along. Let's welcome the Smiths."

The two walked over to where the black man and his wife stood. They had not been able to see it all, and even now they did not know what the vote had been.

Jordan introduced Colin, then said, "It's all right, Cato. You and Rosie are going with us."

The words seemed to strike Cato Smith as hard as one of the blows that had been struck in the fight. He swallowed hard then looked down at Rosie, who held onto his arm. Something warm came to the face of the black man, his dark brown eyes fixed on the pair. "I thank you, suh. And you, Miss Jordan."

"Yes. We can't ever thank you enough," Rosie whispered.

"I'll make it up to you, Mistuh Bryce. You see if I don't."

Colin Bryce looked at the huge hand that was shoved toward him. He put out his own at once and felt the power of the man's grasp, although there was no attempt to manifest it.

"You don't owe me anything, Cato. My wife here, she's the one you've got to thank."

The fight had built some walls, and pulled others closer together. As they finally rolled out and left Laramie behind, Colin said little. All day long he drove, silently thinking about what had happened.

That night, after the trains pulled into the circle, he had been strangely quiet as Jordan fixed steaks. Dave Minton had slaughtered one of his beef cattle and shared the meat with the rest of the train.

Colin had eaten hungrily and then sat around the fire taking little part in the conversation. Les and Paul Leverett had come over to share in the beef, and Les had talked the most. He was a witty man and could see into people better than most. He spoke of his time on the stage, for he had been an actor, and he drank from a small flask that he carried. The liquor seemed to increase his faculties rather than dull them, as was true with most drinking men.

"I drink too much," he remarked at one point, then grinned. "Paul has spent a lifetime getting me out of trouble."

Paul Leverett cast a glance at his brother. His crisp brown hair was mussed, and his sharp gray eyes were on the younger man. "You've been hard to raise. That's sure enough."

Les laughed. "He never would get married because he knew he had to take care of me." He listened then to the music that had started over near the Lee's wagon. He could hear Jesse Lee's fiddle and Mary's zither, and voices began to be raised in song. They were singing a hymn, and Les grew silent. "I remember that hymn. Don't you, Paul?"

"Yes, it was Mother's favorite. 'Rock of Ages.'"

The plaintive hymn seemed to lift itself above the train and surround it. The strong voices of Jesse and Mary Lee blended together, and the old song touched the entire train.

Rock of ages, cleft for me,
Let me hide myself in thee
Let the water and the blood,
From thy wounded side which flowed,
Be of sin the double cure,
Save from wrath, and make me pure.

Could my tears forever flow,
Could my zeal no languor know,
These for sin could not atone;
Thou must save and thou alone.
In my hand no price I bring;
Simply to thy cross I cling.

While I draw this fleeting breath,
When my eyes shall close in death,
When I rise to worlds unknown,
And behold thee on thy throne,
Rock of Ages, cleft for me,
Let me hide myself in thee.

For some reason the hymn brought a silence to Les Leverett. He rose suddenly without another word and walked away.

"You're very different from your brother, Dr. Leverett," Jordan said.

"Yes, I've always been the dull one."

"I expect you're lively enough. Doctors don't have to be lively, do they?" Colin said.

Leverett laughed shortly, then got up. "I guess I'll go to bed. No, doctors don't have to be lively. They can be as boring as a stump."

The doctor turned and walked away into the darkness, and Jordan remarked, "They're a sad pair. Unhappy, both of them."

"I guess so. I think I'll go to bed." Colin rose and went to the wagon. Pulling off his boots, he lay down on the mattress that they had managed to make that covered the supplies. He lay there for a long time, it seemed, and then he felt the wagon sag. He kept his eyes closed, but he was aware of Jordan as she undressed, and then he felt her warmth come to him.

"Colin?"

"Yes."

Colin felt the softness of Jordan as she put herself against him. Her arm came over and stroked his cheek. "I was so proud of you today."

"Not much to be proud of."

"Yes, there was." Her hand ran down his side and then touched his chest. He had removed his shirt, and now her arm went around him in a suggestive fashion.

Colin turned to face her. He put his arms around her and whispered, "I was pretty much of a sorehead."

"Yes, but you did what was right."

Colin ran his hands down the shapely lines of her body. She wore only a thin nightdress, and Colin realized what a prize he had. All the quick curves of her healthy, sup-

ple body reached out to him, and he whispered, "Do I deserve a reward?"

Jordan came to him with a fierceness
then, whispering, "Yes!" And the two clasped
at each other with a hunger that shocked
them both.

SIXTEEN

The sound of the sentinel's gunshot broke into Mark Ellencourt's sleep, pulling him out of an uneasy rest into the busy world that he had learned to dread. He lay on his thin mattress, listening to the sounds that occurred every morning: people pouring out of their wagons and tents, hatchets breaking up firewood and branches for the morning cooking fire, and the snorting and chuffing of the riding stock as the party of hunters began to draw them out of their corral.

Carefully Ellencourt pulled himself up to a sitting position, but the movement, as cautious as he had been, pulled at something in his chest, and he was racked suddenly by a series of short, hoarse coughs. He struggled to restrain the spasm but was unable to and thought, *Lord, I sound like a dog barking!* The spasm passed, and he finally got control of himself, feeling weak and nauseated as he always did after such an attack.

The gray light of morning suddenly flooded the interior of the wagon as the canvas cover was drawn back, and he heard Leah ask anxiously, "Are you all right, Mark?"

"Sure. Just a little coughing." With an effort he threw back the blanket, rolled over, and crawled to the rear of the wagon. Leah's face was filled with concern, he saw, as he eased himself down. He saw her reach out to help him then draw her hand back. She was a thoughtful woman and knew that he needed to do as much for himself as he could.

"Breakfast is almost ready. I'm fixing pancakes."

"Good. That always makes me think of home."

"Sit down and have some coffee while I finish them. Ty said he'd be back to join us."

Sitting down cross-legged before the fire, Ellencourt took a small sip of the coffee. He did so cautiously, for swallowing had become a challenge for him, often bringing on the cough that had troubled him for weeks. The coffee was hot and black, and he savored it, nursing it along as he watched Leah flip a pancake in the air and catch it on the cooked side.

A smile came to Ellencourt. "I never could see how you do that."

"Long practice." Leah turned, tall and strong, a woman with a will. Her green eyes studied him thoughtfully, and he thought what an attractive woman she was. She had a round face, ash-blonde hair, and startling green eyes like the green of the sea.

"You're a good-looking woman, wife."

Leah's face flushed, and she laughed aloud. "I'm gritty, and grimy, and sunburned, and my hair is dirty—but I appreciate the compliment."

At that moment Jos Ellencourt came running into camp barefooted and wearing a pair of brown trousers and a linsey shirt that had once been blue but now was faded almost white. His blonde hair was uncombed, and his blue eyes were large as he said, "Pa, Ty says he's going to take me to Independence Rock."

"Is he? Why, that'll be fine."

"He says we can carve our names in the rock, and people who come along afterwards will see it. He says there's about a million names already carved up there."

Mark reached over and ruffled the boy's hair, affection in his brown eyes. The hand he placed on Jos's head was thin and not entirely steady, but he spoke warmly. "That's good. You carve 'Josiah Ellencourt, age eight.' Maybe you'll come back here when you're an old man with a long, white beard, and it'll still be there."

"Oh, I'm not gonna have a beard! Ty don't have one."

The two adults exchanged glances, and Mark smiled faintly. "You and Ty have gotten to be great friends."

"Sure. He's gonna teach me how to make a bow and arrow just like the Indians, and then teach me how to shoot it."

Even as the boy spoke Sublette came striding into camp. He never made any noise, somehow, when he moved. Some holdover from his days in the mountains among the Indians, Ellencourt supposed. "Hello, Ty."

"Mark—Leah." Sublette squatted down before the fire and grinned at Jos. "I bet I can eat more pancakes than you can."

"Bet you can't."

"Breakfast is all ready," Leah said. "I've got a treat for you this morning."

"What's that?" Mark said with interest. He had little appetite himself, but he tried to eat as much as possible to regain his strength.

"Here, take your pancakes, and I'll give it to you."

Leah dispersed the pancakes, two for Sublette, one for the others. When they had taken them she moved over to the wagon and pulled a jar out of a box. Coming back she held it up. "Pure sourwood honey. Straight from home, Mark."

His eyes lighting up, Mark said, "That sounds great. I'm partial to honey."

"So am I," Ty said. "Out in the mountains that's about the only sweets you get. Once I robbed a bee tree. Got some honey all right, but the bees stung me so bad around the eyes I couldn't see for two days."

"How'd you get around? Did somebody lead you?"

"Sure did."

"Who?"

Sublette had been pouring honey over his pancakes, but now he paused. "My wife," he said quietly.

"Your wife? Where is she?" Jos said.

"She and my boy died some time ago."

"Oh," Jos said and studied the face of the tall man. "I'm sorry."

Mark noticed that whenever his wife was mentioned Sublette grew silent. It was obvious that he still loved the woman and the son but did not want to talk about them.

Mark bit into the pancakes after sopping a morsel around in the amber-colored honey. "This is like home," he said. "I'll miss the honey."

"Lots of bees in Oregon," Ty offered. "We might even get you some hives and raise your own."

"I think a different kind of bees live in hIves, not the wild ones," Mark observed.

"So we'll get whatever kind of bee it takes," Leah said. She came over to sit next to Mark and listened as the two men spoke of Oregon. She could not help but contrast the two men. Physically they were so different. Ty stood over six feet with a strongly built body, while Mark was a small man with mild brown eyes and a thin, almost delicate face. Before she had married Mark she had always been partial to big men, but Mark had come courting her, and she had been fascinated by his mind. She also was inclined toward him because she herself was a devoted Christian. She had not one time regretted the hardships that a Methodist preacher's wife endured.

"Well, I guess you and I better go have a

look at that rock," Ty said. "You can ride behind me. Think you can hang on, Jos?"

"Sure I can!"

"Let me get this stock hitched up and
we'll take a look-see."

Mark watched as Sublette yoked the
oxen with an ease that brought some envy
to him. He respected Sublette and admired
him, but the big man's strength and en-
durance made him feel even more frail than
he was. When the stock was yoked and the
wagon was ready to go, Sublette grinned at
Mark. "I'll bring him back after he does
some name carvin' on that rock."

"All right, Ty. And thanks."

"My pleasure. He's a fine boy."

After the two left Mark got up and began
to move carefully, washing the dishes and
getting ready to go. Leah did not attempt to
stop him although she could have done it
quicker. She saw how slowly he moved, and
every day she worried about him. It had
been Mark who had felt the call of God to go
to Oregon. She had felt apprehension about
his health, but he had insisted that they
must obey God. And now as she went about
her work she kept a sharp eye on him and
prayed an oft-repeated prayer, "Lord, give

him strength to get to Oregon and preach your Word there."

"I hate my hair!"

Rita Farr pulled a comb down through her thick mass of bright red hair and stared at herself in the small mirror that she had braced against the side of the wagon. She had risen at the first sound of the sentinel's rifle fire, and had helped her mother fix breakfast. Now she stared at herself with dissatisfaction. "I don't know why I couldn't have brown hair like Pa."

Ellen Farr laughed. She paused long enough to say, "Because you got your red hair from me, and it's beautiful."

"Everybody makes fun of it."

"They did the same thing when I was your age, but all the same young men like red-haired women."

Rita turned to face her mother. She was on the verge of womanhood. At the age of sixteen, some of her childhood friends were already married and two of them had babies. "I know, Ma," she said. "I just get tired of listening to people talking about it."

"Lots of girls would love to have their hair

talked about like you do. Now, if you're going to go carve your name on that rock, get going."

"All right. I'll catch up with the wagons later."

"I want to go, too," Payton said.

"You're too little," Rita answered. She left the camp in the midst of Payton's angry questioning of why he wasn't old enough to do anything that Rita did.

Rita stopped long enough to ask her grandmother, "You want me to carve your name on the rock, too?"

"You won't have time to do that." Dorcas Farr, thin and gaunt, had amazingly bright blue eyes for a seventy-one-year-old. "You'd better hurry up. Don't let some injun get you."

"I won't, Gran." She left, noting the hunters a long distance from the line of march. Independence Rock was a hallmark along the trail. It stood high over the Sweetwater River, giving a panoramic view, and as Rita moved swiftly to the base and then began climbing she passed Ty Sublette, who was advancing at a leisurely fashion with young Jos Ellencourt beside him.

"Hello, Rita," Sublette said. "Going to carve your name on the rock?"

"Yes, sir."

"Be careful. There's snakes out there."

"I'll be careful, Mr. Sublette."

Rita left the pair behind. She was a fleet young woman able to outrun many of the young men of her own age. She had learned not to do so, for it made them angry, but when one displeased her she would always put him to shame by outrunning him. Now as she mounted quickly, she began to see names that were already carved, along with dates. It was a balmy day, and she was enjoying the trip immensely. She had youth and strength, there was excitement and adventure, and she did not mind the hard work. Now as she reached the top of the massive pile, she was thinking of what Sublette had told her father the night before. He had said, "About seventy miles west of here there's a bed of ice. You only dig down about a foot, even in midsummer. We're about seven thousand feet high here and almost at the South Pass."

Rita wished that they could go by the ice slough, which was what Sublette had called the place where the ice lay. It would be nice to have a drink with ice in it, but it was too far away, Sublette had said.

When she reached the top of the rock, Rita stood looking down at the scene before her. The Sweetwater River made great sweeping curves, and the sunlight glinted on the surface of the slowly moving stream. Far away she could see a fort of some kind, but she did not know what it was. In the other direction a great column of dust rose high in the air as wagon trains approached. Still farther off she could see the rise of the mountains in all directions, and they were a delight to her, for she had come from a country that was mostly flat.

Knowing she had to hurry, she began studying some of the names and the dates. She saw one that intrigued her. "Carl loves Rachel" with the date "May the sixth, 1847." And below it, inside and not quite so deeply, "And Rachel loves Carl."

Rita ran her fingers over the crudely carved names, and a smile turned the corners of her lips upward. The wind blew her hair, and then she shook her shoulders and chose a spot. She had brought a chisel and a hammer and began carving her initials.

She had finished with the first letter and was started on the second when someone spoke to her. "Hello."

Turning quickly, Rita saw Cornwall Barnhill. "Hello," she said rather shyly. One night the people had gathered for a dance, and Rita had noticed that Cornwall kept his eyes on her although he had never come to ask her to dance. She had wondered why then. He was a tall, lanky boy and was not yet filled out to full manhood. "I'm Cornwall Barnhill."

"I'm Rita Farr."

"I know. I've seen you before."

Rita studied the young man who seemed almost paralyzed by shyness. He was not bad looking although his face was thin, and his body was like a lathe. He seemed strong and healthy, and his face was tanned. His hands looked strong and there was an able look about him.

"Carving your name, are you?"

"Just my initials."

Cornwall struggled for something to say and finally muttered, "That's a good thing to do. You'll be able to come back later and see it."

"I doubt if I'll ever come this way again. It's too far."

"You never can tell."

"Well, I'd better get busy."

"Sure," Cornwall said quickly. "You mind if I watch?"

Rita laughed. "No, I don't mind. You can use my chisel if you want to and do your own name."

"All right."

The next half hour went by very quickly. Cornwall borrowed the chisel and with firm strokes put a CB into the rock. Handing the chisel back, his hand touched hers, and he flushed slightly. "Reckon we'd better get back," he said. "The train's already started."

"I think so."

"I'd better go with you. There might be some Indians."

Rita smiled at him. "I don't think so. Pa would never have let me come if there were any danger of Indians. And Mr. Sublette says that we're safe enough here."

"Well, there might be a snake then." Corny was wearing a pistol at his side and put his hand on it. "Never can tell."

"All right, you can shoot all the snakes we see."

The two made their way down the mountain, and as they approached the train, Corny said, "I seen you at the dance."

"Yes, I know it."

Corny gave her a startled look. "You saw me?"

"I was wondering why you didn't come and ask me to dance."

Cornwall shook his head. "I'm just not much of a dancer."

"You won't get any better without practice. Next time"—she smiled—"you ask me."

Cornwall brightened up considerably, and as they approached the train he looked up and said, "There's my brother Ace."

Ace walked over. "Hello, Corny. Who's your lady friend?"

"This is Rita Farr."

"Well, Miss Rita, I'm glad to know you."

"I'm pleased to meet you."

"Corny, you'd better move on. I'm going to steal your girl."

Corny dropped his head and muttered, "All right, Ace." As he moved away Rita said, "You'll hurt his feelings."

Surprise showed in Ace's handsome face. "Why, I wouldn't do that. He's a good kid." He stepped closer to her and smiled down. "You got the prettiest red hair I ever saw in my life."

"Don't tease me!"

"I'm not teasing. Red's the prettiest color there is for a woman's hair."

"You're just saying that."

Ace was experienced and practiced with women. Now as he saw the blooming, youthful beauty of Rita Farr, he accepted it as a challenge. His back arched, and his eyes glowed as he said, "You're the prettiest girl on the train. I don't know how I let that get by me."

Rita felt helpless and unable to speak. She had heard that Ace Barnhill was quite a ladies' man. She was pleased at his attention and yet somewhat apprehensive. "I've got to go," she said.

"Sure. But the next dance we have, I'm claiming you for it. Don't forget."

Rita suddenly smiled at him. "All right," she said and turned away. She found that she was breathing more rapidly than usual, and she turned once and looked back to where Ace stood. He was still watching her, and she waved at him.

I wonder if he'll ask me to dance, she thought. *I hope so!*

* * *

Colin Bryce stood looking out over the moving mass in front of him and shook his head in wonder. "Must be a million of those things, Ty."

"Maybe so. I never stopped to count." Sublette looked over the milling herd of buffalo. "I don't think a man could live long enough to count all the buffer in this country."

The two sat their horses, listening as the bulls bellowed and the calves cried for their mothers. The sound filled the entire prairie, and to Colin, it seemed that the earth was alive and moving. He murmured, "It's almost like the sea, Ty, when it moves. Sometimes the sea seems almost alive like that."

"Well, this bunch is alive. They won't be here for long. Not the way we're moving in on them."

The red buttes rose bare and naked over the two men, and the sun shone down brightly. Colin had been amazed that the buffalo didn't run. "Aren't they afraid?" he asked. "They just mill around like cattle."

"No. Not unless somethin' scares 'em."

"You know, I wouldn't have believed this if somebody had told me about it." Colin shook his head, staring in disbelief. "This is some country," he said. "I never saw anything like it or expected to. Either there's no buffalo at all or there's a million of 'em."

"Yep, that's about true. That's the way it was when I was a mountain man. You either starved to death or had too much meat."

The two made their way slowly along, Sublette speaking now and then, and Colin listening carefully. He was a man who liked to learn things, and this was a new thing to him. The wagon train had stopped for repairs, and now as he looked back in the distance the train seemed very far away.

"I hope a storm doesn't blow up," Sublette observed, looking over to the west.

Colin looked and squinted his eyes. He was used to checking the weather at sea, and he could tell that there was a slight darkening of the sky. "Why?"

"If it storms while we're close to the buffalo, they could stampede us."

"What sets 'em off?" Colin asked.

"Sometimes a bolt of lightning. Or a roll of thunder. You never can tell." He glanced over at Colin and grinned. "I reckon we'd better shoot a couple of these." Pulling his rifle out, he handed it over and said, "Why don't you do the shootin'?"

Startled, Colin took the rifle and even

though he was somewhat apprehensive he took aim. The bull was not more than thirty feet away, and he could not miss. When he pulled the trigger the shot seemed very loud, and the kick against his shoulder was hard.

"Missed him!" he said in disgust. "How could I miss at this range?"

"You didn't miss. Just watch."

Colin watched as the bull ambled on seemingly unhurt, then suddenly he stopped. His legs began to collapse, and he fell down, raising a great cloud of dust, uttering a hoarse grunt.

"You got him dead center. Good shot."

"Well, that's not hunting. That's just butchering."

"That's the way buffalo hunters do it. That's how some men can shoot two hundred a day. They shoot until their shoulders are blue the next day from the kick of the rifle."

They stopped, and Sublette showed Colin how to bleed the animal. Colin was enjoying his day. He had grown short-tempered and impatient, for he liked action. This had been the bane of his life as a sailor when there had been day after day and even month after month of very little happening except for routine. He had left the sea hopeful of finding adventure, and this sort of thing, shooting buffalo, was enough to hold his attention. He helped butcher the buffalo, finding out that it was hard work.

Sublette looked over at him once while they were taking the hide off the animal and grinned. "Hard dirty work. Not much glory in skinning a buffer."

"Same way at sea. Just hard work most of the time. Once in a while something beautiful would come along. Even the storms were beautiful there, I thought. I always loved a storm."

"Well, I don't love this one comin' up." Sublette threw a glance west, where the darkening had turned more definite.

The wagon train was almost up to them now, and Horace Farr came over, a worried look on his lean face. "What kind of weather's comin' up, Ty?"

"It looks like a blow."

"A bad one?"

"Can't say. Looks like it, though."

Farr glanced at the milling thousands of buffalo. "What about these critters? What will they do?"

Sublette shook his head, but his gaze

was alert. "No way of telling. Sure wish I'd steered the train away from them."

"If they stampede toward the train, they'll wipe us out."

"We'll have to keep 'em away from it. I'm gonna go around and tell the men what to do in case of a stampede."

Sublette left, and Horace looked down at the butchered buffalo. "Good meat," he said. "Sublette shoot it?"

"No, I did. Not much fun in it. Like shooting a steer."

The two men spoke, but their minds were both on the dark cloud that was approaching. A low rumble of thunder came and then a bolt of lightning outlined itself against the darkness of the cloud. Both men looked instinctively toward the herd of buffalo and saw a ripple run over them as the massive animals lifted their heads, and a slow moaning began.

The stampede came so suddenly that few of the drivers had a chance to prepare for it. One moment the herd was milling around moaning, and the next they seemed to have all been touched by some sort of madness.

Sublette knew that there was little chance of saving the train unless they took action. He called out loudly, "Everyone! Come over here! Bring your rifles, pistols, anything!"

The train had been pulled up into a circle, and now as the mass of buffalo charged toward them Sublette raised his rifle and shot into the herd. It seemed a puny effort, but he cried out, "Everybody shoot! Shoot!"

The herd seemed not to notice for a moment, and then slowly it divided. Sublette shouted, "They're splitting! Drive them off! Any kind of noise!"

The men were all there, and the sound of the muskets and pistols and rifles made a popping sound. Buffalo fell and slowed the animals somewhat.

How long this went on no one could actually remember, but like a river the mighty herd split, and for what seemed like an hour they followed the path, leaving the wagons untouched.

Finally Colin rode up, his face pale. "You think that's it, Ty?"

"Looks like it. They're slowin' down."

Even as he spoke a cry startled most of them.

"Billy! Billy!"

Sublette wheeled to see Orville Crane run straight toward the buffalo. Quickly Sublette ran and grabbed the man. "Don't get out in that herd, man! They'll kill you!"

"It's Billy!" Orville Crane's thin face was tortured. "He ran out to get his dog right in the middle of the buffer."

Sublette cast a quick glance and knew it was hopeless. He held Crane, who would have gone after the boy. "It's too late, Orville," he said quietly. He turned and led the man back where Fanny Crane was holding onto her baby. The smaller children were huddled around her, their eyes wide with fear.

The Cranes were the poorest people on the train with probably less of this world's goods than anyone. Now something twisted in Sublette as the scrawny form of Orville straightened, and he went over and put his arm around his wife. "He's gone! Billy's gone, Fanny!"

Unable to bear the scene, Sublette turned away. He walked away far enough that the cries of the Cranes were muted, but still they struck him with a blow. He looked up to see Leah Ellencourt approaching.

"What's wrong, Ty?"

"It's Billy Crane. He got caught in the stampede."

Compassion swept over Leah's face. "I'd better go help them as best I can."

"There's nothing anybody can do for them. The boy's dead—and I'm to blame for it. I should never let the train get this close to buffer with a storm blowing up." Bitterness tinged his voice.

"We all lose things, Ty. But God can give us comfort if we'll let him." She saw her words strike against him, and knew he was thinking of the dead boy—and of his dead wife and son. He did not answer, and she started for the grief-stricken family.

Mark Ellencourt stood with his Bible in his hand. A silence had fallen over the crowd that had gathered for the funeral. The boy had been mangled almost beyond recognition. Gus Dabney had fashioned a small coffin out of spare lumber that he could gather, and the Cranes had not been permitted to view the remains. Mark and Leah had stayed with them almost constantly, and now as the preacher stood lifting his head, the only sound was the weeping of Fanny Crane and the crying of the baby, who seemed to be aware of his mother's grief and agony.

"Of all the miracles that Jesus performed," Mark said, his voice clear on the stillness of the air, "the one that has always touched me most is recorded in Mark's gospel, the fifth chapter. This chapter gives us the picture of what the life of Jesus was like at times. It begins with Jesus encountering a man with an unclean spirit, who lived in a graveyard. He spent his life crying and cutting himself with stones, but when Jesus came, the poor man ran to Jesus and worshiped him. And Jesus cast the demons out of him. They entered into a herd of swine, and they all ran off a steep cliff and killed themselves." Mark nodded, and remarked, "It's strange that human beings will live with demons in them, while hogs won't!"

Sublette stood back from the crowd. He'd helped to dig the grave, and had been touched by the hymns that the crowd had sung. Now he kept his eyes fixed on Mark Ellencourt, listening intently.

"After this a ruler of the synagogue named Jairus begged Jesus to come and heal his daughter. Jesus agreed, but on the way to the house of Jairus, a sick woman with an issue of blood reached out and touched the garment of Jesus—and was healed instantly. She'd spent all her money on doctors, but none had been able to help her. But one touch of Jesus, and she was healed! He's a mighty Savior!"

As Ellencourt continued his sermon, Sublette glanced at the Cranes. They were in front of the crowd, the husband and wife clinging to each other, and the children looking frightened. It touched a chord in Sublette, and he could not bear the sight of them. *They loved Billy as much as I loved my son.* The memory of his own lost boy was a sharp knife twisting in him, and he pressed his lips together tightly, and gave his attention to the words of Ellencourt.

"When Jesus had healed the woman, some men came to tell Jairus that his daughter had died. I've thought of this story so often. What would I have done at that moment, if I'd been Jairus? I think I'd have given up. But Jesus said, 'Be not afraid, only believe.' And that, friends, is always the word of God to any whose heart is broken—'Be not afraid, only believe.' Now let me read the rest of the story to you from the Bible.

"'And he cometh to the house of the ruler

of the synagogue, and seeth the tumult, and them that wept and wailed greatly.

"'And when he was come in, he saith unto them, why make ye this ado, and weep? the damsel is not dead, but sleepeth.

"'And they laughed him to scorn. But when he had put them all out, he taketh the father and the mother of the damsel, and them that were with him, and entereth in where the damsel was lying.

"'And he took the damsel by the hand, and said unto her, *Talitha cumi;* which is, being intrepreted, Damsel, I say unto thee, arise.

"'And straightway the damsel arose, and walked; for she was of the age of twelve years. And they were astonished with a great astonishment.

"'And he charged them straitly that no man should know it; and commanded that something should be given her to eat.'"

Ellencourt paused for a moment, then said in a gentle tone, "In this case, the damsel came back from the dead at once. That's what we would all like for Billy. It's what we want for all our loved ones who cross over. But God's timing is not ours. Sometimes, in his infinite wisdom, he takes from us that which we love best. We will know why someday, I believe, but in this life, we do not. But I believe that Jesus gave us the truth about all death when he said, 'Be not afraid, only believe.'"

"Billy will rise again!" Ellencourt's voice was strong now, and he lifted his Bible high. "All who have taken Jesus Christ into their hearts will rise again!"

Sublette was moved by the fervor of Ellencourt, and kept his eyes fixed on the man's face. He saw the victory there that most men miss, and he knew that somehow the words from the Scripture had entered into his own heart. For years he'd been bitter over the loss of his wife and son, but now he felt a strange peace that he could not explain. He felt the presence of God, and at that moment he knew that he would see his wife and son again.

Finally Mark ended his sermon, and he went over and put his hand on the thin shoulder of the dead boy's mother. Sublette felt the need to say something, and finally, after Ellencourt had left, he moved over to Mrs. Crane and said quietly, "I am deeply sorry for your loss, ma'am."

* * *

The death of Billy Crane had sobered Horace Farr considerably. He sat talking about the boy's death to his wife, Ellen. "I hated to lose that boy, but we're lucky we haven't lost more."

"Yes, we are."

Farr looked around thoughtfully. "Well, this is the South Pass. Not what I thought it would look like."

"What did you think?"

"I've heard Ty talk about how it's the only way through the Rocky Mountains, and I thought it would be some kind of a gorge or valley cut out of high mountains. But it's just sort of a high rise in the trail."

They had stayed the night at Pacific Springs, and they were approaching the eastern boundary of the Oregon Territory. Horace said, "You're tired, aren't you, Ellen?"

"No more than anyone else." Actually she was discouraged and sick of the trail. When they had left home she had thought more about the dangers of Indians or cholera, but now she had learned that that was not the enemy, but distance. Day after day plodding through the same kind of country, they seemed to be stuck in one place. The wheels were turning on the wagons, but they were not going anywhere—every day was the same with the skyline forever unchanged.

But she would reveal none of these thoughts to Horace. He had enough weight on his shoulders. She pointed. "There's Sublette."

"Probably coming to talk. We have to make a decision before we leave tomorrow."

"What's that?"

"Whether to take the long way around to Fort Bridger or take Sublette's Cutoff."

"Which should we take?"

"I don't know. Ty says that Sublette's Cutoff would be faster, but it's a real rough trip." Horace stared at the horizon and shook his head. "I wish I didn't have this job, Ellen."

Ellen Farr moved to put her arm around her husband. "You'll always have a job like this, Horace. Whatever makes men trust other men, you've got it."

"I wish I didn't!"

Paul Leverett looked at his brother with distaste. "You shouldn't drink so much, Les."

"Mind your own business."

"You are my business. You're my brother."

"I wish you'd forget it." Les had been drinking heavily all day, and now he simply turned and walked off into the darkness.

Paul watched his brother go and shook his head. He regretted that he had allowed Les to bring a large supply of liquor on the trip. He had tried to get him to bring only a few bottles, but Les had rebelled and refused to make the trip unless he had his way. It was time for a meeting, and now here was Les acting like a child. No, worse than a child. A child would have more judgment. Disgust rose in him, and he shook his head, then made his way to the group that had gathered in the center of the wagons. Everyone was there, and he saw that, as usual, the Barnhills and the Grattons were grouped together. Al Catlow, the mountain man, stood talking to Ace Barnhill, and his brother Theodore, as always, was close to him.

Instinctively Leverett drew away and went to stand beside Jesse Lee, whom he had come to like a great deal. Their music added a pleasant note to the camp. "Hello, Jesse."

"Why, hello, Doc." Jesse turned his blue eyes and fair smile on the doctor. Others had lost weight, but Jesse and his wife, Mary, somehow seemed to have kept their weight even on the thin rations. Leverett suspected they had brought sweets and other such things in their stores. He turned to face Jennie Town, marveling again at the calm peaceful look on her face. "Good evening, Jennie," he said, making sure his lips formed the words so that she could read them.

"Hello, Doctor."

"You're looking very well. Travel agrees with you."

Jennie smiled and nodded. "Everything agrees with me pretty much."

"I wish everyone were so easily pleased."

"What's this meeting about, Dr. Leverett?"

Knowing that the young woman would not be able to pick up on everything, Leverett said carefully, still facing her full face, "We can take a turn here and go to Fort Bridger. That's over that way."

"Is it really a fort?"

"Not an army fort. Just sort of a trading post. I've been talking to Ty about it. He won't say one way or another. But if we don't go that way, we can take a cutoff. It's called the Sublette's Cutoff."

"Named after Ty?"

"No, after one of his relatives, a mountain man named William Sublette. Anyway, it's an easy road to Fort Bridger but a hard one on the cutoff. Thing is, we'd save several days on that cutoff."

"I hope we take the cutoff. I'm anxious to get to Oregon."

"What will you do there, Jennie?"

"Oh, I don't know. The same as everyone else. Work. Get what I can out of life."

"That's a good philosophy," Leverett said. He liked this young woman very much indeed. If she had her hearing, she probably would have married and been a mother several times by now.

The meeting did not last long. Farr got up and laid out the decision that had to be made, and he ended by saying, "So, it's an easy trip to Fort Bridger but plumb out of the way, and we'll lose several days."

Dave Minton turned to Ty, who stood over to Farr's right. "What's the road like on Sublette's Cutoff, Ty?"

"It'll be hard going. Water's the problem. We might lose some of the weaker stock."

"Can the wagons and the oxen make it?" Ira Barnhill demanded.

"I think so, but I'm warnin' you, it'd be a tough trip."

Pete Gratton shook his head. "I don't

know about this. We're pretty worn down, Farr."

Farr himself was not sure which direction to take. He did not argue but listened as the talk went around. Finally a vote was taken, and it was overwhelmingly in favor of taking Sublette's Cutoff.

"All right. We leave in the morning then," Farr said rather heavily. As the crowd dispersed, he turned and found Ellen standing close to him. Horace put his arm around Ellen, leaned over, and kissed her. It was an unusual gesture, for he was not publicly demonstrative. "You know, you're a good-lookin' woman. I may give you something for being the best wife in the train—and you should give me something for being the best husband."

Ellen laughed up at him. She had been despondent, but somehow he had the ability to raise her spirits. "All right. I'll give you an apple pie."

"I need somethin' sweeter than that."

Ace Barnhill drifted closer to the Farr family. He waited until they turned back to their wagon and intercepted Rita. "Maybe you and I could take a walk."

Rita did not know how to answer him.

She hated her lack of experience, and could only say, "I guess you've had a lot of girls."

"Not so many."

Rita laughed. "That's not what I hear."

Ace grinned, and his handsome face was alert, almost like a fox. "Why, I like pretty girls—and you're the prettiest."

Rita simply shook her head. "You say that to all of them." It was not what she wanted to say, and she felt awkward, and hated herself for it. She longed for attention, and though she knew Ace Barnhill was a dangerous man for young girls, she could not bring herself to say the words that would turn him away.

Ace saw that longing in the girl, and said, "Don't forget to save me a dance like you promised."

"I never promised that!"

"Come on, Rita, be kind to a man, can't you?"

Rita flushed and said, "I'll have to see." She turned and left, and Ace smiled. *She's like a ripe peach, ready to fall to the first man that reaches for her!*

Ty Sublette was silent at dinner that night, but the Ellencourts were lively. "We're nearer than we were when we left," Mark said, smiling.

Sublette grinned back. "That's like saying, 'I feel a whole lot more like I do now than I did before I felt like this.'"

Leah was glad to see Mark cheerful. "What happens now?" she asked.

"We go on to Fort Hall. We ought to be there in about a week."

"Fort Hall. What kind of place is that?"

"It's a trading post operated by the Hudson Bay Company."

"Is there much there, Ty?"

"No, but we'll have to make another decision. Some people may want to cut off there and go to California. Others will go on to Oregon."

"We won't argue about that, will we? I mean, nobody's going to want to go to California."

"You might be surprised," Ty said evenly. "People change their minds. For one thing, the climate in California is better—at least it's drier. It rains nine months of the year in Oregon, and some folks can't take that. Then getting to Oregon is harder than getting to California. By the time folks get this far, some of them are played out—just want to get someplace and settle down."

"What about the government?" Mark asked. "The Spaniards are in California, aren't they?"

"Sure are. But it might be that Oregon will wind up being British. Some folks don't like the British, so they head for California." Sublette shrugged, saying, "I'll take Oregon. The land's wet, but it's more my kind of country."

Jos had been sitting beside Sublette. "Tell me another story about Indians."

"You want a true story or a big lie?"

"You don't lie."

Sublette laughed and squeezed the boy. He winked across the fire at Mark and Leah. "I wish everybody had the good opinion of me this young man has." He leaned back and began a long tale, taking pleasure in the bright eyes of the boy, wishing he still had some of his faith in tomorrow and the days afterward.

SEVENTEEN

The train had begun to feel the strain of Sublette's Cutoff. The sun overhead grew as hot as a woodstove, throwing its pale, dry beams down on the oxen and the cattle as they struggled along. The dogs who accompanied the train seemed to feel the strain, for they no longer dashed along barking and chasing each other.

At times they traveled far into the night, bumping over sagebrush and following the beds of old lakes that were now dry as the dust itself that composed them. Each day they stopped and doled out water for the animals and turned them loose for the little graze that sparsely covered the floor of the desert. They breakfasted on dried meat and drank water so alkalized that even after one had drunk his fill his stomach seemed to swell.

At last they came to the Green River. The oxen and the stock smelled the water and broke into a stumbling lope as they approached. Jordan felt grimy and longed to strip off and plunge herself into the clear water. Some of the men and the boys did exactly that, going upstream for their baths. She could hear the faint sounds of their laughter floating on the air. "I wish I could go swimming," she complained.

Several of the women had gathered to wash dirty clothes—Mary Lee, Jennie Town, Leah Ellencourt, and Ellen Farr. "Why don't we, Jordan?" Jennie smiled. "We could go downstream and find us a place."

"All right." Jordan nodded. "Let's do it!"

"You better stay put," Ellen warned. "Could be Indians around here."

"I'd as soon be scalped as be filthy," Jordan announced. "Come on, Jennie."

The two women gathered soap and towels, then made their way downstream. They arrived finally at a curve in the stream sheltered by a clump of cottonwood trees. "This will do." Jordan nodded with satisfaction. She slipped out of her dress, then her underclothes, and waded into the stream. Settling down, she sighed with pleasure. "When we get to Oregon I'm going to have a bath twice a day!"

Jennie laughed, and as she waded in to sit facing Jordan, she said, "You'll be all puckered, Jordan."

The two women soaped and scrubbed, then they washed each other's hair. Finally they came to the bank, dried off, and dressed. They sat in the sun, letting their hair dry, and Jennie said, "It's funny how the people in the train have made little groups—just like in a small town."

"That's right," Jordan agreed. "The Grattons and the Barnhills keep together, and won't have much to do with the rest of us. And there's our group—Colin and me, you and your folks, and the Ellencourts."

"And the Farrs are close to the Mintons." Jennie nodded. "But some people seem so alone. Dr. Leverett and his brother, Les, they seem left out."

"So do Cato and Rosie," Jordan murmured. "We try to be as close as we can, but they're so shy around us."

Jordan pulled the brush through her hair, then remarked, "I've wondered why you never married, Jennie. You must have had chances. You're so pretty."

Jennie looked away, then rose quickly and said, "Guess we better get back. I've got lots of washing to do."

* * *

The late afternoon sun was almost down by the time the wagons were drawn into a circle. The Leverett brothers had bathed with the rest of the men, and now Les cooked the supper, which was not exciting, to say the least. One of the hunters had shot a buffalo, but the two men were tired of the steady diet of nothing but meat.

"I'd give anything for a plate of vegetables," Paul muttered. "Just for a plate of beans or cabbage or something green."

Les had eaten little, and now he pulled a flask out of his pocket and took a heavy pull on it. He saw the look of disapproval in his brother's eyes and smiled cynically. "Go on. Deliver the sermon."

"I didn't say a word, Les."

"You don't have to. I know what you're thinking."

"Wasn't thinking anything at all." Paul Leverett pulled a stick from the ground and poked the ashes of the fire.

The flames threw their reddish gleam on the face of Les. He took another swallow from the flask, capped it, and put it away.

The night had closed on the train, and the blackness was a reflection of the darkness in Les Leverett's soul. He had long ago outlived any hope of a good life. Samplings of the world had been enough to convince him that, for him at least, there was no nice, happy ending. From time to time he would watch a family, such as the Farrs, and wonder how it was that he had missed everything that Horace Farr had. A longing buried deep down rose up in him from time to time, and it came now. He turned and studied the face of his brother and wondered why God had made them so different—if it indeed was God. He had been proud of Paul, for his older brother had struggled to qualify as a physician.

Les said suddenly, "You've wasted most of your life trying to reform me. Quit thinking of me and think of yourself; I'm a lost cause."

A rebellious look settled in the rather sober features of Paul Leverett. "You know I'm not going to do that. You're a young man yet. You'll find your way."

"I don't think there's any way to find. I think we're just a bunch of cold carbohydrates headed for destruction."

"You know better than that," Paul argued.

"No, I don't, not for me at least. It's different for you."

Somewhere far away a wolf lifted his voice. It was one of the most mournful sounds the two of them had ever heard, and suddenly the wolf was joined by others, making a chorus that sounded funereal.

A touch of fear came to Les. Paul had practically dragged him away from the city, hoping that a new setting away from the temptations of civilization might offer a better life, but now he knew that it was not the outside that ate away at him—it was something deep on the inside.

Les listened to the wolves and murmured, "Listen to those fellows. They've got a simple life, haven't they? Just something to eat, a full belly for today. They don't even worry about tomorrow. Human beings don't have it that easy."

"It'll be better when we get to Oregon."

"There's nothing there for me, but there is for you." Les's face suddenly underwent a change, and words rose in him that he longed to say. At last, when the cry of the wolves had died down, he said, "You're a good man. Find a good woman, marry her, and raise children. Be happy."

"Sure, both of us should do that," Paul said. He waited for Les to say more, but the younger man rose suddenly and walked out into the darkness.

* * *

The train fared better after leaving the cutoff, and finally they reached Soda Springs on the sixteenth of June.

Ty Sublette stopped at Horace Farr's wagon. "Time for some lemonade." He lifted his hand and said, "See that water over there? It's got somethin' in it that bubbles. Tastes a little bit like beer."

Ellen Farr laughed suddenly. She nudged Horace with her elbow. "You'd better stay away from there. I'd hate to have you get drunk on springwater."

Payton Farr, age ten, said, "I'm gonna go get some lemonade. Can I, Pa?"

"I guess we'll all sample it."

Indeed, the entire train stopped to sample the water. Rita dipped a cup into it, then turned to find Corny Barnhill standing beside her. He was watching her, and she smiled at him. "Have you tried the water?"

"Not yet."

Rita handed the cup to him and said, "Taste it." She watched as Cornwall tasted the water and suddenly smiled. "Mighty good."

"I'm going to make some lemonade—mix

it with citrus syrup and some sugar." She
liked Cornwall, who was, Rita knew, a much
better man than his brothers, Theodore and
Ace, who were totally selfish—as was their
father, Ira. Corny followed Rita to the wagon,
carrying the bucket she had brought, and
watched as she mixed up something that
vaguely resembled lemonade. When Corny
tasted it, he smiled shyly. "That's mighty
good. You must be a good cook."

"Anyone can make lemonade!" Rita
laughed. She drank deeply from the cup.
"What are you going to do when you get to
Oregon, Corny?"

"Farm and raise cattle like everybody
else. What about you?"

"Oh, I'll do the same thing I did back
home. I miss the farm," she said suddenly.

Corny was rather tongue-tied in the face
of the young woman who had the red hair
and blue eyes of her mother. He had watched
Rita shyly, admiring her clean-run-
ning lines, and now she seemed to have ma-
tured even on the hardship of the trail. Her
hips seemed to be more rounded, and her
hair, as red as hair can get, was glossy and
hung about her shoulders. He noticed that
her firm young bosom filled out her dress

and turned his eyes quickly away. He was a young man who thought a great deal and talked little, but somehow in this girl he found what he admired most—pride and a joy in living. "Maybe we'll have a dance."

"You didn't dance with me the last time."

"This time I will." He laughed at himself then. "You'll be sorry. I'm not much of a dancer."

"I'm not either."

Then they were surrounded by members of Farr's family, and Corny felt strangely embarrassed. Horace Farr, tall and raw-boned, nodded and said, "Good mornin', Cornwall. Tryin' the lemonade out?"

"Yes, sir."

"How's your cattle doin'?" The Barnhills had the biggest number of cattle that followed the train, Ira Barnhill being, probably, the wealthiest man.

"They're mighty fine. I get tired," he said, "of eatin' their dust, but somebody has to trail the herd."

"Why don't you get Theodore or Ace to do it?"

Cornwall shook his head and did not answer. His two brothers used him miserably, he knew, but he had assumed that because he was the youngest that was the way things were.

Dorcas Farr, Horace's mother, was a thin, wiry woman. She studied the young man and something came to her spirit. She was an herb woman, and back on the farm people had come for miles to be treated by her, often preferring her ministration to the doctors that were available. She believed in signs and was superstitious. And now as she watched Cornwall Barnhill, something came to her. *Something in this boy. I don't know what it is.* She waited, and the feeling became even stronger. *Somehow he's tied in with this family. We'll have to wait and see.*

"Ma, will you be glad to get to Oregon?" Horace asked.

"I'm glad to be alive."

Horace laid his hand on his mother's shoulder. "I'm glad, too. I feel bad draggin' you away from the homeplace."

"One place is pretty much like another." Looking up, Dorcas Farr studied her son's face. She was proud of him, although she had difficulty phrasing the words. He was slow talking, with little education, but she knew that men listened to him and that he was a natural-born leader. He had wanted to be a schoolteacher but there had been no money for that, and now he had settled down in his life. Her eyes went over the two boys—Payton, unformed and brash at the age of ten—and Jack, seventeen and longing to be a man.

Rita stayed around the fire after the others had left, helping her grandmother do the cooking. She loved her grandmother and had a respect for the deep wisdom that lay in the old woman. Now she smiled at her and said, "Helen Mabry said if you cut your hair in the dark of the moon, you'll go bald. She said it was a fact."

Dorcas looked at the young woman and thought of the hope that was in her and the pure joy of living, and suddenly the feeling that had been gnawing at her became somehow larger and more ominous. *Trouble ahead for this girl, but I don't know what it is*, she thought.

"Sounds like nonsense to me."

"She said if she found a crooked feather in her hair, she'd marry a hunchback."

"More nonsense."

Rita removed the biscuits from the Dutch oven and smiled at her grandmother. "Nobody makes biscuits like you do, Grandma," she said.

"Lots of people do."

Rita outwardly paid little attention to superstitions but in secret she had put a four-leaf clover in her shoe, for she had heard that the young man she met immediately afterward would be her future husband. She had been chagrined when the next person she met had been an old man named Denton who certainly would not be a flt mate for her!

"I'm going down and get some more of the soda water, Grandma," she said. She left, and the blue eyes of the old woman followed her, and the feeling that ran through her she could not explain to anyone.

Gus Dabney saw the steer running right towards the woman, and instantly he shouted, "Look out!" The woman made no move, and he broke into a run. Yanking off his slouch hat, he yelled and caught the steer's attention. The woman still didn't turn, but the steer, a powerful animal with one horn turned up and one down, wheeled and made a pass at Gus. Gus dodged the horn, struck the steer in the face with his fist, and then he caught a wicked blow in the side from the up-turned horn. The force of it knocked him to the ground, and he expected the steer to attack him. But for some reason, the animal wheeled and galloped away, leaving a cloud of dust.

Getting to his feet, Gus snarled at the woman who had turned to face him, her hands full of wildflowers. "Are you deaf, woman?"

"Yes, I am."

Gus had never felt quite so foolish. He had seen the young woman at a distance, but he had no idea that she was the deaf girl that he'd heard about. Now he noticed that her eyes were wide-spaced and were blue-gray. Her dress fell away at her throat, showing the smooth ivory of her complexion. She had a fair and smooth and rose-colored complexion, and the light sliding across the golden surface of her hair was strangely attractive. Gus noticed also that her face was a mirror that seemed to change slightly as she studied him.

"Don't be embarrassed," she said. Her voice had a strange quality, almost toneless, and now Gus understood it was because she herself could not hear her words.

"Well, I'm glad you're all right," he said lamely.

"My name's Jennie Town."

"I'm Gus Dabney." He took a deep breath and suddenly winced.

"You're hurt," Jennie said quickly.

"Not bad. He just slapped me in the ribs with those horns of his. I should have shot him. He's nothin' but a troublemaker." He saw that the woman kept her eyes fixed on his lips. "Nothin' to worry about."

"I'm sorry you got hurt."

"Nothin' to that. Which wagon are you with?"

"My sister and her husband. That's Jesse and Mary Lee."

"Yes, the heavyset folks."

"That's right."

"They're the ones that play the fiddle and the zither at night sometimes."

"Yes, they're very musical."

"They play real good."

"I suppose so."

Gus felt that he'd made another blunder, but knew no way to make it right. At that moment a large, flop-eared hound came up stiff-legged and bared his fangs at Gus. "Hey, boy, cool down!"

"Bo, be quiet!" Jennie reached over and put her hand on the dog's head. "This is Gus," she said. "He's a friend."

"Your dog?"

"His name is Bo."

"You got a family—besides the Lees, I mean?"

"No." The word came quickly, and the woman reached over to pick up her bag as if the question bothered her.

"Here, let me help you fill that bag up."

Jennie Town gave him her smile again. "That would be nice of you."

As Gus helped her fill the sack with buffalo chips, he found himself acclimating his ways to hers. He always turned his head toward her when he spoke, and he deliberately pronounced his words with more care. She fascinated him. Finally when the sack was full, he said, "I'll carry it back to the wagon for you."

"It's not heavy."

"No trouble."

Fifty-five miles beyond Soda Springs lay Fort Hall, built by a man named Nathaniel Wyeth, but now operated by the Hudson

Bay Company. A few miles west of Fort Hall at the Burnt River the trail to Oregon suddenly branched off and wound its way down to California. It was a time of decision that was troubling, for some in the train had been discouraged.

After the train had settled in, several of the men met, squatting around outside the dried mud buildings that Paul Garnett used for his office. Garnett was a big man, English to the bone, and had been long employed by the Hudson Bay Company. He had been helpful enough to the train, trading some fresh oxen for those that had been worn out by Sublette's Cutoff. He took other sore-footed oxen and allowed up to twelve dollars for them.

Now Garnett sat down on a cane-bottomed chair, listening as Horace Farr and the other members of the council spoke of the road to come.

"Some of our folks are thinking about taking the road to California," Farr said, speaking slowly, with a thoughtful look in his eyes. "I'd hate to see us split up. What's the road like on ahead to Oregon, Garnett?"

"Pretty tough," Garnett said. "Lots of folks don't make it."

"How about the trail to California?" Farr asked.

"Much easier. The trail to California has a couple of high passes, but they've been cleared. There's water for the stock all the way, and the weather will be good. The trouble with going to Oregon is that you've got long dry marches where you'll lose stock. And when you get to the Columbia River, you'll have to build rafts and float your wagons through some white water—pretty dangerous." Garnett tipped his hat. "Gentlemen, I wish you well as you make your decision," he concluded. He turned and went back inside the store.

Pete Gratton brushed his tow-colored hair back from his eyes. "Well, there's a cheerful one, I've got to say."

Ira Barnhill shook his head. "It sounds pretty bad up ahead. What about it, Sublette?"

Colin put in. "He's making the trail ahead sound pretty bad."

Sublette smiled. "He doesn't want us to go to Oregon. He wants us to go to California."

"Why's that?" Colin asked.

"He wants Oregon for the English. Could be a war over it some day."

"What about California?" Dave Minton spoke up. "Maybe we ought to go there."

"It's your say." Sublette shrugged.

"What would be the difference? Isn't the land good in California?" Colin asked, his eyes on Sublette.

Sublette shrugged his shoulders and gazed up at the sky thoughtfully. "Only thing about California—it's been settled a long time. It's set in its ways, you might say. Lots of Spanish there. Oregon, now, it's pretty wild, but a man can make of it what he wants. Doesn't have any models to follow."

"Well, as for me," a tall thin man with curly hair spoke up, "I'd just as soon go to California." His name was Mort Johnson, and he had been a complainer on the trail.

Farr put his eyes on Johnson and said, "If that's what you're thinkin', that'll be fine."

Johnson rose stiffly. "I been talkin' with some others. It looks like there'll be eight families of us going to California." He turned and walked off without a backward look.

"Seems like some folks are pretty discouraged," Paul Leverett said. "But as for me, I'm going to Oregon."

"So am I," Orville Crane said. His face showed the sadness that marked one who had lost a child. The Cranes had less than anyone, but there was some backbone in the short, skinny man, some determination in him that pushed him on.

"All right. We'll go then."

"Well, we made it to the Snake," Ty observed. "We're getting there."

"It looks like a pretty rough river to me, Ty." Paul Leverett stared at the river doubtfully. "Don't see how we're going to cross it. I was expecting something like the Platte."

The Snake River was not wide and shallow like the Platte. It was a newer river, with steep sides and fewer meanders. The brown water rushed through the channel, cutting away at the sides, and something ominous lurked in the muted roar of the rushing waters.

"Must be an easier place than this to cross," Les said. "No wagon could get across here." He glanced up to see Sublette riding his gelding along the bank. When he pulled up, Les shook his head. "This river is nothing to fool with, Ty. How are we going to get across?"

Pulling his hat off, Sublette wiped his forehead with his sleeve. His eyes were narrow, and he shook his head. "Never saw the Snake this high. Must have been some big rains up in the headwaters."

"Can we cross it, do you think?" Les asked.

"Have to, Les, or go back to Missouri. But there's a ford upstream, not near as deep as this." He shook his shoulders in a weary gesture, then pulled the gelding aside. "Reckon we're going to camp tonight."

Horace Farr rode up and stood looking at the Snake River as it wound around. It was roiling and muddy brown, and Farr, always cautious, shook his head. "No way we can stay on this side?"

"Nope. We've got to get west of it, Horace. It won't be too bad. I've found a ford that seems pretty safe."

"Well, we might as well do it then."

Sublette knew that the wagon master was worried. "This is the worst we'll have to cross until we get to the Columbia. It'll be all right."

Sublette rode back to the Ellencourt's wagon and found Mark reading his Bible and Leah sewing something. She put her green eyes on Sublette as he came forward. "Are we going to cross, Ty?"

"Either that or turn back. Me, I'd rather cross."

"So would I. Is it going to be bad?" Mark asked.

"Hope not." Ty suddenly reached over and snatched up Jos Ellencourt, who was playing with a wooden wagon in the dirt. He tossed him high in the air, and the boy shouted, "Do it again, Ty!"

"Can't do it. You're gettin' too big and heavy. By the time we get to Oregon you'll be tossin' me up in the air."

"Where are you going now?" Leah asked.

"I saw a tribe of Indians back over at that Indian camp." Sublette pointed over. "I thought I'd go ask them about the trail on the other side."

Sublette left, and as he moved toward the camp, Jordan suddenly came up to him on her mare. "Where are you going?"

"Over to visit the Indians."

"Can I go along?"

"Sure." He walked along beside her, and she sat her horse until they reached the camp. The visit was a disappointing experience to Jordan. She said nothing, but listened as Ty spoke with three of the men. The camp stank to high heaven, and she had never seen such dirty people in all of her life. They were friendly enough and talkative but apparently slow-minded and dirty and naked.

When they left and were out of earshot, she laughed shortly. "Well, there goes all the romantic notions I had about Indians."

"How's that?"

"Well, I've been reading Cooper, about how noble the savages are, and I had an idea that they were tall, bronze, strong people with piercing eyes. Not like these at all."

"You're talking about the Plains Indians, like the Blackfeet. These fish eaters are altogether different." He looked down at her and added, "You ought to see what they eat besides fish—lizards, grasshoppers, anything you thought would choke a man."

"I wish I hadn't gone with you."

Sublette glanced at her. Suddenly he said, "You remind me of my wife."

"But she was Indian."

"Oh, not in looks. I meant she was like you in her ways."

It was the first time that Sublette had ever brought up his Indian family, and now Jordan felt free to say, "Leah told me you were married—but she was an Indian. How was she like me?"

"She liked life," Sublette said simply. "No

matter how rough things got she was always cheerful."

She studied Sublette's face, noting that the planes had been cut into his features by hardship, and she said softly, "You loved her very much, didn't you?"

"Reckon so."

Jordan said no more, but she filed this away. In some way, it seemed to her that Ty Sublette was lost. She knew other men who had lost their families to come through it and manage to move on, but this was not true of Sublette, and it grieved her.

The ford, such as it was, looked slightly better than the rest of the river. It was broken by two islands that sat like low rafts in the stream.

"It don't look too deep, Ty," Horace Farr said, gnawing on his lower lip nervously.

"Maybe deeper than you think. The water here is clear so it makes the bottom look close."

"Well, we'll have to try it then."

Les Leverett, for once, did not start drinking early in the morning—a fact which Paul noticed. *Maybe he's getting better,* he thought. Aloud he spoke his thoughts. "I don't like the looks of that ford."

Les looked at the river and said with some surprise, "It doesn't look too bad."

"I don't know. I just don't like it."

For several hours that morning preparations were made to cross. Finally Ty said, "I guess we're ready. I'll go across with your team, Horace." He moved to the head of the oxen and waded his sorrel out belly deep. "Come along." He waved his hand, and Horace Farr spoke to the oxen, who plodded obediently into the stream. The water, as Ty had feared, was much swifter than it appeared. There was a deceptiveness about it, and he hoped that there had been no holes cut out for the oxen to step in. They would drag the wagon with them down the stream, which was bad business. But the crossing went well, and soon Farr was on the west side of the river. He nodded at Sublette. "It wasn't too bad."

"I've seen lots worse."

The crossing went well for most of the morning. The Leverett brothers sat on the wagon seat together. As the power of the water seized the animal, Paul, who held the lines, said, "I don't like this. That river's strong. It could suck us right away."

"Everybody's made it so far," Les said cheerfully. He looked as if he were enjoying the sensation and suddenly put his arm around Paul and hugged him. "You're just an old worrywart," he laughed.

The weight of his brother's arm felt good to Paul Leverett. He enjoyed the feel of it and turned to say, "We're going to make it, Les. Both of us."

"Sure we will."

Even as he spoke a cry suddenly rang out. A woman screamed, and both men stiffened and whirled to see that a family named Lawton was in trouble. The oxen had stepped into a hole, and the wagon was skewed around sideways. Then Paul gripped Les's arm and said, "Look, there's a child! The river's got him!"

The doctor saw the child being thrown head over heels by the power of the river. "He'll drown!" he cried.

"I'll get him." Les pulled his boots off and leaped out of the wagon. He was a strong swimmer, but the water was powerful. There was a bend here, and they caught the full force of it.

Paul Leverett urged the team across, but by the time he got there he had lost sight of his brother and of the boy. Throwing himself off the wagon, he ran along the bank calling out, "Les—Les!"

The river rolled on, and frantically Paul searched it. He thought, perhaps, Les had come out on the other side, and then he saw a small group of people who had run down on the opposite bank. They were holding a small boy and waving frantically. "Where's Les?" he shouted, but got no answer.

Running back, Paul got on his saddle horse and rode back across the river. When he got there he found the family holding the boy, who was no more than three years old. The father, a short muscular man named Dick Lawton, could not speak. He glanced at his wife, who was holding the boy fiercely, but said nothing.

"Where's my brother?" Paul cried out.

"I think—" The man tried to speak and shook his head. "He got Toby there to the shallow water, and I waded out and grabbed him. I thought he was right behind me, but when I looked back the current took him. It—it carried him off, Doc."

Paul Leverett could not accept this. He

rode up and down the river looking frantically. Finally he looked up to see Sublette approaching him. "I can't find him. He's got to be here somewhere, Ty!"

Sublette pulled his horse up and compassion was in his eyes. "Bad news, Doc. We found him—but he's dead."

"He can't be!"

"I think he hit his head on a rock or something. He was drowned, and we couldn't bring him back."

Paul Leverett sat tensely on his horse. "Take me to him," he said hoarsely. "He can't be dead."

Sublette nodded, and the two went back to the small crowd that had gathered beside a form that was far too still. The doctor fell off his horse and stumbled to the body. "Les!" he gasped, unable to believe what had happened.

Ty Sublette watched silently as the doctor held the form of his dead brother. He had been at such a point in his life, and now he knew that nothing anyone could do or say could bring comfort to Dr. Paul Leverett.

EIGHTEEN

The death of Les Leverett struck the train hard. The dark truth that a young man in the prime of life could be snuffed out in a moment sobered the train. There was less singing, and it seemed that even the children played with less enthusiasm.

The train wended past landmarks along the way—Birch Creek, Burnt River, the Powder—and each day increased the sense of misery for all of them. After such days men and women alike would arrive at camp with no energy left for the work. Still, work they did, the men going through their chores with a slow motion as weariness pulled at them. They tended the stock, trudged along wearily as the animals plodded toward the distant goal, and the women cooked and washed when there was water. All looked to one goal—the Dalles—a small town nestled on the banks of the Columbia River. There they would build rafts and float down to Fort Vancouver. From there they could reach Oregon City, and their journey would be finished.

Late one Thursday afternoon, the sun was a huge red globe sinking down into the flatness of the desert country. Avis Barnhill, always alert to beauty and seldom finding it, wandered away from the camp, allowing her husband's hired men to cook the supper for once. As always, she had been careful to do her share of the work, for she wanted no one to accuse her of not holding up her end of the marriage.

The thought of her marriage depressed her, and she walked more swiftly into a grove of stunted evergreens that masked off the mountains that lay to the east. The same stream held the wagons in a crook as with an elbow. She thought of her past without willing it, and wished bitterly that she had never laid eyes on Ira Barnhill, but what was done was done. She had been willing to do anything to escape the grinding poverty that she had known for her first eighteen years, but it had taken only a few weeks for her to learn that some things are worse than poverty.

As she moved into the brush, the scrub pines grew thicker, and the sounds of the camp were muted. She forged ahead until she came to a stream, then stood listening to the sibilant chafing of the water on the stones. For a time she stood there trying to blot out the miseries of the trip. The death of Les Leverett had moved her, for she had seen the sadness in his face. He had been a failure—and this gave her a kinship with him. She thought of Billy Crane killed in the stampede, dead without having the life that had been owed to him.

At each turn of the trail tragedy had reached out and struck the train, and Avis knew more dark times lay ahead. As she regretted marrying Ira, she regretted this trip with every fiber of her strength.

Unhappy with herself and her thoughts, but helpless to resist them, Avis turned and followed the meanders of the stream. She had not gone far, however, when she started suddenly. An unusual sound had caught her, and fear raked across her as she thought of Indians. Alert in every nerve, she stopped and held her breath.

A movement caught her eye, and she turned to lean around a six-inch-thick fir. There she saw a man seated beside the stream, his head down on his folded arm. There was still enough light for her to see that it was Dr. Leverett, and drawing a sigh of relief she moved forward and said, "Hello, Doctor."

Paul Leverett wrenched himself around, and Avis saw with a shock that tears were running down his face. The men in her family did not cry, and the thought occurred to her, *That's what he's doing here. He's come away where no one can see him—and here I am interrupting him.*

For a long moment, Avis stood still, ready to turn and leave Leverett, but the sight of his face touched a deep chord in her breast. Moving forward, she saw that he did not even rise and knew then how badly he felt. He was, she had observed, a man of innate good manners and would rise for any woman in the train no matter how ancient or homely. She was now close enough to see him clearly, and she had never seen such misery on a face. The muscles of his cheeks seemed drawn, and yet there was a twitching around his mouth that he could not control. Without invitation she sat down beside him and took her eyes away from his face. She watched the clear water swirl over the mossy green stones and waited for him to speak. When he did not, she said quietly, "I didn't tell you, but I'm so sorry about your brother."

He did not answer and neither did she speak any more. She had not known Les Leverett well, but she had long understood that Paul and Les Leverett were as different as two men can be. Les had been a man with trim good looks and soulful blue eyes. He had never tried his wiles on her, but she well understood that it was in him. Now she turned her head and studied Paul's face—not at all handsome, but a face that people could trust. A straight nose, rather thin features, and sharp gray eyes now dull with an ache that brought a quick feeling of pity to Avis.

"It—it was all my fault."

The words were halting, and Avis turned so that she could see him better in the falling darkness. "It couldn't be your fault. He was trying to save that boy's life."

"You don't understand. He—he didn't want to come on this trip."

"I didn't want to come either."

"But you had a choice."

"No, I didn't."

Her words fell on Leverett, and he glanced at her briefly before saying, "I should have left him back in the city. He hated discomfort."

"Why did you want him to go, Doctor?" It

sounded formal to call him that, but she felt uncomfortable using his first name.

"He was in trouble, and I wanted to get him away from it."

"I take it it wasn't the first time."

Surprise leaped into Leverett's eyes. The woman had a penetrating insight, and he bowed his head and whispered, "All his life he's been in trouble. He was my kid brother, and I tried to keep him out of it from the time we were in short pants. But I—I couldn't do it."

A breeze rose, whispering in the tops of the stubby pine trees, and the two of them sat there for a long time. Avis felt she had to say something. Indeed, a surprising compassion arose in her. She felt herself wanting to reach out to him, and the desire became real. She reached over and took his hand in both of hers. It was the first time she had voluntarily touched a man in years, and she felt a gust of surprise at her own impulse. "You mustn't blame yourself. You meant well, and that's all any of us can do."

Leverett's eyes had opened with surprise when she had taken his hand. He was not a man who was good with women, but this one had some quality that touched him. He

needed a woman's compassion and tenderness, and now the simple act of touching
broke down the walls of his self-restraint. He
could not stem the agony of regret that rose
in him. Clamping his teeth together, he struggled against the sobs that came to his throat.

Avis Barnhill did something that she
would not have done for any other man she
knew. He seemed almost like a small child
struggling against his tears, and she thought
the better of him for it. Her husband, she
knew grimly, would not cry if every one of
his sons and she herself were killed by Indians. He would grow angry and fight and
curse—but he would not weep. The very
fact that Paul Leverett could do this caused
her to reach over and put her arms around
his neck. He turned with surprise to face her,
and she laid her cheek on his. And the fact
that it was wet with tears somehow touched
her greatly. "It's all right to cry," she whispered. "I do it myself sometimes."

The words loosed something in Leverett
that had been held back. With a strangled
cry he threw his arms around her and put his
face on her shoulder. She felt the pressure of
his face against her neck, and she held him
tightly, stroking his shoulder with her free

hand and making small comforting noises. Her lips were tender as she held him that way for some time. The sobs shook his body as if he were being struck by mighty blows.

Avis could not remember a moment like this. She had known everything but gentleness in men, but now she sensed it in this one—who knew so much but was not strong physically. He could not use a gun nor fight, but she was sick of that. She held him until finally the sobs ceased, and then she whispered, "That's good, Paul. We all need to cry sometimes."

Leverett straightened up slightly, but still her arms were around him, and his one arm was around her waist. She looked into his eyes and saw that something had replaced the grief, and she knew the sorrow would return. But for now she had managed to exorcise the demon that was tearing him to pieces.

"I—I never did that before."

Avis did not move. She was pressed tightly against him, and she understood at that moment that he put his grief aside only to be made conscious that he was holding a woman in his arms. Any other man would have taken advantage, but she saw that his

innate shyness would not permit him to do
so. Still, the desire was in his eyes, and
when he moved forward and put his lips on
hers, she placed her hand on the back of his
neck and received his kiss. There was
something in it that no other man's kiss had
ever had. She knew she had used no wiles
to draw him on, and there in the falling darkness she understood that she could stir him
easily enough. She was a woman with a
woman's dreams and desires, and none of
these had been fulfilled. Suddenly she gave
herself to him with a soft, wild, half-giving of
her body, and then knowing that she was on
the brink of something that she would regret—and that he would regret, too—she
put her hand on his chest and turned her
head away.

"I'm—I'm sorry," Paul whispered.

"Not your fault. You're just at a bad time
right now, Paul."

Carefully she drew her arms back, and he
moved back also, but he was watching her.
"I don't want you to think," he said haltingly,
"that I'm the kind of man who would take
advantage of a woman."

"No." She smiled. "You're the kind of man
that women will take advantage of."

"What?"

"You don't know women very well, do you?"

"No. I suppose I don't."

"I don't want you to think I'm the kind of woman that would let any man that walks along kiss me."

"Why, of course not!"

"I guess I've been alone too long. I didn't mean to kiss you. Any woman can do that to a man."

"You're not any woman, Avis."

Avis sat there and knew that if she stayed longer, both of them would be in danger. He was weak from the loss of his brother, and she had been weakened by the blows that life had dealt her. He was a man, she understood, that would be kind, but he was still a man with his desire.

Quickly she rose and said, "I've got to get back." She waited until he stood in front of her and then nodded. "Don't be grieved. Or if you must grieve, don't let it destroy you."

"He had so much good in him. He could have been so much!"

"He saved a boy's life. That's more than most of us do in a lifetime. Maybe that's why he was on this train."

The words interested Leverett. "Do you believe that, Avis?"

"I don't know. The preacher would say so."

"It helps hearing you say that."

She smiled then, and her smile was a small lightness around her mouth. She should have been a laughing woman, rich and self-possessed, but she had had much of that crushed out of her by circumstances. Now she turned from him and did not speak again.

Paul Leverett stood there looking after her and knew that when he was an old man he would still remember this moment. He would never forget her gentleness—nor the touch of her lips. He gave her time to get back, then his lips tightened, he nodded as if making a decision, and he walked back in the direction of the camp.

NINETEEN

Ty threw up his hand, and when the train halted, he pointed toward the town that lay ahead. "Well, there it is, Horace—the Dalles."

Horace Farr stared at the small collection of buildings, and suddenly snatched his hat off and threw it high into the air. "Thank God! We made it!" He turned to Ellen sitting beside him on the seat, and yelled, "We done it, Ellen—we done it!"

Farr's yell echoed down along the line of wagons, and people came running from all along the line. The cries of those in the lead echoed back to those in the rear of the train, and soon a crowd stood looking at the settlement. Ty sat his horse, smiling slightly at the sight. It had been an easier trip than he had anticipated, but he knew that none of these farmers could understand that. He dismounted and led his gelding to where the Ellencourts stood looking at the town. "Looks pretty good, doesn't it?"

Mark laughed, his face more relaxed than Sublette had ever seen it. "You did it, Ty! You got us here!" he exclaimed, and came to throw his arms around the tall man.

Sublette was touched by the gesture, and held on to Ellencourt, conscious of the fragility of the man. Releasing him, he grinned and winked at Leah. "I reckon the good Lord had a little something to do with it." Then he bent and picked up Jos and ruffled his hair. "Wonder if any of the stores in this town has any candy. I'm nigh starved to death for a little sweetening."

"I betcha there is, Ty!"

Leah watched her son's face and remarked, "Don't you make him sick, Ty."

"Boy ought to get sick on good things once in awhile." Ty grinned. "And I'm inviting the preacher and his whole family to supper tonight at the Umatilla House—finest café in the Dalles." Ty nodded and gave Jos a squeeze before putting him down. He smiled at Leah, enjoying the light that danced in her eyes. "We'll all make ourselves sick."

"You're a bad man, Tyler Sublette!" Leah suddenly laughed and then lifted her arms high in the air. "I just want to shout!"

"Reckon that would be all right." Ty nodded.

Mark came and put his arms around

Leah, and Sublette was touched by the joy that filled the couple. "Get your menfolks washed down and dressed in their best, Leah," he said. "I'll come by about five and we'll do the town."

"All right, Ty." Leah held tightly to Mark, and as Sublette moved away leading his horse, she said, "We owe Ty so much!"

"Yes, we do." Mark looked down at Jos, smiled, and said, "Be sure you wash your neck, son. We're dining in style tonight."

Jos grinned at his father. "You, too, Pa," he said. He whirled and ran to join a group of young boys who were gathered to stare at the town, and Mark said, "The Lord has brought us here, Leah—with the help of Ty Sublette. I have to admit that my faith got a little shaky at times."

"Yes, and he's going to do great things with you. You'll see!"

"Well, we're here, thank God!"

"Some of us aren't," Leah whispered. She was thinking of the lonely graves that marked their journey.

"That's right, and they'll be missed. But it'll be all right now."

"Do you really think so? There's so much to do!"

"We'll do it together," he said. "You and Jos and me." He smiled and leaned over to kiss her cheek.

Jordan and Colin cleaned up and went into town as soon as the train had made camp. There was a holiday atmosphere, and Jordan said happily, "Every one is so happy, aren't they?"

"Sure. It's been a tough trip," Colin agreed, then added, "We're not in Oregon yet. Still have to float that river. And even after we get there, we have to work like mules for years."

"We'll do it," Jordan said quickly. She glanced at Colin and saw that he was under some restraint. She was disappointed and could not understand why he was not as ex-cited as she was. Everyone else was beam-ing with joy, and those who were on their way to town were laughing. She took Colin's arm. When he turned to face her, she said, "I thought you'd be happy the trip was nearly over."

Colin put his arm around her. "I'm just an old grouch," he said, and found a smile for her. "I am happy, sweetheart." He motioned toward the town and said, "Ty told me this place was a Methodist mission once. It was no more than a mountain niche—a breathing space between the heights and the river. Nobody but the Indians knew about it until the Methodists built a mission."

"I wonder if the mission was a success."

"Ty said it hasn't changed the Indians too much."

"Mark and Leah will be interested. Maybe they'll stay here and help with the mission."

The two moved into town, and the influx of people from the train soon filled the streets. No one had a great deal of money to spend, but just the knowledge that the dangers and hardships of the trail were mostly behind them loosened both men and women. Colin grew more cheerful, and Jordan was pleased that he seemed to have shaken off the dark mood that had been on him for the past weeks.

For two hours they roamed the streets, Jordan going into every store and looking at merchandise. Since there were very few stores, they found themselves with little to do as the afternoon drew to a close. Finally Colin left to join a group of men who were meeting to discuss the building of rafts. Jordan was joined by Avis Barnhill, who said, "Not much of a town, but it looks good to me."

"Maybe Fort Vancouver will be better—or Oregon City."

"I suppose so." Avis glanced over at the Wild Horse Saloon across the street, and remarked, "I suppose the men will get drunk." She laughed, saying, "I don't suppose you and I could join them, could we?"

"I don't think so." Jordan smiled. The two women walked the streets and observed the sights. "Look, Avis, there's Ty and the Ellencourts."

Avis followed Jordan's nod, and saw the group going into the Umatilla House. "Going for a meal without flies all over it," she said. Then she saw Paul Leverett coming down the street. "Hello, Doctor," she said. "Glad to be in a real town?"

"Yes, I am. I'm looking for a barber."

"If you don't find one," Jordan said, "let me do it. I cut Colin's hair. You can take it off my bill when I come in for my first baby."

Leverett smiled. "Will that be pretty soon?"

"I hope so. I love babies."

"Nasty screaming little things," Leverett

teased. He turned to Avis and was ill at ease, remembering the incident when she'd found him grieving over his brother. He could not forget the sweetness of her as she'd held him, but he was embarrassed that he'd broken down. "Are you two spending all your money?"

"No," Avis answered. "Just glad to be someplace besides on the trail."

"Everyone is relieved." Leverett nodded. "The trail took something out of all of us." A sadness crossed his face, and both women knew that he was thinking of his brother.

"Come along with us," Avis said quickly. "You can help us shop—and you can tell us what you're going to do when you get to Oregon."

"I'm not much on shopping," Leverett protested, but allowed himself to be pulled along the boardwalk. "As for what I'm going to do, that's no secret. I'll start a practice in Oregon City."

"That will leave us without a doctor," Avis said.

"No, it won't. I'll get a wagon and make rounds pretty regularly."

"That'll be good, Paul." Avis smiled at him. "Something we'll all look forward to."

Leverett accompanied the two women for a time, then said, "Guess I ought to get that haircut—or really I ought to be with the rest of the men. I didn't think I'd be much help, though. I don't know a thing about building a raft."

"Neither do they." Jordan smiled. "I think they're meeting at the saloon just to get their drinking done."

"Well, I'm not a drinking man—but I guess they deserve it. Anyway, I'll go listen."

"Did you hear that Mark is going to have a service tomorrow?"

"No, I didn't."

"He said it will be short," Jordan said. "It'll be at the camp about ten in the morning. You be there, you hear?"

"I'll be there."

The two women watched the doctor cross the street headed for the saloon, and Avis said, "I feel so sorry for Paul."

"Why is that? He's got a profession that he loves."

"He has no one to share it with. He should be married."

"I wonder why he hasn't."

Avis didn't answer for some time, then said, "Nobody knows about things like that."

She saw that Jordan was looking at her strangely, then added quickly, "Come on, let's go have a cup of tea. I want someone to wait on me for a change."

The arrival at the Dalles brought a loosening to the spirits of everyone, it seemed. Most of the men did visit the saloons and let off steam, and the women patiently endured this as a part of life.

Gus Dabney had gone to the saloon with the other men, had downed a few drinks, but had not gotten drunk. He had been interested in talking about how the rafts would be constructed, and had slept well.

The morning sun shone brightly, and Gus fixed breakfast and ate. Afterwards, he sat drinking coffee. Theodore Barnhill came by and sampled the coffee. The two men talked, and finally Gus said, "Well, we made it."

"Just barely." Theodore was usually a silent man. Now a sly smile lifted the corners of his broad mouth. "Doc Leverett's pretty sweet on Avis. Did you notice?"

"Shut your mouth, Theodore!"

Theodore stared at Gus, then snorted and

turned around. "Well, I'm sorry! I didn't mean to offend you! Pardon me for speakin' the truth!" He turned and stalked away, his back stiff with anger.

Gus Dabney was an observant man and had watched Paul Leverett after his brother's death. He knew the doctor was more sensitive than most people and therefore grief would hit him harder. He had also noticed that Leverett's eyes always followed Avis Barnhill. That had not surprised Gus, but her response had. He saw that the two had some sort of magnetism, and it troubled him. *Doc's a fine man. I hope he don't take after Barnhill's wife. That's a shootin' business.*

He put down the wagon wheel that he was working on and walked out to the edge of the crowd. It was Sunday, and Mark Ellencourt would be preaching in an hour. The crowd was beginning to gather to socialize beforehand, and Gus noticed that Jennie Town was standing at the back of the circle. Gus moved over to stand beside her. When she turned to him, he moved his lips to frame the words, "Do you like preaching?"

"Yes."

"I reckon Reverend Ellencourt's a good one."

Jennie studied Gus for a moment, then a smile came to her. "Do you like preaching?"

"Good preaching."

"What's that?"

"I'm not so much on hellfire and damnation, though I don't have a doubt about it, but the preacher up there, he talks about the love of God. I like that."

Jennie regarded the homely man carefully. She had studied him on the trail, and now she said, "I want you to do me a favor."

"You name it," Gus said eagerly.

"The Smiths have got to build a raft, and Cato doesn't know how. Nobody else on the train is going to help him. Most of them don't like black people, but I bet you could help."

"Build a raft? Why, you bet! I've got to build one, too, for the Bryces. I'll go see Cato. I kind of like him."

"They're good people."

Gus had noticed that Jennie spent a great deal of time with the dark-skinned couple. He had felt good about it, for many of the travelers had nothing to do with them. Sublette was not one of them, and Jordan Bryce was often seen taking a meal with the Smiths.

She turned to face him, the structures of her face making definite and pleasing con-tours, and finally she said, "Your whole name is Gus?"

"It's really Augustus, but that's too long a handle." Dabney grinned at her and said, "I like your name, Jennie."

"Why, thank you." The compliment seemed to please her. "It is pretty, I think. Why are you going to Oregon, Gus?"

The question surprised Gus. He pulled off his hat and ran his hand through his hair, which was down almost to his shoulders now. "Why Oregon? I don't know. Just some place to go."

"You don't have a wife or a family?"

"No. Never have."

"Why not?"

Gus suddenly laughed. His teeth were very white and gave his homely face almost an attractive appearance. "You ask a lot of questions, but I guess that's like a woman. Why are *you* going to Oregon?"

An expression that Gus could not read flashed across the woman's face. "I didn't have much choice. I had to go with my sister and her husband."

Gus chewed his lip thoughtfully. "Well,

you'll probably like it there." She grew quiet, and he changed the subject. "I see you reading sometimes."

"Yes," Jennie said, and she smiled. "The only time I ever argue with Jesse, my brother-in-law, is about my books. He says they weighed too much, but I have to have my books. I read a lot."

"What do you read about?"

"Oh, everything. I like novels, travel books." She gestured. "Come along. I'll show you something."

Gus followed her to the wagon. She went to the rear of it, reached over, and pulled out a flat leather case. She opened it and took something out, then said, "Look."

Gus took it, and his eyes widened. "Why, that's me!"

"Yes."

Gus was staring at the drawing. He could not believe it. The sharp lines, and the features that she had captured were him, even to the old hat that he wore. He looked up and smiled. "You didn't make me very pretty."

Jennie dropped her head for a moment, then looked up. "I just draw what I see. You can keep it."

"Why, thanks, Miss Jennie." Gus could not get over the drawing. "You've got some more?"

"Oh, yes."

"I'd like to see them."

Jennie got another bundle, and for the next half hour Gus took delight in the drawings. She had drawn a great many scenes of wagon train life, and Gus was amazed. "Look there. There's Ty Sublette to the like! And that there is Al Catlow. He's a bad one all right. You caught that. How do you do that with just a pencil?"

"I don't know."

Finally Jennie said, "I didn't mean to bore you."

"I'm not bored," Gus said. He was not a man who was comfortable around women, but somehow he was around this one. He took a deep breath, then said, "You never had a husband?"

She was silent so long that Gus thought she missed his question, but he did not want to repeat it.

"No. I'd not make a good wife. A man wants someone that can hear him." She took the drawings and rose. "I think the preaching's about to start."

Gus watched her leave, then went to stand beside Jordan. He told her what had happened. "She can draw like nothin' you ever saw, Miss Jordan," he said, showing her the drawing she'd given him. "But she said a husband wouldn't want a wife that couldn't hear him. I don't see that."

Jordan studied the homely face of Gus Dabney. "I like Jennie a lot, Gus. She's a very fine woman."

"Yes, she is. I'm sorry she can't hear—but there are worse things than that in a woman."

One of the small pleasures of the hard trek had been the preaching services along the way. Almost all the train, even those who had little religion, had come to listen to Mark Ellencourt preach. He was not a fire-eating sort, but something in his manner pleased those who came to hear him.

"I won't preach a long sermon, folks, for I think what we need is a time of thanksgiving." Ellencourt spoke clearly, and his voice carried to the back of the crowd. "I went through my Bible last year, trying to find out what the worst sin was, and I was surprised. I thought it would be murder or adultery, but it wasn't. I found three sins that are worse than any of those according to the Word of God. One of the sins that God hates is pride. Another is unbelief—and the other is ingratitude. Over and over the Scripture mentions these as the sins that do most to destroy us. And you know that these are 'invisible' sins. A man or a woman can be eaten up with doubt, but never show it. The same is true of pride. The book of Proverbs states that 'Six things the Lord hates, yes, seven are an abomination to him.' And the first sin it mentions is 'a proud look.'

"As I read through the Scripture, I was rebuked by the Holy Spirit, friends, for I found all three of those terrible sins in my own heart—especially ingratitude! Why, we ought to get up shouting thanks to God for his goodness to us! Just to be able to walk around, to see and hear, think what it would mean if we lost these things! I marked every verse in the Psalms that spoke of giving thanks, and I was shocked. I think that's the reason David was 'a man after God's own heart.' He was a flawed man, but he did give thanks to God. He danced before God with all his might, the Scripture says, and I know that God loves that spirit of thanksgiving."

A silence had fallen over the crowd, and Ellencourt spoke eloquently for some time. "We can't all be great speakers, and not all of us have great faith—but we can all give thanks—"

Suddenly a voice broke through. "We don't need your preachin', Ellencourt!"

Mark turned quickly to see Al Catlow. He was wearing his greasy buckskins as usual, and there was a brutal look in his eyes. He appeared to be drunk. "Shut up about all that stuff! It ain't true anyhow."

Mark Ellencourt did not raise his voice. "Why don't you join us, Mr. Catlow?"

"*Mr.* Catlow! Well, now, ain't you polite! No, and I don't want any more preaching— so shut up!"

A wave of disagreement brushed through the crowd, for everyone liked Ellencourt. He had not gotten better physically on the trip, and it had been an effort for him to preach. Gus saw his face was pale, and he saw also that none of the men on the train were about to challenge Al Catlow. The man was bull strong, mean, and strong enough to ruin most men in a fistfight.

The disturbance swept through the crowd, and then Sublette walked across to stand in front of Al. He was taller, but he seemed small beside the bulk of the other man. "Shut your mouth, Al." He spoke quietly enough, but everybody heard the words.

"You're tellin' me to shut up?"

"Either shut up or leave."

Such a blind rage filled Catlow that the crowd was startled. He had no gun on him, but if he had, he would have reached for it. Catlow's body tensed, and he stared through half-lidded eyes at Ty Sublette. Finally Catlow cursed and turned and shoved his way out through the crowd.

"Go on with your sermon, Reverend," Ty said. He went back to stand beside Cato Smith and his wife, Rosie, who were on the outskirts of the crowd.

After the service was over, Cato Smith said, "That's one mean man, Captain. He ain't gonna forget what you done."

Sublette smiled. "I hope he does. You and Rosie ready to build a raft?"

"I don't know much about it."

The black man's face was troubled, and at that moment Gus Dabney walked up. "Well, Cato, I got some ideas about gettin' these wagons downstream. If we all work together, I think we can do it."

Relief and surprise washed over Cato's face. "That would be mighty nice of you. It purely would. I don't know anything about no raft buildin'."

"We'll make it up to you, Mr. Gus," Rosie said.

"Why, no trouble at all," Gus said. "We've all got to hang together."

The raft building proved to be simpler than everyone had thought. The forest was crowded with tall, straight fir trees, and the men soon had enough for rafts. Gus Dabney built the first one, and the others were built on the same model. Once they were built and fastened firmly together, the wagons were rolled on them by muscle power, and then the wheels were removed and the wagons tied down. Everyone was cheerful and the work went quickly. According to Sublette they had reached the river at the best time to make the trip. "In the spring this river gets plumb rambunctious," he said as they were all lined up, ready to shove off. "But now it's quiet. We just float down, and first thing you know we'll be in Fort Vancouver."

Two days later every wagon was taken

apart and placed on rafts, the wheels off. The animals were aboard except for the herd, which would be taken around the river passage on a narrow trail. Cato Smith came to look up at Dabney as they fastened the last tie-down. "You don't know what it means to me, Mr. Gus."

"Why, Cato, it wasn't nothin'."

"Maybe not to you, but it was to me and Rosie. If you ever want anything from us, you just say."

"I reckon you and me better start fishin' together, Cato."

Cato Smith took a deep breath. Rosie's eyes were on him, and their glances met. They had known much cruelty from white people, but this one was different. "I'd like that mighty well," Cato said. "I purely would."

"Look, there's Fort Vancouver." Colin was standing at the front of the raft with a long pole to guide it through the shallows. He turned to Jordan and said, "I'm glad to get here."

"So am I, Colin."

Remorse swept through Colin at that moment. He had not been pleasant company for the last half of the journey. He was a man that demanded change, and the long hard grinding labor of the trip had made him cranky. He put his arm around Jordan and said, "Sorry I've been such a beast."

"You weren't a beast." She turned her face up to be kissed, then she said, "I've got a present for you."

Colin smiled at her. "Where did you buy a present?"

"I didn't buy this one."

"Well, all right. Did you make it?"

"We both did." She watched something change in his face and then laughed aloud and put her hand on his cheek. "I can't give it to you until about March."

Colin Bryce was not a man easily surprised, but when what she had said sank into him a tremor went through him. "You mean—a baby?"

"Yes."

Colin put his arms around her and kissed her. "I never even thought about it."

"That's what happens when people get married." Jordan had been hurt by his callous treatment of her during the past few weeks, and now her voice trembled as she said, "You don't mind, do you, Colin?"

Colin held her more tightly. "Mind! It's the best news I've had since I got a wife." He took his hat off, waved it around, and shouted, "Hey, everybody, I'm going to be a father!"

Gus Dabney, steering the raft at the back, let out a shrill cry. And Cato Smith, who was on the raft out further in the stream, yelled also. "That's mighty fine, Mr. Colin!"

Jordan had worried about telling Colin this news. She herself was delighted, for she loved babies and children. The trip had been hard on her, but the hardest thing had been Colin's inability to adjust. Now that they were almost there she knew that things would be better.

"It's a new land for a new baby," she said. "Oh, Colin, I'm so happy!"

He held her tightly, glad that the long journey was over. "I'm happy, too, Jordan," he whispered, and he held her as the raft slowly moved toward the land.

PART THREE

TWENTY

"Look, Ma—it's a real town!"

Leah Ellencourt looked down at Josiah, then reached out and ruffled his fine blonde hair. "Yes, it's Oregon City—a real town." She smiled. "Are you glad to see it?"

"Yes," Jos said fervently. "Can I have some candy?"

"I expect so. Look, there's a store over there. Why don't you go in and pick it out? Your father and I will be there in a few minutes."

Mark Ellencourt smiled slightly as he watched Jos run across the wide street. "I wish everyone were as easy to satisfy as Jos is," he remarked. "Just a little candy or a few toys, and he's content."

The train had reached Oregon City on September twenty-first. They were all worn down by the journey, and when Leah reached over and took Mark's arm she was momentarily shocked by the thinness of it. He had continued to lose weight on the last half of the journey, and his eyes seemed to be sunken deeply into their sockets. She said nothing of this, however, but observed instead, "It's a sight for sore eyes, but it isn't much of a town, is it?"

Oregon City, which had been the El Dorado of their journey, the goal which they'd looked forward to over the long months on the trail, was indeed not much to look at. It was the first town except for the Dalles and a couple of forts that the pair had seen since leaving Independence, but the town itself looked good to them, as rough as it was. Oregon City consisted of some fifty houses and had not been laid out with a great deal of thought. The roughly built structures seemed to have been scattered across the rise and fall of the land, and as the two walked slowly along, Leah studied the main street. She noted a hotel, a dressmaker's shop—which surprised her somewhat—several saloons, and a bank. Other businesses were spaced on the edge of the wide street, and she caught the smell of fresh-baked bread emerging from a café right next to the general store where Jos had disappeared.

"I'm glad we're here, Leah."

"So am I. It's been a hard trip. You're going to have to rest up."

"I don't think I'm going to be able to do that."

"You have to. You've got to pace yourself, Mark."

Ellencourt turned and studied Leah. She was one of the strongest women he had ever known—not just the physical strength in her full-figured, tall body—but in her spirit. He had known from the very beginning that in many respects this woman was stronger than he. She had never intimated any such thing, but at times Mark Ellencourt wished that he were stronger for her sake. "A woman needs a strong husband," he had said to her once, to which she had responded instantly, "And I have one."

"We've got to find a place to start a church," Ellencourt remarked.

"Plenty of time for that. We need to find something to live in—if there's anything available."

"Well, come along. Let's buy Jos candy, and then we'll look around."

The pair entered the store that was identified by a weathered sign that announced "Jonah Smallwood General Store." When they entered, Leah saw Jos standing on tiptoe and peering at the candy in a glass case.

A thin man sporting a heavy mustache nodded in greeting. "Evenin'. I'm Jonas Smallwood. You folks get in with the train?"

"Yes, we did. I'm Mark Ellencourt. This is my wife, Leah."

"Well, I'm pleased to welcome you to Oregon City." Smallwood smiled, revealing two gold teeth. His eyes went down to Jos, and he winked at Ellencourt. "I think a young man that's made a trip all the way from Missouri deserves a reward." He leaned over and smiled. "Pick out what you like, son. On the house."

"Really?"

"Sure enough." Smallwood watched as Jos studied the candy and shook his head. "That boy's just like all of us. Can't make decisions too good. I'm the same way myself." His gray eyes studied the pair, and he asked, "Are you going to settle on a place?"

"No, we're here to start a church, Mr. Smallwood."

"Do you tell me that! Why, that's mighty fine! We had a preacher here, but he moved on. We just been waitin' for the Lord to send somebody else."

Mark Ellencourt took a deep breath and

turned to smile at Leah. "Didn't I tell you that God would go before us?"

"Do you have a church already started, Mr. Smallwood?" Leah asked eagerly.

"Well, I guess what we got mostly," Smallwood said, judiciously stroking his sweeping mustache, "is a bunch of little lambs running around without no shepherd. I won't say all of them are true sheep, but there's a few good folks here. Maybe you'd care to come and preach for us this comin' Sunday."

"I would indeed!" Mark said warmly.

"Well, the trouble is we ain't got no church building. We used Sy Huggin's barn, but it burned down. So we've been meetin' out-of-doors mostly. But if you're the man that God wants here, maybe we could start thinkin' about a real church house. Need to get one in before winter, too."

"I believe the Lord has brought me and my family here. Of course, you don't know anything about me, and you'll want to hear me preach. But I hope that God puts us together as a people and a pastor."

"Well, amen to that, preacher! Now, boy, you pick out *three* kinds of candy there. And, preacher, I want you to pick out somethin' you been real hungry for on the trail as your first offering from one of your new flock. And, Miz Ellencourt, you go find a bolt of cloth you like, enough to make a new dress."

The Ellencourts thanked him warmly, then moved around the store and made their selections. Leah whispered to Mark, "Isn't it wonderful? God's gone before us."

"Yes, it is. I know God's going to do great things in this place." A cloud passed over Mark's face. "I just hope I'm strong enough to hold up to it."

"God will give you strength."

"He gave me a good wife and a fine son."

Such remarks always touched Leah. She said cheerfully, "Look at this cloth. Do you think it's too colorful for a preacher's wife?"

"Not for this preacher's wife."

"I may look like a honky-tonk girl."

Ellencourt laughed. He was feeling relieved that the door had been opened for his work. He reached over and hugged her and whispered, "You're a wonder, Leah."

Jordan stood at the back of the circle which had arranged itself. The men had formed a small group within the center of the wagons. Now Jordan's eyes went around the faces, and she saw the tiredness there. The trip had sapped their strength so that they were not what they had been when they left Missouri. They moved almost with the care of old people. Their weakness had caught up with them, whatever it had chanced to be. *We're worn out. This land out here isn't free like they say. Every one of us paid something for it.* Her eyes touched on Orville Crane and his wife, Fanny, and she knew that even though they had five other children, they still grieved over their son Billy.

Actually the meeting was almost accidental, for Farr had not called it. It was as if those who had clung together for strength on the long trip now were drawn as a magnet draws filings, so that the small group waited expectantly to hear what Farr would say.

Horace Farr looked around and said in a quiet tone, "Well, we made it this far, but now we've got to make a choice."

He went on to speak about some of the possibilities, and his eyes went around the group as if weighing the strength that they had left. The men and the women and a few of the children listened carefully, and Jordan knew that their decisions would affect their very survival. Some sort of order would have to be imposed on the mountains and the hills and the prairies for them to live. They could not live alone, and the urge for companionship, for friends, for union with others, brought them together.

"All of us will have to make our own decisions," Farr said. "But I'd like it if most of us could stay together." He looked around the train and smiled slowly. "We've become neighbors on the trail to Oregon, and I think it would be comforting to me to know that my neighbors were just over the next hill."

Pete Gratton spoke up quickly. "I've been talking with some of the folks around town. From what I hear the area around Blue Creek might be good."

"I've heard about that. I've been talkin' about that place, too," Jesse Lee said. "But according to what I hear, Blue Creek gets under water part of the year, and so does the land around it. You can't farm from a rowboat."

"I like what I've heard about the Tulatin Valley," Farr put in. "I'm thinking that's the driest ground around."

The talk went on for some time, the men

arguing mildly. Jordan saw Ty Sublette turn and walk away, and was curious. He went to sit beside Leah Ellencourt, and interest quickened Jordan's eye. The pair of them made a striking couple. Sublette was over six feet, strongly built, weathered with a capable look that seemed made for a land such as this. Leah was Jordan's idea of attractiveness in a woman. She admired Leah's ash-blonde hair, green eyes, and quietness, sometimes broken by a flash of humor that made her a woman that men would notice. Jordan's eyes went then to Mark Ellencourt, who stood back. Since the Ellencourts were not going to stake out a claim, they had taken no part in the discussion about the best place to settle. Nevertheless, Mark listened carefully, and Jordan noted how thin he had become on the trip. They made a rather strange couple, and she had wondered about their relationship. Now she glanced back at Sublette and Leah, and the thought came unbidden. *Anyone walking by here would pick them for the couple—not Leah and Mark.*

Such thoughts as this came to her quickly, for she was an imaginative woman. She had gotten rid of some of her romantic notions on the trail. She had looked forward to the trip as being a romantic interlude, filled with idealistic pictures in her mind on what the West would be like. She smiled now as she thought of her earliest hopes. She had pictured the train peopled with men and women nicely dressed, faces shining and glowing with happiness. She had thought the animals would be healthy, and the people would make the trip singing and convening around campfires at night. She had thought of young people falling in love and getting married, but the reality had been much different. She remembered now the grinding pressures of the trail, the heat and the mosquitoes, the danger of Indians, death, and sickness always peering in on them at odd moments. Now she thought of how foolish her ideas had been. *It's not like it is in the books, but I like the reality better,* she concluded.

Finally the meeting broke up, and Gus Dabney drifted over to the Lees. He liked the couple a great deal. They were a good-natured couple and were the only individuals that the journey had not whittled down.

Somehow they both had stayed plump and rosy-cheeked despite the heat and the monotonous diet and the long hours of work. "Well, Jesse," Gus said as he stopped to stand beside Lee. "We made it to Oregon."

"We purely did," Jesse said. He hummed a fragment of a tune and shook his head. "Wuz a few times I had my doubts."

"I reckon all of us did."

"Why don't you stay to supper tonight? I'm so tired of dried buffalo I got to have something else, so I bought us some chickens."

"How do you like your chicken?" Mary Lee said.

"Cooked."

"I know that! But do you like it stewed or fried or roasted?"

"Any way I can get it," Gus smiled. "I appreciate the invitation. Maybe, while you're doing that, I can fix somethin'. You got somethin' that needs fixin'?"

"Well, that wagon tongue's about ready to fall off. If you could brace it, I'd be much obliged."

Gus at once began to work, and soon the couple started cooking. From where he worked he could see Jennie plucking the chickens, and he found a satisfaction in watching her. She wore a simple faded blue dress, and a bright green ribbon tied her auburn hair. He finished bracing the tongue of the Lee's wagon, then stood up and moved to stand over Jennie. She looked up and smiled at him. "Hello." Gus had ceased to notice how odd her voice sounded.

"How are you today, Jennie?"

"Good. I'm looking forward to chicken."

"Let me help you pluck those things."

"Oh, that's woman's work!"

"I think work's just work, no man or woman to it." Gus squatted down and began plucking the fine feathers that remained on one of the birds. He noticed that she kept her eyes fixed on his lips, and he kept up a running conversation about small unimportant things. Finally he asked her, "Think you'll like it in Oregon?"

"It's a good country. I think I will. What about you, Gus?"

"What about me? Why, I like it fine."

"Are you going to settle a claim?"

"Hadn't thought to."

"You should."

"What would I do with a claim? I'm just a rolling stone, and I ain't gathered much moss either."

Jennie gave him her full attention. There was a habitual repose in this girl, a stillness that Gus thought was probably due to her deafness. She seemed to be in a world all her own. Somehow, what she was pulled at him, and he was drawn toward the mystery that he found in her. Suddenly she looked at him with a strange expression in her eyes. Some sort of a challenge was there, and for that brief moment Gus Dabney understood something of what was in her heart. There was a poignancy there, a shadow of hidden sadness, and without meaning to he felt himself wishing that he could do something to bring joy into her life.

The two finished plucking the chickens. After Jennie had surrendered them to Jesse to cook, she said, "I want to show you something."

"All right." Gus followed her to the wagon, where she pulled out the box where she kept her sketches. She opened it up and handed him a single sheet of paper. Gus stared down at it, and then his eyes flew open with surprise. "Well, look at that!" he said softly, wonder in his voice. "Look at that!"

He kept his eyes fixed on the sketch with

disbelief. It was a sketch of Gus himself sitting on a wagon holding the lines. His hat was pushed back, and his face was alert. The details were not filled in, but the figure of Gus himself had been caught as perfectly as if she had used a camera. "I don't see how you do it." He shook his head. "This is better than the first one you gave me."

Jennie was pleased. Her smile made a change in her face, and she said, "You can keep it if you like."

"Keep it? Why, I'll have it framed and hang it over a mantel—if I ever have a mantel to hang it over."

"You will some day, Gus. You go make a claim."

"What would I do in a cabin all by myself?"

Jennie Town gave him one look that was unfathomable. She shook her head, then turned and went to help Mary at the cooking fire.

Corny Barnhill had walked around the town taking in the sights. He had passed by a saloon and glanced inside where he saw a woman with too much makeup on standing beside his brother Theodore. Theodore had suddenly reached over and put his arm around her and kissed her.

Corny moved on, displeased by the sight. He was accustomed to his brothers and their affairs with women. At times he felt in-clined to join them. Indeed, Ace had already tried to get him to go to a brothel back home, but Corny had refused. Although he was a hard worker and could ride better than his brothers, he had doubts about him-self as a man. He had grown up in the shadow of Theodore and Ace and somehow felt inferior, though he could never explain why.

When he spotted Rita Farr walking along the street with several packages in her arms, he moved quickly. "Let me help you with that, Rita."

"All right, Corny." Rita surrendered sev-eral of the packages. "Where are you going?"

"Just walking around. What about you?"

"Me, too. I'm glad to be here."

The two walked along, and Rita did most of the talking. Finally she said, "Your family won't have much trouble building a cabin with you and your two brothers."

"Well, I guess not." For some reason he added, "I'm not as tough as either of them."

Rita Farr looked at the young man. "Don't put yourself down, Corny. You're not as old as they are."

Her words brought a flush to the face of Corny Barnhill. He smiled at her, feeling warmed by her interest. "All right," he said.

"Come along. You can help me find a ribbon."

They moved across to Smallwood's store, and Corny found himself speaking more easily and feeling more comfortable with this young woman than he ever had with any other. She held a ribbon up to her hair and said, "Do you like it?"

"Yes, it looks real good."

"I wish I didn't have red hair."

"I'm glad you do. I always liked red hair."

"You tell all the girls that. You tell blonde girls you like blonde hair and brunettes you like dark hair," she teased him.

"No," Corny said, utterly serious. "I never told a girl that!"

Rita, at fifteen, was in some ways more mature than Corny, one year her senior. She saw the innocence in the young man and was touched by it. "Well, I appreciate

the compliment. Do you need to buy anything?"

"How about some sarsaparilla?"

"That sounds fine."

Colin and Jordan lay side by side on the
bed in the wagon. "I'll be glad to get a real
bed and a real mattress," he said.

"That'll take a little while. We'll be sleeping in this wagon for a time."

Colin reached over and pulled her around
to face him. As always the touch of her firm
body pressed against him stirred him, and
he kissed her, her lips warm and soft under
his.

"I'm going to build a big house, maybe
two stories—and we're going to have a big
yard with real grass, and windows with glass
in them."

Jordan lay quietly smiling. His arm was
under her head and the other around her
waist, and he pressed her closely against
him. She was proud of his strength and
proud that she was bearing a child that
would have his name. She had been troubled
by his behavior on the trail, for he had shown
irritation and shortness of temper. He did not

take boredom well, and she was well aware that some boredom lay ahead of them.

"We'll have a nice cabin. Some day we'll have a big house, but for now a cabin is fine," she said.

"All right, but one day we'll have a big house."

"Have you thought of what to name the baby?"

His hand ran up and down her back as he seemed to ponder, then he said, "If it's a boy, I've got the perfect name for him."

"What?"

"We're going to give him the same name that Isaiah the prophet gave his son."

"I don't remember that."

"You don't? It's a fine name. It's Maher-Shalal-Hash-Baz."

"What! We'll not name a baby Maher-Shalal-Hash-Baz!"

"Sure we will, and we can call him Hash."

Jordan reached up and grabbed his thick hair with both hands and shook his head. "You're crazy!" she laughed. "But we're not calling him Maher-Shalal-Hash-Baz!"

"How about . . ." Colin seemed to ponder and then said, "We can name him Melchizedek. We can call him Mel for short."

"I'm not talking to you if you can't be serious."

"And if it's a girl, I'll tell you what. We'll call her Jezebel."

"You wouldn't call a sweet little baby girl Jezebel!"

"I guess not. I'd like to call her Jordan, for that's the sweetest name for a woman I ever heard." He pulled her closer to him, and as he kissed her she was drawn into his passion. She clung to him fiercely, but one part of her was separated and saying, *Lord, make him content!*

TWENTY-ONE

The oxen lumbered forward beyond the town out into the rolling country. The prairie schooners made their way, hugging a steep red stone cliff that crowded the train against the river. When they reached the top of a rise, the country flattened out, and soon they were passing through the dense forest, broken, at times, by prairie, with softly waving grass in the October breeze. Most of the men were pleased, for the land was good. Finally the column began to break up, wagons angling off in different directions, all searching for the homestead that would be theirs for a long time—or so they all prayed.

That night, Jordan and Colin shared dinner with Gus and Sublette. Jordan chattered on about what would need to be done first when they found their land. "First thing I want is a decent privy dug!" she declared. She looked over at Colin, who was drinking coffee out of a tin cup. "Do you hear that, Colin?"

"Sure. I'll see to it."

"Don't forget."

"For heaven's sakes, Jordan, I won't forget!" Colin exclaimed.

"Must be nice to have a woman bossing you all the time," Sublette said. His voice was soft as the summer breeze, and there was a glint of humor in his eyes. "Was she always as bossy as she is now?"

"Born that way," Colin drawled, letting his left eyelid droop slightly in a wink.

"Oh, you two! Why don't you go out and do something worthwhile—wash the dishes, maybe."

"I'll do it." Ty got up and gathered the dishes.

"I'll help you there, Ty," Gus said.

Jordan said, "I didn't mean that. Go sit down."

"No, ma'am. We've got us some dishes to wash." Sublette and Gus disappeared into the night, moving down toward the creek.

Jordan watched them. "What will Ty do, now that we're here?"

"I'm not sure. He doesn't have any ambition. I don't know if he'll stake a claim or not."

"He ought to. He'll marry one day."

"I wouldn't be too sure," Colin said mildly.

"He may be a one-woman man." Jordan went over and sat down beside him. "That's what I am," he drawled. He grabbed her so she fell across him protesting, but he stopped that with a kiss. "I'm lucky to have you, Jordan," he said.

It was the kind of thing that Jordan loved to hear, and she stroked his chin. "You need to shave," she whispered.

"What for? Nobody out here to see us except varmints."

"There's me."

"That's right. There's you." He nuzzled her neck, which always made her shiver, and laughed. "I'll shave tonight before we go to bed."

Sublette crouched by the stream, scrubbing at the plates, while Gus swished water around in a pot.

Gus said, "You gonna stake out a claim?"

"I doubt it."

Gus chewed on his lower lip. "I been thinkin' about stakin' one out. The land's here. Might as well claim it."

"You ought to do 'er then, Gus. You know anything about farmin'?"

"I know it's hard work."

"Maybe you ought to go back to the circus and throw knives at people."

Gus laughed shortly. "Nope, I've been there and done that. I been thinking I'd like to try somethin' different."

"You're not thinkin' of gettin' married, are you, Gus?"

"Why not?"

"Oh, I don't know. I just didn't figure you for the marryin' kind."

"Well, I ain't been—but maybe it's time."

"Who you got your eye on? You ought to find yourself a nice widow with kids. Save a lot of time and work courtin' and havin' babies and such."

"Oh, hush, Ty!" Gus protested. "I ain't interested in your foolishness."

The two worked in companionable silence. Finally Gus said, "Maybe you'd help me find a place, Ty. You've got a good eye for the land."

"Be proud to."

"And why don't you stake out one next to me? We could be neighbors."

Sublette set the last clean dish on a rock and leaned back. "That'd be something," he said finally. "Farming."

Gus glanced at him taking in the full, long lips, the light blue eyes, and the heavy nose. "How'd you get that nose broke?" he asked.

"Foolishness."

Gus grinned. "I got some scars come from the same source. Anyway, you think about it, Ty."

"I'll think on it."

The forest echoed with the sound of axes from dawn until darkness made clearing impossible. Logs fell with a crash and then were skidded to the various cabin sites. Quickly the varied talents of the new settlers became apparent, and crews came together, the men specializing in chores. They became efficient and the cabins seemed to rise up. The men worked doggedly felling the logs and peeling them. Once the logs were downed, they were raised in place by an active crew. Some men became experts at notching the logs so that they did not even have to measure. Others were good at splitting the cedar or oak shakes. Fireplaces at first were built of sticks and mud, there being no time to haul rocks. Once the reach poles and the shakes were in place, the crew moved on to another cabin.

Ira Barnhill's older sons, Ace and Theodore, complained, wanting something
more elaborate, but their father said briefly,
"Not now. We'll worry about buildin' somethin' better soon enough. It ain't practical to
waste much time on these cabins. When we
get time we'll have a big house, and this will
just be a pantry or an extra room."

There was no variety in the cabins. The
thing was to get four walls and a roof up as
quickly as possible before winter. None of
them was any larger than the rest; all were
sixteen feet long by ten or twelve feet wide.
There was little comfort in them, and when
the larger families bedded down they covered the entire floor.

The floors were hard-packed earth, and at
first the only door that existed was a blanket
or piece of canvas tacked up over an opening. Most of the cabins had one wall dominated by a massive fireplace.

The few pieces of furniture that had survived the trip were set in place, while some
were quickly manufactured out of the wood
of the forest. A bed was one peg put in the
angle of a corner with two saplings at right
angles fastened to the walls, with a mattress
hauled from Missouri thrown on top of it.

By the time two weeks had gone by, everyone on the train was exhausted. They were all glad to see the Ellencourts pull up in a wagon. "I thought you needed a break," Mark Ellencourt said. "There'll be a Thanksgiving service next Thursday—and it'd be nice if the ladies would cook up a big meal."

"We ain't got time for such foolishness," Ira Barnhill said shortly.

"I think it'd be nice," Avis said.

Barnhill stared at her for a moment with resentment, but could not think of an answer. He had married her because of her youth and attractiveness, and in truth she was a good worker. He could not fault her there—but something was wrong. She had not come to him as a woman comes to a man. She never refused him in bed or argued, yet there was a passivity in her that displeased him. "All right," he said shortly. "Won't take long, I guess."

Cornwall, who witnessed this, grinned at his stepmother. "I'm thankful for a break in this work. I'm tired to the bone."

Avis came over to stand beside the boy. He was taller than she, lean as a sapling. She reached out and took his hands and saw that they were scarred with blisters. "Come along and let me put something on those hands."

Corny submitted, and as she put a lotion on them that was cooling and soothing, he studied her. He was a shy young man and at that fork in the road where he would either become good or bad. Suddenly he said, "How do I tell a girl I like her, Ma?"

He was the only one of the boys that ever called her "Ma," and it touched Avis. "Why, you just say, 'I like you, Helen,' or whoever it is."

"You mean just come right out with it and say it?"

"Why not?"

Corny shuffled his feet nervously. "Well, I don't know as I can do that."

Avis reached out with affection and brushed his hair back from his forehead. It was lighter than his brothers', and there was a gentleness in his eyes that was lacking in Theodore and Ace. "Who is it?"

"Aw, nobody."

"Come on. Tell me."

"Well, it's Rita Farr."

"A very pretty girl."

"Lots of fellows in the train think so. I just get all stopped up every time I get around her, Ma. I can't talk."

"It will come with time. You're a good boy, Cornwall, and she'll see that. She comes from a good family. Her mother and her father both have good sense, and I think she does, too."

"Just walk up and tell her?"

"Well, not out of the blue," Avis laughed. "Just sometime say, 'That's a pretty dress.' Something like that."

"Thanks, Ma."

Avis saw the relief wash across his youthful features and hope dawn in his eyes. He turned away, and she watched him thinking of how difficult it was to grow up. She wondered what she could do to keep Corny from becoming what Ace and Theodore had become.

The Thanksgiving service was well received. Everyone was tired, and they pooled their resources to make a communal dinner. Everyone gathered at the Farr's cabin, and the men built a pit of coals to roast the meat, mostly venison, but also two young pigs.

The women shared the food they had and cooked together.

Dorcas Farr, darkened by the sun, looked all of her seventy-one years, but her eyes were bright. She threw onions, flour, salt, and pepper randomly into a pot.

"Don't you ever measure anything, Gran?" Rita asked.

"A pinch of this and a pinch of that."

"I can't cook like that," Rita protested. "I've got to know what to put in."

"You'll learn," Dorcas Farr said.

Dorcas Farr studied her granddaughter carefully. The girl was blooming, and at that instant a strange feeling came to the old woman. She would have described it as "someone walking over my grave." There was nothing in Rita Farr to cause such a thought, for the girl was attractive, lively—a good girl, one who always did her work without complaining. *But she's young—and she wants attention. That's a bad combination.*

When Rita left to go get more water for the tiny amount of coffee they had, Dorcas turned to Ellen. "You ever worry about Rita?"

"About Rita?" Ellen Farr stared at her

mother-in-law. "Well, just like all women think about their children."

"I worry about her."

"Why? Have you seen anything, Dorcas?"

"Not everything kin be seen. She's a good girl, right enough, but she's got a woman's weaknesses. Best woman in the world kin fall iffen things fall thet way." Her wise old eyes held Ellen and she nodded slowly. "Men tell as how a woman kin bring a man to grief—but it works t'other way. Lots of good girls been ruined when they had no notion of goin' thet way."

Ellen Farr knew the old woman's moods, but still she was troubled, for Dorcas Farr had a way of being right about things. "We'll watch her," she said. "And we'll pray."

"It's a turrible thing to be old," Dorcas said. "The only thing wuss is bein' young."

Ellen laughed. "You like me to think you're wise, don't you?"

Dorcas pushed her mood away and laughed shortly. "None of us knows much."

Mark Ellencourt preached a good sermon, and afterwards the settlers fell on the meal like starved wolves. They ate rapidly, and Jennie Town watched with a smile. She had enjoyed being with the women. Cut off in her silence, she missed much of what went on. She could only understand the one person she was looking at, but she had learned the ways of the women of the train. She knew that Ada Minton, wife of Dave Minton, was terrified of having a baby. And she knew that Cornwall Barnhill was falling in love with Rita Farr.

Jennie picked up a bucket for washing dishes and went down to the creek. When she reached the creek, she put the bucket in the water and waited until it filled, then turned back toward the cabin. She had almost gotten there when a man stepped suddenly out of the shadow of the trees. Startled, she turned and saw that it was Al Catlow, the mountain man. He was smiling as he came to her, but she had always been apprehensive about him. There was a wildness in the man, and she saw his lips move as he said, "Well, hello, Jennie. That's your name, ain't it?"

"Yes." Jennie started to move toward the clearing where Jesse and Mary Lee had started playing, and the singing had begun.

"Don't be in such a hurry," Catlow said.

He took her arm, and Jennie felt the strength of the man. She tried to pull away, saying, "I've got to get back with the water."

Catlow ignored her words. He reached out and pulled her forward, and before she could help it he kissed her.

Jennie tried to turn her head, but the strength in the man was frightening. He ran his hand over her body, and fear ran through her. She wrenched her head away and cried, "Help! Somebody help me!"

"They can't hear you." Catlow grinned. He enjoyed hurting things that were weaker, and pleasure stirred in his dark eyes as Jennie struggled like a bird to escape his grasp. He started to kiss her again, but suddenly a hand on his arm caught his attention.

"Let her alone!"

Gus Dabney had appeared and others had somehow seen the struggle. The music stopped, and Catlow suddenly without warning reached out and struck Dabney a terrible blow that caught him where his head joined his neck. It drove Dabney sprawling backward, and he rolled helplessly on the dirt.

Catlow moved forward. "I'm going to kick your head off!"

"Hold it, Al!"

Ty Sublette had moved in closer. His hands hung down at his side, but there was something in his face that caught Catlow's attention.

These two were a different breed from the settlers. They had lived a hard life where the weak men died easily. Both had learned to fight in a way that these settlers never knew. Catlow's pride rose in him. "Stay out of this, Sublette!"

"If you can't behave decently, the best thing for you to do is to go off by yourself. Go back to the mountains."

"You're tellin' me what to do?"

Sublette moved closer, his eyes locked with those of Catlow. A silence had fallen, but everyone had come to witness the conflict that exploded in their midst. Jennie stood silently without speaking, then she moved over and knelt down beside Gus. He was still dazed, and she helped him to a sitting position. Gus shook his head, then got to his feet. "I'll get my gun, Catlow."

"There's no need of that," Horace Farr said. "There won't be any shooting."

Catlow seemed not to have heard. He was staring at Ty Sublette with a wildness in his face. Then without warning he threw himself forward with a wild yell. He struck Sublette, and the two hit the ground rolling. They fell against Dave Minton, who went down with a yelp and scrambled to his feet.

Sublette felt a kick in his kidney and caught the foot of Catlow and twisted it. Catlow fell to the ground but came up like a cat. The two men circled each other for a moment, and then Catlow came in once again. This time his blow missed, and he was struck in the mouth by a blow with all the weight of Ty Sublette behind it. It stopped him dead in his tracks, but he was a tough, hard man and aimed another kick at Sublette's stomach. Sublette took it on the hip, and it staggered him. Catlow roared forward, throwing blows from every angle. Several of them landed, bloodying Sublette's face.

The two men fought wildly, each of them trying for a killing blow, and both were bloodied. The crowd made a loose circle, and the faces of the men reflected a savage desire that shocked some of the women.

The end came when Sublette swung his arm and caught Catlow in the nose. The nose broke, and Catlow staggered backwards, but Sublette did not let up. He rained blow after blow on Catlow, who tried to defend himself, but finally he fell backwards.

Sublette, breathing hard and with blood trickling down from a cut over his right eyebrow, said, "Get out, Al."

Catlow struggled for breath. His nose was flat, and he spat out a tooth. His eyes were dimmed with the pain, and he stood up wavering. Without a word he turned and headed to where the horses were tied. Sublette followed him, and people moved quickly to see the end of the drama.

"Stay away from decent women, Catlow, or I'll take you off at the neck," Ty said flatly.

Catlow untied his horse and pulled himself into the saddle. "This ain't the end, Sublette," he muttered.

"You heard what I said." Ty turned and started to walk away.

Suddenly Catlow's hand darted down inside his coat.

"Ty, look out!"

Sublette knew he should not have turned his back. He threw himself to one side and a shot rang out, but it did not strike him. He whirled to see Al Catlow sitting in the saddle, but there was a black spot just over his right eye. Quickly Sublette wheeled to see Colin Bryce lowering his revolver.

Catlow sat in the saddle without moving, the revolver still clutched in his hand. His eyes were open, and he seemed to be caught with some sort of thought. Then he suddenly collapsed, and his body fell off, striking the ground loosely.

Jordan had watched the fight with a sinking heart, and now she turned to Colin who slipped the revolver back into the holster at his side. She had not even realized he was carrying a gun.

Sublette walked up and said, "I reckon you saved my bacon, Colin."

Colin's face was somewhat pale, and he said soberly, "I guess that makes up for what you did for me in Laramie."

"It's a little different. That gambler wouldn't have killed you, but Catlow would have got me for sure."

Horace Farr said, "We'll have to take him to town and report this to the sheriff."

"All right," Ty agreed.

The party broke up then, and Ty rode back to Oregon City with the body of Al Catlow. There he found Sheriff Joe Meek in his office. Meek, a muscular man with a pair of alert, gray eyes and a thick beard, had been a mountain man himself. He listened as Sublette explained what had happened, and then shrugged his massive shoulders. "Clear case of self-defense."

"Yes, it sure was."

"Don't you fellows make a habit out of shootin' each other. I might have to take notice of that."

Sublette grinned. "I'm tryin' to quit."

Meek slapped his meaty thigh and nodded. "Let me know if I can do anything for you, Sublette."

Jordan said little, but when she and Colin were alone in the cabin, she said, "That was a terrible thing."

"He was a bad man."

Jordan said, "Does it bother you, Colin—killing a man?"

"Not a bit." Colin turned to face her. "Would you rather he had killed Ty?"

"Oh, no! You did the right thing."

She set about some meaningless task, but she knew she would not soon forget the sight of Al Catlow sitting in the saddle with a bullet in his brain from her husband's gun.

The violence that had risen in Colin was a part of him that she did not know, and it troubled her deeply. She knew that part of his early life had been hard, but it distressed her to think that taking a man's life meant so little. With an effort she pushed her doubts away, but knew they were implanted on her memory.

TWENTY-TWO

Ty Sublette straightened up and arched his back to ease the strain. With his right hand he held a plane and with his left he reached down and ran his fingers over the floor that he had just smoothed with the tool. It gave him a sense of pleasure somehow, this small luxury of having a smoothly planed wooden floor, instead of the hard-packed dirt that most cabins had. He had spent several days in a saw pit making boards with the help of Gus Dabney, and now one chore was out of the way.

Getting to his feet, Sublette glanced around the cabin, and somehow the sight of it amused him. "What's a wandering fellow like me making a nest for?" He spoke aloud and the sound of his voice startled him. From outside the cabin he could hear faint sounds coming from Colin's place, but other than that he inhabited a place shut off from the world. Others, he knew, would clear their fields, but he had no intention of doing more than a minimum. He had chosen a spot of higher ground covered with tall, stately oaks, chestnuts, and beech. It gave him great pleasure simply to walk through the woods, and sometimes at night he would go out and sleep under the open sky rather than sleeping in the cabin.

Sublette left the cabin and saddled up his horse. The gray light of dawn was beginning to break through in the east, and he felt good as he always did in the mornings. The gelding was full of life and pitched several times, which made Sublette laugh. "Go on, you hammerhead! Jump all you want to. I'll take some of that steam out of you." He kicked the horse's flanks, and the gelding shot out of the clearing down the rather steep slope at full speed. Sublette kept him at a fast gallop until he passed the Bryce place, but no one seemed to be stirring, so he let the animal run another half mile before slowing him down to a trot. The trot was harder on the rider but easier on the animal. He was on his way to Oregon City to see how the Ellencourts were doing. He had not seen them since the Thanksgiving feast, having spent every day from first light until after dark helping with more cabin raising, but he had thought of them often.

He arrived in Oregon City midmorning and stepped out of the saddle in front of a house with a small sign over the door proclaiming "Dr. Paul Leverett." He stepped up on the porch, knocked on the door, and waited. When it opened, a large elderly woman with iron-gray hair stood before him. "You need to see the doctor?"

"Guess I do."

"Come in." The woman stepped aside and said as Ty entered, "I'm Mrs. Bishop. You wait here. I'll see if the doctor will see you."

Ty noted that the woman had a proprietary air about her, as if the doctor would not see a patient she herself didn't approve. Paul appeared at once, smiling. "Ty! Good to see you."

"Will you be needing anything else, Doctor?" Mrs. Bishop asked.

"No, Mrs. Bishop. Thank you." Seizing Ty's arm, Paul pulled him down the hall, and when they were inside a large room, he laughed. "Mrs. Bishop ask you what your complaint was?"

"No, she didn't."

"She usually does. Nosiest woman I've ever seen. She's a good cook, though, and a fine housekeeper."

"Nice place. You getting lots of patients?"

"Oh, sure. When a new doctor comes, lots of people will come, just to see what he's like. What brings you to town?"

"Ada Minton wants you to come and see her if you can. Got some sort of ailment. And I wanted to see how Mark and Leah are doing—maybe take Jos out for some fun."

"I'll probably go out to see Ada and the other sick folks day after tomorrow. Come back here for supper if Leah doesn't ask you."

"How's Mark doing?"

Leverett grew serious. "Not well. I'm worried about him, Ty. He's not getting any better."

The two men stood silently, then Ty said, "I'll see you later, Paul."

Ty pulled his gelding up beside the small white house that the Ellencourts had rented. Tying the animal to the hitching rail, he stepped up on the porch and knocked on the door. It opened almost at once, and Jos grinned up at him. "Hello, Ty," he said.

"Hello, Jos. Where are your folks?"

"Across the street working on the church."

"What are you doing here?"

"I just came to get something to eat. Come on in."

"No, I think I'll go over and see if I can lend a hand with the church." He saw the disappointment in the boy's face and knew that the lad was hungry for companionship. "I passed by a big creek," he commented. "Just outside of town. I'll bet it's full of fish. Reckon I could persuade you to go bait a hook with me after I help with the church a while?"

"Sure! That'd be great!"

"Okay, we'll catch a couple of whales."

As Sublette moved across the street, he could hear the sounds of hammers on the inside. The building, he noted, had once been some sort of storage building. There were no windows in it across the front, and the boards, warped and free from any sign of paint, had turned silvery gray by the passage of time and the heavy hand of Oregon weather.

Stepping inside, Sublette saw Mark Ellencourt hammering weakly on some boards. Leah was opposite him, and with the din of the hammers they did not hear him approach. "You two need a helping hand?"

Mark turned quickly and got to his feet,

pleasure on his face. He put out his hand, and when Sublette took it he was shocked at the frailness of the man's grip. "Glad to see you, Ty. When did you get in?"

"Just came riding in. I went over across the street."

"It's good to see you." Leah smiled. She was wearing a faded gray dress, and her ash-blonde hair was tied back with a ribbon. "How are things out at your place?"

"Fine as frog hair," Sublette said cheerfully. "Thought I'd come and do a little church building."

At once Leah said, "Good, I'll be the boss. Mark, you go over and help Jos with his lessons."

"Why, I can help here!" Mark protested.

"I'm the boss," Leah smiled. She reached over and took his arm and turned him toward the door. With a gentle push, she said, "You might fix us something to eat."

"All right, I'll do that."

"Jos and I are going fishing when we get through here if it's okay with you, Mark."

"Why, that'd be fine. I may go with you."

"Good. Go fix us a little something to eat, and I'll let this woman of yours boss me."

As soon as Mark left, Ty turned to Leah

and saw that her face was troubled. "Mark doesn't look too well," he said. "He doesn't need to be doing this kind of work."

"I know. I told him that. Jonah Smallwood has got a group of the men coming to do this work. I tried to get Mark to wait, but he's so impatient to get it finished."

"What are you building here?" Sublette asked.

"We need a platform to put the pulpit on."

"Well, I can't cook worth a hoot, but I'm a pretty good carpenter. Let's get it done."

The two worked together for an hour, and then Leah straightened up and surveyed the results. "You *are* a good carpenter, Ty!"

"My father was a carpenter. He taught me a little bit." He looked around and commented, "This will make a good building. You might need to put a couple of windows in it to let in some light."

"Jonah Wheelright says he'll do that. He's such a fine man. He's one of the deacons, and there are other good men of the church." She bit her lip, and discouragement was evident in her face. "I'm worried about Mark."

"Have you had him down to see Leverett lately?"

"Yes."

"What'd he say?"

"He didn't say anything to Mark, but afterward he talked to me. He's afraid that Mark's got consumption."

An involuntary grimace crossed the tan face of Ty Sublette. "That's a bad one," he murmured. "Maybe he's wrong."

"I hope so, but he's been sick for so long—and now he's getting weaker."

Sublette studied the woman. Soberness came to him and an innate sadness that he usually covered up with a light manner and a smile. "You know, Leah, we're pretty weak, frail things. We can be healthy one minute and the next minute drown or get hit by a bolt of lightning or burn in a fire."

"Don't talk like that," Leah said quickly, and there was hurt in her voice. "Don't ever talk like that, Ty! Life is good. We have our hard times, but there are so many wonderful things in the world."

Sublette turned his head slightly to one side, and he seemed to hear a falling cadence in her words that struck him. Something in him stirred, and he reached out and took her upper arms with his hands. Her flesh was firm under his grasp, and he said,

"Don't be sad, Leah." He saw that his words touched her, and she suddenly reached up and put both of her hands on his chest. They stood there almost in a half embrace, and when she spoke there was a brokenness in her voice. "I sometimes let myself get down."

Sublette was aware of the fresh, clean smell of her hair and the fragrance of her clothes came powerfully to him. He felt the full womanliness of her form and suddenly put his arms around her and drew her close. She looked up at him, and he saw something in her eyes that he could not identify. Passion stirred within him and also a warning that this must not be. He stepped back, saying hurriedly, "Don't know why we're so serious about all this. Things will be all right."

"That's right." Leah spoke quickly, and he saw that she had been affected by his embrace. She laughed shortly. "We're like a couple of drunks crying in our beer."

"Now just when were you ever drunk and crying in your beer?"

"Never mind. I've got to have a few secrets." She smiled. She studied him for just an instant, and what thoughts passed through her mind Sublette could not imagine. It was as if she were weighing him somehow in her mind. "Come on, let's go see what Mark's got to eat."

As the two walked through the door, both of them somehow felt that they had come close to a precipice and then had pulled back suddenly. Sublette knew that he would not speak of it, and the one thought that passed through his mind was, *I must be a fool acting like that with a fine woman like Leah. I'm old enough to know better.*

"Keep your line tight—don't let him get away, Jos!"

"I got him, Ty! I got him! He must be a whale."

Sublette smiled as he stood beside the boy. The late afternoon sun put lights in the boy's blonde hair, and as he shouted excitedly the fish drew the line across the water, and the pole bent nearly double. Sublette had the impulse to help the boy but knew that that would not do. "Just let him tire himself out, son."

As Sublette watched the boy struggle with the fish, he suddenly felt a sense of the goodness of being alive. It came to him from time to time, and now as he watched Jos grasp the sapling pole with both hands, his eyes wide with excitement, he knew that when he was an old old man with white hair and a beard, perhaps, that he would re-member this time. The sight of the boy's thin body, his sunburned face, reminded him of his own childhood when his father had taken him fishing. He had treasured that moment for years, and now his smile stretched out and pleasure glinted in his eyes.

Jos finally wore the fish out and brought him to the shallows, still flopping but ex-hausted. Stepping out into the water, Sub-lette reached down and grabbed the fish by the jaw and lifted him up. "A fine bass, Jos. Why, he'll go three or four pounds, I ex-pect."

Jos came forward and reached out his hand to run his fingers down the side of the fish. His eyes were filled with a pleasure that was total and complete. "Gosh, Ty, he's a big one, ain't he?"

"Sure is. Why, he'll feed all three of you—your mother and father and you." Sublette knew that anything else would be anticli-mactic so he said, "You're not likely to top this fellow. What do you say we go home, and I'll help you clean them."

"All right, Ty."

Sublette pulled the stringer, filled mostly with bream the size of his hand, and one two-pound catfish that he put back into the creek. "They're too much trouble to clean," he said. "If we got one that weighed about twenty pounds that'd be different."

"Did you ever catch one that big?"

"Sure did, but it was always on a trotline." He had to explain what a trotline was to the boy as they made their way back to the house. Sublette listened as the boy chattered on, and he had to fight back a wave of sadness. *My boy would have been about this age if he had lived.* He had learned quickly to retreat from such thoughts, and he forced himself to speak of his days in the mountains with Jos, who never tired of hearing such stories.

When they were within sight of the house, Jos said, "Are you ever going to get married again, Ty?"

"I don't know, son. Nobody knows about things like that."

Jos craned his head sideways and said, "I wish you would."

"Why do you wish that?"

"Because then you might have a baby, and he could grow up, and I could help take care of him and he could be my little brother."

Sublette found the boy's reasoning amusing. "I'll see what I can do."

As the two reached the house, Leah and Mark both came out. Jos ran forward shouting, "Look at the fish I caught! He'll feed all of us, Ty said."

Leah smiled and ruffled his blonde hair. "My, that *is* a fine fish. Why don't we cook 'em all up for supper."

"Looks like plenty for all of us."

"I've got to get back, Mark."

"Oh, Ty, you said you'd help me clean 'em, and it won't take long to cook 'em. Please stay."

Sublette had half turned to leave, but the boy's words caught at him. "Well, I guess I could. Come on, let's get these fish cleaned. Put some grease in the skillet, Sister Ellencourt," he said.

When the two disappeared around the corner of the house, Leah said to Mark, "I don't know what we would have done without Ty."

"I don't either. God surely sent him," Mark agreed.

Leah spoke reluctantly. "He needs to get married."

"Some men are just meant to be alone, I guess."

"But he's not one of them," Leah said quickly. Then, as if she had spoken too much, she turned quickly to go into the house. "I'll make some hush puppies. You always liked them."

Finally January came, bringing 1844 to birth. While the weather did not turn as bitter as some of the old-timers predicted, the temperature went down and thin ice formed in the water buckets and glittered in the creeks and on the surface of the ponds. Far off, the mountains turned white with glittering snow, like huge sharp-crowned hats outlined against the sky. The breath of the horses and oxen turned cloudy in the air, and thick blankets of ice topped the trees. Snow finally came, coating the brown earth like a fairyland with glistening white crystals that glittered like diamonds. It made mounds against the tree trunks and layered the entire land with a crust that the young delighted in breaking, but to the adults it was another hardship of the land.

Colin Bryce had labored through the fall and into the winter. One of the jobs that he hated the worst was clearing land. To make his fields, he simply ignored some of the larger trees, knowing he could plow around them for a time. He concentrated on those that he could handle. He and Gus felled tree after tree, then cut them into lengths that could be moved. Making tunnels underneath the stumps, he started fires and soon learned that stump burning was no easy task. The fires continually went out until finally Gus figured out how to clear a small tunnel that made a draft. After that the work went easier.

It was late on a Thursday night, and Colin had come in exhausted after a fourteen-hour day. He stopped at the door of the cabin abruptly, turning to stare out into the darkness. The stump fires looked to him like the eyes of demons gleaming redly in the blackness of the night. Colin could hardly pick up his feet, for his energy had been drained out of him by the monumental task of clearing the land. He suddenly thought, *Clearing this land has robbed me of four months of my life. I can never get it back.* He looked back at the gleaming red eyes that seemed to glare at him, and disgust fell upon him.

As he stood there with his knees trembling from weakness, he thought suddenly of his life before he had left the sea. He had thought that was out of his system, but now memories came rushing back of the good times that he had known. He remembered the sun glittering on the boundless, endless ocean; that had always pleased him. He thought of the travel and the strange lands he had touched upon. The thoughts of women that he had known in these places rushed in, and he remembered faces and the touch of bodies that had been part of his life.

Colin shook his head, and his wide mouth drew into a grimace. "I got to stop thinking like that," he muttered. Wearily, he approached the cabin, and when he stepped inside the warmth of the fireplace was welcome. Jordan came to him at once and helped him strip off his heavy wool mackinaw.

"Come over by the fire," she said. She was heavy-bodied now and moved slowly and carefully.

It's as if she's carrying some immense treasure, Colin thought. He moved over to the fire, held his hands out, and for some time stood there soaking up the heat. He finally sat down, pulled his boots off, and then his wet socks. He took the clean socks that Jordan had warmed by the fire and put them on.

"Supper's ready."

"All right." Colin moved to the table and sat down. He bowed his head and asked a brief blessing and then began to eat. He was aware that Jordan was talking happily. She had not sensed the darkness of mood that filled his mind and his spirit. He finally put his fork down and bowed his head, staring at the untouched food.

"What is it? Don't you feel well, Colin?"

Lifting his head, Colin met her gaze, and despite himself said in a bitter tone, "I'm sick of this life, Jordan."

The words seemed to strike against Jordan with such a force that she blinked her eyes. "Why—Colin, I can't believe it!"

"Nothing but work all day long—every day! Now we've got to build a road, and that'll take another month out of my life. I'm nothing but a slave. None of us are. It's hard on you, too."

Jordan reached across the table and took his hand. It was callused, and the hard labor of the past months had whittled him down.

There was nothing left but bone and muscle. "I know it's hard now, dear," she said, "but it'll get better. Once we get the fields in—"

"I don't think we'll ever get them in," Colin muttered. He knew he was hurting her but could not help himself. Then suddenly the words boiled over. "We never should have come here. We could have had a better life back east."

"I don't think so, Colin. I think God brought us here. It's just that you're discouraged right now."

"I'm not the only one. We're worked down to the marrow."

He suddenly rose and went to stand before the fire, staring down at the glowing red coals. He was aware that she had come to stand beside him, and then he felt her arm go around his waist. He knew that he was behaving badly but somehow could not stop himself. "I don't think I can last doing this for the rest of my life."

Jordan did not answer for a moment, and then she whispered, "I'm sorry it's so hard on you."

Colin turned and took her arms. "It's hard on you, too—having a baby out in this blasted wilderness. It's too much!"

"Don't say that, Colin!" Jordan said defensively. The words poured out of her as she held onto him. "We're going to have a son or a daughter, and we're building something here that will be for them. I know you miss your life at sea, but there were bad times in that life, too. You've told me about it."

"Not as bad as here," Colin said stubbornly. Deep down somehow he knew she was right, but the monotonous, grinding labor had crushed his spirit. "I don't think I can last at this. We may have to do something else."

Jordan's eyes flickered with fear and apprehension, but Colin did not see it. "We may have to leave this place. I don't think I can take it much longer." He knew that his words cut her, for she was happy here, but he was also aware that he was reaching the end of his rope.

To Jordan's relief, for some time Colin said no more about quitting the homestead, but she knew that he was silent out of a despair that she could not understand. She was getting ready to go to Oregon City, for there was to be a celebration and a dance. It was a combination of a Christmas celebration and simply something to bring laughter and a little joy and companionship into the lives of the settlers. Mark Ellencourt had organized it, and all the settlers were going.

She put on a dress that she had made herself and laughed at the size of her stomach. She was carrying high which meant, according to Dorcas Farr, that it would be a boy.

When she was dressed she turned to the door as Colin entered. He said, "You'd better wear your coat. It's cold as the Arctic out here."

"I'll be fine. I'm all wrapped up."

"It's pretty near your time to be doing all this. You can't dance," Colin observed.

"It's time to be foolish. You can dance, and I'll watch you. Just don't pick out any pretty women to dance with."

The two made the trip into Oregon City rapidly, noting the other settlers all headed for town. When they got to the community building, which served for a courthouse and any other occasion that required room, Colin leaped out, tied the team, and then helped her down. "It looks like everybody came," he said, seeing the large number of wagons and buggies tied outside.

"It'll be good to see everyone," Jordan said.

The two hurried inside and found that the room was already crowded. They were met by Leah Ellencourt, who greeted them warmly. "I'm so glad you could come."

"Where's the preacher?"

Leah's face changed. "He's not well, Colin."

"I'm sorry to hear that," Jordan said at once.

"We'll just have to pray for him," Leah said.

Colin took Jordan over to a line of chairs, and Horace Farr stood up at once. "Here, take this seat, Miss Bryce."

"I think I want to stand a little bit. That was a long ride," Jordan said.

Rita Farr moved closer to smile at Jordan. "You're looking so pretty. I think having a baby agrees with you."

"Why, thank you, Rita. And don't you look pretty tonight."

Bryce suddenly said, "My wife has forbidden me to dance with any pretty girls, so just to show I'm my own man, I'm asking you, Rita."

Rita was, indeed, very pretty in a bright

green dress. She smiled shyly and said, "That would be fine, Mr. Bryce."

"We'll have to watch out for my wife here. She's liable to pull out a gun and shoot one of us. She's very jealous, you know."

His mild teasing pleased Rita, and the two moved out on the dance floor. The music was loud, and Jordan enjoyed speaking to her friends, almost all of whom came over to greet her. Paul Leverett came, wearing a new gray suit, his face lit with pleasure. "It's good to see you again. My favorite patient." He took her hand and asked her how she had been.

"Fine, but I'll be needing you fairly soon."

"Don't waste any time," Leverett said. "You send for me even if I have to come and stay a week."

"That's good of you, Doctor."

Rita Farr was having a wonderful time. She knew she looked very well, and she was besieged with offers to dance. She danced once with Cornwall, but then he was crowded out by others—most of them older than he. Rita felt sorry for him and was about to go ask him to dance again when suddenly someone came up before her.

"I believe this is our dance, Rita." Ace Barnhill was, without a doubt, Rita thought, the handsomest man in the community. His hair was black as a raven, and his eyes so dark that they seemed to have no pupils. His skin was smooth and tanned, and his teeth looked very white as he smiled at her.

Rita had no chance to reply, for he simply pulled her to the dance floor, and she listened as he told her, "You're the prettiest girl here, Rita."

"How many girls have you told that to tonight?"

"None. I'm tellin' the truth. I've laid it on pretty thick with some young ladies, but I don't have to lie about that. You are the prettiest. Where'd you get that dress?"

"Ma and I made it. The cloth was a birthday present from Pa."

"Well, you did fine."

Ace looked appreciatively at the young woman. His eyes took in the firmly blossoming figure, the glowing complexion, and the laughing eyes. "I'm gonna beat old Corny's time. He's too young for you. You need an older man to be sure you don't go astray."

"*You're* going to keep me from going astray? That's not what I've heard about you. That'd be like puttin' the fox to guard the chicken house."

Her remark amused Ace Barnhill, and he swept her around the floor, pulling her closer.

"You're holding me too tight."

"Can't help myself. You shouldn't be so pretty."

As the dance progressed, Rita became aware that Ace was courting her. She danced several more dances with him and was flattered at his attention. He was amusing, but several of her girlfriends whispered, "You'd better be careful about him."

Rita shook her head. "I can take care of myself. I know what he is."

The hours flew by, and finally Rita found herself dancing with Ace again.

"This is the fourth time, or the fifth, that I've danced with you," Rita laughed.

"I wish it was just me and you," Ace replied.

Rita listened to his talk, and finally when he said, "Let's go outside. It's warm in here," Rita hesitated.

"You're not afraid, are you?" Ace taunted.

The remark challenged Rita, and she said, "Just for a minute."

The two went outside and walked down the boardwalk. The noise became muted, and Ace suddenly stopped in front of the livery stable. He took her in his arms as she had known he would, and he kissed her. "You're the prettiest girl I ever saw. I reckon I'm downright in love with you."

The words weakened Rita, and when he took her in his arms and kissed her there was a wildness and a passion that she had never known. It was not in him alone, but in her also. She struggled and tried to get away, but he was strong, and his lips sought hers incessantly. She was aware that he had opened the door to the livery stable, and then she cried as he pulled her down into the hay on the floor. But he kept caressing her, and finally something she had never known stirred within her, and she fell against him moaning, "Oh, Ace!"

TWENTY-THREE

The morning sun threw a yellow gleam though the single window in the cabin, and a cheerful fire crackled in the fireplace, throwing its warmth on Colin. He sat on a three-legged stool intent on the newspaper, turning slightly so that the flickering tongues of flame could cast their light on the paper, noting that the date was January 12, 1844. *That's what's wrong with living in the backwoods—reading a newspaper two months old,* he thought. Still, any reading material was valuable in Oregon, so Colin was glad enough to have even an outdated newspaper to read.

The front covered the election of William McKinley as the twenty-fifth president of the United States, and another story noted that Daniel Webster had retired as Secretary of State. Politics were a mystery to Colin Bryce. He had never been interested in them, but now as he turned the page he found a discussion of the dispute over Oregon boundaries. An international argument was raging concerning the boundaries of

Oregon—which land would belong to the United States and which to Great Britain. This had been one of the key issues in the presidential campaign, and there seemed to be no end to the dispute.

Turning over to another page, Colin sat there with the silence unbroken save for the crackling of the sap bubbling from the rich pine. It made a pleasant sound, and the aroma was pungent in the room as Colin read a story that *did* interest him. It described the voyage of the SS *Great Britain,* the first propeller-driven ship to cross the Atlantic. A wave of nostalgia came to him then as he thought of his days at sea. At the time the voyages had seemed hard and boring, but after the bone-cracking labor of the past few months, he would have welcomed a voyage almost anywhere!

His thoughts evaporated when he heard a faint cry from Jordan, who lay in bed buried under a pile of blankets. March had been cold, and she had complained lately of this.

Quickly Colin rose and moved to stand beside the bed. As soon as he caught a glimpse of her face by the pale light streaming in through the window, he knew something was wrong. "What is it, Jordan? Is it time?"

"Yes." Jordan's face was squeezed together, and a tremor swept across it as pain struck her. "You'd better—you'd better go get Dr. Leverett."

Alarm ran through Colin, and he bent over and kissed her, then whirled away calling out, "I'll get Ty to go. I'll be right back as soon as I can get him started."

Grabbing a coat, he raced out the door. Quickly he saddled his horse, then flung himself on and kicked him in the side to get more speed out of him. He had been dreading this moment for months now, and fear raced through him. *What if something happened to Jordan?* When he came within sight of Ty's cabin he saw the smoke curling up and heaved a sigh of relief. *Thank God he's there*, he thought. When he was a hundred yards away he began yelling, "Ty—Ty, get out here!"

As he pulled his horse up shortly, Sublette stepped outside the door and at once took it all in. "Is it Jordan?"

"Yes—the pains are starting. They came on real quick. Go for Leverett, Ty."

"I'll make a fast trip, Colin. You go back and stay with Jordan."

"All right. Break that horse down if you have to."

"I will. Now you go on back." Sublette whirled at once and ran toward the shed that sheltered his horses. He saddled up with the speed of much practice and stepped into the saddle.

"Come on, boy," he said to the gelding. "If you ever made a fast trip, now's the time."

Ty galloped through the narrow forest trail and toward the river. The hooves of the gelding echoed over the new bridge, and Ty swerved the horse to the right with a hard pull on the line. He was passing by the Barnhill place. He called, "Hello, the house!"

Ira Barnhill was in the corral, and he came forward. "What's wrong, Sublette?"

"It's Jordan. She's about to have her baby."

Avis stepped out onto the porch. "Are you going for the doctor, Ty?"

"Yes, but I'd feel better if you'd go over, Avis. She needs a woman with her."

"I'll go right now."

"Thanks, Avis." Sublette wheeled the gelding around, kicked him, and shot off, the hooves throwing mud high into the air.

"Hitch up the wagon for me, Ira," Avis said.

"All right." Barnhill hitched the wagon, and when she came out, he said, "Will you be gone long?"

"I don't know. I'll stay until she has the baby. It may be a while."

"Get home as soon as you can," Barnhill said gruffly.

"All right." She waited until he brought the wagon out of the barn, then climbed up on the seat. She slapped the lines on the team, which stepped out at once. She did not look back, and Barnhill watched her, his eyes narrowed, as the wagon moved down the road and bent around a clump of trees.

When Ty reached Oregon City he drove the horse now flecked with foam down the street. The ten-mile ride had seemed like a long trip to him, and he was worried. He fell off the gelding, ran up the steps, and banged on the doctor's door. "Leverett! Leverett!" he called.

The door opened very soon, and Leverett blinked only twice, then said, "Somebody hurt? Who is it?"

"It's Jordan. The baby's coming."

Instantly Leverett nodded. "Go saddle my horse."

"Have you got another one for me?"

"Yes, but there's no need for you to go."

"I guess I will. I'll saddle the horses."

He moved to the small barn at the back of the house and saddled the two horses—one a tall long-legged mare and the other a rather stubby but strong-looking roan. He led them out, and when he reached the front Leverett stepped outside. He had his black bag with him, and he said, "You take the mare." He strapped the bag to the saddle horn of the roan, and as he stepped into the saddle said, "Now remember, Ty. It won't do any good to get me killed. I'm not much of a rider."

"You set the pace, Doc. We need to be there before dark if we can."

"All right. Let's go!"

Leverett piled off his horse, his face flushed. His fingers fumbled with the strap that held his medical bag, and when it came free he went at once to the door of the cabin. He was met by Avis Barnhill, whose face showed relief. "I'm glad you came, Paul. She's having a hard time."

Ty did not go in. He stood outside, loosened the cinches on the horses, and walked them, for they had been run hard. Finally when it was safe enough he watered them from a bucket, measuring out a little at a time. The cries from the cabin disturbed him. He knew that Jordan Bryce was not a crying woman, but this was different. The sounds came through the walls of the cabin and struck Sublette hard, almost like the blow of a fist. He had gone through this before when his Indian wife had borne his son, but she had uttered hardly a sound. *Blazes, I wish it was over!*

The time passed slowly, and finally Colin came outside, his face ashen and his hands unsteady. "Thanks for getting the doctor, Ty," he said in a muted tone.

"How is she?"

"The doc says it's hard. I don't know much about it. I hope I never go through this again!"

The two men remained outside the cabin. Finally, after what seemed like an eternity, the cries became less agonized. Finally a silence fell, and when the door opened Avis smiled. "You can come in now, Colin. You come, too, Ty."

Colin swallowed hard, then walked to the door. When he stepped inside he saw the doctor standing beside the bed. Jordan was lying still with a pale face marked with strain—and holding a small bundle. Her voice was very weak, but she managed a smile. "Come and see your son, Colin."

Colin advanced gingerly, and Ty moved over to one side watching as Colin bent over the bed. It pleased him that he did not look at the baby but first kissed his wife. Then he saw Colin gaze at the red face and become absolutely still.

"Isn't he beautiful, Colin?" Jordan whispered.

"Yes. Are you all right?"

"Of course I'm all right."

"She did fine." Dr. Leverett nodded. "A little trouble, but she came through it like a trooper."

"Do you want to hold him?" Jordan asked.

Colin reached out and took the swaddled form. The baby seemed very small, and he pulled the coverlet back from the baby's head. Jordan had called him beautiful, but Colin saw a red wrinkled face. As far as he could remember, this was the first brand-new baby he had ever seen. He smiled at Jordan. "I'm proud of you, sweetheart. He's a fine boy."

"Can we call him Michael?"

"Yes. You have kinfolks by that name?"

"No. He's the first Michael, but it means 'one like to God.' I prayed that God would use him in a special way."

"Michael it is." Colin held the baby, his eyes on the infant's red face, then turned to Sublette. "Come admire your godson, Ty."

Sublette moved forward, reached out, and touched the baby's cheeks. "Hello, Michael," he said. He went around to Jordan and put his hand on her hair, which was damp. "You did real good, Jordan—real good!"

Her hand came up and covered his, and her eyes smiled up at him. "Thanks for all you've done, Ty."

Sublette was embarrassed by her gratitude but leaned over and kissed her forehead. "I think you need some rest. You had a hard job."

The baby had come at almost sundown, so Colin begged the doctor to stay overnight to make sure his wife and baby were all right. Leverett agreed, and Ty, about to head home, said, "You come on when you get ready. I've got an extra bunk at my place."

"I'll be along. I just want to take one more look at Jordan," the doctor said.

Leverett moved inside and found Colin sitting beside Jordan holding the baby in his arms. He went over and looked down at the trio and smiled. "How do you feel?"

"Fine," Jordan said. She reached out her hand, and when Leverett took it she squeezed it. "Thank you, Dr. Leverett."

"It's what I do." Leverett shrugged. "Most of the time I'm not much help. Set a bone, pull out a bullet, bring a baby into the world. But it's times like this that make me glad that I'm a doctor."

He stared down at them, and then Avis's voice came. "Come and eat something, Dr. Leverett."

Leverett walked over and sat down at the table. She had scrambled eggs, fried bacon, and reheated some biscuits. There was coffee, and as he sat and ate, he suddenly discovered that he was ravenous.

"You eat like a starved wolf, Paul."

"Are you going to stay here tonight, Avis?"

"Yes. It's too late to go home in the dark."

"Will Ira be worried?"

"I don't think so."

Something in her tone caught his attention, and he looked up. He did not speak more of this, but the two did converse quietly. When he was finished he nodded. "That was a fine meal."

"Let's go outside and give them some privacy," Avis suggested.

The two went outside. It was a fine March evening. Overhead the sky was a solid canopy of black, but it was lighted by millions, it seemed, of lights. The moon was full and seemed to smile down upon them as they walked over to the barn. "Beautiful night, Avis."

"Yes. I love the stars. I wish I knew all their names."

"I know a few of them." He took her arm and turned her to the left and, still holding her, pointed up to the sky. "That's Orion up there."

"Where?"

"Right there. You see those four bright stars at the corners of sort of a trapezoid?"

She laughed softly. "I don't even know what a trapezoid is."

"Well, look right there. Now look along my arm." He held his arm up, pointed at the sky, and she laid her cheek against it. "Right there. There are four points, and see those three stars coming across it? That's Orion's belt. And there, going down from the belt, is another group. They're faint, but that's his sword."

He was very aware suddenly of holding her arm, and when she turned her face was only a few inches from his. The moon poured down its silver light, seeming to gild her face with an argent glow. He was not a man who knew women, but he did know that this one had stirred him as no other woman ever had. He suddenly felt awkward and unsure and would have released her, but she reached up and put her hand on his cheek. He knew she must have seen his awkwardness and clumsiness, and this was her way of saying that it was all right—that she didn't mind. She put her face up and smiled and let her hand remain on his cheek.

Finally he whispered, "I love you, Avis." The words shocked him. He had not intended to say that, and yet those were the words that came to his lips and suddenly the speaking of them freed him from a restraint. He pulled her closely and buried his face in her hair and felt her tremble in his arms. "I love you, Avis," he repeated in a husky tone.

She did not move for a time, and then she turned away from him and stood absolutely still. She finally turned to him, and he was shocked to see tears in her eyes. She said, "It's too late for us, Paul."

She turned quickly and walked back toward the cabin door, leaving him standing there in the darkness. It was as if he had been wounded in his heart, in a vital organ, and he knew that no matter where he went he would carry with him the scent of her hair and the feel of her firm body against his.

Slowly he turned and made his way toward the horse, and it seemed a labor to climb into the saddle. He turned the horse toward the road, and when he looked back he saw that she had turned at the cabin door and was watching him. He could not speak nor lift a hand, for he knew that what she had said was true. She was a married woman, and although he had learned long ago she did not love her husband, he knew that she had spoken the truth. It was too late for the two of them.

The emptiness that filled Rita Farr was immense. She felt it now as she waited outside the Smallwood General Store. She had seen Ace Barnhill come out of the saloon down the street, and as he approached, her heart beat faster. Her mouth was dry as dust and her knees were weak. She waited until he was about ten feet away, stepped out, and said, "Ace, can I talk to you?"

Ace stopped and blinked with surprise. "Why, sure," he said cautiously.

"Not here."

"Well, where then?"

"Just walk with me."

She turned and began walking slowly, and they turned the corner. The streets were nearly empty, only one old man sitting on a chair tilted back in front of the blacksmith, and he seemed to be asleep. Rita turned and with lips that seemed frozen said, "Ace, I'm—I'm so afraid."

"Afraid of what?"

"You know," she whispered.

Ace's eyes narrowed, and he said, "It's probably your imagination."

"I don't think so. I think it's sure. I'm—I'm going to have a baby."

Ace stared at her. He had seen her only at a distance since the night at the party when he had taken her. He had felt badly about it at first, but then it had passed from his mind. It was not the first time he had led a young woman astray. "What do you want me to do?" he said, his voice hard-edged.

"I—I don't know what to do."

"You don't even know if you're pregnant or not."

"I know I am."

"Well, there's nothing I can do about it. I'm sorry, Rita."

She stared at him. "Sorry! Is that all you can say?"

"It takes two to make a baby. You were willing enough."

Rita could not answer. She had prepared herself for this for many days now, and in her heart of hearts she had hoped and even dreamed that he would show concern and even affection. Now the look in his dark eyes was bleak, and she knew there was no help to be had here. She could not think of another word and turned to go away, her hands trembling.

"Wait a minute," Ace said. "Rita, you're a good-looking girl. Men have been chasing after you. I've seen that. Why don't you get married?"

She thought for an instant he meant to himself, but his next words revealed his intent. "It wouldn't be hard for you. Lots of men would like to have a pretty wife like you."

"To who?"

"Why, anyone. All you have to do is smile a little bit. Show you're interested." He was suddenly disturbed by the look in her eye. She reminded him of a deer that he had once wounded but was still living. The same reproach was in her soft, gentle eyes, but he turned and said, "I'm sorry, Rita—but there's nothing I can do."

Rita dropped her head. The humiliation was now complete. She could not think straight, and she had to get control before she could go back to the wagon. Slowly she stumbled down the road and climbed into the wagon.

When her brother, Jack, came out of the store, he found her sitting in the wagon. "You ready to go?"

"I guess so."

Jack spoke to the team and slapped the lines on their backs, and the wagon moved forward. They were halfway home when Jack said, "You haven't said a word. What's wrong? Are you sick?"

"No. I'm all right."

"Not like you to be so quiet." Jack was a tall young man, almost eighteen. He studied his sister's face and started to speak but then changed his mind.

They rode the rest of the way, and when they arrived at the cabin Jack leaped out. "If something's wrong, you can tell me, Sis."

She looked at him and tried to smile. "Thanks, Jack. I'll be all right."

She left and went into the cabin where her mother and her grandmother were preparing the evening meal. The weather was warm so she took off her coat. Suddenly she felt her grandmother's eyes on her. Dorcas Farr, her grandmother, was a woman who could penetrate her thoughts. Dorcas came over and without speaking stood before the young girl. A flush came to Rita's face, and then she heard her grandmother whisper, "It'll be all right, honey. It'll be all right."

She threw herself into her grandmother's arms and began to sob.

Ellen Farr turned from the fireplace with surprise to see Dorcas holding her daughter. "What's wrong?" she said. She went over quickly, and Dorcas turned, and there was something in her face that demanded understanding. "It's Rita. She's in trouble."

Ellen Farr loved her daughter with all of her heart, but for one instant anger came. But it was only for an instant, and then she moved over and took her daughter, put her arms around her, and held her as she sobbed. Her eyes met those of Dorcas, and the two women understood something of the pain that now racked Rita. "We'll make it through this," Ellen said, stroking her back. "It will be all right, Rita. I'll tell your father."

Colin Bryce was fascinated by his son. He cut back on his working hours so that he could come in and help, and nothing gave him more pleasure than to simply hold him on his lap and look down into his face.

As for Jordan, she was as happy as she had ever been in her life. She had had lapses of faith before the baby had been born—fears that the baby would not be well, or that something would go wrong during the birth. But he was a fine healthy boy now a month old, and she smiled as she walked by with a pan of cornbread in her hand to put on the table. She said, "You're going to wear him out handling him."

"Not this one, wife." He held the baby up and smiled at him, shaking him gently. "You're all right, Michael. You're going to be as good-lookin' as your ma."

Jordan laughed and sat down to eat. As

she finished her meal, she said, "Let me hold him while you eat."

Reluctantly Colin handed her the baby and sat down. She had found wild greens which he loved, and Ty had brought over a quarter of a deer. She had prepared the venison so that it was tender. He ate hungrily as she nursed the baby, and when he finished his meal she rearranged her clothing and said, "I'd like to take him to church Sunday."

"All right. We'll go."

"I don't believe in sprinkling babies."

"No. That's your Baptist blood." Colin's eyes sparkled. "But he's too young to slap under the water. He'd drown."

"I'd like to dedicate him to the Lord. Just have Brother Ellencourt hold him up and have everybody pray for him that he'll never go wrong. That he'll be a man of God."

Colin watched her carefully. Her faith was much stronger than his. He felt himself to be rather weak in his Christian walk, and he was well aware that she knew it. "All right," he said. "If that's what you'd like, that's what we'll do."

"Sunday then. We'll dedicate Michael Bryce to the Lord Jesus Christ."

TWENTY-FOUR

The mild spring had endured for two months, but now June came bringing with it a hot sun that poured down from straight above and turned the air into a thin, still breeze. Heat lay like a thin film on the windless air, and whenever horses moved along the road a fine dust stirred. As Corny moved slowly along the trail, he saw that the sunlight burned against the earth. He noticed the thin flashes on the water of the creek that circled and held the Farr homestead as in the crook of an elbow. From far away came the mournful sound of a dog, and Corny, alert to such things, noticed that it was not the sound that a dog made when he had treed something or was on a trail.

"Just howlin' at the sun, I reckon," he murmured, and then stopped, for he had seen Rita who was walking along the rows of corn looking at the emerald green stalks. Her red hair made a counterpoint to the green of the corn and the azure of the sky, and caught by the beauty that lay before him both in the young woman and in the land and sky, Corny stood totally still.

I can't help it, he thought. *I've got to do it. I can't go on like this.* The thought brought some sort of resolution to him, and tightening his jaw, he walked down the trail until he reached the cornfield. He made his way down one of the rows noting that the corn was healthy, more so than that which he and his brothers had planted. A rabbit exploded under his feet, then ran down the row, his white cottontail a flag that bobbed up and down. Corny watched him as he scooted past Rita, and then she turned and looked at him. A startled look came into her eye, then she smiled and came toward him. She was wearing a simple blue dress, and it was evidently an old one for it was faded and tight on her body. She half turned away from him, then he called her name. "Rita!" And she turned back to face him.

"Hello, Corny." Her voice was somewhat strained, he thought, and it had a falling cadence.

"Rita, I got to talk to you."

She looked somewhat surprised and then shrugged her shoulders. There was in her some sort of sadness that he could not understand. She had always been a young woman full of life. That was part of her attractiveness. Now as she stood there something was evident about her that he had not seen before. He was not sure what it was, but he felt the turbulence of her spirit as a strange current might cut across the wind as it blew. Her eyes and lips were both still, and she did not speak so that finally he kicked a clod of dirt and tried to frame the words that he wanted to say.

"How have you been?" he asked. It was not what he meant to say, and when she replied briefly, he said, "Rita, I been thinkin' about you a lot."

Her eyes studied him for a moment, and then she asked, "Why, Corny? Why would you think of me?"

"You know. I—" Words failed him for a moment, and he cleared his throat and tried to smile. "I'm not much good at talking about things. I wish I could talk like Ace does." Instantly he saw that he had said something that disturbed her. He could not imagine what it was, but she half turned away, and he reached out to take her arm. "I mean I got things inside me I want to say, but I never have been good at talking." She turned to face him again, and he let his hand fall away. They stood facing each other under the hot sun, and desperately Corny blurted out, "I guess you know how much I've always liked you, Rita."

"I like you, too."

The conversation was going nowhere, and Corny Barnhill knew that he was not good enough with words so he said simply, "I—I've come to care for you these months we've been together, and I wanted to know if you'd ever—" He swallowed hard and seemed to find it difficult to finish the sentence. "If you'd ever think about marrying me."

The words seemed to break against Rita's spirit, and in her eyes was reflected a shock that Corny could not understand. He rushed to add, "'Course I know I'm not much to look at, and I really don't have anything. But if you'd think about it, and if you could come to care for me, I'd like it mighty well, Rita."

The silence lay over the field except for some crows that were making their harsh cawing noises over in the next field. Rita stood stock-still and could not answer, it seemed, for a moment. Finally she said, "You don't want me."

"Why—certain I do. That's what I come to tell you."

Something in Rita's eyes puzzled the young man, and he tried to understand what he had said wrong. "I maybe haven't said it right," he said. "I love you, and I want to marry you."

"You don't want to marry me, Corny."

Corny was shocked at the bottomless misery that lay in the girl's eyes. This was not the Rita he knew, for her eyes had always been laughing. He had noticed lately that she had been quiet, but he had not seen her a great deal. Now he shook his head and began to speak. "Like I say, I'm not much, and I know you could have lots of men older than I am who have got money. But I'm a hard worker, Rita. If we got married, I could stake out a claim, and we'd build a cabin there. It would be just you and me." He continued to speak earnestly, his eyes alight, but at the same time he was puzzled, for she was showing no sign of responding.

At last his words wound down, and he concluded, "Well, I had to come and ask. I wanted you to know how I felt."

Rita Farr studied the young man and then said simply, "I can't marry you, Corny." Her words dropped at the end as she spoke his name, and then she straightened herself up and looked directly into his eyes. "I'm going to have a baby."

Rita's words caught at Corny, and he could not believe he had heard her right. He started to ask her to repeat it, but seeing the misery in her face he knew something of what was in her heart and spirit. She was crushed and broken, and he could not think clearly. Then the words rose swiftly. "Who done it?" he said almost harshly.

"It doesn't matter." Her words were flat and lifeless, and she turned to go away, but Corny swung her around.

"Tell me who done it!" he said gritting his teeth together. "I'll show him!"

At that instant Rita realized that she could never let Corny know that his brother Ace was the father of her child. *If he finds out, he'll go after Ace and either kill him or get killed himself,* she thought. She stood looking into his eyes, thinking of his gentleness and knowing that she could not let him be destroyed. Then she thought of her brother, Jack, whose strong sense of justice would make him want to avenge any man who wronged his sister. *I can't ever tell anybody, not ever!*

And so Rita closed the door forever on the subject and said, "It wouldn't do any good. Let me go, Corny."

Corny released her, and she turned and walked slowly down between the rows of corn. He watched her for a moment, then could stand it no longer. He whirled and ran blindly from the field. Anger, fierce and white-hot, rose in him, and for that one moment he hated this girl who had shattered the one dream that he had ever had.

"What's the matter with you, boy?" Ira Barnhill snapped. "You're walkin' around like you're half drunk or half asleep."

"Nothin'," Corny said shortly. He had been helping his father clear land, and he had kept up with the strokes of the saw, or so he had thought. But now he looked up to see his father staring at him. Barnhill wiped the sweat from his face and shook his head. "Are you sick?"

"No, I'm not sick."

"Well, what is it then? You're gonna walk off a cliff the way you been actin' the last few days."

"Nothing's wrong with me." Ordinarily

Corny was a cheerful young man, but now there was a sullenness in his thin face and in his words. He stared at his father defiantly, and Ira Barnhill finally shook his head. "You need a good beltin' is what you need."

"I'm too old for that."

Ira Barnhill blinked. He had played this scene out with his other two sons, Theodore and Ace, and the time had come when they had both challenged him. This younger son of his was a softer, gentler kind, and now Barnhill was half angered as he said, "You don't think I can thrash you?"

"You can try. I'd hate for it to come to that. I'm seventeen years old, Pa. I'm not a kid anymore."

Ira Barnhill was so accustomed to the gentle ways of the boy that he could not understand the anger that flared in Corny's eyes. For a moment he considered lighting into the boy, but he was not at all sure that he could handle him. He was fifty-one and was not the man he had been. Corny was lean, but very strong and quicker than any of the other boys. The impulse was in him, but finally Ira Barnhill said, "Well, I hope you snap out of it. You're walkin' around like a blasted ghost!"

* * *

"I got to talk to you, Corny."

"Sure. What is it, Jack?"

Corny had finished clearing the land and was saddling his horse when Jack Farr rode into the yard on a gray stallion. He had come off the horse and approached Corny with such intensity that Corny grew wary. Rita's words were still like a raw wound with him, and he imagined at first that Rita had told him about his offer and that Jack had come to warn him off.

"Not here, Corny. Come with me."

The words were almost an order, but Corny was curious as well as apprehensive. He finished saddling the mare, stepped into the saddle, and then rode out to where Jack was waiting. Neither of them spoke as they rode together along the dusty road. When they were out of sight of the house, Jack suddenly turned. "I've got to know something." Jack was the same age as Corny, and the two had become good friends on the trail. But now there was anger in Jack's blue eyes. When he spoke he bit his words off sharply. "Rita's going to have a baby." He waited for Corny to speak, and when the other simply waited, he said, "I'm gonna ask you, Corny, and I want the truth."

"All right. Ask your question."

"Rita's going to have a baby. Is it yours?"

Of all things that Corny had expected this was the last. His eyes flew open with shock, and he almost stuttered as the words fell out of his mouth. "Me! Gosh no, Jack! I wouldn't do a thing like that. You know I wouldn't."

Jack Farr drew a deep breath. Honesty was plain as print across the face of Corny Barnhill. He relaxed and shook his head. "I didn't think so, but I had to be sure."

"I knew about the baby, Jack. Rita told me."

"I didn't know she had told anybody except Gran and Ma."

For a moment Corny hesitated, then he said, "Why'd you come to me?"

"Well, I always thought you liked Rita. I could see something in you when you watched her."

"You was right about that. I do care for her. I asked her to marry me. That's why she told me."

Jack could not speak for a moment. "I didn't know that," he said finally.

"She could have lied to me and not told

me the truth, and I'd never known the difference," Corny said. This truth came to him
then, and his eyes met those of Jack, and he
added, "It wasn't her fault. You can't blame
her for it and put her down, Jack. She needs
you. She needs all of us."

It was at that moment that Jack Farr knew
the real worth of this young man. He had always liked Corny but never more than at this
moment. He suddenly reached out and
squeezed the other's arm. "You're a good
man, and I wish Rita would marry you." He
shook his head. "There's no keeping a thing
like this secret."

"I'd like to talk to your parents, but I don't
know if Rita would like it or not."

"I think you should, Corny. They need to
know how you feel."

"Rita don't care for me like I do for her,
but I figured that if she'd give me a chance, I
could make her a good husband, and she'd
come to love me." Suddenly Corny straightened up and his eyes flashed. "I'm going to
tell your ma and pa."

"Come along. I'll go with you."

The two men rode along silently, each
filled with his own thoughts, and both of
them were experiencing the grief that comes

to young men and to young women as they pass from adolescence into the hard harsh world of adults.

Sublette was on his way out to hunt deer when he heard a horse approaching. He turned in the saddle and saw Corny Barnhill. Drawing up, he nodded and said, "Hello, Corny."

Corny shifted in the saddle. "Mind if I ride along, Ty?"

"Sure. I'm goin' out for a deer. Come along if you'd like."

The two rode along, and Sublette saw that something was eating at the young man. He was wiry and tall and had not yet filled out. He would be a big man when he got his growth, tall like Ace and Theodore, and well-muscled.

"Ty, I got to talk to you."

"Well, I'm here."

"Suppose there was this girl, and she— she got in trouble." Words seemed to dry up, and then he said, "I ain't no good at makin' up stuff, Ty. I guess you'll find out like everybody else."

Ty had observed the way that Corny

Barnhill watched Rita Farr, and suddenly he said, "Is it Rita?"

Corny turned a pair of anguished eyes on Sublette. "Yes, but don't you fault her for it, Ty!"

Sublette turned and looked at the young man, and he felt a quick compassion for him. He had not been blind to the fact that Corny had developed some sort of affection for the girl, but he had not known it was this serious. "She's a good girl. I'm surprised."

"She won't tell me who it is. If I find out, I'll kill him!"

"I reckon you won't do that."

"Then I'll whip him and run him out of the settlement." Corny's face was pale, and he struggled to gain control of his temper. "The thing is, Ty, I—I'm mighty fond of Rita. I want to marry her, but I don't know what to do now."

Sublette turned, and his eyes were half hidden behind the drop of his lids. A day's growth of whiskers glittered like metal filings on his face, but his expression was gentle and filled with compassion. "She's a fine girl—and she made a mistake. We all make them, but it's harder on women."

"I know that, but I don't know what to do." Agony ran across the young man's face, and he looked to Sublette for help.

Sublette knew the boy had no one else to go to. His brothers were careless and rough, and his father was not a man that a young boy with this kind of trouble could talk to. What he needed was assurance, somebody to help him, to stand by him in his thinking. His wide chest lifted and fell, and he wondered if he was doing the right thing. Here was a young man on the razor's edge, and he was, for a moment, fearful of saying the wrong thing—of giving him a push down the wrong pathway, but he knew that Corny needed him.

"Take her," he said as forcefully as he could. "And never say a word about what she's done. It'll be your baby. Yours and hers."

"You mean it, Ty?"

"Of course I mean it! She's a fine girl— none better in the whole settlement. She made a mistake, but you'll make yours, and I've made plenty of my own."

Eagerly Corny studied the face of Sublette, who was smiling with a remote and angular expression. Behind this smile was a toughness that the years had beaten into him.

Corny suddenly cried, "All right, Ty, I'll do it!"

Sublette reached over and slapped him on the shoulder. "You love that girl and take care of her. Never say a word to her about what she's done. Bury it deep."

"I'll do it, Ty!" Corny wheeled his horse around and drove it at a fast gallop. As he left, Sublette pulled his hat off and ran his hand through his hair. "I hope I told him the right thing," he said to himself. "But who am I to tell another man how to live?"

Rita looked up to see Corny riding down the road at a fast gallop. She was sitting in a chair beside her mother helping make soap. The pungent smell filled the air as it bubbled in the black kettle, and Rita glanced quickly at her mother but said nothing.

Rita's heart lurched as Corny stepped out of the saddle and threw the reins down. The horse, trained to stand, did not move, and began chomping at the growth of grass.

"Miz Farr."

"Hello, Corny," Ellen Farr said. "How are you?"

Corny said, "I'd like to talk to Rita if you don't mind."

"Why, sure. I'll go in and see if my cornbread's done."

Rita watched Corny as her mother went in and saw there was something new in him. He had always been diffident and awkward, but now he stood straight, and there was no hesitation when he said, "Rita, I'm sorry for what's happened to you, but I want to marry you."

Rita took a quick breath. "You don't mean that, Corny."

"Yes, I do. I care for you, and I want to marry you. I'd like for you to say you'll have me."

Something swept through Rita as she saw the goodness of the young man. He was so young and so vulnerable! She studied his thin face and saw the plaintive quality in his eyes. "I can't do that, Corny, but I thank you for asking."

"Why can't you marry me? That man, he's not going to marry you, is he?"

"No."

"Then you need a husband, and your baby needs a father. Why won't you do it?"

"It—it wouldn't be fair to you. I don't—" Rita hesitated and then shook her head. The sun touched her bright red hair, and she looked very young as she stood there before him. "I don't feel for you what a woman ought to feel for her husband."

Corny had expected this. "I know that," he said. He reached out suddenly and touched her hair, and his voice was gentle as he said, "I'm believing that will come, Rita. I can make you care for me. I'll never ask you who the father is. We'll never speak of it again from this day. You'll be his mother and I'll be his father."

Tears suddenly formed in Rita's eyes. They ran down her cheeks, and she could not move. He put his arm around her and held her close saying, "I'll tell your pa and your ma, and we'll get married right away."

Rita could not speak for a moment, and then she turned and buried her face against his chest. His arms went around her, and she felt as if her heart would break. She did not know whether this was right or wrong. All she knew was that he was a man who cared for her and would care for her baby.

* * *

Avis Barnhill looked up from her sewing and noted that Corny was riding in at a fast pace. The sun was almost set, and it was behind him so she could not see his face, but there seemed to be something different about him. Even as she watched, Ira came out and stood leaning against the post that held up the roof. "There's that boy again. He's been moonin' like a sick calf."

Avis laid her sewing in her lap as she caught a glimpse of Corny's face. He was the best of the Barnhills and was treated the worst. Her heart had gone out to him even in the midst of her own unhappiness, and now she saw that there was a grim determination that had etched itself on his youthful features.

"Where you been?" Ira demanded.

Corny did not answer. He came up on the porch and stood looking at his father. He was at least four inches taller, and Ira had to turn his head up to look in his eyes, something that always irritated him. "Well, where have you been, I said."

"Pa, I'm going to marry Rita Farr."

Ira Barnhill's jaw sagged, and then he stiffened his back. He cursed harshly. "No, you ain't! I'll not have a woods colt in my family!"

Ordinarily this would have settled the matter, but Avis stood up, for she saw that a storm was brewing.

"You can say anything you want to, Pa, but I'm going to do it. I'd like for you to accept her as your daughter."

"Daughter! Never in this life! Everybody knows she's carryin' somebody's baby. She won't come in this house."

"All right. If that's the way you want it, I'll build a cabin for her. I wish it didn't have to be like this."

Ira Barnhill could not bear to be thwarted. His face was livid. "*You* build a house! You can't even build a shed! You don't have anything, and you won't get any help from me!"

"Yes, he will."

Avis stepped forward and put her hand on Corny's arm. She faced her husband, and determination filled her gaze. "We'll help him. We'll help him build a cabin, and we'll welcome her in this house, and nobody will say one word about what's happened."

"What are you talking about, woman?"

"You listen to me, Ira. I won't live with a man mean enough to cut his son off like you have—and his best son at that!"

Ira could not seem to find words, and then he cursed her. "You'll keep your—"

"Shut your mouth, Ira!" Avis Barnhill's dark eyes seemed to glow with a fire, and she held tightly to Corny's arm. "I'll leave you, Ira, and then you know what people will say? They'll say you're an old man not able to keep a young woman satisfied."

Ira's arm shot out, and he slapped her across the face. Avis staggered, but she did not relent. "If you ever lay another hand on me, I'll wait until you're asleep, and I'll pour boiling water in your face. You'd better listen to me. I'll do exactly what I say. I'll leave you, and I'll go live with Corny and his wife."

Ira Barnhill started to bluster, but suddenly the look on her face shut him down. He knew she was a woman of fierce determination when she set her mind to it. She had never opposed him before like this, but somehow he knew that she would do exactly as she had said. He was a man sensitive to what his neighbors thought of him, and he had come in his own rough way to care for this woman. She had not responded to him as he had wished, but he still had hopes. But now he saw that if he took one false step here, everything was over. He was not a stupid man and understood at once that Avis had the best hand.

For a long moment he stared at her face, and then he nodded slightly. "All right," he said. "It'll be as you say."

"That's fine, Ira," Avis said at once. There was a calmness about her that almost frightened Ira. He knew that she had been ready to do whatever was necessary, but he had weathered it.

"You go ahead, boy, and marry the girl," he mumbled. "It'll be as your ma says. I'll never say a word to her, and we'll help you get started."

"Thanks, Pa," Corny said quietly. He turned to Avis, and his lips that had been tight with strain suddenly relaxed. He reached out and took her hand and held it for a moment in both of his. "Thanks, Ma." He turned and walked away.

Watching him, Avis said, "She's a good girl. She made a mistake."

"You would have done it, wouldn't you?" Ira said. "Shamed me in front of everybody!"

Avis looked at him and said quietly, "Yes, I would."

She turned and walked into the cabin leaving Ira there watching her—wondering what kind of woman he had married.

"Hello, Rita."

Turning quickly, Rita stood silently for a moment in front of Ace. She had been walking alone in the woods, along the path that led from the cabin to the creek, occupied with her thoughts. "What do you want?" she said.

Ace had said little to Corny when the young man had told him of his intention to marry Rita. He had muttered, "Well, now, that's fine, Corny."

But he had not been able to get away from thoughts of the marriage. Finally he had ridden out to the Farr place and kept himself out of sight until he saw Rita leave the house and enter the trail that led through the pines. He had followed her, and now as she faced him, he found he didn't know what to say. He waited for her to speak, then when she remained silent, he said, "Corny told me about you two getting married."

Still Rita didn't speak. She was thinking of

how selfish this man was—and how generous Corny had proven. Finally she said,
"We'll be in the same family, Ace. I haven't
told anyone who the father is—and I never
will. I ask just one thing—never come close
to me and never mention what happened.
I'm ashamed of myself—but I did find out
what kind of a man you are. Corny's twice
the man you'll ever be."

Ace's pride was wounded. "He's just a
kid. You don't love him."

"You're wrong about both of those
things. He's a man! And I do love him." To
her surprise Rita suddenly knew that her
words were true. She had thought of nothing but of Corny's love for her and the way
he came to offer himself, and a great tenderness had grown in her heart for him.
Somehow she knew that this love would
grow, and this knowledge made her bold.
"From now on, you're just a brother-in-law
to me. Corny and I are going to be man and
wife, and we're going to have a fine baby.
It'll be ours, and we'll love him or her. Good-
bye, Ace."

A sense of anger and shame mingled in
Ace as he watched her walk away. He almost called out to her, but what would he

say? As she disappeared into the deeps of the woods, he turned and moved to his horse. He mounted and rode away, but he could not get away from the pride and scorn that had been in Rita's eyes. He knew he never would, and he thought, *She's right— Corny is a better man than I am.*

TWENTY-FIVE

Jennie Town stood smiling down at the new litter of pigs, then with a swift motion she placed her hand on the top rail and vaulted over. The piglets scattered, but she swooped down and grabbed one up in her arms. It squealed with a piercing cry, and Gus, who had been watching her with a smile, suddenly saw the huge sow appear and came over the fence in one bound. He scooped Jennie up in his arms, practically lifted her up, and tossed her over the fence. By the time he had accomplished this the sow was almost upon him. She was a monstrous animal reddish in color, and her eyes were red with fury. Gus had no time to leap. He simply dodged to one side, and the sow ran into the stout barricade built of white oak split rails. He turned quickly and ran with the sow right behind him, grunting with every leap she made. Gus made it to the other end and left the ground in a dive. He felt the sow's blunt snout strike the bottoms of his boots, but he turned a complete somersault and landed flat on his back. It drove the wind out of his body, and he sat up trying to suck air in.

Jennie hastily lifted the squalling pig over the rail, and he slipped out of her hands with no harm done. Quickly Jennie ran over and knelt down beside Gus. His face was red, and he seemed to be making sucking noises although, of course, she could not hear them.

"Are you all right, Gus? Are you hurt?"

Gus could not answer for a moment, and then finally he managed to frame the words without actually saying them. "I'm all right."

Jennie's large blue-gray eyes were wide open, and worry etched itself across her face. She waited for a moment and then reached out and brushed the dirt off of Gus's shoulders. He reached up, caught her hand, and managed a grin. "You can get into more trouble than any woman I ever saw." He struggled to his feet, shook his shoulders, then managed a grin. "What did you want to do a thing like that for? Don't you know those sows will fight for their pigs?"

"I didn't even think about it. They just looked so cute."

"Well, that sow doesn't look cute, and if she had caught me, I think she would have stomped a mud hole in me."

His words amused Jennie, and her lips turned upward in a smile. "You looked so funny diving over the fence."

"I would have looked funnier if that big sow had caught me."

Gus had come over to bring the Lees three large rabbits that he had shot early that morning out hunting. They were cooking now, bubbling in a pot inside the fireplace, and Jennie had spent the morning making him a berry pie. When he had asked her what kind of berries they were, she said, "I don't know, but they taste good."

"They're huckleberries. You can dry 'em and use 'em in cakes."

Now Gus took her arm and turned her around toward the edge of the timberline. She looked up at him and said nothing for a time as they walked along, and finally in her husky voice she said, "How are the Bryces?"

"Jordan's fine," he said turning so that she could see his lips. "She's all caught up in that baby of hers. I never saw a woman so foolish about an ugly little red-faced youngun."

"He is not ugly! He's a beautiful baby."

Gus admired Michael Bryce as well as she, but he loved to tease her. "No. He looks like raw meat, or he did when he was first born. He's beginning to un-uglyfie now."

"Un-uglyfie! You talk awful, Gus!"

She stopped and leaned her back against a towering cedar tree, and he lounged beside her putting his weight on one foot and his hands behind his back. From somewhere far off he heard the cry of doves, that soft cooing that sounded so nice. He remarked, "I'll have to go out after some doves. They make good eating."

"Don't you do it!"

"Don't do what?"

"Don't you shoot a dove."

"Why not?" Gus asked with surprise. "Don't you like 'em?"

Jennie shook her head. Her golden hair had been left free, and now it fell down her back—a rich blonde with glints of silver catching the sun. "Doves are in the Bible, and they're always good birds."

"Well, cows are in the Bible, too, but you eat 'em."

"That's different. It was a dove that Noah let out of the ark to see if the floodwaters were gone." She went on to speak of the doves in the Bible, and he listened, charmed by her words.

When she fell silent, he shook his head and changed the subject. "I'm worried about Colin."

"Why is that?"

"He's an unhappy man. He don't smile anymore. He's downright sullen most of the time."

"What's wrong with him?"

Gus shrugged. He made a rawboned, angular shape as the shade fell across him from the branches of the cedar tree. He reached out and pulled off a strip of the shaggy bark, held it for a moment, then let it drop to the ground. "He's always been a free man, out at sea doing what he wants, and now he can't handle all this work it takes to clear land. I don't think he's cut out to be a farmer."

"You think he'll go back to the sea?"

"I don't know. I don't think that would please him either. He's got a wife now and a baby, and a seafaring man don't make a good husband for a woman."

Smiling at Gus, Jennie asked innocently, "What kind of man does make a good husband?"

Taken off guard by the question, he glanced at Jennie and saw that she was making fun of him. "My kind of man!" he said. "A man who'll take a stick to a woman the first time she don't have his meal on the table at suppertime!"

"You'd never beat a woman." Jennie smiled.

"How do you know?"

"I just know, that's all."

Jennie was wearing a light brown skirt and a blouse of some soft material dyed a light aqua. It matched her blue-gray eyes somehow, and she made an attractive picture as she stood before him. She asked, "How are things over at your claim?"

"Cabin's up. Right empty though. Haven't had time to make furniture yet. Still doing a lot of work helping Colin clear land."

"I'd like to see it."

Gus's head lifted. "Well, why don't we? It won't take long."

Jennie nodded. "All right. I'll go tell Mary where we're going. I'll bring my paper and some pencils, too. Maybe I can draw a sketch of it."

"I wish you'd draw a sketch of somethin' else."

"Of what?" Jennie said, pausing to look at him.

"Of yourself."

"Of me?" Jennie's lips turned upward in the corners. "All right. I'll get in front of a mirror and draw my own picture. I've never done that before."

"Good. Now let's get going."

As soon as Jordan looked up, she knew something had happened that had pleased Colin. His dark blue eyes were wide, and he was smiling. His trim mustache gave him a rakish air, and as he stepped inside the cabin there was a lift in his step and an excitement in his voice that she had not witnessed since they had left Independence.

"Sit down, wife. We've got talking to do."

Jordan sat down on one of the cane chairs that Gus had woven for them, and Colin sat down in the other one. He leaned forward, slapped his hands together with excitement, and rubbed his palms. "I've got something to tell you."

"You're excited. What about?"

"I met an old friend of mine in Oregon City. His name is John Dawkins. I've known him for about five years. He owns a ship—the *Corsair*." Colin laughed and shook his head. "The name's a lot fancier than the ship. She's pretty old now but still got good ribs and good wood in her. I sailed on her once around the Horn carrying a load of whale oil mostly, although she's not a whaler."

"Is the ship in harbor here?"

"Yes. I saw her out there, and I knew her as soon as I laid eyes on her. Brought back old times."

"Why didn't you bring your friend home with you?"

"Maybe I will, but he's busy now getting the *Corsair* ready for a voyage." For a moment Colin hesitated, and then he said, "That's what I've got to talk to you about. I've got a great chance here."

"To do what?"

"Dawkins wants me to take the ship to Africa."

"To Africa! Why, that's a thousand miles away!"

"More than that, but listen to this." Colin pulled the chair forward, picked up one of her hands, and held it in both of his. "We're breaking our backs here, both of us, Jordan. I've been losing my mind trying to figure out some way where we could get ahead enough to hire some of this work done."

"We've got Gus."

"But we're about broke, too. We can't keep on paying him. And you know that there's no market for wheat around here. Most of the time we have to trade it just for stuff to live on."

Something very like fear began to rise in Jordan, for she knew that Colin had already made his mind up. "But, Colin," she said. "You'd have to leave us for how long?"

"Maybe six months."

"You don't really know that, do you?"

"Well, it could take a little longer," Colin admitted. "But look at this. On this one trip, why, I could make enough money to build us a proper house—one with lots of real glass windows!" He dropped her hand, got up, and began striding back and forth. "I'll be going on shares with Dawkins. He's already got a pretty good crew, and she's a good ship. We could make ten thousand dollars or more."

Suddenly a thought came to Jordan, and she demanded, "What's the cargo?"

Colin seemed reluctant to speak. He chewed on his lower lip for a moment, passed his hand over his brow, then said, "Well, it's slaves. Black ivory, they call them."

"You can't do that, Colin! It's not right."

Colin's jaw set in a stubborn line. He said,

"I knew you'd take it like this, but I've got to do something. I don't like slavery any more than you do, but it's going to be done whether I or another man captain that ship. It's going to Africa and coming back with a load of slaves. They'll be delivered in the South, and then I can take a ship around the Horn."

"That'll take another three months. You'll be gone a year. You'll be gone while Michael's growing up."

Colin waved away her protest and said, "If I were talking about going back to the sea full time, that would be different. But I'm not. A lot of wives, and even those with small babies, send their husbands off to sea. They come home and stay for a month or two, then they're gone again for another year. Sometimes a whaler will be gone two years."

Jordan felt her hope sinking. She knew Colin well, and he had his mind set on this. The more she argued, the more adamant he got.

Finally he said, "I don't like for us to be apart, but I've got to take care of you and Michael the best way I can. If we stay here like this another five years, we'll be old and worn out. With this one trip I can buy you anything you want. The finest house, nice clothes . . . We'll have enough money to take care of Michael. I've got to do it, Jordan!"

Suddenly Jordan knew that he had already made his decision known to Dawkins. "You've already agreed to do it, haven't you, Colin?"

"I had to," Colin said defensively. "The ship leaves day after tomorrow."

Panic ran through Jordan, and she went to him and put her arms around him and laid her head down on his chest. "Please don't do this! Don't leave me here alone with Michael. I need you, Colin."

Colin shook his head. "I'm sorry that we don't agree, but I have to do what's best. That's what a man does. I can't take care of you like this. I'm not cut out for it, and I hate it. It would be nice if you'd see it my way."

"I love you, Colin—but I think you're wrong."

The two days passed swiftly in a whirl of preparations, and now the time had come to part. Colin had come outside to saddle his horse and pack up his few belongings in the saddlebag. At the sound of hooves, he looked up and greeted Sublette as he rode into the yard. Ty was going with Colin to Oregon City to bring his horse back once Colin boarded the ship.

Sublette dismounted. "Ready to go?"

With a glance over at his cabin where Jordan waited inside, Colin said, "Jordan isn't taking this well."

"You're not surprised by that, are you?" Sublette said. "I don't want you to go either. I think you're making a fool mistake."

With a shake of his head, Colin said quickly, "I know you both think so, but it's the one chance I've got to make enough money to take care of my family. I've got to go, and I want to ask you a favor."

"All right. What is it?"

"I want you to watch out for Jordan and Michael."

Sublette studied the face of Colin carefully. "All right," he said slowly. "I'll see that they're all right."

"They might get sick or something. You're their closest neighbor. Would it be too much to ask you to look in every day?"

"That won't be any problem."

"Gus can put the crops in. I've left enough money with Jordan that they ought to be

able to make out until I get back. I'm hopin'
to be back in less than a year if we're lucky."

Sublette nodded. "No man can live another man's life. If it were me, I wouldn't go.
But if it'll set your mind at ease, I'll promise
you as long as I'm on my own two feet,
they'll never want for anything."

Relief washed across Colin's face. With a
gusty sigh, he said, "That takes a load off
my mind, Ty. I know they're in good hands,
and I appreciate it." He turned to go to the
cabin to say his final good-bye, and then a
thought came to him. He turned around and
said in a different sort of voice, a little
strained, "The sea's a dangerous place.
Ships go down. I've lost good friends out
there." He was silent for a moment, and then
his eyes met with those of Ty Sublette. "If
anything happens to me—" He hesitated for
a long moment. The silence seemed to run
on, and finally he said, "I want you to do
whatever you can to take care of my family.
Anything! Will you promise me that, Ty? I—I
know it's asking a lot."

Sublette was surprised at the vehemence
and the urgency in the voice of Colin Bryce,
but he did not hesitate. "You saved my life,
Colin. Of course I'll do it. You go on out

there, get rich, and get back to your family."
He slapped Colin on the shoulder and
squeezed it with his powerful grasp. "I'll take
care of things here."

Colin swallowed hard, and his eyes
blinked for a moment. "You're a good man,
Ty Sublette," he said huskily. "I hope I can
do something for you some day."

Colin turned then, and as Sublette
mounted his gelding, he went inside.

Jordan was standing holding Michael in
her arms, and for one instant the look in her
eyes and the grief that was etched on her
face almost caused Colin to change his
plans. He had felt anxious to go, but now a
strange reluctance took him. He came to
stand before her, and the struggle within him
was fierce. To be separated from this woman
that he loved and this child that had come
into his life and taken such a place in his
heart dominated him for a moment. But he
knew that he had to go, so he reached out
and took Michael and held him in his arms.
He looked down at him for a long time, then
kissed him and reached out and drew Jordan
with his free arm. He kissed her, and she
clung to him tightly. So tightly that he had to
free himself by pulling her arm loose.

"Here. Take Michael." Colin waited until she had him and then said, "I love you and Michael, but I've got to do this."

Jordan could not speak, her throat was so full. She swallowed hard and then said, "God go with you and bring you back to us safely."

"Good-bye, sweetheart. Good-bye, Michael." He turned and walked out of the cabin, not daring to look back. Quickly he walked to the horse where Sublette held him, mounted, and then said huskily, "Let's go, Ty."

The two men turned their horses, and Colin kicked the sides of his animal. As they reached the clump of oak that the road bent around, Colin Bryce turned his head. The last thing he saw was Jordan standing in front of their cabin holding Michael in her arms.

He shook his head, gritted his teeth, and slapped the horse with the reins. The gelding, startled, leaped ahead, then drove down the road at a dead run. *It's for the best! I'll make it up to them.*

PART FOUR

A humming sound caused Jordan to lift her head, and she caught sight of a hornet that had sailed in through the open door. He flew directly to the small nest that he and his kind were building on the roof beam of the cabin, hesitated, then entered the egg-shaped structure. She had watched them build the papery nest and had chosen, on Ty's advice, to simply leave it there. "They'll keep the place clear of flies," he'd said. At first she had been apprehensive, but he had been right, as he usually was, about such things. The hornets flew overhead, busily coming and going all day, but did not offer any harm to Jordan or Michael. Even now Michael, who was sitting on the floor across the room, paid no heed as the hornets darted about in the bright sunlight that flooded in through the window and the upper doorway.

Dipping the tip of the goose quill in the bottle of ink, Jordan placed the date, September 2, 1845, at the top right-hand corner, then began writing:

*Dear Mother and Father and all you
dear ones,*

*A friend of Ty's is leaving tomorrow
to return to the east on horseback. He
is a fast rider, Ty says, and this letter will
get to you much faster than it would by
ship going around the Horn.*

*Michael and I are both well. He is al-
most eighteen months old now and so
much like Colin it startles me sometimes! He has the same dark hair and
eyes, but he has your mouth, Mother,
and your way of tilting his head, Father.
But he's Colin in miniature and not only
in appearance but has his temperament, too.*

For a moment Jordan hesitated, not
quite sure how to put into words what was
troubling her. She sat there, her eyes going
to the world outside. Through the open
door she could see the birds and heard
their twitter and chatter, their shrill cries
and whistle notes. One of them made a
pure flutelike call, and all of the sounds
were blended together in a way that
pleased her.

Impatient with herself, she hurried on,

putting down words which she knew would be misunderstood.

Colin has been gone for fourteen months now, and most people around here assume that he died at sea, but I won't believe that. I realize, of course, that by now he's probably had time to make the trip and return, but he told me once that ships sometimes get be-calmed for weeks or even months. Sometimes the storms batter them so badly that they have to put into a port and refit. I pray to God every day that he will return, and to keep him fresh in Michael's mind, I tell him stories about his father every night.

I could not have made it through these months without the help of Gus and Ty. Ty brings meat by regularly, and Gus is always available, for Colin left enough money to pay him. But many of the things Gus won't take pay for. It's not just helping me that Ty has been so good about—he's been so good with Michael! He takes him out almost every day, and at night he often has supper with us and plays with him until he falls

*asleep. What I would have done with-
out him I can't say.*

She wrote for some time, relating those
things which had become important to her,
and finally closed on a more personal note.

> *Something has happened to me
> since I left home and became a wife
> and mother. I look back on what a fool-
> ish girl I was, my head literally stuffed
> with romantic notions! I won't say that
> they're all gone, but a trip across the
> Oregon Trail with all its hardships and
> the everyday business of just simply
> keeping a homestead going doesn't
> leave much time for romantic notions. I
> haven't read* Ivanhoe *since I've been
> here, but I suppose I will. Living on the
> edge out here has made me put ro-
> mance into perspective. Read about it,
> enjoy it in books, but do not let it get
> mixed up with reality.*
> *I miss all of you dreadfully and know
> that one day either you will come here
> or I will come home for a visit. Please
> pray for me and Michael and especially
> for Colin.*

Dissatisfied with what she had written, Jordan stared at the words as the ink dried. She had not been able to say what she felt. Every day since Colin had left had been hard, and the time had stretched her thin. She well knew that if it had not been for Ty and Gus, she would not have survived.

In the quietness of her room at night, she wept the tears she could not show to anyone. She had prayed every single day that God would bring him back, and at first faith had been relatively easy. But as month after month passed small doubts began to form.

Small doubts at first, but then they grew more insistent, filling her heart and mind. Fear was an emotion she had not known to a great degree, but as the days crawled by with no sign of Colin, she found she could not sleep, and keeping a smile during the day became impossible.

What if he's dead?

The thought refused to leave, and at times she wanted to scream out, "God, why have you let this happen? Don't you care?"

These outbursts took place in her own breast, for she was careful not to voice her doubts to anyone. But she remembered how her pastor in Missouri had warned her that she'd never gone through any real trials, and she realized now that he had been wise. Her religion had been sufficient while things were going well, but now that the trial had come, she knew how weak she was in faith. This drove her to her knees night after night, seeking God. But nothing seemed to help, and she could only weep and beg God to help her—and to bring her husband back.

A sound caught her attention, and she rose quickly and went to the door. A wagon rounded the clump of trees to the south, and she saw Avis and Leah Ellencourt sitting on the seat waving at her. She stepped outside and waited until the wagon pulled up before saying, "Well, where are you two headed?"

Avis secured the lines tightly, then leaped to the ground with a single swift movement. "I'm taking Leah back to Oregon City. Would you like to join us?" Leah had hitched a ride out to visit her friends at the settlement, and now it was time for her to return.

Leah got down more carefully, and she and Avis came over to stand before Jordan. "We want you to come with us, Jordan. You haven't been away from this place all summer."

"Oh, I don't know if I can do it. There's so much to do."

Leah shook her head impatiently. Her green eyes matched the light green dress that she wore, and she insisted, "We came to kidnap you."

"But Michael—"

"Bring him along," Avis urged. "He needs to see some new sights too."

"All right. But first, come inside. I made a cake yesterday."

Leah said, "Where's Michael?"

"Ty took him down to the creek. He whittled out a boat for him last night."

"I'll go get him," Leah said firmly. "Save some of that cake until I get back."

Avis and Jordan went inside, and Jordan said, "I've just been writing my people." Moving to the fireplace, she set the kettle on the fire. She stirred the fire until it blazed up, then she came back over to sit down at the table across from Avis. "It's hard to write to them, Avis," she said quietly.

Avis Barnhill studied Jordan carefully. The two had become very close over the past months. Avis was near enough to make visits regularly, and the two had worked hard on a quilt that was the talk of the community.

Avis leaned back and said quietly, "Missouri is so far away. I don't suppose you've gotten many letters from them."

"Only once, and that's been months ago. They expected Colin would be back by this time, and I had to tell them that he hadn't returned." Leaning forward, she placed her hands flat on the table and studied them. She did not speak for some time, then when she lifted her eyes, there was a sadness in her countenance. "I—I get so discouraged sometimes, Avis."

"So do I, but you mustn't give up."

"Most people already have. Some are saying that something must have happened to Colin, that he's dead."

"They can't know that. You know how erratic ships are," Avis responded quickly.

The kettle whistled a shrill note, and Jordan rose to retrieve the kettle and make sassafras tea. The two women sat there drinking it, and Avis said finally, "The wheat looks good and the corn, too."

"Yes, Ty and Gus have done well." She said nothing for a time but sipped her tea, and finally, in a tone filled with something close to despair, said, "I get so lonely, Avis!"

"You have Michael."

"Yes, thank God! I think I'd lose my mind if it weren't for him. Every day I tell him about his father. He looks so much like him it breaks my heart sometimes."

Avis leaned forward. "Have you given up on Colin?"

"No! I pray every day that God will bring him back to me."

"I suppose you've heard people saying that it's time for you to move on, to think about making another life for yourself."

"I won't do that." Jordan straightened up and tried to make herself sound more cheerful. "Colin will come back. I know he will."

"I hope so. You and he were so happy together."

Jordan studied the woman across from her. She had admired Avis now for a long time, and although the woman had never spoken of her situation, Jordan knew she was imprisoned in a miserable marriage. More than once she had wanted to ask Avis why she had married a man like Ira Barnhill, but she never had. A curtain of reserve masked what Avis really was on the inside, and Jordan dared not penetrate it.

Suddenly Jordan thought of Paul Leverett. She had noted the way that Leverett looked at Avis and was sure that Avis, being as astute as she was, had not missed it. It was a hopeless situation, of course, and pity came to Jordan. Quickly she changed the subject, speaking of their trip to Oregon City.

"Well, you two haven't drowned yet, I see."

Ty heard Leah approach and stood to his feet. Michael was seated on the creek bank, his feet in the water. He looked up briefly and then went back to pushing the small boat around.

"Hello, Leah. What are you doing way out here?"

"I came to see what you and this big, fine man here are up to." Leah reached down and ruffled Michael's hair. "What a nice boat. Show me how it works."

She watched for a time as Michael pushed the boat around. He was wearing only a pair of short pants, and the summer sun had left a darkness on his skin. As he moved downstream intent on the boat, Leah whispered, "He looks enough like Colin to startle me."

"I never quite get over it," Ty agreed. "Some families are like that, aren't they? I mean, all the children look alike."

The two stood there, the sunlight making a pattern on their faces as it filtered through the large oaks that shadowed the stream. Ty felt, as always, a special calmness when talking with Leah. From time to time he looked at her, noting that she had changed little since the first time he had seen her. She wore a simple light blue dress, and he noted, not for the first time, what a strong woman she was.

"How's Mark?"

A shadow seemed to touch Leah's eyes. She did not answer at once but reached up and tucked a lock of hair away from her forehead. "Not as well as I'd like."

Ty knew that she was not a woman to say a great deal about her problems. "You're worried about him, aren't you?" he pressed.

"Yes, I am. He hasn't really been well since we left Missouri. I thought when the spring came he'd get better, but he hasn't."

"Has Leverett taken a look at him lately?"

"Yes, but he couldn't tell us much." She suddenly turned and faced Ty. "I get the feeling he doesn't think Mark will live."

"We'll hope for better things than that."

The two stood there talking, watching the boy as he poked along the creek. Finally Leah said, "What do you really think about Colin?"

Quickly Ty lifted his eyes. "Every day the chances look worse. I think he's dead," he finally said. "If he'd been alive, he'd have been back by this time, or at least sent some word."

"There's always a possibility that he got delayed."

"That's right. That's what Jordan's praying for."

"I pray for it, too."

Ty turned his head to one side, ran his hand through his sandy hair. "I wish I were a praying man."

His statement surprised Leah. "Why aren't you?" she asked quietly, her eyes fixed on his face.

"It's hard to know about things like that, Leah. I've had a hard life, and I suppose I've been discouraged. I saw some folks who call themselves Christians who didn't act like it."

"You're a smarter man than that, Ty. There are some Americans who aren't faithful to this country, but that doesn't mean it's not a good country."

"You're right, of course," Ty said. "It's just I can't say what I feel."

"Mark's worried about you. He prays for you every day."

"That's the kind of man he is, but I can't say as I'll ever change."

"I think you will. You just haven't found your way to God yet." She suddenly reached out, put her hand on his arm. "I'll pray for you, too."

"That's like you, Leah. Well, with folks like you and Mark praying for me, I guess I've got a chance."

The two stood there quietly, and finally Leah said, "I worry about what would happen if Colin didn't come back."

Quickly Ty said, "I promised him I'd take care of Jordan and Michael. I owe him that much."

"Why, you have taken care of them, but if he never came back, that would be different, wouldn't it? You can't take care of her the rest of her life, I mean, if Colin's dead."

"Yes, I could. I gave him my word."

"You're a man with strong convictions, Ty, but you have your own life to lead."

Ty suddenly laughed. "My life's never gone in a straight way, Leah. I've just been a wanderer."

"You were married though. That must have been a good time for you."

"The best time I ever had. She was a good woman. I think a lot about the boy I lost. I guess I sort of pour myself into Michael as a substitute."

"It's been good for him and good for you, too."

Leah's words seemed to reach out to Ty, and he turned to look into her eyes. She did not move nor did he. Each ceased to be conscious of the wind blowing softly through the trees, of the chattering of the boy as he played in the creek. They were looking at each other as a man and a woman, and both were startled by the intensity of the moment.

Leah broke away first saying, "Well, come along, you two. Avis and I are going to take Jordan and Michael to town. They need to get away."

"That would be good. It'll take her mind off things."

Michael protested, but Ty simply swooped him up and put him on his shoulders. Michael's chubby legs dangled down on his chest, and as he looked up, Ty said, "Grab a good hold there, son."

Leah moved to walk beside Ty as he headed back toward the house. She was disturbed about the feeling she had had, and she had seen that Ty Sublette had looked at her the way a man looks at a woman. She knew she would not mention it to anyone, but she was also certain that she would not forget it.

TWENTY-SEVEN

Almost every night it had become a habit for Ty and Gus to take the evening meal that Jordan cooked for them. The two men would sit on the porch in front of the cabin when it was warm enough or beside the fire during the cold days while the cabin itself was filled with the smell of meat cooking or stew bubbling in the pot.

One evening when Gus had taken Michael outside to play, Jordan took time out from the cooking to come and sit beside Ty at the table. He was reading a newspaper so old it was falling apart, and she laughed, putting her hand down on it. "The news is old."

He looked up at her and smiled. "I guess so. I'll have to start reading your books next."

"Good, you can read *Ivanhoe.*"

"What's it about?"

"Oh, it's a love story about a knight who has to make his choice between two women."

"Only two?" he teased her. "A man ought to have more choices than that. What'd he do, flip a coin to see which one he'd have?"

"I'm not going to tell you. One of them was fair with blonde hair and an aristocrat, and the other one was a dark mysterious lady with beautiful black hair."

"A man can't pick a woman by the color of her hair! Which one did he pick?"

Jordan reached over and picked up one of his hands suddenly. She ran her hand over his callused palm and shook her head. "I've made a slave out of you."

"Not so's you'd notice it. Are you going to tell me?"

Jordan looked up with surprise. "Tell you what?"

"Whether he married the lady with the blonde hair or the black hair."

"No, I'll give you the book."

He sat there as she held his hand, then suddenly she released it as if embarrassed. She reached up and ran her hand over her hair. A small dimple appeared at the left of her mouth, and a light danced in her eyes. "Have you ever read a book all the way through, Ty?"

"One or two. History books mostly."

"I used to hate history. The schoolmaster would make me read geography and history and do arithmetic, and all I wanted to read was romances and fairy tales."

The two sat there talking, and suddenly the thought came to Jordan's mind, *Why, we're like man and wife sitting here talking.* She was shocked at the thought, for somehow it seemed disloyal to Colin. She thought about him every day, but the power of memory had lost some of its potency.

She studied Ty's face, and he made a vivid image there so solid and so thoroughly masculine. She knew his smile so well after all these months, and she knew him. She had learned that he showed the world a serene indifference, yet there was a sadness in him. Even as she spoke, his head tipped forward, and his features turned heavier. She had seen this mood in him many times, as if a weight had suddenly come upon him, and as the light struck him from the window, she was moved by the solid irregularity of his features.

Then he looked up and smiled, and his mood seemed to change. "The wheat's going to be good this year and the corn, too."

"I loved watching it grow this summer. Sometimes at night I could almost hear it pushing itself up out of the ground. Next year let's put a stick in the ground and mark off how much it grows each day."

"All right."

"You always agree with me no matter what I say," Jordan smiled. "You spoil me, Ty."

"I guess I do. Maybe I'll take a stick to you one day to keep you in line."

Jordan's eyes grew dreamy. "I love to think of the crops growing, corn getting higher every day, the heat of the sun flowing into it all day long. I love to watch the blades swing in the wind, and the tassels when they first come on the corn—so tender, and everything is so perfect just like God makes it. I read in a book once that an elm tree will make half a million leaves in a single season." She shook her head slightly. "I can't even make one."

"I guess if a woman could make a leaf, she could make a million. Making the first one's the trouble," Ty said.

A log burned in two in the fireplace, settled with a sigh, and Jordan jumped up. "I've got to get supper on the table. You men will starve to death."

After supper Ty and Gus walked in the darkness across the field toward their cabins. Gus was strangely silent. As they reached Ty's cabin, he said finally, "You got a minute? I need to talk to somebody, Ty."

"Come on in. You want to make up a fire and brew up some tea?"

"No, just talk."

The two men went inside, and Ty lit the coal oil lamp. It cast a flickering light over the interior of the stark cabin. There was nothing there but a bed, a table, and two rough chairs. Ty's few belongings were thrown carelessly against the wall or hung from pegs. "What is it, Gus?"

"Well, I'll tell you, Ty, I'm about to go crazy." Gus Dabney moved restlessly, taking several steps along the wooden floor of the cabin, a gangling, rawboned man, homely and as uncertain of himself as Ty had ever seen him. He admired Dabney, who could work with any man cheerfully.

Ty said, "Well, spit it out, Gus. What's bothering you?"

"All right. Here it is. I'd like to marry Jennie Town."

Ty waited for Gus to add more, but when the man stood there silently staring at him as if waiting an answer, he said, "Well, what's the problem? Nobody else courting her, is there?"

"No, it ain't that. But look at me, Ty. I'm older than she is. I'm forty years old and gettin' too old for her. I can't read, and I'm ugly as homemade sin."

Ty had been aware of Gus's affection for the deaf girl. During every meeting that the settlers had had together Gus had placed himself close to Jennie. He understood that Gus needed reassurance.

"Well, blazes, man, you're a fool if you don't marry that girl!"

Gus looked up, and his eyes gleamed. He asked eagerly, "Do you really think that, Ty?"

"'Course I think that! She's a fine girl. I'm surprised she hasn't married before."

"She thinks no man would want her because she's deaf."

"Well, she's foolish. She understands every word you say as long she can see your lips. She needs a man, and she needs children. Go after her."

Gus took a deep breath and nodded. "I know people will think it's wrong—me marrying a pretty woman like that."

"Who cares what they think!" Ty laughed and reached over and struck Gus on the upper arm with his fist. "I approve of it, and if you can get her to say yes, that'll be all there is to it. Why, man, you've already got a cabin built. She'll be lucky to get a good man like you, and you'll be lucky to get a woman like her."

The next day Ty related to Jordan what Gus had told him. Gus had disappeared at midafternoon, and now Jordan walked alongside Ty through the cornfield, with Michael toddling ahead. When he finished relating Gus's intentions, he stopped and turned to her. "What do you think? Did I tell him wrong?"

Jordan looked up at him, the wind blowing her hair, and her cheeks reddened by it. "No, you told him right. I don't know why he's waited this long. I think Jennie's been disappointed."

"Why, a man needs some encouragement."

And then something came to Jordan that had been on her mind to say for some time. "You ought to think about doing something like that."

He stared at her. "Like getting married?"

"Yes."

Ty stared at Jordan, somehow disturbed

by her suggestion. "Why would you say that?"

"A man needs a wife, and he needs to have a family."

"Not all men marry."

"No, but you should. You're not one of those who can grow old alone. I know that much about you."

Ty's face showed a sudden feeling. He reached up and touched his nose, and then he said, "I made Colin a promise that I'd take care of you and Michael."

"You've done that, Ty, but you can't keep us for the rest of our lives."

She stood before him in a simple gray dress, and the afternoon sun made a slit across the copper surface of her hair. Her lips lay together almost willful, for she had been planning this for a long time. She had no idea what she would do if he left her, but she urged him saying, "You need people around you, Ty. You've been alone too long."

Ty reached out and took her by the upper arm. He pulled her close and shook his head. Leaning forward, he kissed her on the cheek. It was not a passionate kiss but rather expressed the affection and respect that he had learned to have for her. "I reckon

I can last a while longer at taking care of you and Michael," he said.

She said no more but turned, and the two continued their walk through the corn. Overhead a red-tailed hawk sailed gracefully, making a beautiful arch, and then dropped to make his kill. Jordan noted this, but her mind was on the scene that had just taken place. She would say no more, but a sense of the innate goodness of the man came to her. She felt safe and secure, and somehow knew that Tyler Sublette had brought this feeling to her heart.

Jennie drew the lines carefully on the piece of paper. The charcoal followed the will of her eyes, and she looked up from time to time at the squirrel that sat above her calmly. Jennie took pleasure in taking one animal and drawing it from every angle, and now she turned her head to one side and nodded, pleased by the picture.

A movement caught her eye, and she turned her head quickly to see Gus Dabney, who was coming down from the cabin. Jennie rose, glad as always to see Gus. "Come and see what I've drawn, Gus." She waited until he drew near, then handed him the sheets of paper. She watched as he looked at them and knew that he would praise them as he always did.

Gus studied the drawings and, as usual, shook his head and said, "I don't see how you do it, Jennie. It's something that the good Lord's put in you."

"Come on inside. We'll fix something for supper. You're off early, aren't you?"

Gus did not answer. He put his hands behind his back and dropped his head. Nervously he pulled his hat off and twisted it around in his hand.

Jennie watched all this carefully and knew that something was amiss. He was normally one of the most cheerful individuals she had ever met. "What's wrong, Gus?" she asked.

"Nothing's wrong."

"Yes, there is. I can tell." Jennie reached out and put her hand on his chest. "You're worried about something."

Gus put his hand over hers and held it there. He saw surprise leap into her eyes and swallowed hard. "I'm not a fellow who's good with words, Jennie. I wish I were." The words seemed to stick in his throat, and then he knew there was no easy way. He had made up a speech as he had walked over from the field, and now he took a deep breath and spoke the words slowly.

"There's no way for me to deserve a woman like you, Jennie, but maybe you know I've cared for you for a long time. I want to marry you and take care of you."

He watched her eyes, expecting the rejection to appear there first. To his shock and amazement, suddenly Jennie uttered a small cry. Her lips parted, and she threw her arms around his neck. He held her as she clung to him, and a great gladness came to him. He waited for a moment, then he drew back. When he saw her face, he said, "You'll have me then?"

"Gus, I've been waiting such a long time!"

"I guess I've been a fool, but I do love you, Jennie." He kissed her, and she came to him in all the fullness of a woman. He felt the strong curves of her body and knew that for once in his life he had done a good thing.

Jennie drew back, reached up, and touched his cheek. "Come on, let's go tell Jesse and Mary."

TWENTY-EIGHT

The yard in front of Jesse and Mary Lee's cabin was packed. The sound of a fiddle carried on the afternoon breeze, and men and women formed into a square dance. Over a pit that Jesse had dug, the carcass of a large pig was turning over hot coals. Long boards laid out on trusses held the food that had been partly furnished by the Lees, but everyone had brought something. Paul Leverett stood with a group of men talking until the square dancing was over, and then when a slower tune started, he moved over at once toward Avis. "Will you dance with me, Avis?"

Avis had danced several times already. Ira did not dance but gathered with a group of the older men as they talked about crops and political matters. "Yes," she said. She came to him, and the two began to move around the packed earth in front of the cabin. "Everybody loves a wedding," Paul said.

"Yes, they'll make a good couple."

"I never would have figured it out—Gus and Jennie. I thought Jennie had pretty well given up on marriage, and as for Gus, I thought he was a confirmed bachelor."

Avis Barnhill moved easily in his arms. "I guess it's never too late. There was one couple in the town where I grew up. The man was seventy-two, and the woman was sixty-nine. They got married."

"Did they have a house full of children?" Paul smiled.

"No, no children." Her lips turned upward. "But they had a good life together. It was the sweetest thing, Paul. They held hands almost all the time everywhere they went."

"A thing like that is good to hear."

As her body moved beneath his hands, Paul Leverett took in her face. "You're looking very well, Avis. Beautiful, I might say."

"You should say that to the right woman."

"What do you mean by that?"

"Everyone in the community wonders why you're not married. They think you're wasting a woman. There are plenty of women who need husbands."

He did not answer for several moments, then he said, "You know how I feel about you, Avis."

"And you know what I said. It's too late for us, Paul. Some people find happiness, and others miss it. You and I missed it, but it's not too late for you."

"How could I go to another woman when I love you?"

"You'll have to take what comes," Avis said so softly that he could hardly hear her over the music. "I wish it were different, but it's not."

Across the yard a tall man in his early thirties claimed Jordan. He introduced himself. "I'm Mel Ott, Mrs. Bryce."

"You know my name?"

Ott smiled. "I always find out the name of handsome women."

Jordan was surprised. "You're very forward."

"I suppose I am. I'm new in the community. I'm a lawyer."

She studied him more carefully. "Where do you come from, Mr. Ott?"

"Just call me Mel. From Virginia."

Ott was a fine dancer, and finally he said, "I would like to come calling on you, Mrs. Bryce."

Jordan was so surprised she could barely speak. "Don't you know who I am?"

"Why, yes. You're the widow Bryce—at least so I was told."

The widow Bryce.

"My husband has been on a long sea journey, but he's not dead!" she said half angrily.

Ott blinked at her expression. "I apologize, Mrs. Bryce. I was misinformed."

From across the yard Ellen Farr was watching standing beside her husband. "That'd be a good match for Jordan. He's a fine man, Ott is."

"I've wondered why she hasn't married Ty," Horace murmured. "They seem to make it well together."

"She ought to. I guess everyone expects it. She needs a man."

"She's just being careful, I suppose."

"Careful! Why, he's been gone over a year. He's dead. He has to be."

"Maybe he's not."

"He'd have come back by this time. You know that," Ellen insisted. "He loved her very much."

* * *

Rita held Lisa tightly, for she had caught sight of Ace, had noted that he was staring at her. She ignored his glance, suddenly thankful afresh that he had not married her. She took Corny's arm, and when he turned to her, she smiled and said, "I have the handsomest husband in the valley."

Corny blinked with surprise. "What brought that on?"

"Oh, the wedding, and . . . I just wanted to say it." Rita studied his face and added, "I'm so in love with you I could squeal!"

For one moment, Corny's face seemed to break, for he had longed to hear this from Rita for a long time. Their marriage had been difficult at first, but ever since Lisa had been born, he had noted that there was a freedom in Rita that changed her completely. She had clung to him, showing her affection in ways she never had before.

"I love you more than I ever thought I could love a man," Rita whispered. She saw his eyes moisten, and he turned his head away. She took his arm, squeezed it, and leaned against him. "When we get home, I'll find some way to show you how I feel."

Corny laughed and put his arm around Rita. He looked down at Lisa, then said, "Prettiest daughter a man ever had!" He leaned over and kissed the baby, then kissed Rita firmly. "I love you too," he said, and at that moment each of them knew that what had come to the two of them was real—and that it would never pass.

The wedding was over now, and the people all were headed home. Mark Ellencourt found it difficult to get up into the wagon. When he did, he began coughing violently.

Leah had come up to the seat beside him and knew there was nothing she could do. *These coughing fits are getting worse*, she thought. *He's so much weaker.*

Mark finally gained control of himself, picked up the lines, and spoke to the horses. "It'll be dark by the time we get back home," he said in a tight voice, and she knew he was trying to keep from coughing again.

"We should have left earlier."

"Had to get Gus and Jennie married. It did me good," he said, turning to face her. "They can help each other."

"Yes, he's a good man, and she'll make a good wife for him," Leah said.

Mark did not speak for ten minutes, and then finally he turned to her and said, "Leah, we haven't spoken of it, but we're in God's hands. If I should die of this thing, I wouldn't want you to mourn me as some women do."

Leah was surprised. She put her arm around him and held to him tightly. "Don't speak of it, Mark."

"Now, Leah, you've always been a sensible woman, but we both know I'm getting worse." Jos was riding back to town with a neighbor boy, his best friend, so they were alone in the wagon. "I think about Josiah. He needs a good father, Leah."

"I won't hear this," she said firmly. "God is the great healer."

"Yes, he is, and I may live to be an old man with a long white beard." He reached over and put his hand on her knee and squeezed it. "Just put it in your mind somewhere. Tuck it away."

Leah Ellencourt changed the subject immediately. She began talking about the church members and how well the church was doing. She knew that Mark would never speak of this again—and she knew that she would not forget what he had said.

TWENTY-NINE

Another winter went by and 1846 came with no word from Colin. Michael turned two in March, but his birthday celebration was muted. As the months passed, Jordan had gone from deep pain to numbness to a sort of resignation—or even acceptance of her lot. She focused on her everyday tasks and tried to keep life as ordinary as possible.

The most difficult thing about Oregon to Jordan had been the rain that seemed to come constantly. Almost every day, though the skies might not produce a downpour, one could be sure of a drizzle. Jordan, at first, was terribly disturbed by it. She seemed to be walking around in her own atmosphere of muggy, wet, damp climate that never left.

As time had gone by, however, she had become accustomed to it so that now, in the middle of May, she hardly looked up when the sky became so dark that it could have been night. She'd been so intent on her fishing that she hadn't been conscious of the dark canopy overhead as it became thick and furred as a blanket. The air had the sharp metallic taste of a coming storm.

The sky suddenly glittered with the first splash of lightning and then was followed by the sharp crack of thunder. Large drops began drumming against her scalp, and then the rain sheeted down. Holding her bucket of perch, she ran toward the house, and by the time she got to the porch she was completely soaked. Going inside, she found Michael seated at the table playing with the wooden toys that Ty had carved for him out of soft pine. "Wet!" he said, his eyes sparkling. At that moment he looked so much like Colin that Jordan could not speak. He had the black hair of his father with a slight wave, the same dark blue eyes, and the thick black lashes that would have been the envy of any girl.

Forcing this thought out of her mind, Jordan shook her hair and said, "Yes, I got wet. I'll have to dry off and change clothes now."

Slipping into the bedroom, she stripped out of her wet clothes, dried off, and put on clean underclothes and a different dress. She moved back into the main part of the cabin and built up the fire in order to prepare the evening meal. She was expecting Ty, who had gone over to Dave Minton's to borrow a big saw to cut down more trees.

As the fire began to crackle, she interlaced it with chunks of white oak. Then, moving across the room, she picked up a letter from the table under the window. Sitting down, she unfolded it and read it again. She almost had it memorized, but as she read the words again, her brow wrinkled.

You really should come home and live with us, Jordan. It's just too hard for a woman with a small child to make it on the frontier. You haven't complained at all about the difficulties of it, and I know Ty has been a great help to you, but you can't go on like that indefinitely, can you? I mean, sooner or later, Ty will marry, and you'll be alone.

Jordan lifted her eyes and stared out the single window of the cabin. Rowena had grown into a large beautiful cat but had not grown especially intelligent, it seemed. She still could not believe that the brown thrashers that lived in the thick brush to the west of the cabin could be so mean as to peck her head. As Jordan watched, she saw one brown thrasher suddenly appear, swerve, and dive straight down on Rowena. The big white cat closed her eyes and began creeping away, but not before the thrasher had pecked her severely on the head. "Are you never going to learn, you silly cat?" Jordan said, then continued reading the letter.

Colin has been gone now almost two years. It was right of you to wait, but you must, by this time, have accepted the fact that he died on his journey. Please think about it. Your father and I would love to have you back again. We long to see our grandson and, of course, you. The children are growing older, and they would be delighted to have you back. Please think about it. If you agree to come, we will pay all the expenses.

A sudden sharp sound plucked Jordan's attention from the letter, and she looked around to see Michael banging the table with one of the wooden toys. "Stop that, Michael, you're going to break it."

"No, I won't!" he argued.

"You mind what I say. Ty worked hard to

make those toys for you, and I won't have them broken."

Getting up with a swift motion, Jordan folded the letter, put it back on the table, and then began making dough for biscuits. She had become a good cook of necessity since leaving her home, and as she expertly mixed the ingredients and then stirred them with a wooden spoon, she thought about the letter from her mother. It had disturbed her greatly, and she had told no one about it, not even Ty. She had considered going back, but somehow she knew that would not make her contented. Part of that, of course, was the fact that she still clung to some faint hope that Colin would come home again. And what would it be like if he came and found his wife and son gone?

The rain beat a tattoo for a time on the cedar shingles and then became muted. The smell of wet grass came through the open door. As she cut the biscuits using a tin can to form them into perfect circles, she thought about how different Ty was from Colin. Ty Sublette was, she had long ago decided, the steadiest man she had ever seen. He set himself on a chore, and he did not look back until it was finished. *So different from Colin,* she thought. The thought seemed disloyal to her, but Colin, despite her efforts, had faded somehow in her mind. *Almost two years and not a word. If he had just died in an accident, and had been buried, that would have been an end to it, but it's been the not knowing that's been so hard. I can't go on like this forever. It's not fair to Ty,* she thought, and resolved to speak to him that night.

"You catch all these fish today, Jordan?"

It was suppertime, and Jordan, Ty, and Michael were enjoying a meal of fresh perch. She had fried them whole so that the sweet crispy flesh fell off in chunks under her teeth. They also had her biscuits, which Ty loved, and fresh green onions from the garden gave the meal an extra spice.

Jordan nodded. "They were really biting. All you had to do was throw the bait out, and they went off with it. It was fun."

Ty smiled. "I remember the first time I taught you to clean a fish. You acted like it was something awful."

"That seems like a million years ago," Jordan murmured.

"I thought I'd plant that field over by the line in sorghum cane. And there's a new shipment of young fruit trees available, Dave told me. Be nice to have a whole orchard—peach, apple, pears."

"Oh, that would be good! Just imagine being able to have fresh fruit any time you wanted it."

"Oranges! Plant an orange tree, Ty," Michael piped up, his blue eyes sparkling. "I like oranges."

Ty laughed and leaned over and ruffled the boy's raven black hair. "Oranges won't grow around here, son. I wish they did."

The simple act somehow wrung Jordan's heart, and she thought of how Ty took Michael with him on every opportunity. And Michael, of course, loved it. Jordan loved to look out her window and see her son riding on Ty's broad shoulders as he plowed or as he simply moved around. A well of thanksgiving came to her as she realized how terrible it would have been if she had been alone.

The meal was finished, and the evening went pleasantly. After cleaning the dishes, Jordan sat down to read *Ivanhoe* again. She had lost count of the times she had read it, but curiously this time the romance of it was distant from her. She remembered how as a young girl she had entered into the stories of chivalry and loved forgetting the whole world about her. Now she got her chief pleasure out of different things, such as cooking for Ty and Michael.

From time to time she looked over to where Ty was sitting on the floor with Michael playing with the wooden soldiers he had made. The sight of them gave her a good feeling, and she, more than once, found herself experiencing a sense of security and strength as she watched the two.

Finally she got Michael ready for bed despite his protests. After Michael was dressed in his nightshirt, he went to Ty, who leaned over, picked him up, and tossed him in the air. He squeezed the boy and gave him a kiss on the forehead. "You go along to bed, big 'un. Tomorrow we'll see if you and I can't catch some fish out of the creek."

"Okay, Ty," Michael said.

When Jordan put Michael down in his bed, she prayed over him, and he smiled up at her sleepily. "Good night, Mama," he said and reached up and touched her cheek.

She went back into the room and found Ty

standing at the door looking out. Going over to take her place beside him, she looked out and saw the stars. After the rain the skies seemed clear, and the earth smelled fresh and fruitful. Ty smiled down at her.

Jordan suddenly turned toward him and said almost breathlessly, "Ty, what would I have done without you?"

Her words caught at Ty, and for a moment he did not speak. Then he reached out and put his hand on her cheek. It felt hard and strong, and she covered it with her own.

"What would you think about marrying me?" His voice was quiet and almost matter-of-fact, and he turned his head to one side waiting for her answer.

Jordan felt a strange shock run through her. She had been expecting something like this for a long time. Perhaps she had even been a little disappointed when he had made no mention of such a thing, but now as it came, she suddenly understood his patience all these months. All the labor and work and responsibility of caring for her and for Michael! Most men would have demanded something in exchange, but until this moment Ty Sublette had not said a word.

"Is that what you would like, Ty?"

"I would like it very well." He put his other hand on her cheek, leaned down, and kissed her. And when she returned the kiss, he put his arms around her. Jordan felt the pressure of his lips and knew that his hunger for her was real—and she understood also that she had hungers and desires of her own. She clung to him for what seemed like a long time, and finally he lifted his head and said, "I expect it would be the best thing, but I don't want to rush you. Why don't you think about it, Jordan?" He released her then and said quietly, "Don't let this be a burden to you. If it doesn't please you, we'll go on just as we are."

Jordan stood motionless as Ty picked up his hat and left the cabin headed for his own. She watched him as he disappeared into the darkness, and then she put her hand over her heart and thought about what he had said. And she thought about how she had grown to depend upon him. She looked up at the sky, and saw the bright star glittering. *That's my star, Sirius.* She thought of the night that Colin had told her the name, and how she had claimed it, but the memory was not as clear as it had been once. She turned slowly and shut the door, knowing that she would sleep little that night.

For two days Jordan did little except think about Ty's proposal. She spoke to no one about it but went about her work, and yet her mind kept going back to the scene. She knew that people would call her foolish if she refused Ty's offer. What kept going through her mind was the memory of Colin, but now she felt that he was dead and like any other widow she must do what was best for her and for Michael.

She had gotten up early on a Thursday morning and had just finished breakfast when she heard someone coming. Going to the door, she saw Leah Ellencourt in the small wagon that she and Mark used to visit their parishioners. A woman sat beside her, but Jordan could not make out who it was.

Leah pulled the wagon to a stop in front of the cabin and called, "Jordan, I've got a surprise for you!" She got out of the wagon, and Jordan saw the other woman get out on the far side. When she turned to face her visitor, Jordan was so shocked she could hardly speak.

"Jordan, it's me!"

"Jolie!" Jordan ran forward and embraced the laughing young woman. She would not have been more surprised if the president of the United States had suddenly appeared! She clung to Jolie so hard that the young woman protested, "You're squeezing me to death!"

"Jolie, what in the world are you doing here?" Jordan stared at the young woman, who was wearing a stylish outfit. "I can't believe my eyes!"

"Why, I've come to visit my best friend." She suddenly turned and saw Michael, who had come out of the cabin and was watching her with his intent stare. "My gracious, is that your boy?"

"Yes. Michael, come here." Michael came at once, and Jordan put her hand on his head. "I want you to meet my very good friend and cousin Jolie Doucett."

"Why, what a handsome boy you are. I'll bet you like candy, don't you?"

"Yes, ma'am."

"Just so happens that I have a bag of it. We'll give you so much that your mama will be mad at me."

Leah Ellencourt stood to one side smiling.

"Jolie came in on the *Victor* yesterday, Jordan. She just got off the ship and started asking for you, and someone brought her to me. She stayed with us last night, and I brought her out today."

"How long can you stay?"

"Only two days. We'll have to make the most of them."

"Two days!" Jordan exclaimed. "No, I can't let you go that soon!"

"I was lucky to get that much. We have only that long before we leave for San Francisco."

"Oh, fuzz! Well, come in. I was just starting to fix breakfast."

"I've got to get on back," Leah said. "It's good to see someone from home, isn't it?"

"Yes, it is. Thank you, Leah."

As Leah got into the wagon and drove away, Jolie got the small bag that she had set on the ground. "You cook, and I'll eat, and you can tell me all about yourself." Jolie smiled.

But it was Jolie who talked mostly as Leah prepared breakfast and as the two ate it together along with Michael. "I went on the stage, so I'm a genuine actress now."

She went on to tell how she had joined

with Brian Defoe's company when he had come to New Orleans. She had toured with them all over the South, and now they had come to San Francisco.

"I knew if I ever got that far, I'd get up the coast, so I just told Brian I'd have to leave and come and see you. He kicked up a fuss, but here I am."

"I can't believe you're actually on the stage. Do you like it, Jolie?"

"It's not as exciting as I thought." Jolie shrugged her trim shoulders. "Of course it was at first, and I still like it, but I won't be doing it forever. It was romantic enough, but it's not what I want for the rest of my life. Now, tell me about yourself."

The two young women talked, the words falling out, until Ty arrived. When he came in, he was surprised to see the visitor, but upon being introduced, he said, "Well, you'll have to tell me all the wicked things this woman did when she was a girl."

Jolie smiled up at Ty. "I could tell you lots of things. You wouldn't believe what a wicked girl she was."

Jordan shook her head. "Don't believe a word she says, Ty. Now, sit down and eat something."

* * *

The two days went by quicker than Jordan would have believed possible. Jolie seemed genuinely glad to see her, and she, of course, demanded to know exactly what was going on in Jordan's life. She listened as Jordan spoke of Colin's decision and his disappearance. Finally on the second day Jordan confessed, "Ty asked me to marry him, Jolie."

"Well, why doesn't that surprise me?" Jolie smiled. She reached over and pinched Jordan's arm. "When's the wedding?"

"Why, I haven't said yes."

Jolie stared at her. "You haven't said yes! Why not?"

"Well, I'm just not sure."

"Are you still in love with Colin?"

Jordan looked down at her hands and did not answer for a moment. "I'll never forget him," she said softly, "but he's gone."

"That's wise to accept that," Jolie said quickly. "But how do you feel about Ty?"

Jordan's eyes widened, and she shook her head with a smile. "I've never met anyone like him. He's altogether different from Colin, of course. He's slower and thinks

things over more. He's more—solid, I suppose you might say, and he's been so wonderful to me and to Michael."

"Marry him, Jordan," Jolie said, and at
that instant her face was totally sober. She
reached over and grasped Jordan's wrist.
"He's a good man. I've seen that, and he's in
love with you. That's not hard to pick up on
either. I don't know why you hesitate."

Jordan sat quietly for a moment, then she
said, "I know you're right. It's just a hard decision."

"No, it's not. It's an easy decision. It's the
right thing to do, Jordan."

On Saturday Ty and Jordan and Michael
took Jolie back to Oregon City. There they
put her on a ship bound for San Francisco.
Jordan said good-bye almost painfully, for
she knew it was not likely the two would
meet again soon.

Jolie hugged Ty and then turned and gave
Jordan a kiss and hugged her fiercely. She
whispered in her ear, "Take him, Jordan.
He'll make you happy."

Jordan thought about that as she sat with
Ty in the wagon as they left the dock. She

knew then what she had to do. She reached over and put her hand on Ty's arm. He turned to her with a questioning look, and she said simply, "Don't go home yet."

"You have a stop to make? Something at the store?" he asked.

"No, I want us to go by and see the pastor." She smiled and reached up and drew his head down and kissed him. "I want to go home a married woman."

Ty's entire face lit up. He put his arm around her, crushed her, and said huskily, "That's all I want to know."

The new family arrived back at their cabin later that evening. Jordan put Michael to bed, and then she came and stood for a moment looking at Ty, who had been reading. He looked up and smiled and said, "How are you, Mrs. Sublette?"

"I'm very happy."

"So am I."

"I'm going to get ready for bed," she said. She turned and left before he could answer. Going into the bedroom, she undressed, and she put on a gown that she had brought all the way from her home in Missouri. It was white and clung to her. She turned the covers back and got into bed. She pulled the sheet up, covered herself, and waited for what seemed like a long time. She lifted her voice and said, "Ty, where are you?"

He came into the room, looked down at her, then went over and blew the candle out. She heard sounds as he undressed, then when he slipped into the bed beside her, she turned to him. His hands sought her, and he kissed her, then he whispered, "I reckon I've cared for you a long time, Jordan."

She replied, "Husband, hold me."

She didn't know what it would be like, being married to Ty. She had expected he might be rough and demanding in bed. Instead he held her with a gentleness that pleased her. It was she who finally stirred and pulled him forward with a passion that she thought had left her long ago. He came to her, and Jordan found that she had married a man who was tough on the outside but who had a gentle heart. And she knew that she was happy.

THIRTY

For Jordan the boundaries beyond Oregon were dim and faint. Great things happened, no doubt, and great men and women made their mark on the earth, but for her the world was the cabin, the homestead, the fields, and the immense forest that rose like a green boundary. As summer passed, she found herself content and happy. The small things became important—making her husband happy, watching Michael grow as quickly as a weed. The kings and princes might make their mark elsewhere beyond this place she had found for herself, but for her the coming of a new baby tooth to Michael was more important than the treaties and the kingdoms so far away.

The land was untouched and untouchable that lay around her. It was time for the rains to come, and now as fall came the leaves turned amber and crimson and gold. There was a satisfaction in life at its simplest level. She had not dreamed that such peace could come, and now she made ready for winter. Soon it would be time for the lights to shine out onto the cold earth, and the house had to be made close and warm. The year's work had been almost performed, apples packed away, meat salted and smoked. She had seen to it that the vegetables were carefully put away, the corn dried and milled, the flour sacked in the pantry. It had been a good harvest, and now it was past time for rain and for winter to come, and she felt the fatness and goodness of the land and often gave thanks to God for his keeping of her and Michael—and now for Ty.

A blazing fire kindled on the hearth gave life to the cabin as Jordan sat darning a pair of Ty's socks. She sat quietly only occasionally looking over at Rowena, who lay in a box nursing her litter. It was her fifth litter, actually, and the father was a mystery cat— but then he always was. Rowena licked one of the kitten's fur as he nuzzled against her.

"I think this is the best litter that Rowena's ever had, don't you, Ty?"

From where he sat in a chair tilted back against the wall, Ty looked up from the gun that he was cleaning. He studied the cat for a moment, then said, "I expect we'll be run over with the pesky little varmints."

"No, everybody wants one of the kittens," Jordan said quickly. She put her knitting down, rose, and walked over to stroke Rowena's fur. She smiled as the cat opened her mouth and meowed loudly. "You are a nice mother, I must admit, Rowena."

"I'm surprised she made it all the way across from Missouri," Ty said. "I thought a dog or a coyote or maybe even a wolf would get her. I still don't see how she's made it."

"That's because God loves good kitties."

Ty grinned broadly. "You didn't think she was all that good when she ripped your nice dress to bits."

"Wasn't her fault. She was trying to make a nest for her babies."

"I declare, Jordan, you'd make excuses for Judas!"

"Well, you're the same way about that horse of yours," Jordan said quickly.

"A horse is good for something. You can ride on him."

"Cats are good for something, too!" Jordan argued. She stroked the silky white fur and smiled down at the litter. "They are beautiful kittens. I'm going to keep this tiger-striped one. She reminds me of one I had when I was a little girl."

"I suppose they do earn their keep catching rats and mice."

Jordan picked up the morsel of flesh and fur, held it up, and touched her nose to the kitten's. She meowed loudly, and she laughed. Walking over to Ty, she held her out. "Look how pretty!"

Ty reached out and stroked the kitten with a forefinger. "He is a pretty tough-looking fellow."

"It's not a he. It's a she."

Ty suddenly reached out and put his hand behind Jordan's head. He pulled her close and kissed her right between the eyes. "I always like to kiss you right between the horns," he said cheerfully.

Jordan hesitated, then she said quietly, "I guess Rowena's had some kind of influence on me."

Ty looked up puzzled. "What do you mean by that?"

Jordan suddenly laughed. "You are so dense! You are the dullest man I've ever known in my life. I'm going to have a baby, and you haven't even noticed."

Ty grew stone still for a moment, and then a glad light came into his eyes. "A baby! Are you sure?"

"Yes, I'm sure."

Ty came to his feet, and the rifle clattered to the floor. He reached out, took her in his arms, and she held the kitten up so that she would not be hurt. He squeezed her and then leaned forward and kissed her. There was a proud possessiveness in him, and when he lifted his head, he said, "When will it come?"

"It won't be an *it*. It'll be a he or a she." She smiled. "Sometime in March or April, I think. You didn't waste any time."

Ty released her but excitement rose in him. "I never thought I'd be a father again," he said.

"That's what happens when men get married. I'm surprised you hadn't noticed," she teased.

"Well, I hope he has a little bit more respect for his father than you have for your husband."

Ty began to pepper her with questions. She put the kitten back down, and the two talked for a long time.

"Do you want a boy or a girl?" Jordan finally asked.

"Any baby of yours will be nice. A little girl would be fine with me."

The two sat close together, pulling two chairs up in front of the fireplace. He put his arm around her, and as the fire finally began to die down, she said, "Ty, I worry about you sometimes. About your soul."

Ty turned to look at her. "I know you do. I guess I worry myself about it."

"Why haven't you ever become a Christian?" The question had been in Jordan for months or even longer than that. Ever since she had known Ty Sublette, she had wondered what kept him from God. She knew there was an innate kindness and goodness in him, but she was also aware that that was not enough.

She saw now that he was trying to frame his answer, and he finally shook his head. "I can't say about that."

"Have you ever wanted to become a Christian?"

"I suppose so," Ty murmured. "It just never came to me."

"I wish you knew the Lord Jesus, Ty. That's the one thing that gave me some peace about Colin. He was a Christian so I don't have to worry about where he is now."

"That's a good thing. I'm glad, and I wish I had something of that in me, but I had a preacher once who said that a man can't come to God until God calls him."

"Where was this?"

"Oh, it was a long time ago. I went to a camp meeting, and this preacher quoted a Scripture. I haven't been able to forget it. Don't know where it is."

"What does it say?"

"He read it out, and it was Jesus talking, and he said, 'No man can come to me except the Father which hath sent me draw him.'"

"I remember reading that, but I think God draws all men."

"Maybe in a general way, but this preacher said every man and every woman has a time, and God would pull them. I guess I've been waiting on God to pull me, Jordan, but he never has."

"Maybe he's waiting for you to look to him before he starts to pull you."

"It could be so." He looked at her, and there was a tremendous seriousness in him. "I've seen a lot of men and a few women go out to meet God. You can't watch a thing like that without wondering where they're going. And I do think about it."

Jordan longed to urge him, but she knew

somehow that it was not the time. She simply took his hand and held it between both of hers. "You'll find Jesus. I know you will, Ty. I want my children to have a Christian father."

Ty squeezed her hand and murmured, "We'll just have to see. I've got to feel God calling me."

Leverett had just risen and was completing his shave when the loud knock came at his door. He had learned to accept the fact that most of the knocks on his door meant trouble, sickness, or an accident. He placed the razor down carefully and turned to go answer it. When he opened the door, he saw Leah Ellencourt, and from the look on her face, he knew what it was. "Is it Mark?" he said.

"Yes," Leah answered swiftly. "I found him on the floor. It looked as if he had tried to get up and had fallen."

"I'll be right with you, Leah."

"I'm going back to him. Be as quick as you can, Paul."

Leverett quickly wiped the lather from his face, not even taking time to finish. He pulled on his coat, jammed his hat on his head, and grabbed his black bag which he always kept ready. He left the house and hurried down the street, his breath making a white incense as it rose. When he reached the Ellencourt house, a white-framed structure next door to the church, he did not knock but went in at once.

"In here, Paul." He heard Leah's voice and went into the bedroom. Mark Ellencourt lay flat on his stomach on the floor. His arms were flung out, and quickly Leverett knelt beside him. Without attempting to move him, he put his hand on his wrist. As he counted the pulse, he said, "Was he all right last night?"

"He was very tired. He went to bed early."

"What time did you find him?"

"I got up very early. I was going to let him sleep. When I came back I found him like this."

"His pulse is very weak. Let's get him into bed." The two managed to get the sick man back into bed, and Leverett made a quick examination. He listened to the lungs, and when he turned to face Leah, his face told her the story.

"It's the consumption, isn't it?"

"Yes, but I'm afraid it's a little worse than that, Leah. I think he has pneumonia."

Leah's face changed then, and he saw that she was prepared for the news. "Is he going to live?"

Leverett shook his head. "I can't say, but you have to prepare yourself."

"I'm worried about Jos."

"Does he know how sick his father is?"

"I think he tries to block it out. He won't talk about it."

"I think you'd better talk to him, Leah. Or maybe it would be better if I did."

"No," Leah said quietly, "I'll go tell him."

Leverett watched Leah go, then turned and looked down on the face of Mark Ellencourt. He had seen the signs of death on Ellencourt's face months ago. He had advised him to leave Oregon and go to a hot, dry climate, but Ellencourt simply said, "I've got to stay where God puts me, Paul."

Leah found Jos awake, and when she spoke to him saying, "Your father's ill," fear leaped into his eyes.

"Is he going to be all right, Ma?"

Leah, ordinarily, would have answered as optimistically as she could, but she had seen the shadow of death on her husband's face, and she knew that it would not be fair or right to deceive him. "He's very ill, Josiah. I think we have to be prepared to lose him."

"Oh, Ma, he can't die!"

Leah went forward and put her arms around Jos. She held him tight and stroked his hair. *Why can't I think of anything to say? But there never is anything to say when a time like this comes.* "Come along," she said. "I'll fix you some breakfast."

"Can I see him?"

"He's not awake right now. When he wakes up you can."

Leverett pulled the mare up in front of Ira Barnhill's cabin. It was a larger cabin than most of the settlers had. The man's ego had demanded it. Getting out of the wagon, he went to the door and knocked. Avis answered it, and her eyes had a question mark in them, but she said only, "Come in, Paul." She waited until he was inside and said, "I've got coffee on the stove."

"That sounds good." He looked around and said, "Where is everybody?"

"The boys are gone hunting, and Ira's gone over to look at a pair of mules." She put the coffee in front of him and poured her own cup and sat down. "What is it? Is there trouble?"

"I had to come this way. I got word that Ada Minton is pretty sick." He sipped the coffee and studied her. "How have you been, Avis?"

"Just the same. How are things in town?"

"Have you heard about Mark?"

"No, is he sick?"

"He's been sick a long time." A grimness touched Leverett's lips. He took it as a personal affront whenever he was unable to help a patient. "But this time he's not going to make it."

"Oh, no, Paul, don't say that!"

"I wouldn't say it if it weren't true. Haven't you seen how he's gone down? Why, he hasn't been able to preach half the time."

"I know, but I thought—well, I hoped he would get over it."

"He was a sick man when he joined the train. I saw it in him then, but I didn't say anything."

"Poor Leah and Jos!"

"It'll be harder on Jos. He thinks the world of his father."

Avis was moved by the news. She had

learned to respect and admire Mark Ellencourt as much as any man she knew. She
was not herself a Christian, but Ellencourt's
gentle witness had meant a great deal to
her. He had not attempted to bully her into
the kingdom, but his love and concern had
been unmistakable.

"He's one of the few men I trust." Realiz-
ing how that sounded, she added quickly,
"That doesn't sound very nice. I trust you,
too, Paul."

Paul suddenly reached out and captured
her hand. "You shouldn't trust me. I'm weak
where you're concerned. You know I want
you, Avis. Why won't you say yes?"

"What kind of a life could we have? Hiding and sneaking? I won't do it."

"You love me. I know you do."

For the first time Avis openly admitted
what she felt to him. "Yes, I do love you. I
don't know how love comes or why it
comes, but I do care for you, Paul. But it's
for that reason that I won't have an affair."

"Why not? We'd have something at
least."

"It wouldn't bother me as much as it
would you."

Paul Leverett stared at her, pain and puzzlement in his eyes. He had never loved a woman before, and he was old for a first love. It had disturbed him and consumed his thinking. Now he said, "What does that mean?"

"I know you're a good man, Paul, and you're a Christian. I won't make an adulterer out of you."

"Let me worry about that."

"I can't do that, Paul. If I loved you less, I might. But I'm a married woman, and that's all there is to it."

"You made a mistake. You should never have married Ira."

"I knew that even a week after I was married, but it was too late."

He got to his feet, came over, and pulled her up. He held her and tried to kiss her, but she turned her head away. "Please don't, Paul," she said. "It's hard enough as it is. Don't come here anymore. I'd like to be strong, but I can't."

A dark pessimism descended on Paul Leverett. He released her at once and turned to pick up his hat. He moved to the door but turned and said, "Good-bye, Avis."

"Good-bye, Paul. You're a good man. Find a woman who's free."

"I won't look for another woman," he said bleakly. He turned and left.

Avis stood looking at the door and knew that somehow something had ended in her life. "I want you, Paul," she whispered, "but it would end up being your ruination."

Ty stared at Leverett, who had pulled up in front of his cabin door and given him the news about Mark. "When did this happen?"

"Yesterday," Paul said. "Ty, I know you're close to Mark. You'd better go in and see him."

"Is it that close a thing?" Ty said quickly.

"He's living on borrowed time. He's only awakened twice, and there's nothing I can do. The pneumonia's taken him. You'd better go quick."

"Thanks, Doc. I'll go right away."

Ty went inside and told Jordan the news. "I've got to go to him, Jordan."

"Shall I go with you?"

"If you like."

"All right. Maybe I can be of some help to Leah. We'll all go."

* * *

Ty had sat beside Ellencourt's bed for over an hour. He had seen no sign of movement, but he could tell that death was near. Leah had been glad to see them, and now she and Jordan and the boys were in the other room. The bedroom was dim with the one oil lamp throwing its amber corona over the face of the dying man. Outside a wind was rising, and the cold was beginning to grip the land. Ty reached out and pulled the cover over Mark, and as he did, Mark's eyes opened. He stared for a moment without recognition and then whispered hoarsely, "Hello, Ty."

"Hello, Mark. I heard you had a bad spell."

Mark did not answer. He had to struggle, it seemed, simply to stay awake. "I'm glad you came, Ty," he whispered, his voice a husky, thready sound. "I—" He began to cough, and the cough seemed to tear him in two.

Helplessly Ty stood beside him waiting until the spell passed. "Shall I get Leverett?"

"No, he's done all he could. It's my time, Ty."

The simple words seemed to strike Ty almost like a blow. He had seen so many men die, and he knew now that he was in the presence of death. He reached out and put his hand on Mark's thin shoulder. "I guess it comes to all of us, but I hope it won't be now for you."

"No time for small talk, Ty. God's been good to me. I've had a good family. I've been able to serve the Lord Jesus. Two things I'd like to ask of you."

"Anything, Mark. Just ask."

"I want you to listen to God."

"Listen to God? What do you mean?"

"God's going to call you one day, and when he does I want you to be ready. I think he's already been calling you."

Ty bowed his head. It hurt him to have to say, "I wish I were a man of God."

"The Lord has assured me that you will be. I'd like to see it now, but I won't. But you remember that God gave me a promise that you'll come into his kingdom. Will you remember that, Ty?"

"Sure, Mark. What's the other thing?"

"The other thing is Leah and Jos. They'll need some help after I'm gone."

"You don't worry about that. I'll be here and so will your other friends. You've made so many good friends, Mark."

"I remember when I was sick in that wagon in Missouri. Didn't have any hope. I could hear someone telling Leah that we couldn't go, and then you came and you stood for us. It's meant a lot to me, Ty. It always has." He closed his eyes and then said, "I know you'll do your best for them. It's hard for a young fellow to grow up without a father. So do your best and be kind to Leah."

Ty felt tears in his eyes. "I'll do it. I promise." He knew then that that promise would be kept no matter what it cost. And as he sat beside the dying man, he knew that what he had just said was a vow unto the God he had not yet accepted.

For over an hour Ty sat beside the dying man, feeling more helpless than he'd ever felt in his life. Finally Leah and Jos returned, and giving her one drawn look, he left. He sat alone until Jordan came and sat beside him. "He's going, Jordan."

"Yes, but he's ready," she whispered.

The two sat without speaking, and when Leah came out, one look at her face told them both that it was over. "He slipped away, like he was going to sleep," she whispered. Diamonds were in her eyes, and Jos clung to her. She looked down at him, hugged him closely, and could say no more.

Jordan rose at once and went to put her

arms around Leah. She whispered gently the things people say at such times. Ty went down on one knee and put his hand on Jos's shoulder. The boy turned a tearstained face to him, and Ty said huskily, "We'll miss him, Jos, both of us." Jos came to him, and Ty held him closely.

Both Leah and Jordan saw the breaking of Ty's face, and then he said, "You'll always have me for a partner, Jos!"

For several weeks after Mark's death, Ty was more silent than usual. He went often to Oregon City to visit Leah and Jos, taking Jordan when she could get away. Finally one morning, he came to stand before Jordan as she washed the breakfast dishes. "I've got to do something for Leah and Jos," he said. "They don't have anybody."

Jordan turned to face him. "It's been hard for them since Mark died. They really don't have anything. I know Mark didn't have any money, and they don't own the house they live in. It'll be for the new preacher."

A new minister had been engaged but had not yet arrived. When he did come everyone expected that he would live in the

house that the church had bought for the Ellencourts.

"What do you want to do, Ty?"

"I didn't tell you, but the last time I talked
to Mark I promised him I'd do what I could
for his Leah and Jos, and I've been thinking
of something."

Jordan came up to stand beside him.
"You're always thinking of others just like
you thought of me after I lost Colin. What do
you want to do?"

"I want to give her my claim. We've got
this place. We don't need two homesteads. It
would be a place for them to call their own."

"Why, Ty, that's wonderful!" She reached
up and put her arms around his neck and
kissed him. Her eyes glowed. "They'll be
neighbors! We'll be able to see them all the
time."

"You don't mind then?"

"Mind! Why should I mind?" Jordan was
sincerely puzzled. "Did you think I would?"

"Well, actually it would have been yours if
anything had happened to me. It's half yours
at least. I couldn't do it unless you were willing."

"Of course I'm willing! Then go to her, Ty. I
know she's been worried though she hasn't

said anything. And just think, you'll be close to Jos. The two of you have always been good friends. And Michael will enjoy having him around."

Ty's face cleared. "That's right, isn't it? We'll have two boys around here. I think I'll go now. Will you come with me?"

"As big as I am? I'm big as an elephant!"

"You're a beautiful elephant," he said. He kissed her and left the room quickly. Saddling his horse, he rode at once directly to Oregon City. Going to the Ellencourt house, he came out of the saddle, and when he knocked on the door, Leah answered. "Hello, Leah."

"Why, Ty, come in."

"Is Jos here?"

"No, I sent him to the store. He'll be back soon."

He stepped inside and saw that traces of sorrow were still on her face, but she was a strong woman, and he knew she would bear this as she had to. "Leah, I don't know what this will sound like. I've got something I want you to do."

"Me? What can I do for you?"

"Well, before Mark died I made him a promise." Ty went on to explain what he had promised, and then he said simply, "I want you and Jos to have my homestead."

"Why, I can't take your place!"

"I don't need it, Leah. Jordan and I have a good place. The other one is just standing empty. It'll be good for you, and Jordan and I have talked about it. We'll be neighbors, and Jos will be right there. As I told her, I'll have me two boys instead of just one."

Tears leaped into Leah Ellencourt's eyes. She bit her lip and tried to control herself, but she could not help it. "Oh, Ty," she said, "what a kind man you are!"

Moving forward, he reached out and took her by the shoulders. When she lifted her eyes, he said, "Don't cry. It'll be good for all of us. When can you leave?"

"We're ready now. I want you to tell Jos, Ty. He'll be so happy. He's been worried."

She reached up then and put her hands on each side of his cheeks. "You're a good man, Ty," she whispered.

Tears rolled down her cheeks, and he reached into his pocket and pulled out a handkerchief. He wiped the tears away and said, "It'll be good for all of us."

* * *

On April the twenty-first, 1847, Jordan went into labor. She had an easy time, and when Ty entered she held the baby in her arms. "Come and see your son, Ty," she said summoning a smile. Moving over, Ty knelt down and looked into the red face. "Can I hold him?"

"Yes, of course."

Ty Sublette took the small bundle. It felt so fragile, and he still knelt beside Jordan. "What shall we call him?"

"You name him, Ty."

"I've always been partial to David."

"Then David it is."

Ty looked down. "David Sublette." He smiled and leaned over and kissed Jordan. "You did fine—real fine! Now," he said, "I've really got something to work for! Two boys and a fine wife!"

THIRTY-ONE

From far away, from somewhere deep in the hills, a wolf made a symphony to the full moon. Always a lonely sound to Jordan, she hugged David closer to her breast and took pleasure in the touch of his small body. She began to sing softly:

Pappy's gone to get a rabbit skin
To wrap the little baby in.
It wouldn't be a might of harm
To keep the tiny baby warm.
Shoot a fox or shoot a bear
To keep the little baby there.

She put her gaze on Ty, who was sitting at the table reading a three-month-old newspaper. He was big boned and long armed, and there was no fat on him. She liked the way that his eyes were deep-set, and she liked the way his jaws were sharp against his heavily tanned skin and wondered again about the break in his nose, for he had never told her what put it there.

And then without warning unexpectedly a memory of Colin came to her, him who had been so alive and now was gone. She had thought about his death so many times. How he lived out his span, grew up, had known things, and then, like the last spark of a fire put out, he had died, and there was not even a grave to show that he had ever drawn a breath.

The thoughts troubled Jordan, and to distract herself she said, "You ought to have that paper memorized by now, Ty."

"I'd like to read a new one for a fact. I wonder how the army's doing down in Mexico." The United States had sent troops into Mexico the year before, but they hadn't heard much about it. "It says here there's a potato famine in Ireland," Ty went on. "People starving to death." He shook his head and sadness came to his eyes. "It's a shame that we can't share with those folks."

They sat quietly speaking, and finally Ty went over and began working on his musket balls. It was a task he loved, melting the lead down, pouring them into molds, and then when they cooled trimming them to the exact size with his knife. As he worked, he said, "I expect we'd all better stay pretty

close to the cabin, Jordan, for a time anyway."

Quickly Jordan looked up, catching from
the tone of his voice that this was not idle
talk. "What's the matter? Is there trouble?"

"I'm worried about the Indians."

"The Mololas? You've told me often
they're peaceful."

"They're no trouble, but a big tribe of Klamaths have joined them. They're a tougher
tribe. I don't want you wandering around."

Jordan held David closer to her breast and
a small fear touched her. The Mololas had
never been threatening. But she had heard
Ty's tales of the cruelty of some of the other
tribes. "Do you think they'll break out?"

"Always possible. We'll just have to be—"
He broke off abruptly and lifted his head. Always alert, he rose quickly and went to the
door. "Someone coming," he murmured. He
waited, keeping back from the doorway but
peering out into the darkness. "A lone man.
Who could be roaming around this time of
the night?"

"Maybe it's Gus."

Ty did not answer but stood balanced and
waiting. He half lifted the musket and then
stepped back clear of the doorway. Shoot-

ing a glance at Jordan, he shook his head as if to insure her silence. Jordan watched this and rose quickly and moved over to the far side of the cabin away from the door and the window.

A silence seemed to fill the room, and Jordan could hear the sound as someone approached. She almost held her breath, and then a voice called out, "Hello, the house!"

Something touched Jordan then, and she could not identify it. She stared into the darkness, and a form took shape. A man came and stood just outside the door. He did not move for a moment but stood looking in. She saw Ty lower the rifle and say, "Come in. Show yourself."

And then the man stepped across the threshold. He was thin and wearing a floppy hat that covered his head and a beard that covered the lower part of his face. His clothes were worn and ragged.

Then he stepped forward and pulled off his hat. "Hello, Jordan."

For a moment the room seemed to reel, and Jordan could not speak. And then she knew. "Colin!" she whispered, her throat so tight she could hardly speak. She could not seem to move, and the silence seemed to be deafening in her ear. A great feeling of joy came to her, and turning she put David down and then advanced. She came to stand before him. "Is—is it you, Colin?"

"It's me." He put his hands out and touched her hair and then let his hand fall. He turned to glance at Ty and spoke quietly. "Hello, Ty."

Jordan saw that Ty was as shocked as she herself. She looked closely at the man who stood before her who little resembled the one who had left three years ago. With his hat off she could see a terrible scar that began on the left side of his face and ran all the way down his cheek, pulling his features awry so that his left eye drooped. His cheeks were sunken, and his eyes were somehow different. And he was thin. He had always been so strong and so well-built, but now his flesh seemed to have shrunk away, stripping him down to the bare bones.

Ty spoke finally. "Where have you been, Colin?"

Colin dropped his head and speech seemed to catch at his throat. "A prisoner," he said finally. He looked up, and his eyes were on Jordan. "Whose child is that?"

Jordan glanced quickly at Ty, then faced

Colin squarely. "It's David," she said quietly. "David Sublette."

For a moment Jordan did not believe that Colin had understood her. He did not move nor blink, and then a shadow seemed to sweep across his face. He swallowed and turned to look at Ty for a moment, then over at the child in the cradle. "What about Michael?"

"He's asleep."

"Could I see him?"

"Of course. He's in the other room that we built." She picked up the lamp and moved out through the door that led to the extra room that Ty had built. She moved stiffly and felt, somehow, as if she were in a dream. Her mind was not working clearly, and when she stood over the bed she turned to watch as Colin came to stand and look down at the sleeping child. "He's three and a half now," she whispered.

Colin looked down silently at the boy. He did not speak, but pain was in his face. Reaching out, he touched the hair of his son very lightly, and then he turned quickly and walked back into the kitchen area.

"Sit down," Jordan said quickly. "There's some stew."

"I'm not hungry, but I could drink something. Water maybe."

Glad to have something to do, Jordan moved to get the water. She poured it into a tumbler and put it before him, and for a moment he held it looking at her, a wondering light in his eyes. Jordan trembled, for the enormity of what had happened was beginning to come to her. When he emptied the tumbler, she filled it again and said, "Where have you been, Colin?"

Ty came over then where he could see Colin's face. "We heard you were dead," he said, and there was an edge to his tone. "It's been three years."

Jordan felt she could not stand, so she took a seat and stared at the face of Colin. "We thought you were dead—that your ship went down."

Colin nodded. He held the tumbler in his hand and turned it around, speaking so quietly that Jordan had to strain to hear him. "The ship did go down. Only two of us made it to shore. A typhoon it was, and it tore the ship to bits. Sollie Goodman and I, we made it somehow. But he was all cut up from the coral that the sea drove us through. He died the next day."

"Where was this?" Ty asked.

"It was off the coast of Africa. I nearly died on the beach. I was cut up almost as bad as Sollie, and when he died, I tried to walk away, but I'd lost too much blood." He looked up then at Ty and added, "If I hadn't been found, I would have died there."

"Who found you, Colin?" Jordan asked.

"A tribe of slavers. The leader was a man named Hakeem. They raided throughout Africa taking whole villages."

David began to whimper, then cried. Jordan went over at once and picked him up. She sat down again holding him and rocking him slightly. "What happened then, Colin?"

"Like I said, Hakeem was a slaver. He patched me up and fed me—and then he made a slave of me."

"And that's where you've been all these years?"

"Yes. He knew I was a sailor in from the wreck. He had a ship. He used some of the slaves to man the oars, but when he found out I could navigate and knew the sea, he kept me."

The lonesome sound of the wolf's cry came again and stirred the still air. Colin looked at Jordan and seemed about to ask a question. He did not, however, though his eyes went to Ty and remained there for some time. Finally he said, "They kept me chained night and day. When I was on land they would chain me to a stake hand and foot. At sea I was always chained to the vessel itself. If it had gone down, I would have gone down with it. He hid me when other ships were around—didn't want anyone to pressure him to let me go."

Ty said almost harshly, "Did you try to escape?"

Colin's eyes went to Ty, and something passed between the two that Jordan could not understand. "I did try, Ty. I tried three times, and they caught me. They beat me so bad I thought I'd die. My back's nothing but scars now."

Jordan listened as Colin spoke for a long time about his attempted escapes. Once he had killed a man, his guard, and when he had been recaptured they had beaten him with rods until his back was nothing but blood and muscle and raw nerves. Another time he had managed to throw himself into the sea but had been caught very quickly.

"How did you get free, Colin?"

"A British frigate caught Hakeem's vessel. Came out of nowhere. I was chained, of course, and when they opened fire there was no chance. The shells blew the ship to pieces. It blew my chain loose, too. The captain sent boats in, and they picked me up." His face relaxed a little, and he smiled. "The captain's name was Simms. He was pretty shocked to find an American in that boat. He was a big help to me though. He put me on a vessel making its way back to this country. It took a long time. The ship didn't come directly." Colin suddenly straightened his shoulders and turned to face Jordan. "You didn't wait? You're married?"

"I waited almost two years, Colin. We thought you were dead. Everyone said you were. How could I take care of myself and Michael? I had to have someone."

Ty spoke up then. He looked big and somehow rather dangerous by the flickering amber light of the lamp. "You asked me to look after them. I gave you my word that I'd take care of them the best way I could. You remember that, don't you? Well, that's what I've done."

Colin's body seemed to sag. "I've thought about it. I thought about it all the time I was chained over there. What would happen to you and to Michael." He took a deep breath, then shook his head. "I did the best I could to get away. I never should have gone. Both of you were right."

Ty took a step closer. He shook his head and said tensely, "It's too late, Colin. She's my wife now."

And then a trace of the old Colin appeared, a flash of his dark eyes, and despite his thinness and poor condition he stood to his feet. "She was my wife, and Michael is my child."

"It's too late for that. You'll have to go away, Colin. You were dead, and it's best you stay that way."

Colin stood to his feet and would have answered sharply, but Jordan suddenly cried out, "Both of you leave!"

Both men turned to Jordan. Her eyes were filled with something neither of them had ever seen before. Her lips were trembling, but she stilled them and said, "Both of you go from this place! Neither of you can stay here!"

"I expect that's best," Ty said. He seemed

to have gotten control of the anger that had flared out, and he said, "You can go stay with Gus Dabney, Colin. I'll go with you. He's got a claim not far from here."

He gave Jordan a glance that she could not read. "I'll go stay in the barn at my old place."

Colin took one last look at Jordan and then said, "All right, Ty." He turned and moved slowly outside, weak and scarred by his experiences.

Ty followed him and turned to say, "We'll talk later."

Jordan watched them leave, and then she went to the door, shut it, and bolted it. Her limbs felt weak, and she could not think clearly. Flashing thoughts raced through her mind. "What am I going to do? What *can* I do?" she cried aloud, then clutched David tightly to her breast and fought back the tears.

Leah heard the slight sounds of tapping and got out of bed. She was wearing a thin cotton gown and grabbed a robe and belted it around her. She moved toward the cabin and picked up the pistol that Ty had given her for protection. Pulling the hammer back, she said, "Who is it? Who's out there?"

"It's me, Leah. Ty."

"Ty? Wait a minute. I'll unbolt the door."

She laid the pistol down, unbolted the door, and swung it back. Ty stood there outlined against the darkness, and she said, "Come in." She moved over and turned the lamp up that was burning low, and the light blossomed in the room. As soon as she turned and saw Ty's face, she said, "What's wrong? Is Jordan sick or one of the children?"

"No, it's not that." Ty stood in front of her, and his face was more serious than she had ever seen it. He stared at her for a moment, then shook his head. "Colin's come back."

For a moment Leah thought she had misunderstood him, and then she knew she had not. "How can that be?" she whispered. "Where has he been?"

She listened as Ty briefly outlined the story of Colin's captivity, then he said, "I'm going to sleep in the loft out at your barn."

"Where's Colin?"

"He's staying with Gus and Jennie."

Something in Ty's face warned Leah of

the suffering that he was going through. She came closer and almost timidly reached out and touched his arm. "Are you all right, Ty?"

"No, I'm not."

Instantly Leah knew that guilt was eating away at the big man. "There's no fault in it. You've done nothing wrong."

Ty stared at her, then shook his head. "There's no happy ending to this story, Leah. Not with two sons and different fathers. If it weren't for David, it might be different."

"Come and sit down."

Ty hesitated, then he moved over and sat down. She busied herself stirring up the fire, and neither of them spoke as she put water on to heat. Finally, when she had tea made, he began to speak, telling her the details of Colin's captivity. Leah listened and felt a great wave of pity for all three of these people that she loved.

"I don't know what to do, Leah. I've never heard of such a thing."

Leah said, "You'll be all right. So will Colin and Jordan. God will make a way."

"I can't believe that."

Leah leaned forward. They were sitting at the table, and she took his hand in hers.

"This is the worst time of your life, Ty. It's the time, I think, that God's been waiting for. Now's the time for you to let God into your life."

Ty felt the warmness and the firmness of her hand, and it gave him comfort. He whispered, "You know, Leah, God's been speaking to me ever since David was born."

"I know. I've seen it in you, and I've been waiting for you to let him have his way."

"I don't know how, Leah."

Leah began speaking then, and she spoke for a long time of his need for God's forgiveness. She quoted Scriptures that she knew so well and saw that he seemed to be drinking her words in. "You've got to give yourself up to God, to make a surrender to him. I don't know how this problem can be solved, but I know that if you'll let Jesus come in and be what he wants you to be, you'll find peace. God will help all of you if you'll trust in him."

"Do you think so, Leah?"

She squeezed his hand and felt the strength and at the same time sensed the terrible guilt that he felt. Again she said, "You've done no wrong, Ty. Neither has Jordan. God will work it out if you put your faith in him."

"I'll think on it," Ty said. He rose and moved toward the door. He turned and tried to smile. "You're a comfort, Leah Ellencourt." He disappeared then, and as he left her alone in the room, Leah felt that she had failed. She went over by the fire, knelt down, and began to pray.

Gus had been stunned to see the two men who had appeared the previous night. He was so shocked at Colin Bryce's appearance he could not speak for a moment, but then he had covered it by going over and shaking hands. He had felt the thinness and the weakness of Colin's hand, and when Ty had explained the plan, Gus had said, "Why, me and Jennie would be plumb glad to have you. Come on inside."

Now morning had come, and Colin was outside washing up. Jennie had fixed eggs and fried ham and made fresh biscuits. Gus had warned her that Colin was different. "He's like a man that's been all shot up in a war. You can see it in his eyes. Terrible things happened to him, Jennie."

"What will they do, Gus?"

"You mean Jordan and about both men bein' married to her?" Gus had shaken his head. "I don't know. It's beyond me. They're all such good people—" He broke off as Colin entered, saying, "Sit down, Colin, and eat."

Colin ate sparingly, and when Jennie urged him to eat more, he smiled and said, "I guess I'm not used to such good cooking, Jennie." He looked at the two and said, "No need to ask if you are happy."

"We're very happy," Jennie said. She went over and put her hand on Gus's shoulder. He was sitting at the table, and her eyes went down to him fondly. "He's the best husband I ever had."

Gus laughed at that. Reaching up, he captured her hand and said, "I guess I am at that." He looked over then and said, "Do you mind talkin' some more about what happened to you, Colin?"

Colin knew that this would happen again and again. He sat at the table speaking of his experiences until finally Gus turned his head. "Someone comin'," he said. He got up, went to the door, and said, "It's Jordan and the boys."

At once Colin stood to his feet. He came to the door and stepped outside. Jordan had walked over and was carrying David and holding Michael by the hand.

"Hello, Colin," she said. "Good morning, Gus—Jennie."

"Come in and have some breakfast," Jennie said with a smile.

"No," Jordan said. "I won't stay. I've already eaten." Jordan said, "Michael, this is your father."

Michael's bright blue eyes were alert. He pulled away from his mother's hand and stepped closer. "Hello," he said. "Are you really my father?"

Colin could not speak for a moment, then he smiled. "I really am," he said.

"Mama told me you got killed."

"That's what she thought, but I didn't die."

Jordan said quickly, "I thought you two might get to know each other."

Colin looked at her. "That's like you, Jordan."

"Why don't you two go for a walk. Maybe I will have a little breakfast."

"There's a creek down there. Me and Michael go fishin' some time," Gus said.

"Why don't you go down and see if the fish are bitin'."

"Will that be all right, Michael?" Colin asked, his eyes fixed on the boy.

"Sure, let's go."

At once Colin moved across the yard, and when they disappeared, Jennie said, "I'd forgotten how much Michael looked like him."

"Colin looks terrible," Gus said. "Come on in. We can have some coffee anyway."

As Colin walked down the path with the boy, he was aware that Michael was giving him a close examination. "What happened to your face?" the boy asked.

"I got into some trouble, and a man cut it with a knife."

"Did you fight him back?"

"No, there wasn't much of a chance of that. My hands were tied."

"Why were your hands tied?"

As the two walked on, Colin spoke of his voyage and finally said, "You were just a baby when I left. I know you can't remember me, but I remember you. I remember holding you and rocking you when you had a stomachache."

"Did you really do that? I don't remember it."

The two reached the small creek, and Michael, at once, began pointing out the spots where he and Gus and Ty had caught fish. Colin could barely answer him he was so moved by the sight of his son. He was such a handsome boy and so much like he himself when he was that age. Finally the two sat down, and Michael turned and said, "Why did you go away and leave me and Mama?"

"I made a bad mistake, Michael. I never should have left."

"Ty is my second father. That's what Mama said."

"He's taken good care of you and your mother."

"Why did you go away?"

The question came again, and Colin repeated, "As I said, son, I made a bad mistake."

"Are you gonna stay here now?"

This was a question that Colin Bryce could not answer. He put the boy off saying, "Let's get some lines, and maybe you and I could catch some fish."

"All right, and maybe you and me and Pa can come sometime. That'll be three of us."

The boy's words wrenched at Colin, but he only smiled. "That'll be fine."

* * *

The news of Colin Bryce's return spread like wildfire. Nothing had happened like this before in the experience of the settlers. It was a drama such as they had never encountered. Jordan kept to herself for several days. She saw Ty rarely, for he would come to check on David and then leave. He was spending much time in the woods hunting, and there was a constraint between him and Jordan.

The same was true of Colin. He spent time with Michael, taking him fishing every day or walking through the woods.

But nothing was really settled. No one dared to come and ask Jordan directly, and she kept to the house doing her work mechanically.

Finally, on a late Tuesday evening, Leah had set the table for herself and Jos and Ty. They had just finished supper when Jos said, "Look, there comes Miz Sublette."

Leah rose at once, as did Ty. They went out on the front porch, and Jordan was alone. "Jennie's keeping the children," she said. "I need to talk to you, Ty."

"Come on, Jos, let's go back inside,"

Leah said quickly. As soon as she and the boy were inside and the door had closed, Jordan faced Ty and said, "I'm going to live alone, Ty, until I know what to do."

"I think that's probably best."

"You come and see the boys all you want, but I can't be with a man." Tears rose in her eyes, and she said, "I don't know what to do."

"I don't either. Leah says God will have to settle this."

"I think she's right. Come anytime you want to see David or Michael."

Ty watched her leave, then turned and went back inside. Jos was watching him carefully, and he knew that the boy was as aware of the situation as any grown-up. The two of them had gotten very close, but he waited until Jos left to go do the milking before he turned to Leah and said, "Jordan is going to live alone."

"I think that's the right thing to do until this is settled. It's hard for all of you, but it's harder for Jordan."

"I couldn't sleep last night. I guess whatever happens it's going to be painful for all of us." He looked at her thoughtfully. "I haven't forgotten what you said about letting God into my life. I've got to find the right thing to do, Leah!"

Leah wanted to put her arms around him and comfort him as she would Jos. He was so big, but he seemed so fragile and so helpless. This would not do, but the impulse was strong. "You will, Ty. God will make a way."

THIRTY-TWO

Avis moved around the table serving the men, who ate like starved wolves. As she moved over toward the stove, she heard Ace laugh and turned to watch him.

"Why, I'd say Jordan's got it better than most. She's got two husbands to take care of her now. She'll never have to hit another lick of work."

Theodore had stuffed his mouth full of fried pork, and he talked around it in a mushy fashion. "That's right, ain't it, and when it gets cold she'll have a man on each side of her to keep her warm."

Ace looked up to see his stepmother staring at him. "Well, that's a good thing, ain't it, Ma? Those fellows may have to take turns, but there's—"

"Shut your filthy mouth!"

Avis moved quickly to stand to the left of Ace, who was staring at her with astonishment. "Why, I didn't mean nothin'."

"You have a filthy mind and a filthy mouth, Ace, and you're worse, Theodore! In this house you'll keep your mouth shut about decent people. They've got enough problems without people like you."

Ace's face turned suddenly red. He got up, stared down at Avis, then without a word he marched out of the room.

"You can go, too," Avis said to Theodore, who was staring blankly at her.

"But, Avis—"

"You heard what I said. Get out of here!"

Theodore, a slow thinker, had never seen his stepmother this angry. He got up without a word, cast one look at his father, and then left the room.

"A little bit hard on the boys, Avis, weren't you?" Ira said.

"I didn't notice you jumping in to make them keep their mouths shut."

Ira suddenly grew angry. He had a hot temper, although he usually kept it for others rather than his wife. "There's talk going on all over the valley about Jordan and her two husbands. You aim to go around to every cabin and tell people to keep their mouths shut?"

"No!" Avis turned to face him. "But I'm going to tell you just like I've told Ace and Theodore. There'll be no more of that kind of talk in this house."

"You've decided to wear the pants in the family."

"Since you won't, I will!"

Ira started to speak, then clamped his lips tightly together. He had married Avis because she was attractive, and he needed someone to keep his house. He had thought keeping the house was the most important thing, but ever since they had married he had been dissatisfied with his bargain. He wanted more from her than just meals on the table and a clean cabin. Now he stared at her and said, "I don't think you're anyone to be giving advice. You're cold as a stick."

"I've never refused you," Avis said.

"No, you haven't, but you've got no love in you."

"You didn't ask me for love. You asked me to keep your house."

"I thought it was understood that a woman would love her husband."

"Then why didn't you ask me if I loved you? If you had, I would have told you I didn't. I've never lied to you about that, Ira. I needed a home, and you needed a woman to keep your house. I've done that, and I've never refused you in your bed."

Ira Barnhill met her glance, then he shook

his head. "I'd like a little tenderness, but you're a cold woman, Avis."

He turned and left the cabin, leaving her standing staring after him. She did not move for a time, and then she sat down and put her head on her forearms. She had not wept for a long time, but now she could not hold the tears back. She had a love for a man at last, the first that she had ever known, but she knew that there was no way that she could ruin the life of a man like Paul Leverett. If it were just herself, she would take her chances and seize what happened as she could. But she loved him too much to bring him into that kind of wrong.

"Something's got to be done, Preacher."

Horace Farr shifted himself in the straight-backed chair and looked across at his pastor. Houston Land was, in many respects, different from his predecessor, but in the short time that he had been pastor he had proven himself to be a man of wisdom, insight, and compassion. He was a tall man, lean, almost lanky, with shaggy brown hair that refused to stay combed.

Farr leaned forward and said, "Everybody

in the valley's talking about this situation. We've got to do something."

Land had received two of his deacons and was not surprised when they had announced that they had come to speak with him about Jordan Sublette. He did not know Jordan well, but had been impressed with her quiet sincerity. The Sublettes had been in his mind an ideal family, and now this situation had simply exploded.

Land turned to look at Mel Ott, a lawyer he had called in for legal advice. "What do you think, Brother Ott? What legally, I mean, about this thing."

Ott said quietly, "I don't think it's a matter for courts."

"Not a matter for courts!" Farr exclaimed. "But the woman's got two husbands. There are some who're saying she's a bigamist."

"That's nonsense, Horace, and you know it," Ott shook his head. "The man was gone for nearly two years before she married again, and by every report was dead. It's just an unfortunate circumstance."

"You came across on the trail with all three of these people, Brother Farr," Reverend Land said. "What do you think of them? I've heard nothing but good."

"They are good people. Colin was not as steady a man as Ty, but he was a good man. He made a mistake going off to get involved with that slavery business, but you've talked to him. What did he say?"

"He said it was the worst mistake he ever made, and having been a slave, he's now about as staunch an abolitionist as you'd find. He hates it."

"But that doesn't solve our problem," Horace said. "Something's got to be settled."

Ott shook his head. "It won't be settled by the courts. We don't have all that much law out here anyway. And even if there were a more sophisticated system, what could they say? Mrs. Sublette married both men legally. There was no way of knowing that her husband didn't die."

The three men sat there for a time, all of them anxious to find a solution to the problem. They were well aware of the talk that went around the community. Finally Horace Farr said, "My grandfather was an overmountain man. He left Virginia to settle in Kentucky, and he was a storytelling man. I hadn't thought of this for years, but he told stories of three times that this same situation happened. You got to remember in those days men went out to fight the Indians, and if they got killed, their bodies weren't brought back. A lot of them were captured by the Indians. Men and women for that matter. In the three cases he knew of a man was thought dead and when he came home, the wife had remarried."

"What did they do, Horace?" Ott asked quickly.

"They left the choice up to the woman as to which man would be her husband."

Mel Ott said instantly, "I think that's what is going to have to happen here. It's not a legal matter. Reverend, I think you ought put this to Mrs. Sublette."

"That's right," Horace agreed. "You can tell her, Reverend, that it's Mel's legal opinion that either man she chooses will be her real husband."

"What about the other man? The one she doesn't choose." Reverend Land shook his head. "Not going to be a happy ending, but you're right, and I'll go see her right away."

The weather was cool, for September gave hints of the winter to come, but the sun was warm at midday when Jordan looked up from her washing and saw Colin walking quickly toward her. He had shaved the beard off so he looked more like himself, and he had gained some weight. Not much but enough to fill in the cavernous hallows of his cheeks. Her heart went out to him, for she remembered him as the handsomest man she had ever seen. No one would call him that now, not the way his face was scarred. She spoke cheerfully to greet him. "Hello, Colin. Did you come for Michael?"

"If it's all right. I'd like to take him fishing."

"You two have become good friends in a short time."

"He's a fine boy. I see a lot of you in him, Jordan." Colin smiled crookedly. "You've done a fine job of raising him."

"He maybe is a little like me, but he looks so much like you. I'll bet you looked exactly like that when you were three years old."

"I think I did. Where is he?"

"He's out in the back digging a hole. I don't know what for. I think he's going to bury a treasure in it and come back in years and find it."

"He's very imaginative."

"I guess he got that from me, but I hope he's not as wildly romantic as I was."

Colin smiled, looking for a moment like his old self. He was wearing a gray linsey shirt, a pair of Gus's old trousers, and a pair of rough shoes. He looked at the cabin and then around at the garden and then at the cattle that grazed inside the pasture. "You know, Jordan, this place—and you—that's all that kept me alive. I almost killed myself twice, but then I'd think of you, and I'd put it off."

"I'm so sorry, Colin." Jordan went closer to him. She reached up and touched his scar. It was the first time she had touched him since he had returned, and he stood very still. "I'm so sorry that you had to go through all of that."

Colin reached up and put his hand over hers. "It was all my own fault. I deserved this," he said.

The two stood there for a moment. Something passed between them, and then Jordan withdrew her hand. "It's good for you to spend time with Michael."

For a moment Colin stared at her, then he ran his hand over his black hair. It had been roughly cut and shaped by Jennie. He hesitated, then said quietly, "I've been thinking, Jordan. It would have been better if I had died in that wreck or in one of my attempts to escape."

"Don't say that, Colin!"

"It's true enough. I've brought nothing but trouble to you, and that's not what I want. I'm not the same, and you're not the same." He looked off to the hills for a moment, and when his eyes came back they were filled with infinite sadness. "I heard someone say once you can't step in the same river twice."

"Things have changed, of course, but we didn't know. We all did the best we could."

"There's a kind heart speaking, but you always were kind." He suddenly said, "Have you talked to Reverend Land?"

Jordan dropped her eyes. "Yes, he came by yesterday."

"He came to see me, too. I know he talked to Ty. I suppose he said the same thing to all of us."

"I suppose so."

"It's the only way, but it's hard on you." Colin reached out suddenly and took Jordan's hand. He held it for a moment, then looked into her eyes. "I want you to be happy, Jordan. I've lost you—and I didn't know how much I loved you—until it was too late."

Tears rose to Jordan's eyes, and she dropped her head. At that moment Michael came around calling out, "Pa, are we going fishing?"

Quickly Colin released Jordan's hand, reached down, and grabbed the boy and picked him up. "My, you're getting to be a big one," he said. "Won't be long before you'll be able to pick me up."

"Let's go fishing. I bet I'll catch a whale."

"All right, we'll go."

"I'll—I'll have supper cooked for you when you come back," Jordan said quickly.

For a moment Colin almost refused, but then he smiled. It was a crooked smile, for his lips were twisted on the left side by the vicious scar, but it was the same smile that she had loved. "All right," he said. "I'll look forward to that."

A full moon rode high in the sky, and a few small clouds drifted closer to it. Leah watched for a time wondering if they would hit or miss the moon. They covered the face of the silver disk for a moment and then were gone.

She turned as Ty came from the direction of the barn. He had his powder horn on and his musket in his hand. "It's time for supper," she said. "You're late getting in. What did you find out?"

Ty had left early to meet with the militia that had been called by Horace Farr. The Indian situation was getting more tense, and now as Ty went inside, he leaned his musket down, stripped off the powder horn, and sat down. "No trouble so far, but there may be."

"I kept things warm for you. I haven't eaten either."

The two sat down and ate, but Ty seemed to have little appetite.

"Where's Jos?"

"He's over at the Blantons staying with Roger. Those two are getting to be closer than two ticks on a hound."

"Roger's a good boy. I promised them both that I'd take them fox hunting."

"Why would you want to hunt foxes? You can't eat them."

"Just an excuse to get away, listen to the dogs holler, sit around a fire. We never kill the fox. They were some of my best times when I was Jos's age."

"Jos misses Mark."

"So do I. He's got good stuff in him, Jos has—his father and his grandfather." Ty smiled then. "And, of course, there's you."

The two finished the meal, and he helped clean up, then they went out and sat on the porch. They talked of small things, but Leah knew that he was troubled. Finally he turned to her and said, "I don't know why it is, Leah, but I think about God all the time."

"I think trials bring us closer to God—some of us, that is."

"I've known some it drove away. When hard times hit they blame God."

"You're wiser than that," Leah said.

Ty Sublette shook his head. They were sitting on the steps, and he turned to her. "I'm lost, Leah, in every way."

She turned to him quickly and saw such loneliness and misery in his eyes that she could hardly bear it. *Why, I care for him!* The thought shocked her, but at that moment she realized that she had had a strong affection for this man even when she had been married to Mark.

She put that behind her, however, and said, "You're struggling with a terrible problem, Ty, and you can never solve it."

"What can I do then? I thought about just leaving—packing up and going away."

"You can't do that. You've got a son, and he needs you no matter what you and Jordan decide. He's your son, your flesh and blood."

"I know it. That's what keeps me here." He suddenly put his head down and covered his face with his hands. "I don't know what to do. I just don't know."

"You've always been a strong man, Ty, able to handle your own problems. But you can't handle this."

"You're right about that, Leah."

"I've seen so many men and women, too, that ran from God, and that's what you've been doing." Suddenly a strong impulse came to her. She was a woman of deep spiritual discernment, and now it was almost as if a voice had said, *He's ready. Tell him the Gospel.*

Leah began to speak then, and she spoke simply of Jesus. She knew this big man, so strong in so many ways, was not able to go on as he was. She spoke of how Jesus came, laying aside his glory and becoming a man. "And he had troubles, Ty. The Scripture says, 'There is no temptation taken us but such as is common to man.' Jesus knew what it was to be hungry. It seems he was terribly lonely, for nobody on this earth understood him, only his Father in heaven." And then she spoke of his death and said, "I don't know how it is, Ty, but when Jesus died on the cross, somehow that became the hope for all of us. I was only twelve years old when I called on God. He came into my heart, and I don't know to this day how he did it, but he's given me peace. He's forgiven all my sins, and he wants you to know that peace."

Ty turned suddenly, removing his hands, and Leah was shocked to see tears in his eyes. She took his hand and said softly and gently, "Now is the time."

"What can I do?"

"I want us to pray. God answers prayers, and as we pray, you forget me, you forget Jordan, you forget David. Forget everything. Just go to God and tell him that you're lost and that you want peace in your heart. And he'll give it to you."

Without waiting, Leah bowed her head.

She felt Ty's shoulders shaking as she leaned against him, and his hand convulsively clutched hers. She prayed aloud at first, and it was quiet except for his attempts to muffle the sobs that came to him. Finally he cried out, "Oh, God, I'm nothing! I don't know how to find you. I don't know what to do, but I believe that Jesus is the Son of God, and I ask you, in his name, to help me. Save me from the man I am."

Leah's heart leaped as Ty continued to pray, and finally he ceased. The two sat there quietly. She was still holding his hand, and now his grip seemed loose. She turned to him and tried to see his face by the moonlight. When he did turn to face her, she saw that the tears had left tracks on his cheek. "Are you all right now, Ty? Did you ask Jesus to come into your heart?"

"Yes," he whispered. "Is that all I do?"

"No, there's much more. But I know that God has forgiven your sins. Now, we have to pray that Christ will be absolute Lord of your life, and that every day you'll love him more."

"I don't know how, but this is real, Leah. I don't remember crying since I was seven years old."

"It's all right to cry. Jesus did." She smiled and squeezed his hand. They sat there in the moonlight, and from time to time he would speak, and she would answer. It was a holy time and a special time, and Leah knew that she would never forget it.

THIRTY-THREE

The sun had lifted itself above a line of trees as Jordan walked over the ground that sur-rounded the cabin. It seemed to her to be a pale argosy sailing across a tawny sky. It would be a cool day, for there was a gray devout atmosphere about the world, and far off the western hills, in their sullen haze, seemed to be brooding over some brutal thought.

As she moved slowly, deep thoughts dis-turbed her, as they had for days now. She tried to shake off the problem that had come to take full occupation of her life. She glanced to the east where the trees stood in disorganized ranks—a regiment at ease. They shouldered the sun out of the way, and the sun let long fingers of light through them so that the strong, pale light pooled beneath the trees.

She looked overhead and saw a hawk turning on one wing in a geometric curve. Behind him the sailing clouds shifted their shapes, and farther on down four crows rose shaking their heavy wings, leaving four shadows on the shorn hay. The crows seemed ominous to her, and she shook her shoulders slightly to rid herself of her dark mood.

As she turned to go back to the cabin, she saw Colin emerge from the woods following the trail that led to the Dabney place. He was carrying a sack of some kind flung over his shoulder and the same floppy hat that he had worn when he had appeared out of the night. Something about him seemed different, although she could not put it into words. He seemed more purposeful, and when he approached her and she greeted him, she saw that his face was cast in a solemn almost fixed look. "Hello, Colin."

"Good morning."

"Michael's not up yet. You two stayed up so late last night that he overslept." She smiled slightly thinking of the long hours that Colin had stayed playing games with Michael. He had gotten on the floor and played with the wooden figures that Ty had carved out of pine, and then when the boy had grown sleepy he had sat down, pulled him on his lap, and told him stories of his seafaring days as a young man until finally

Michael had simply passed into uncon-
sciousness. The memory touched her, and
she stood before Colin, watching him with
softness in her eye.

As for Colin, he stood stiffly, and his eyes
were cloudy as he watched her. Something
about him quickened her breath. So much,
Jordan knew, lay between them, and she
had thought so much of the early days of his
courtship and of the first days of their marriage when passion had almost melted them
together. Many things warm and good lay
between them back in the past, and it kept
coming out more and more.

She saw the fugitive shadows, chasing
themselves in and out of the corners of his
mouth and of his eyes. She kept waiting for
him to speak, and finally he said in a voice
that seemed held steady only by his will,
"I'm leaving, Jordan."

"Leaving! What do you mean?" His words
stabbed her, and she was shocked at the
depth of feeling that ran through her. "You're
not going back to sea, are you?"

"I don't think so. I've got to get away,
though." He looked down at the ground for
a moment, and when he lifted his head, he
said, "I remember a verse from the Bible. It

says, 'I see through a glass darkly.' That verse has been coming to me for some reason or other." He suddenly half turned and looked over the homestead, his dark eyes taking in the cabin, the smoke rising from the chimney that he himself had built. He seemed to be soaking in the sights and the smells and almost the touch of the place. "God gives us so much in the world," he murmured. "He gave me such wonderful things, pressed down, shaken together, and running over, and I threw it away."

"No one intended for all this to happen, Colin," Jordan said quickly.

"No, it's like a very bad accident. No one intends for it to happen—but after it does people are hurt, and they have to pick up the pieces. Sometimes they've even lost limbs or their sight, but people have to go on. I thought I'd come home, and we'd pick up where we left off. But I see that can't be."

His words had a ring of grief, and she saw that he was holding himself together with an effort. "I don't know how we'll solve it all, but we will," she said gently.

"It's too late for that," Colin said, "and I've been thinking hard. It's not fair to put the burden on you. I don't know a better man in the world than Ty Sublette. I did ask him to take care of you, and you waited nearly two years. You had no reason to think I was alive. I don't fault you or Ty. You're blameless, and I don't ever want you to be hurt or grieved, but—"

Jordan could not speak she was so overwhelmed. For a moment she simply stood trying to think. She finally whispered, "It can't end like this."

"Somebody has to be hurt, and I'm the one who brought it all about, so it's only right that it should be me."

At that moment Jordan knew that this man who stood before her scarred and filled with suffering was not the same man that she had married. The Colin she had known would never have spoken like this! She had always known he had a bit of selfishness in him, but that was now gone. He had been thrown into a furnace that had burned away his youthful indiscretions and impatience, and she knew suddenly that this was a better man who stood before her.

Colin said quietly, "If you have to leave a place that you've lived in and loved, then it's best to do it the fastest way you can. That's what I'm going to do, Jordan. I know I can never forget you no matter how hard I try, but I don't want you to grieve. So I've come to say good-bye. I don't think you should wake Michael. I—I don't think I could face up to saying good-bye to him—but I'll write him a letter and try to explain as best I can."

Jordan came forward and put her arms around him. "My dear man," she whispered, "things are so hard!" She clung to him and felt her arms go around him, and with her face against his chest she could not help but remember that he was the first man that she had known, her first love, the one who had awakened her from adolescence and with whom she had first encountered the joys of marriage. Now she could only keep her eyes shut and try to will away the thing that was happening. She lifted her head and looked into his eyes, and when he did not move, she pulled his head down and kissed him. The kiss brought back memories of times long gone, and she could not keep back the waves of regret.

It was Colin who pulled away, and she looked at the terrible scar on his face and knew that behind his expression was a hunger for her and for his son and for this land. He said in a strained voice that seemed to come from deep within, "Good-bye, Jordan. I'll always love you, but it's best that I go."

He turned and walked away stiffly. As she watched him go, Jordan felt a pang, sharp and keen and painful, touch her deep inside. She could not move or speak, and as he moved away, she stood as stiffly as if she were before a firing squad. She whispered his name, and when he disappeared down the path into the trees, she felt that part of her had died.

"Reverend Land, have you got a few minutes?"

Houston Land had answered the door and found Ty Sublette standing there. He said at once, "Why, of course, Mr. Sublette. Come in." He stepped back, and when Ty stepped into his office, he seemed to make the room smaller. "The place is a mess. I'm not much of a housekeeper. Just take those books off that chair and sit down."

Ty moved several books from a wooden chair, sat down, and waited until Land took his seat. "I've got to talk to you."

"Glad you came," Land said quietly. "I've

not been able to advise you. I've not got that much wisdom."

"It's a hard thing," Ty said slowly. "Hardest of all on Jordan. I've never had to face anything like this before."

"Very few people have. I've been concerned about it and so have all the members of the church. You're not a member yourself, are you?"

"No, and that's what I've come to see you about."

Instantly Land's attention sharpened. His eyes grew narrow, and he said, "How's that?"

"I've never been a man of God, but just recently I've called on the Lord, and I asked him into my life." Ty struggled with his feelings for a moment and then said with a gusty sigh, "It's been different from anything I've ever known."

"Tell me about it. It sounds like wonderful news." Land listened as Sublette told him about calling on the Lord. He was interested that Leah Ellencourt had been the means used to bring him to the Lord. When Ty finished, he said, "Leah Ellencourt is a very wonderful woman. I wish I'd known her husband."

"He was a good man and so was his grandfather. In any case, I don't know what to do next. I'll be attending church now, and it's in my heart to serve God. Just tell me," he said simply, "what to do."

"Well, this is wonderful indeed!" Houston Land got up and walked around the desk. He put his hand out, and Ty took it. "I can't tell you," Land beamed, a smile wreathing his features, "how fine this news is. Always good to see someone find the Lord. As for telling you what to do, why, I'll do what I can." He hesitated, then said, "Would you agree to being baptized?"

"Oh, yes. Leah has already told me that that's the next step, and I'm agreeable." He hesitated, then said, "It's awkward, Reverend. People don't know what to say to me. They look at me as if they're afraid they'll say something to hurt my feelings. Even my good friends."

"I suppose it's natural they should feel that way." Land kept quiet for a moment as he thought. "One of you is going to be hurt badly when Jordan makes her choice."

"That's right, and I'm ready for that. She loved Colin long before she ever loved me. The problem, of course, is the two boys."

"Something will be worked out. Suppose we pray about it right now."

Ty nodded in agreement. "I need all the prayer I can get!"

After his conversation with Land, Ty went to the store and bought some black powder and a sack of cornmeal. He turned to go outside, and as soon as he stepped out into the bright morning sunlight, he saw Colin walking along the line of stores. He saw Ty at once. He came forward and said, "I need to talk to you, Ty."

"Sure, let's go over under that tree—get out of the sun."

The two men moved across, and Ty could hear the ringing of the smith's hammer on the anvil. "You come to town to get some supplies?"

"No, not for that," Colin said. He looked fully at Ty and said without preamble, "I'm leaving, Ty. It's not fair to put Jordan in this position, so I'll be moving on."

Shock ran through Sublette as he heard these words. He stared at Colin and said, "But Jordan hasn't said what she wants."

"It's not fair to put it to her, Ty. I felt that all

along. A man has to pay for his mistakes, and I'm paying for mine."

Sublette had thought that this would be welcome news, but it made him uneasy. "I don't think you ought to do it, Colin. Give it a little bit more time."

"We can't both have her, Ty, that's plain, and I forfeited my chance. You've made a home for her, and all I ask is that you look after my boy. I'll maybe be able to come and see him when I get settled a little bit."

Ty could not believe what he was hearing, and a great respect for Colin seemed to birth itself in him. He said quietly, "Look, Colin, I don't know if you've heard yet, but I've had an experience I never thought I'd have." He went on to tell him about his calling on God, and now he said, "I've given everything to the Lord, and I don't know what God wants. But I'm willing to wait, and I think you should, too."

Colin smiled a strangely crooked smile due to the scar that marred his face. "That's like you, Ty. I'm glad you've found the Lord, but I'll be leaving."

"Have you told Jordan?"

"Yes, we said our good-byes."

Sublette started to speak when suddenly

the sound of a rapidly approaching horse came to him. He turned quickly and saw Jack Farr lashing his horse at a breakneck speed. "Something must be wrong, Colin," he said. "Jack isn't one to treat a horse like that."

He turned, and the two men ran quickly. Ty reached up as the horse was pulled to a halt, his flanks white with froth.

Jack said, "It's the Indians! They've gone on a rampage! They're all the way down from the Masters place. They attacked Ronnie Masters."

A crowd had gathered, and Ty demanded quickly, "Which way are they headed?"

"Masters said they seemed to be headed north. He forted himself in, and they couldn't get to him. I got to get the doctor there. Miss Masters, she's hurt."

A crowd began to gather quickly. Pete Gratton said, "We've got to stop 'em." He looked at Ty. "You're the only one that ever actually fought the devils. I'll go with you, and you tell me what to do."

Instantly the voices of the men began to agree with this. Ty said, "All right, they're probably headed for Barnhill's place. Everybody get a gun and plenty of ammunition. I'm leavin' in five minutes."

Colin started and said, "Ty, Jordan was taking the boys for a visit to Avis."

Ty's mouth tightened, and he said, "Let's get going."

Colin turned to Dave Minton and said, "Dave, do you have a horse I could ride?"

"Sure I do, Colin."

The five minutes passed, and twenty-two men rode out heavily armed with Ty at their head. There was a coldness in his heart, for he was the only one who had seen what the Indians could do when they were on the rampage. *We've got to shut 'em off quick*, he thought, and drove his horse forward as fast as the gelding could travel.

"There they are, in the bush," Colin cried out. He had managed to keep up with Ty, and now the two drew their horses up.

"We'll go after 'em on foot," Ty said. "Pete, you take half the men and take 'em around that bluff over there. We'll go right in after them. If we whip 'em, they'll probably run that way, and you cut 'em off."

"All right," Pete said. "Come on, fellas."

The remaining men tied their horses and drove at once toward the woods. They shoved their way forward, and Ty called, "Keep scattered out. At the first sign of a shot get behind a tree."

They encountered no resistance, but Ty caught the smell of smoke. "Something's burning," he said. "Come on, we don't have time to wait." He broke into a dead run, and the others followed him. They thrashed their way through the thickness of the woods and finally emerged into a field where Ty cried out, "The barn's on fire, but I don't see them!"

They raced across the field, and Ty said, "There's one of them that didn't make it." He pointed to a dead Klamath who lay on his back, blood over his chest as he stared up sightlessly into the heaven. They found two more bodies, but the barn fire was raging beyond control.

"Hello, the house!"

The door opened, and Theodore Barnhill stepped out. He had a bloody rag tied around his left arm, and his eyes were hard. "Good thing you got here. They would have had us."

Avis came out, and Ty said, "Did Jordan come with the boys?"

"Yes, they went down through the woods going to the river just before they hit us."

"They killed Ace," Theodore said dully. "And Pap, he's dead, too." A dull fury shook the big man, and he said, "Let's go get 'em."

Ty thought quickly. "Dave, you take this bunch and take out after the Indians. Colin, come on. We'll go look for Jordan and the boys." Without waiting for an answer, he turned and ran away at full speed. Colin came as best as he could, but he could not keep up with the big man. Finally they reached the edge of the thick forest.

"Come on. We have to go careful now. There may be some Klamaths in here," Ty said. They pushed forward, and Ty Sublette's eyes were everywhere, but he saw no sign. They had pressed forward no more than five minutes when suddenly two Klamaths appeared. One of them lifted his rifle and fired. The shot grazed Colin's side, but he raised his own rifle, and his shot killed the Indian.

The other Indian raced forward; evidently his rifle was not charged. He raised it over his head and struck at Ty. Sublette parried the blow with his own rifle, then shoved the muzzle into the Indian's side and pulled the trigger. The Indian grunted and was not mortally wounded. Ty smashed the butt of the

rifle against the Indian's forehead and saw
the light go out in his eyes. "Come on," he
said, "but look out, Colin, there may be more
of them."

The two men raced forward and then
suddenly they saw Jordan step forward out
of a clearing where the creek had made a
way. She had David in her arms, and
Michael was clinging to her skirt. Sublette
inwardly gave a deep sigh of relief, and he
started forward, gladness in his face, but he
was suddenly pushed aside and nearly
stumbled. He heard Jordan cry out, "Colin!"

He saw Colin racing forward, his hat flying
off, and he was crying out, "Jordan, oh, Jordan!" He saw that Colin was crying, great
tears running down his cheeks, and he
came to Jordan. He threw his arms around
her, and as Ty Sublette stood there, he saw
Jordan put her free arm around Colin. He
came forward, but he did not speak until finally Colin stepped back. The tears ran
down his face, and Ty saw that Jordan's
face was pale, but her eyes were for Colin.
She reached up and wiped his tears away.
"Don't cry, Colin," she whispered. "We're all
right."

Colin reached down, picked up Michael,

and hugged him, his shoulders shaking. "Thank God—thank God," he kept saying.

"Are you all right, Jordan?" Ty asked. "They didn't find you?"

"No, we heard the firing and their screaming so we stayed in the woods, but I was so afraid. Are the Barnhills all right?"

"No, Ace and Ira are both dead, and there are probably more. We don't know how many. Come along," he said. "You need to get out of this."

As Ty Sublette said this, he could not get the picture out of his mind. He had gone forward anxiously enough and filled with joy that Jordan was all right—but it had been Colin who had run forward weeping.

And it was Colin's name she had called when she saw them both.

THIRTY-FOUR

Ty and Colin sat their horses watching as Lieutenant Seaton directed his troopers in rounding up the Klamaths. Seaton was a young man with dancing blue eyes. He had brought his group of cavalry to join with the militia, and after five days of throwing a circle around the area, they had managed to engage the renegade Indians in one brief but rather bloody battle. Only one trooper had been killed, though several were wounded, and of the militia only one man had been hurt seriously.

Ty watched the faces of the Klamaths and murmured, "They're whipped for now, Colin."

"I feel sorry for them. They're unhappy people."

Ty Sublette shifted in the saddle and put his gaze on Colin. The chase had been hard, and Colin had struggled to keep it up. When rest time came, he had simply stepped off his horse and collapsed, and now he was at the end of his tether.

Ty said quietly, "We'll be out of this soon, and I'm glad of it."

Lieutenant Seaton said, "All right, Sergeant, take them to the fort." He wheeled his horse and galloped him across the open ground, pulling him to a stop in front of the two men. He smiled briefly, his teeth white against his heavy tan. "Your men did well, Sublette. I don't think you'll have any more trouble. This was a swan song for the Klamaths, I think."

"You've got good troops, Lieutenant." Ty nodded. "I hope you're right about the Klamaths."

"What will happen to them, Lieutenant?" Colin asked.

"We'll take them back to the fort. They'll be good Indians for a while, then we'll turn 'em loose, and they may try again."

"They have nowhere to go, don't they? We took their land, and now they don't have a home."

Seaton had a soldier's mentality. It was his job to fight Indians, and he stared at Colin without comprehension. "That's not my job," he said briefly. "Well, you men can go home now. As I say, you did a good job."

Colin and Ty watched as the procession left. The Indians marched on foot, and the troops flanked them on each side, carbines drawn. Ty shook his head. "They don't have much ahead of them, do they? Well, let's get home. I'm beat."

The rest of the militia had already departed, so the two men were alone. "I'm just about past going," Colin murmured. "I thought I had more strength. I thought I was a better man."

"You're not over the captivity yet, Colin. You did fine."

The two men rode along following the easiest path through the forest. Ty knew the country well, and as they rode along, he was deep in thought. The clash with the Indians had driven other things out of his mind, but now in the morning sunlight he was more aware of the problems, and he began to think of the days to come. He saw that Colin was troubled and rode silently and attempted to get through to him.

"Sometimes things just drift along for years and nothing happens," Ty observed. "Just summer, winter, and spring, and then all of a sudden a cloud gathers, and you know there's a storm coming. But now that the Indians are settled, I think it will be better for everybody in the valley."

"I hope so," Colin said briefly. "I looked at those Indians, and it made me sad. I didn't used to be like that. Maybe I'm getting older."

"I guess we all are." Ty grinned. He looked up and said, "Did you ever think how close heaven is for all of us, and yet when we lift our hands to touch it, we can't make it."

"Well, I reached up a lot when I was in chains," Colin remarked. "There were times when I wanted to just end it all."

"It'll be better now," Ty said.

"I hope so, Ty. You know it feels good just to be alive. We ought to just thank God every day for the moment."

"You're right about that. Something I've just begun to learn. I'm beginning to find out that even the bitterest moments in life are for some reason. A man was made to sweat, to laugh, to have joy, and to have sorrow, too, I guess. If you don't do those things, you grow small and shrivel up on the inside. Something about the way we are makes us try for these things."

"I think that's right," Colin said. He guided his horse around a large thornbush and said,

"I feel like I came out of something and all behind me is over. I don't know what's ahead."

"None of us do, but we've all got to go on."

The two rode on, and neither of them spoke what was most pressing on their heart. In each of them was the longing to speak out, but they were men who had grown up hard, and it was not simple for them.

The two kept a steady pace speaking quietly from time to time, stopping once at a cabin where they were fed by an elderly couple who were anxious to hear the story of the battle with the Indians. Ty paid for their food by speaking of it, and when the two rode on, he remarked, "That was a good meal. Did you notice that old couple, how they looked at each other?"

Colin glanced at Ty and smiled. "Yes, I did. You don't think about an old couple like that being part of a love story, but every time she passed him, she had to reach out and touch him—patting his shoulder or touching his hand. It's good to see."

The shadows began to grow long, but Ty said, "We'll make it before dark."

Colin did not answer. He had fallen into some sort of depression. He was worn out from the chase, and it was practically all he could do to sit on his horse. He nodded finally and said, "It'll be good to get off this animal."

"This pie's not much, Avis," Jordan said. "It was sort of an experiment." She made a face and shook her head. "Most of my experiments in cooking don't turn out well."

Avis took the plate with the apple pie in it, picked up a fork, and tasted it. "It's fine," she said. "You put yourself down too much."

Avis had come an hour earlier driving up in her wagon, and the two women had spent the time talking in the kitchen. Now as Jordan sat down and tasted her pie, she thought of the funeral for Avis's husband and stepson Ace. It had been sparsely attended. Since many of the men were off with the militia, the crowd was mostly women and children. The pastor had done his best, but it had been difficult for him. Neither man had ever made any profession concerning God, and it had been hard on everyone.

Finally Jordan pushed the plate aside and

leaned over to say, "Is it very hard for you, Avis?"

For a moment Avis did not answer. She was wearing a dark dress, and her face was etched with strain. "It is hard, but not for the same reason that most women have it hard."

"Why is that? I don't understand you."

Avis dropped her eyes, stared down at her hands, and then she looked up. "Ira and I were never happy, Jordan. We never should have married. It's hard for me to look back and think how little I did to bring happiness into his life."

"I'm sure you did more than you think."

"No, he was a lonely man. He didn't love me, and I didn't love him. I think both of us knew it shortly after we got married. And for poor Ace, I feel grief for him. He was a lot like his father, but there was time for him to change. Now he's cut off, and I grieve for him."

Jordan murmured some comfort, and finally Avis met her gaze. "You probably will be shocked, Jordan, but I've been in love with Paul Leverett for some time."

Jordan could not think of a proper reply, and finally Avis shook her head. "Oh, we've not had an affair. He's such a good man. I wouldn't want to spoil his life with something like that."

"Do you think he really cares for you?"

Avis hesitated, then said quietly, "Yes, he does."

Jordan reached over and put her hands on those of Avis. "Then some day he'll be coming. We have to put things behind us." A cloud crossed her mind, and Avis saw it. "I wish they'd hurry and get back," Jordan said as she withdrew her hand.

"I'm sure they're all right. With the cavalry to help them, the Indians won't be that much of a problem."

The two women sat there, both of them with their own tragedies, comforting each other as much as possible. Their lives had gotten off track somehow, and neither of them knew how to deal with it.

Less than an hour after Avis left, Michael cried out, "Horses coming, Mama."

Quickly Jordan leaped to her feet. She ran to the door, and Michael scrambled to get ahead of her. When they came outside, Jordan's heart gave a queer lurch, and she could not speak for a moment. Michael ran forward on his short legs waving his hands and crying out excitedly to Ty and Colin, who pulled up and stepped off their horses. Michael went at once to Colin, who picked him up, and there was such weariness on Colin's face that Jordan's heart went out to him.

"Did you kill all the Indians, Pa?" Michael demanded.

Colin shook his head. "No, but everything's all right. They won't come back."

"It's all over then?" Jordan asked. "The Indians are contained?"

"Yes, they're on their way to the fort," Ty said. "You don't have to worry anymore."

"Come inside. I'll fix you something to eat."

Jordan went inside and began setting the table quickly. As she cooked a quick meal, she listened as the men answered the questions that Michael peppered them with. She was aware of a strange feeling as the two men sat at the table. She had been sleeping very little lately, and the decision that pressed on her seemed to drain her strength.

The meal was quickly ready, and the men

ate hungrily. Michael did most of the talking and kept the two men busy. Ty was strangely silent, Jordan noticed, and she had to force herself to make conversation.

After the meal, Michael at once said, "Come on, I want to show you the pet coon I got."

Colin rose and gave Jordan a slight smile. His face was pale, and Jordan thought, *He looks so weary, so tired.* She watched as the two left, and at that instant David began to cry. "He's hungry," she said, and she went at once to get him. She held him in her arms, and as she nursed him, Ty sat silently at the table.

Finally Ty said, "Colin's wore out. A time or two I didn't think he would make it. It was all he could do to climb into the saddle."

"He's still weak from that terrible time," Jordan said.

The two sat there, and finally Ty asked about Avis. She told him about the funeral and then said, "She'll be all alone now."

"She'll be all right. She's a strong woman," Ty said.

Finally Ty got up and walked to the door and looked out across the fields. He was silent for a long time. When David was satisfied, Jordan rose and came to stand beside him. "Was it very hard, Ty?"

"The fighting? Not as bad as a lot I've seen." He turned to her then and said, "I've got to go, Jordan."

Surprised at his abrupt manner, Jordan said, "You don't have to go so soon."

Ty reached out, and when she handed the baby to him, he cradled the child in his arms. With his free hand, he touched his silky hair and said, "You know, Jordan, I've always been suspicious when I heard somebody say, 'God told me to do this.'" He looked up, and his eyes were filled with something she could not grasp. He seemed peaceful, yet at the same time there was something in him that was different. "I think I can understand a little better now how people can say that."

"What do you mean, Ty?"

"I mean that God's been speaking to me about us, about you and me and Colin. It's been the hardest thing that's going to ever happen to any of us, but I know what to do now."

Suddenly Jordan grew very still. Her breathing grew faster, and her lips parted. "Why—what do you mean, Ty?"

"Colin is your husband. I'll be leaving."

For one long moment Jordan could do no more than simply look at the tall man who stood before her holding the child. Her heart was filled with pain, but she saw in his features something that stirred her and gave her hope. Quietly she said, "I think I knew that this would happen, but I haven't been able to do it. I don't want to hurt anybody, Ty."

"We acted as we thought was best, and there's been no wrong in it, but it's time for us to separate."

"Oh, Ty—" Jordan could not speak for a moment her heart was so full, and then she got a grip on herself. "David will always be David Sublette, and Michael—why, you've been a father to him."

Not wanting to prolong the moment, Ty handed David to Jordan. When she took him, he gave her one last long look and murmured, "I'll be going away."

"Not for good. You can't."

"I don't know for how long, but I've got some praying to do and some thinking." He moved then to pick up his hat and his rifle. He stood there for one moment filling the doorway, and then he smiled. "You and Colin will have a good life." He turned without another word and left. Jordan watched him as he swung into the saddle and rode away. He did not look back, and she fought back the tears.

"Ty's leaving?"

Jordan turned around and saw that Colin had come from behind the house. "Yes, he's gone."

Colin caught something in her voice. "What's the matter?"

Jordan faced him squarely. "He said that you're my husband, Colin. He's leaving for a while, at least."

Colin stood absolutely still. They could both hear Michael as he chattered out behind the house talking to the coon. Jordan saw pain leap into Colin's eyes, and then he said slowly, "You're not getting the best man. Ty's a better man than I am."

And at that moment, Jordan knew that this was the right thing. The old Colin never would have said something like that. She went to him at once and reached up with her free arm. His arms went around her, and she drew his head down and kissed him. The very feel of his arms brought back old memories, and she whispered, "You're my husband, Colin."

"What about Ty?"

"David's his son. He'll always have him."

Colin's thin face was suddenly changed. "What about us, Jordan? Can a man and a woman go back?"

She reached up and touched the scar on his cheek and then laid her palm there. "Of course we can. We loved each other once more than anything in the world, and we'll find that love again."

THIRTY-FIVE

The countryside had broken into riotous colors as fall swept across the land. Paul Leverett lifted his eyes and took in the flaming reds and the milder, more soothing yellows of the hardwoods and then settled himself back into his wagon. The rain had come earlier in the morning leaving behind a fresh smell of damp earth and the rich odors of the forest. The mud spattered from the hooves of his mare, and he looked up at the sky wondering if the rain would come again.

As the road turned, he looked over to see the cabin nestled in the elbowed crook of a line of walnut trees, and he slapped the reins on the back of the mare saying, "Get up, Clara, you're getting lazy!" As the mare broke into a trot, he thought of the news that had come to him in town that Ty Sublette had taken matters into his own hands, and now Colin Bryce had moved back with Jordan. "Oh, what a tangled web," Leverett murmured. "It'll make things awkward. Jordan will be Mrs. Bryce again. I wonder how they'll adjust to that. How will they ever explain it to Michael that he's got a new father that's really his real father."

A six-point buck suddenly appeared at the edge of the timber, bounded out, then whirled and ran across the field in the most graceful of all gaits. Leverett watched him go and shook his head. "They'll make out, I suppose, but I feel sorry for Ty." He kept the mare at a trot until he pulled up in front of the cabin and stepped down out of the buggy. She was trained to stand, so he simply tossed the lines on the seat and moved toward the cabin door.

The door opened, and Colin Bryce stepped out. He smiled briefly. "Hello, Doc."

"Hello, Colin. I'm glad you got back from that Indian raid with no damage."

"We were lucky. If it hadn't been for the cavalry, I don't think we would have gotten off so easily. Come on inside."

Leverett stepped inside and took off his hat, hung it on a peg. He looked around the cabin and said, "Jordan's not here?"

"She's out back in the garden pulling some corn if the deer left any. Pesky things."

"She sent word for me to stop by and look at David. Has he been ailing?"

"Why, I think he had a stomachache, but it seems to be gone. But maybe you ought to look him over anyhow." Bryce turned and walked over to the cradle and picked the baby up. He turned around and smiled down into his face. "Doctor's come to see you, partner." He walked back, and Leverett smiled. "He looks healthy enough to me." He reached out and touched the infant who looked up at him with owlish eyes and then suddenly broke into a toothless grin. "He's a charmer, Colin."

"Yes, he is. He looks like Ty, don't you think?"

The easy reference to Sublette somehow made Leverett feel better. "A little bit, but he's got Jordan's eyes. He's a big fellow. Well, while I'm here let me look him over."

Leverett stripped the child and poked and prodded and then looked up as Jordan walked in. "Well, you've got a fine boy here, Jordan. Can't find a thing wrong with him."

Jordan smiled and came over and looked down at David, who immediately began to kick and gurgle. "He is fine, isn't he? He's such a good baby, Dr. Leverett."

Colin asked, "Where's Michael?"

"Oh, he's out teasing that coon. I wish

you'd go out and see if you can prize him away."

Colin nodded. "I'll see what I can do."

He left the cabin, and Jordan said, "Why don't you stay for supper. It's getting late."

"No, I need to get over to see the Barnhill child. Rita said she's worried about him."

"She and Cornwall idolize that baby. I hope nothing's seriously wrong."

"No, I don't think so. You know how it is with the first child. Mothers tend to worry. I could take a glass of water though."

"How about some buttermilk?"

"That would be even better."

"You hold David, I'll go out and get some from the springhouse." She left and came back almost at once bearing a jar. She opened the top, poured a large glass up to the brim, and then took the baby. "Drink all you can. It's real fresh."

Leverett drank the milk. "That's good, Jordan." He drank another several swallows and then looked at her carefully. "Are you feeling all right? You look a little tired."

Jordan caught his glance and said evenly, "I suppose I am. I didn't sleep much while Colin and Ty were away on the raid. I was afraid for them."

"Ty left suddenly. Do you know if he's coming back?"

"I think he will. He left to make it easier for me. I suppose tongues are wagging that I swapped husbands."

Leverett said, "Those that love you wouldn't look at it like that, and those that don't, it doesn't matter."

Jordan had thought a great deal about Leverett and Avis Barnhill. She had grown very fond of Avis, and she had always liked Leverett. She had, as a matter of fact, felt sorry for him. He seemed so lonely, and after the death of his brother even more so. For a moment she hesitated, then she said, "Have you seen Avis since the funeral?"

"No, I haven't."

"Maybe you should, Paul."

Something in Jordan's voice caught at Leverett. He had been about to take another swallow of the buttermilk, but now he lowered the glass to study her more carefully. "What do you mean?"

"You'll have to forgive a woman's nosiness, but I'm very fond of Avis and of you, too. I know a little bit about the life she had with that husband of hers."

Leverett did not answer for a moment,

then he said, "You're very quick, Jordan, you always have been, and I'm not good at hiding my feelings."

"Neither is she. You two have been honorable, but honor is sometimes a cold bedfellow."

Leverett suddenly laughed. "Well, that's speaking right out!"

Jordan said, "Life is so brief, Paul. We shouldn't waste any of it."

At that moment Colin and Michael's voices sounded, and they entered the door. Michael came up and said, "Come and see my coon, Dr. Leverett."

"All right, I'll do that. Then I have to go." Leverett extended the glass, and when Jordan took it, he said quietly, "Thank you, Jordan."

"You're welcome."

Leverett went outside to admire the coon then returned to the wagon. He got in and drove away, but he could not get away from what Jordan had suggested. He thought about it all the way to the home of Cornwall and Rita Barnhill, and when he pulled up, he saw another wagon. The door opened, and Cornwall came out to greet him. "Doc, good to see you."

"You got a sick baby, Corny?"

"Just a bad cold. At least that's what Avis says. Come on in."

Leverett entered the cabin and was met at once by Rita, who was holding the baby. He smiled at her, but his eyes went at once to Avis, who stood at the stove stirring something. "Hello, Avis," he said.

"Hello, Paul. I'm glad you've come."

"It's too late for you to go on, Paul," Corny said. "You look over that daughter of mine, and then stay for dinner and the night."

"Please stay," Rita urged. "We've got plenty of room since Corny added onto the cabin."

"Well, I really should be getting back."

Avis had come over from the stove and was wiping her hands on the apron she wore. "I wish you would stay, Paul," she said quietly.

Leverett caught something in her voice and hesitated. "All right, I will." He smiled at Rita. "I've heard about your cooking from Corny here. So, you're on trial."

"It's good, Doc. Look over Lisa there, and tell me if she ain't the finest young lady you ever saw in your whole life."

Avis watched as the doctor examined the baby, and then he pronounced Lisa as fine a girl as he'd ever seen.

When the two women had finished cooking, they all sat down to eat a hearty supper of venison, sweet corn, yams, hominy, and a delicious blackberry cobbler.

"You got yourself a fine cook," Leverett said.

Rita flushed with pleasure. "Corny and I will do the dishes," she insisted. "Avis, why don't you show Doc Leverett the new calf."

Avis rose. "Come along, Doctor. We'll see if you're as good a calf doctor as you are a people doctor."

The two put on their coats and left the cabin, and Avis led the way to the barn. She was holding a lantern in her hand, and when they stepped inside, she proudly said, "Isn't that a beautiful calf?"

Leverett stepped forward and took the lantern from her. The calf was indeed beautiful, and he said so. He turned then and hung the lantern on a nail, then reached out and pulled her to him. He saw her eyes grow wide, and her lips parted. He kissed her, and she came to him willingly. When he lifted his lips, he said, "Jordan told me life was too short to be wasted. We could wait a year or two years, but I've been lonely long enough, Avis. I know people will talk, but I don't care."

Avis suddenly laughed. "I don't care either. Let's do something scandalous."

"Like what?" he said, loving the sight of her as she glowed under the yellow lamplight.

"Let's elope. Go by the preacher's and get married and then go hide somewhere on a secret honeymoon."

Paul Leverett laughed, a full happy sound, then said with gusto, "All right, we'll do it! It'll give people something to talk about. Tomorrow you'll be a bride."

Avis came to him and laid her head against his chest. He held her tightly and heard her murmur, "I love you, Paul, and I always will."

The boys were in bed at last, and somehow Jordan felt apprehensive. She noticed that Colin had said almost nothing directly to her. He had read stories to Michael until he grew sleepy. One of them had been a fairy story, and when Michael had looked up with big eyes and said, "Is that story true?"

he had smiled across the room at her and said, "Your mother would say so. She's always believed stories like this."

Jordan had smiled at that, but he had hardly spoken to her after that. The evening had passed and now it was late. She did not know exactly what she would feel being with Colin again.

Finally she said, "It's late, and you had a hard time."

Colin was sitting beside the fire staring into it. He looked up to her and for a moment did not speak. The scar on his face was emphasized by his leanness, and he said finally, "It will take a while for you and I to find each other, Jordan. I'll keep sleeping in the attic until we feel more comfortable."

Colin had suggested this when he first moved back into the cabin, but Jordan felt a keen disappointment. "All right, if that's what you think, Colin. Good night."

Turning, Jordan went into the bedroom. She undressed and got into bed, but she could not sleep. For a long time she tossed and turned, and finally she began to think about Colin. *He's been through such a terrible time, and now he's home, and he's still alone. It's not right!*

She threw the covers back and went to the trunk where she kept some of her clothes. Lifting the lid, she searched through the trunk until she found the gown she had worn on her wedding night. She held it for a moment, then stripped off her flannel nightgown and put it on. *All right, Mr. Colin Bryce, you're in for a surprise!*

She left the bedroom and moved across the floor of the cabin to the ladder that led to the loft. She carried the small lantern with her, for it was dark. The rungs hurt her bare feet, but when she reached the top of the ladder she stepped onto the floor and moved over toward the bed that was used sometimes for company. She approached the bed and saw that Colin had sat up. The yellow light flared in his eyes, and she put the lamp down and stood before him. She saw his eyes widen, and he whispered, "Jordan—"

Jordan turned the lantern down and got into bed. She put her arms around him, and he came to her. "I'm your wife, Colin." She drew him close and kissed him and felt him, at once, pull her closer and hold her tightly.

"I never believed much in fairy tales, you know that, sweetheart, but I do now." He held her tightly for a moment, then said, "I dreamed of this for so long, and now you're here."

"I'm here, and we're together, and we'll find each other. I've never stopped loving you," she cried, and then she whispered his name, and he came to her with all the ardor of a bridegroom.

Leah saw the horseman as he made the turn in the road and knew at once that it was Ty. His name came to her lips as she rose from where she was sitting on the porch. It was twilight, and snow was falling gently through the tall pines. But Leah had eyes only for the rider, and when he brought his horse directly in front of her and stepped down, she waited until he came to her, then put out her hands. "You're back, Ty. I'm glad."

"I guess I am. It seems like a long time."

"It's been nearly three months. I've looked for you almost every day. Did you stop by to see David?"

"No, I came from the other direction."

Leah was conscious that he was still holding her hands. His hat was shoved back on his face, and his tawny hair was long and curled down his collar. "Come inside. It's cold."

The two went inside, and she said, "Sit down. There's coffee on, and I'll warm up something to eat."

Ty sat down and watched her as she moved to prepare the meal. "Where's Jos?" he asked. "Not in bed already, is he?"

"No, he went coon hunting with Colin. They've become very close." She turned suddenly and said, "He asks about you almost every day. He wanted to know if you were coming back, and I didn't know exactly what to tell him."

Ty did not answer for a time. He took a sip of the coffee and then said, "It's been kind of a hard time for me, Leah."

"I judge it would be. Wait until after we've eaten, and then we can talk."

When she put the meal on the table, the two ate; she took only a few bites while Sublette ate hungrily. "You always were a fine cook," he said as he finished the meal. "I remember on the trail I'd always try to eat with you as often as I could. A lone man learns who the good cooks are."

"Come on over to the fire," she said.

She rose up, and he followed her over. They sat down before the fire, and she said, "Tell me about it, Ty. I've been praying for you every day."

"I was sure you would be. I went back to the mountains, Leah. I wanted to be sure that I'd done the right thing. I told Jordan that I thought God was speaking to me about her and Colin. I haven't had much experience listening to God." He smiled at her faintly, then shook his head. "So I stayed away, and I prayed, and finally I knew that I'd done the right thing."

"I know why you stayed away." She turned to face him and for a moment was silent. She was a shapely woman, and her eyes mirrored some sort of wisdom. She was looking at him silently, and a woman's silence could mean many things. It pulled at him like a mystery, and after his solitary days in the mountains he felt a slow run of excitement as though he were on the edge of discovery.

"Why do you think I stayed away?"

"I know you so well. It's strange, but I just do," she said simply. "You stayed away to give Colin and Jordan time to become settled. To let people become used to it again." There was an enormous certainty in her, and her strong will was in her eyes and on her lips. She had a pleasantly expressive mouth, and she made a good sight by the lamplight in Ty's eyes. The light ran over the curves of her shoulders and softened the lines on her face.

"Maybe that was it," he said. "Are they doing all right?"

"Yes. It was hard for them, I know, but they're doing fine. And David, he's growing so fast."

"And how have you been doing, Leah?"

She looked startled. "Why, I'm fine."

Ty looked at her and said, "You know, I've always admired you. Back on the trail even. I knew that you were a strong woman."

"Not so strong, Ty. You don't know how afraid I was after Mark died. I had no place to go—and then you gave us this place." She suddenly stood up and walked over to the fireplace and stared down into it. She was moved by his presence. It brought her a swift rush of feelings that caught her unawares. Staring down into the fire, she whispered, "I don't know what I would have done if it hadn't been for you."

Ty rose and walked over to her. He reached over and turned her around. "You don't have to be afraid."

Leah looked up at him, and there was a vulnerable quality in her expression. "I'm afraid, not for myself but for Jos. I get lonely, but a woman can learn how to live with that, but a boy needs a father. Will you help me, Ty? You're not going away again, are you?"

"No, I'm not going away. As for Jos, he's a fine boy. I'll do what I can."

Leah was conscious of his lean strength, and a thought came to her. "You know, in a way you have three sons now, Ty."

He blinked with surprise. "Three sons? What do you mean?"

"You were the only father Michael knew for so long. He still looks to you even though he has his own father now, and I think he'll always have an affection for you. Then there's David. He looks so much like you, Ty. I've talked to Jordan several times. She longs for you to be close so that you can help raise him. And then, of course, Jos has always looked to you. You've been like a second father to him already."

"Three sons. That's a lot of boys." He was very conscious suddenly of her presence, and he had thought about her a great deal. Now he knew what had drawn him back, and it was not only David but this woman. "I've always had a feeling for you, Leah," he said, "and I thought I saw something in your eyes for me. Maybe I was wrong."

Leah whispered, "No, you weren't wrong."

She put her hands on his chest and leaned toward him. She was fair and constant and all that a woman should be.

He said, "I'll have to warn you, Leah. I'm a lonely man. I need a family about me."

"Do you, Ty?"

"Yes." And then he pulled her forward and kissed her. Leah put her arms around him and held him tightly. His urges made a turbulent eddy around them both, and he could not hide it, nor did she want him to.

Ty lifted his head and said, "When it's time, I'll be coming to ask you to marry me."

Leah clung to him and knew what she had to say. She whispered, "And I know what my answer will be. You don't know how empty my life's been, Ty. I love you, and I want to be your wife."

"It's too soon. People will talk."

"We'll build us a little world here in this cabin and on this homestead. People will talk for a while, but you'll see. I'll love you so much that you'll forget all about wagging tongues." She laughed and shook her head. "You'd be marrying a shameless woman, Ty."

Ty Sublette laughed suddenly, the lines of tension disappearing. "I expect you'll want a little courting."

"Oh, yes. You can take me places, and people will get used to that. And you'll find out that I'm hard to please."

Ty took her by the forearms and said, "Well, I've got a lifetime to please you, and the sooner I get started the better."

Leah whispered, "You had a terrible time, but I'll try to make it up to you."

Ty held her, and the two stood there. The fire crackled, and outside the snow blew, but they felt sheltered inside the cabin. And they had a world to create and a home and a family to begin, and both of them knew that it would be good.